THE PHANTOM'S OPERA

THE PHANTOM'S OPERA

❀

A Novel

Sadie Montgomery

iUniverse, Inc.
New York Lincoln Shanghai

The Phantom's Opera

iUniverse books may be ordered through booksellers or by contacting:

iUniverse
2021 Pine Lake Road, Suite 100
Lincoln, NE 68512
www.iuniverse.com
1-800-Authors (1-800-288-4677)

Because of the dynamic nature of the Internet, any Web addresses or links contained in this book may have changed since publication and may no longer be valid.

This is a work of fiction. All of the characters, names, incidents, organizations, and dialogue in this novel are either the products of the author's imagination or are used fictitiously.

ISBN: 978-0-595-47236-9 (pbk)
ISBN: 978-0-595-91518-7 (ebk)

Printed in the United States of America

To my many loves without whom
I would not know what this story is all about.

Love must disguise death or else perish at its hands. We cannot really love the dead. We love a phantasm that secretly consoles. What love sometimes mistakes for death is a kind of intense suffering, a pain that can be endured and absorbed. But the idea of a real ending, that cannot be envisaged.

—*The Black Prince,* Iris Murdoch

Suddenly an old man came drifting
   Toward us in a boat, his hair white with decades.
"Woe to you," he began shouting,

Give up all hope of heaven, you depraved shades:
   I come to lead you to that other shore
Where fire and ice abound, and dark pervades.

And you there—the one still alive—stay no more
   With these others, who are dead."
But when he saw me stay and ignore

His order he yelled: "Take a lighter boat instead,
   Leave by another port, cross another way."
"Charon, be quiet," my leader said,

"Put away your anger and listen to what I say:
   Our journey has been willed by one up there
Who does what he wills, and wills what he may."

—*The Divine Comedy, Inferno,* Dante Alighieri

CHAPTER 1

⚜

Worms Have Made Him Their Bed

… shut me nightly in a charnel-house,
O'er-cover'd quite with dead men's rattling bones,
With reeky shanks and yellow chapless skulls;
Or bid me go into a new-made grave
And hide me with a dead man in his shroud;
Things that, to hear them told, have made me tremble;
And I will do it without fear or doubt,
To live an unstain'd wife to my sweet love.

Romeo and Juliet, Shakespeare

A tall sandy-haired boy of six or seven ran to greet the carriage as it pulled in front of his ancestral home. He rubbed his forearm across his face, leaving behind a smear of dirt and grease that matched his chocolate-colored eyes. He had been waiting days for François, his cousin, to arrive from Italy. He could care less about the two-year-old, Laurette, who squirmed in his Aunt Meg's arms. François and he were closer in age, Victor being only five months older than François. Finally he'd have another boy with whom to play and share his room. He'd promptly exile his baby sister, Elise, who was a couple of years younger and much more annoying now that she had begun her lessons and was so precociously advancing in her letters. Unlike his sister, Victor was unable to sit for hours as the governess, Mlle. Villiers, required and was more interested in drawing than in declensions, more engaged in talking than in reading. He excelled at his numbers, but couldn't play any of the instruments his mother kept placing in his hands. In contrast, Elise had already mastered the basics of both piano and violin. He did sing well, though, and had perfect pitch like his mother.

It had been more than three years since their first trip to Italy where he had met his cousin François. Laurette had not yet been born. Victor had liked François immediately in spite of the Italian lilt of his French. Victor, Elise, and François had enjoyed playing together in the vineyard and orchard and had been sad to part. Barely a year later, Victor's mother had taken him and Elise, just the three of them, to visit Meg Costanzi. But this was the first time that his Aunt Meg and the Costanzi children had come to Paris.

A petite, slim woman with blond hair stepped down from the carriage. She had a small heart-shaped face, a narrow waist, long tapered hands and legs. In her arms, clutching a stray wisp of hair, was Laurette. Meg put the child down on the cobblestone path and held her hand to restrain her from running under the legs of the horses. She, too, was blond like her mother with large brown eyes shaded by incredibly long and dark lashes. A taller, striking woman descended after Meg. Her brown hair, streaked by a shock of gray, lay in a tight braid down her back to her waist. This was Mme. Giry, Aunt Meg's mother. Finally, Victor saw emerge from the carriage a tall, dark-haired boy with long, wavy hair and dark brows and deeply green eyes that glanced around cautiously before stepping down. Victor was a little unsettled by the fact that his cousin was several inches taller than he had thought he should be, but François's slender frame gave him hope that he could still overpower his guest if it came to a fight. Forgetting this mild setback, Victor ran forward toward the new arrivals, waving his welcome. His Aunt Meg turned immediately and held her arms out to him. After a momentary hesitation, Victor leaped into Meg's embrace and planted a cool wet kiss on her cheek. Quickly, he pushed away from her and addressed François.

"Come on then! I'll show you my fort."

François looked to his mother for permission, and this having been obtained, the two boys raced toward the woods.

"Christine, you look wonderful. Your color is good. You must be feeling stronger. I'm sure the bed rest is just what you needed." Meg sat by the daybed where Christine was to spend the last two to three months of her confinement. The physician had insisted she have complete bed rest if she expected to bring the pregnancy to term and not risk the baby's health or her own. In spite of Christine's reassurance that she felt fine, Raoul had seconded the doctor in all matters concerning his wife's health.

There had been a couple of frightening incidents. Christine had collapsed on two separate occasions after modest exercise: once on a gentle, meandering walk about the grounds and again one evening while entertaining friends with some of her favorite arias. But the morning she awoke to several spots of blood on the bed linen, Raoul sent for the doctor who had delivered their other children. Dr. Picard had reassured them both, but suggested that a cautious plan would be best—no conjugal relations and complete rest—until the child was safely delivered and the mother out of danger. Christine agreed with one proviso; she dearly wished to have Meg by her side.

Raoul had been reluctant to invite Meg to journey to Paris because of her continued association with Erik. After all, not so many years ago Erik had been known to Raoul only as the Phantom, a man who lived like a ghost in the underground vaults of the Opera Populaire, a violent and troubled man who had become obsessed with Christine. The less contact his wife had with the Phantom, the better. Despite Raoul's misgivings, his wife's ties to Meg far outweighed his objections to Erik. As far as Christine was concerned, Meg was as close to her as a sister, and she would not shun Meg's husband Erik. But Raoul suspected that Christine had always loved her Angel of Music, as she called this man of multiple disguises—phantom, opera ghost, tutor, lover—and even now she was incapable of condemning him for his past crimes, the debacle of the chandelier and the destruction of the opera house itself. If Christine's health had not declined, if the baby's life were not in jeopardy, if Christine had not insisted on sending for Meg, the last thing Raoul would have done was write his old rival and request they visit. Indeed, that had been the only sticking point. He could not very well invite Meg without inviting her husband. To Raoul's relief, Erik declined the invitation on his part but encouraged his wife to travel with the children to be at Christine's side.

Raoul was thankful that Erik had the sense to know that his presence would be awkward, but he imagined that the principle reason Erik did not accompany Meg was that it would be very dangerous for him to set foot in Paris. The Phantom had been hunted down and caught by the police, imprisoned, tortured, tried, convicted, and executed. Raoul himself had assisted in the faked hanging and burial. He had also helped Erik and Meg flee across the border to Italy and to safety. As long as Erik remained abroad, the authorities would most likely continue to believe that the unmarked grave in paupers' field was the final resting place of the notorious Phantom of the Opera. If Erik were to reappear in Paris—and his mask made it difficult for him to blend in with society—the authorities would realize that something was amiss. No, there was no way that Erik could ever return and escape imprisonment and execution. The mask that hid his disfigured face had marked him and always would.

"I'm feeling much better now that you're here!" Christine took both of Meg's hands and squeezed them to her bosom.

"I forgot how much I missed Paris. And, of course, you!"

"Do you mind terribly coming such a long way and staying so long with me? I would never have asked except I can't bear it another day sitting here without someone's company, and you're the only company that I think I can abide! I'm quite out of sorts at times and uncomfortable. And I just miss you incredibly!" Christine's eyes filled with tears even as she tried to wipe them away.

Meg embraced Christine carefully, but warmly. She felt her own eyes begin to water as she recalled how close they had always been when children. It was painful to be separated from Christine, living in another country, rarely able to see her.

"You shouldn't worry! I wanted to be with you. I was glad to have the invitation, and we must find a way to do this under better circumstances. I want you to come to see the new opera house. It is larger than the Opera Populaire and quite modern. Sig. Costanzi spared no expense. We have lifts, Christine!"

Christine's brow lowered in puzzlement so Meg hastened to explain, "Lifts are like dumb waiters, big enough to hold people, that can be lowered or raised from one floor to another. They can transport equipment, props, scenery easily from storage rooms underground to the level of the stage. Erik had read about the principle involved and commissioned one to be built for the opera. He's so proud!"

"You're very happy, aren't you, Meg?"

"Yes," she responded shyly.

For a moment the two women appeared lost in their own memories. Christine was the first to speak. Perhaps thinking of her own impending childbirth, Christine's thoughts brought her back to Meg's last confinement.

"Erik must have been so pleased when Laurette was born. You mentioned once that it was he who insisted on the name. Why 'Laurette'?"

"It was his mother's." The surprised expression on her friend's face was sufficient for Meg to understand the question. "He came upon someone who had known him as a child." Meg squirmed slightly in her seat as she alluded to Erik's sad history before Madeleine had brought him to live in the opera house. Of course, Christine knew the story, so Meg needn't have felt uncomfortable.

Even so, she worried that she was speaking of intimate details that belonged only to Erik and now to her.

Aware of Meg's reluctance, Christine smiled at Meg's blush, took her hand, and squeezed it. "We've never had secrets, Meg, but if you don't want to talk about this, it's all right."

Meg felt relieved. Christine was right; they had shared everything as children and young women. She needn't worry that Erik would mind, as long as she didn't delve into too much detail. "Oh, I don't know why I hesitated. After all, I know you care about Erik. That time he left me he spent wandering around the Italian countryside and eventually ran into a traveling fair, like the one in which he had spent his childhood. It wasn't the same one, but there were a couple of carnival people who had worked in the same fair and knew Erik and his parents. His mother's name was Laurette."

"But how could he name his child after a woman who abandoned him?"

"It's more complicated than that. They said that his mother didn't mean to leave him at the fair. She promised to return for him. Erik's ..." Meg quieted.

"What?"

"Nothing." Meg would not give away all his secrets. She would not talk about the man who had been Erik's father. "There was an accident. His mother was killed."

"How sad! If she had lived, his life would have been different. Perhaps he would have been different."

"Yes, but even though it may be selfish, I wouldn't want him to be any different from the way he is now. I love him! I love who he is. I can't imagine him any other way."

"Of course you love him. I didn't mean that. And after all, you have changed him, you know. But if his early life had been different, I think he might not have suffered so, and he would not have done some of the things he's done."

"Perhaps." Meg understood that Christine was not thinking of how she herself had contributed to his suffering. Would his mother have loved and protected him from all life's cruelties? Anything would have been a mercy compared to the years he had lived like a caged animal, paraded from town to town as the Devil's Child. "Then again, if his life had had a different beginning, he wouldn't have lived in the opera house, and he might never have found his music. Christine, we are what we are because of what has happened to us and what we've done in response to it."

Meg thought of Christine and Raoul. They had clung so tightly to each other in those first weeks and months perhaps because of their encounter with

Erik. What would have happened to Christine after her first child's death if it hadn't been for Erik? And what horrid memories and experiences had Erik called upon in order to help Christine get beyond that grief and want to live again?

"I'm so pleased you're here." Christine interrupted Meg's thoughts.

"You're not worried about the birth, are you?"

"Not now. Not now that you're here."

Erik had not been pleased to receive the invitation from Raoul. But when he read that Christine was in a delicate condition and had asked that Meg come to stay with her, he scowled in concern and reluctantly told Meg she should go.

"Of course the children will go with you. Laurette would be frantic without you, and François will adore Paris." His voice was calm and even, careful not to betray emotion. He kept his back to her, his eyes cast toward the windows that opened on the garden. But Meg could see the tension in his shoulders and the way he folded and unfolded the invitation in his hands.

"Are you worried?" she asked, thinking of Christine. Even now, at times, she wondered what might have happened if Christine had returned Erik's passion. If she had not chosen Raoul instead of the Phantom.

Erik turned away from the windows and toward his wife. She might try to hide her doubts, but they lay just beneath the surface. He drew close and placed his large, square hand behind Meg's head. His fingers woven between the blond tresses, he bent to kiss her sweetly.

She could smell the light touch of cologne he wore and taste a hint of strong tea and honey on his breath. "You're worried about Christine," she insisted.

He took a step back from his wife and studied her expression. "Yes. I could not bear it if anything were to happen to her."

Meg swallowed hard and blinked her eyes rapidly to keep back an involuntary surge of tears. She stiffened and stared at him.

"I daresay you might say the same thing, Meg." It was spoken as if it were a warning of sorts. He watched her curiously before he spoke again. "I've never lied to you."

"Well, perhaps you should!" This time she grew red in the face, angry and annoyed against her better judgment and against her will. In the back of her mind, she observed herself and regretted that he held such a strong sway on her emotions. With everyone else, she was calm, sweet, and rational. But not with Erik. Not when jealousy reared its ugly head. Even so, why couldn't he lie just a little, just for the sake of her vanity, her momentary insecurities?

"Come, Meg." Erik held out his arms to her and gave her a stern look that would not accept refusal.

"No. It's not that easy. I'm sorry. I know you still love her. I know I'm not …" She stopped unsure of what she was about to say.

Erik suddenly had her clutched against his chest, forcing her to look up at him as he admonished her hoarsely, "I love *you*. When are you going to accept that you've won? You pursued me like a hound from hell, and now I could live without you no better than I could live without air! I love you, you silly, infuriating woman." And then he fixed his lips on hers and kissed her hard and deep. He kept his mouth on hers until he felt her body melt against his and heard a low, deep groan rise from her throat. Even then he kissed her, his tongue greedily dipping inside the soft sweetness of her mouth, until the two of them were breathless. Only then did he release her gently, his lips hovering close to her mouth, the two of them breathing each other in, and he softly flicked his tongue along her full lower lip. She wasn't sure whether he had said or thought them, but she knew she heard the words somewhere between his lips and her heart. *I love you.*

Breathless, she leaned against his chest, nuzzled her head under his chin, and placed her arms around his waist. "I don't know if I can bear to be without you for months. I could go later, when she's closer to her time. The separation would not be so long."

"Raoul is concerned, Meg. Otherwise he'd not have written the way he did. It could be serious. She needs you."

Meg swallowed the knot that had formed in her throat. She couldn't imagine losing Christine.

"You're right. I must go. But I will miss you terribly."

Erik was silent. The thought of Meg's absence made his chest tighten.

It was decided that the children and Madeleine would definitely go with Meg. Laurette would not let her mother out of her sight without crying inconsolably, and François was excited to visit Paris and the Chagny children. Christine would be glad to have Madeleine to mother her. Erik had hoped that one day his children might travel to France, even if it were without him. There was no question that Erik would accompany his family. He couldn't return to Paris. Meg understood that it was too dangerous.

As Meg made travel preparations, Erik spent his time at the Teatro dell'Opera, avoiding the hustle and bustle at the Costanzi estate. In anticipation of his loved ones' departure, he was irritable and preferred to stay out of the way. But the night before they were to leave, Erik returned home early. He helped François with his lessons and held Laurette until she dropped off to sleep.

That night, in bed, after they had made love slowly and sadly, Erik asked Meg to come home to him quickly after Christine and the baby were out of harm's way. "I think I won't be myself again until you come back," he whispered as he cupped the round contour of her bottom, unwilling to release her.

Meg rubbed her hand along the dark curls of his chest, down the slope of his abdomen to the sleeping darkness between his thighs. He shifted on the bed, accepting her caresses, and held her closer. "I'll be lost without you, Meg. I need you. Don't stay any longer than you must, please."

Excited by the prospect of seeing Paris once more and being with Christine, Meg teased him, "Three months isn't so very long. After all, we've been separated before." She found that her knowing touch was raising sleeping lions. She relished her power over her tall, commanding husband.

Erik was stroking her body, kissing a path down her neck to her breasts as he replied, "I never want to be separated from you again." He didn't like remembering the time they had wasted when he had wandered hopelessly through the towns and countryside of Italy. He had thought himself unloved and unlovable. But they had found each other again and started a new life in Rome. He had his music, and he was the father of two beautiful children with the woman he loved. He was no longer condemned to hide in the underground cellars of the Opera Populaire, but neither, as Meg had also come to understand, had he succeeded in becoming a part of society. His interaction with others was always tentative, guarded.

She urged Erik to lie back on the mattress. She slid her leg over his groin so that she rested on top of his body. She rose to look down at his unmasked face. He hid it only when among others, never when he was in the intimacy of his family. He didn't need to wear a mask with them. She smiled to see him look up at her in expectation and in trust.

They lay naked in each other's arms, making love until the first rays of daybreak shone upon them through the windows of their bedroom.

François and Elise were taking turns playing the piano in the conservatory. Elise's brown curls danced across her forehead as she concentrated on outplaying her dark cousin. François sat with his back straight, his hands positioned over the keys, elbows drawn in and bent at a ninety degree angle, as if preparing at any moment to join her on the piano, his eyes watching the little girl as she touched the keys with a command that tolerated no rebellion. Unconsciously he observed, as his father had while he played, her poise, her style, her reach, her rhythm, and the precision with which she played each note; patient and pleased, he kept track of comments he might make if she asked him his opinion. But Elise never asked his opinion. She knew she had played the piece better than anyone else in the whole wide world. She only stopped biting her tongue when the last note faded.

As they recognized the look of triumph that spread its wings across the girl's face, Christine couldn't help but smile knowingly with Meg. Meg caught François's eye before he was able to react to his cousin's tour de force, a cautionary glance that said, "be sweet." Not that François had any intention but to be sweet, yet helpful. And to be truthful, Elise had surprised him. She was intent and eloquent, passionate if not meticulous. There were a few aspects that he knew he could criticize, but he recalled one particularly difficult lesson his father had given him.

A precocious child, promising to be as talented as his parents, François had worked on a score by Bach diligently and without stop for nearly a month. He thought that he had perfected it. He had, in the previous week or so, dispensed with the sheet music altogether and played from memory. Erik had confided that a piece was not really mastered until it was written inside the eyelids themselves and could be read without the musical score. It was a technique more than anything that Erik was trying to teach his son.

"How does one make the music come alive?" he had asked his son. "If it's only a matter of translating the black ink into sounds, then where is the art? Where is the musician's contribution to the composition?"

To demonstrate, Erik sat at the piano and played the first movement of the piece François had been practicing for weeks. His father played it from memory, perhaps from having just heard his son play it! Not only did it sound right—that is, it sounded as if he had done it correctly—but the music François heard his father play seemed distinct from what François had played and heard. It had a life of its own.

"There," Erik had said as he rubbed the knuckles of one hand with the fingers of the other. François tried not to look, for he knew that his father's hands were aching. The Bach exercise had not been without pain. François loved his father's hands. They were expressive, strong yet gentle. The slight swelling around the knuckles and the curved bend to several of the fingers were due to injuries Erik had suffered before his son was born. Erik smiled at François and caressed his dark hair with one of those hands.

"You played the piece well. You have it all worked out. But look here at these notes, François. Are these the notes you would have played?" He played the phrase, starting a few measures before and continuing a few beyond. "Or might you prefer to play them this way?" Now he played the same notes with a slight lengthening of one, robbing from another. "Or would it have been nice to put a flat in here?" Again he ran the series making the change he suggested. François's heart sped as he heard his father invent and reinvent the melody. The two of them sat at the piano for the rest of the afternoon scribbling over the original score until they had set down a multitude of variations. That was the day François learned to play music instead of a score.

Now the brown-haired doll that sat beside him on the bench looked at him in tense expectation.

"Elise, you played that song as if you had written it yourself," he said.

It was a compliment that his father had given to him several months after the Bach piece when he had taken a few too many liberties with a new score he was studying. The irony was not lost on the boy, but it confused him. Wasn't that the lesson his father had taught him before? Erik approached his son at the piano and explained, "First you learn it as it is on the paper. You study it so much that it becomes yours, as if you could write the score in your sleep. Only then, when you have paid proper homage to its creator, can you rewrite it, improve it, or destroy it."

A bit flustered, François asked curtly, "And which did I do, Father? Did I destroy it?"

Erik, surprised by his son's challenge, lifted a sarcastic eyebrow and replied, "No, but I do believe you made it groan a few times."

That had silenced the boy. François flushed red and searched through the score to find the sections that he had not taken the time to learn well, the ones that he had guessed or approximated.

Elise smiled sweetly up at François. She had accepted it as a compliment, plain and simple. And she was right in this case. François thought that her playing was technically correct, and yet she had made it sound uniquely her own. His father would have enjoyed listening to her play. He would have smiled at her and asked her to play again. François was about to make the same request when Elise pushed the music over toward him and said, "Can you play it?"

The challenge in her tone did not escape his attention.

∽

My esteemed Count de Chagny,

It is with a heavy heart that I sit to write this note. I could delay it no longer. All hopes have been extinguished alas, and I am forced to beg you to intercede for me with Meg. It is our sad duty—yours and mine—to convey tragic news, and I trust that you and Donna Christine will be able to comfort my little Meg as much as you may.

Several days ago Erik was examining some properties in a section below the dressing rooms in the opera. I don't know why he chose such a late hour to descend several floors to those particular rooms, but as far as I can make out through inquiries some missive he received earlier that evening may have played a role. Moments later several cries for help emanated from the dressing rooms which were fast engulfed in smoke. Shortly thereafter flames were discerned whose origins were traced to the underground storage rooms where Erik was working.

You cannot imagine the chaos and fear! Several people, including members of the chorus and various stagehands were trapped in the west wing, two floors above the storage room. A child of six, our sweet Paulina, was one of these fright-ened souls. Later I learned that Erik somehow found his way to the upper rooms and led those who were trapped through one of his labyrinthine tunnels to safety many meters away from the area of the opera house. He returned several times, in each case carrying or leading more survivors. The last time he emerged from the passageway he was carrying across his shoulders a man who had lost con-sciousness, overcome by the smoke. Although they tried to keep him from return-ing, he said he must be sure no one had been left behind. He never came back. He must have been overcome by the smoke and perished in the fire.

I still cannot believe Erik is dead. I have no comfort to give myself, but rather feel all my thoughts and concerns winding their way to Meg and the children. At this time, overcome with grief, I'm unable to write more. Please let Meg know that I am bereft once more of a son, for Erik had come to be a son to me. As you may know, I conferred upon Erik my family name, and the tomb I intend to erect in my family crypt will bear his name as Erik Costanzi. He will rest next to his brother, Henrico, my other son, now dead these ten years. I pray that Meg will continue to look upon me as a father. She and her children are all I have left in the world, and I will take care of them as I know Erik would wish.

Before closing this letter to you, M. Chagny, I can't refrain from expressing my pride in Erik. Over these few years since Erik has lived and worked with me, he has confided his past sorrows and regrets. In short, I understand now more fully why you were apprehensive and somewhat indifferent—shall we say?—to the dilemma that brought Erik to Rome. Erik himself defended you before my accu-

sations and explained the reasons you harbored ill feelings and distrust toward him. Although much of what Erik revealed appalled me, it was with a father's heart that I listened to his confession. He suffered greatly for his violent nature. I can't help but think that he has made amends in this last heroic deed for some of the pain he inflicted in Paris. He saved all but himself from the fire.

I hope that your wife's condition has improved and fervently desire that you accept my good wishes and the offer of my friendship. In whatever way you deem best to impart this tragic news to Meg, I trust you will cushion it as much as possible.

I remain as ever your humble servant,

Sig. Costanzi

It would be simplistic to say that Raoul read this letter with ambivalent emotions. His eyes returned repeatedly to the line, "He never came back." He could imagine Erik carrying the unconscious man to safety and disappearing yet again into the underground grottos of the Teatro dell'Opera. He tried to imagine Erik disoriented by the smoke, reaching out by feel, calling to anyone who might have remained behind. His eyes watered from the smoke; he crouched low, but turned around and blinded, he collapsed, unconscious, sur-rounded by flames. Although Raoul could imagine all this, he could not see Erik dead. "He never came back!" Consumed by hell's fire, Erik would forever remain in the bowels of the opera house. Ironic that he should meet his end in the underbelly of another opera house. He had grown up in a similar abode under the Opera Populaire in Paris. The fire at the Opera Populaire had augured the end of that realm, but he had built a facsimile of his sanctuary in the Italian opera house. The opera world had been his kingdom, and now it was his grave.

Raoul imagined Meg's life with the Phantom over the past several years as one of compromise between the subterranean rooms of the Teatro dell'Opera and the world of society at Sig. Costanzi's estates in the heart of Rome. Meg and the children belonged to the world of light. Erik, like Persephone, would have spent time in both realms. Whenever he felt persecuted by Italian society, he would disappear into the cellars. There he composed. Each night he would return to the estate to spend with his family. At dawn he would return to the underground.

Meg had once told Raoul that there were times when Erik remained at the estate and joined small dinner parties and mingled with Sig. Costanzi's guests. He had even made friends with a very select number of gentlemen and artists whose company he found pleasant. But his reserves for socializing were meager, and without warning he'd become taciturn and silent—even among his family and friends—and with a look of desperation toward sweet, forgiving Meg bid an abrupt farewell to disappear for days on end. Each time he returned, he'd beg forgiveness and vow he'd try harder. Meg confided that she knew Erik was unable to keep this vow, and told her husband time after time that it didn't matter. She understood his need to return to his sanctuary. She even followed him every now and again and spent time with him in the secret rooms he had constructed and furnished. The two of them would emerge days later refreshed and happy.

Raoul thought perhaps it was fitting that Erik had perished in those rooms. Yet he read the letter over and over as if he could not quite understand something. It wasn't the letter that puzzled him. It was his own reaction. He sat down next to the fire and examined his heart. He was deeply shocked by Erik's death. More surprisingly, he was sad. He didn't know why, for the two of them had nearly killed each other on more than one occasion. They had struck a sort of truce finally, but Erik had been his rival, a dangerous rival obsessed with Christine. It was with great reluctance that Raoul had aided the Phantom of the Opera to escape execution in France and flee to Italy. Several years later Meg had begged his help once more to protect Erik against the unjust accusation that he had stolen a diamond necklace. At that point Raoul had wanted to do the least possible to ensure Erik escaped imprisonment, and he had tried to separate Meg from Erik and bring her back to Paris. Meg had refused, and Raoul accepted defeat. After Erik was reunited with his family, Raoul reluctantly agreed to bury the past. But they were hardly friends. Raoul had trouble deciding exactly what their relationship had been.

Reading the letter, Raoul recognized that he had grown tolerant, perhaps even affectionate, toward Erik. Was it possible that they had indeed become friends? Then again, perhaps it was only compassion that made him regret Erik's death, especially such a painful and violent death. The fact that Erik had saved the lives of others at the cost of his own touched Raoul to the depths of his soul. For the first time, he understood why Meg had loved the Phantom. He even understood why Christine, regardless of the horrible deeds Erik had committed, had always retained some deep seated affection for her mentor and guardian. Christine still loved her Angel of Music, even now after all this time and in spite of her love for her husband and their children. He once had agonized over this fact, but not any longer.

she knew she was dreaming, it had only been a few weeks and her body yearned for his, she lay in the bed, the moonlight streaming across the bedcovers which she kicked away, she was warm and excited, the dream had aroused her to the point that she woke panting, her body covered in a soft sheen of sweat, her hands caressing her breasts, the faint hint of a kiss still on her lips, as if Erik had been with her, in bed, lying across her, his weight sustained by his elbows on either side of her, she trapped under him, his body all muscle and skin and velvet hairs against the fine down of her own limbs, his breath warm on her throat, his knees between her legs spreading them wide, so wide that she felt herself ripping asunder, her legs wrapped around his thighs, then raised to his hips, her heels digging into the tautness of his buttocks, feeling against her lips his hardness slip inside her, thrusting inside her … she woke to find herself alone and unsatisfied, the need of him so palpable that she whimpered involuntarily

Raoul had not told Meg the contents of Sig. Costanzi's letter immediately. He knew it was cruel to hold back such tragic news—Meg had every right to know of her husband's death—but he feared the effects of the news on Christine. His wife's confinement was drawing to its natural end, and any day the doctor expected her to go into labor. The pregnancy had been delicate, and Christine had had difficulty delivering their last child. What if this news threw Christine into a despondency sapping all her energy? What if she went into labor weakened by the emotional reaction to her former tutor's death? Raoul struggled with these fears for two days before, haggard and unsettled, he asked Meg to meet him alone in the park. With him was Sig. Costanzi's letter.

Meg had not been surprised by Raoul's request, but she had been fearful. On several occasions, Raoul had unburdened his heart to Meg in private conversations. He was horribly worried for his wife's health. He had even gone so far as admitting to Meg that he would gladly sacrifice the innocent life of the baby if it jeopardized Christine's. He could not share this with his wife; she would have scolded him severely. It was her wish that the child be saved, no matter what. Although she understood Christine's desire to sacrifice herself for the infant she carried, Meg felt it would be tragic to condemn Raoul to a life without Christine. The child might be forever resented if its life were purchased at the expense of his wife's. So as Meg approached the arboretum at the edge of the park, she was concerned for Raoul and prepared to listen and console him as best she might.

"You wished to speak with me, Raoul?"

Averting his eyes, he nodded silently. Meg could sense his anxiety and wondered if the doctor had told him something frightening about Christine's recent examination. Her sweet smile faded as she studied Raoul's expression. Unconsciously, she worried her lower lip in nervous anticipation.

Finally Raoul turned to Meg. He swallowed audibly and cleared his throat as if to speak. Instead he took her hands in his and drew her to the bench under the canopy of ageless elm and oak. Only when she had sat next to him did she manage to look into his eyes. There she saw only concern and sympathy, not fear. As he began to speak, a cold dread clutched at her heart.

"Meg, you must be brave. I'm sure that's what Erik would say to you. I don't believe that I have any words that would make this easier for you. I'd use them if they existed, but I know how much you loved him."

"Loved?"

"Please forgive me for being the one to tell you this. Erik is dead."

At this, Meg drew in a sharp gasp of air. Her hands dug into Raoul's. She knew he spoke in earnest. She repeated the words several times in her mind. She stared into Raoul's pained eyes, but she wasn't seeing him. She was desperately reaching out with her mind and heart to grasp the meaning of those words. Neither of them spoke for several minutes.

Raoul expected her to cry, to scream, or perhaps to collapse from nervous exhaustion. Her sudden, intense stillness frightened him more than if she had wailed and hysterically berated him. Cautiously he reached out to her and pulled her into his arms. He would never have dared touch Meg in such an intimate fashion unless the circumstances were critical. But Meg allowed herself to be held against his bosom and accepted the slow caress of his hand on the back of her head as he stroked her gently.

Erik is dead, the voice chanted in her mind, and Meg conjured an image of her beloved lying still and pale on satin cushions inside a walnut coffin. A rebellious denial screamed inside her mind, banishing both the words and the image. A resounding "no," not in her voice but in *his* voice, ushered in an image of Erik standing before her, his brow creased, a scowl on his face. Meg pushed away from Raoul's embrace. Tears had made their way down her face; her eyes were swollen, her nose red.

"I don't believe you," she said simply. Seeing Raoul's reaction, she hastened to add, "No. I believe you are telling me what you think is the truth, but I believe you're mistaken or you've been badly informed."

Reluctantly, Raoul took Sig. Costanzi's letter from his pocket. He hadn't wished to let her read it. The details Sig. Costanzi shared with him might overwhelm Meg. They too obviously hinted at what would have been a painful and frightening death. He had planned to share only the fact of Erik's heroism and sacrifice to save others and the fact of his own death. Yet if Meg would insist on a fruitless denial, he was prepared to have her read the words. She would have to believe them. Sig. Costanzi loved Erik, had been present and made all reasonable attempts to verify Erik's role in the drama, and would have left no stone unturned if there were the slightest hope of his survival in the wreckage of the fire. Erik was dead. Raoul had no doubt of it.

Meg stayed his hand as he started to unfold the letter. "No, Raoul. Please. I feel him here." Wishing to impress on him the truth of her conviction, she placed Raoul's hand over her heart. "I would feel his loss if he were dead!"

"And you don't feel it? Your tears tell me otherwise, Meg." Raoul spoke without cruelty, gently, softly, as if Meg were a child. Meg, ferocious and sweet little Meg, was all softness and light. She had taken an irrational, wounded man who had committed barbarous acts and bent him to her will. She had loved what Raoul thought was unlovable and forever transformed a monster.

Unable to sustain her hope, Meg admitted to herself that she could not believe Erik was dead only because she could not imagine her own heart continuing to beat if his had stopped. How could she breathe if his breath were forever stilled?

"I have to go to him!" She stood as if to leave, but Raoul held her back.

"Meg, there's nothing to go back to!"

"What? What do you mean? I need to see him before … Have they buried him already? Has he lain cold and dead so long, and I was here laughing and eating and talking as if my whole world had not crumbled to dust? I'll have his body exhumed! I'll hold him one more time. I'll kiss him one more time! I don't care if the worms have made him their bed, I'll lie with him one more time!" She struggled against Raoul's efforts to comfort her. Her eyes gleamed madly. She wrenched violently away, as he tried to embrace her once more, her hair falling wild across her face and shoulders.

"There's nothing, Meg. There's no grave. There will only be a monument Sig. Costanzi has commissioned. There was a fire, Meg!"

She stopped fighting.

"There was a fire," continued Raoul, more softly. "There wasn't anything left to bury. I'm so sorry."

Her eyes looked up at his so sadly as if pleading with him to have pity on her. She broke into sobs and buried her face in her hands. He sat beside her on the bench once again and placed his arm around her trembling frame and waited.

He had begun to think her sorrow would never abate. The shadows were long, and he shuddered from the cold, somber stillness amid the trees. The tears flowed slowly, the sobs came with less frequency and vigor. Meg leaned solidly into Raoul as if all her energy had been spent. He dared to speak, even though he feared it might set off her anguish. "Sig. Costanzi writes that Erik died while saving the lives of others trapped in the Teatro dell'Opera. As far as anyone knows, he managed to save everyone but himself."

"Oh, Raoul. Why did it have to be by fire?" Her hand clasped his tightly with unexpected strength.

"I don't know, Meg." He had used up all his words. All he could do was hold her, which he did until the last rays of the sun disappeared behind the copse of trees and the night air convinced him that he must take her back to the manor.

Meg kept to her rooms for several days sending word to Christine, lest she worry, that she had caught a chill and didn't wish to pass it on to Christine in her delicate state. Raoul had reluctantly asked Meg to keep the news of Erik's death a secret from Christine until after the birth of the child. It embarrassed him to explain his fear that the news would so adversely affect his wife as to put both her and the child in danger. Meg listened to him with only half her attention, unaware of his discomfort, but she agreed with him that it might cause Christine too much grief and complicate even further her last weeks of pregnancy. She promised not to tell of Erik's death, and that she herself would do everything in her power to act as if nothing had happened.

The promise caused Meg more anguish than she had foreseen when she made it, for it meant that she had to delay telling François and Laurette about their father's death. It tore at her heart to watch them play with Victor and Elise as if their world had not changed for the worst. Raoul had told her of Sig. Costanzi's hope that she and the children would return to live with him, but she wasn't sure she could face living in Rome now that Erik was dead. Raoul had also offered his home to the three of them and promised that he would always consider her his sister-in-law and her children as his nephew and niece. Mme. Giry had always been a mother to Christine, and as such he embraced her as family. Meg would always have a home with the Chagny family.

With some bitterness, Meg accepted his generosity in the spirit in which it was offered even as she thought that had Erik lived he would never have enjoyed Raoul's unconditional acceptance.

Although she was willing to hide her bereavement from her children and Christine, she had to unburden her heart freely to her mother. When Meg fell into her lap, sobbing and telling her that Erik had died over a fortnight ago, Madeleine kept a tight rein on her emotions. She bit back her own tears in order to comfort her daughter.

Later, after Meg had cried herself to sleep, Madeleine stole out to the veranda into the night air and under the stars. There she gave free vent to her anguish. She cried for the beaten and humiliated boy she had rescued from the cage at the fair. She cried for his sadness and incomprehension as he examined his distorted face in the mirror of the dressing room as she picked out costumes and masks to hide his nakedness, but also to hide his ugliness. She cried for the hopeless look of hope in his eyes as she told him she was leaving to make a home, a life for herself with her husband. She cried for her own guilt in his abandonment.

If she had been able to give him just a little more of herself, not only her pity but some of her love, perhaps he would have been able to find some corner of light in which to live. She cried for the child—the young man—who buried himself, his passions and needs, his hopes and desires, in the underground caverns of the Opera Populaire. He had borne her abandonment and her distance—as if it were a judgment against him—and sought to create a world of beauty. He brought her gifts and laid them at her feet, but she had always misunderstood, purposefully misunderstood the gift he asked in return.

She cried for the tragic drama she herself had contributed to when, as a man whose life had never really begun, Erik's gaze fell upon her charge, Christine. It was impossible for him not to love the girl. Madeleine had not allowed him any other hope. It was too late when she recognized his obsession for the young chorus girl. She stood back and watched the course of that ill-fated love. Knowing it must end in Christine's or Erik's destruction, she had chosen to sacrifice Erik.

And she cried for her daughter who had the courage she did not have to woo a wild beast in man's clothing, to find the man trapped inside the monster. She cried because she had loved him, did love him, but had not shown him love when he so needed it, and now would never be able to ask his forgiveness.

It was only later that Christine understood why Raoul had asked her if they could name their new baby girl, Erica.

By that time, out of danger, she had been informed that Erik had been dead for two months. She stared uncomprehendingly at her husband and Meg. Two months he lay cold, and she had not known. Now she understood Meg's haggard face, the small voice that barely emerged when Christine would bring the conversation back to her life with Erik, the gradual loss of weight Meg had suffered, the dimming of her golden light. And not to be able to share her grief with her most loved friend and sister!

Raoul took the brunt of her anger. He explained he had sworn Meg to secrecy. He feared it would jeopardize her health. The baby girl lay mewling in her arms, sensing her mother's distress. Christine looked down at the small miracle, and all her sadness welled up in her breast.

When Meg saw the tears burst on Christine's face, she ran from the room.

CHAPTER 2

❁

Charred and Hollow

How all the other passions fleet to air,
As doubtful thoughts, and rash-embraced
despair,
And shuddering fear, and green-eyed
jealousy! O love,
Be moderate; allay thy ecstasy,
In measure rein thy joy; scant this excess.
I feel too much thy blessing: make it less,
For fear I surfeit.

The Merchant of Venice, Shakespeare

∽

23 June 1877

My Dearest Lucianna,

I have put pen and ink to paper several times without success in an attempt to write you. I regretted your departure. There's little hope that I can tell you in this form how dear you are to me or how grateful I am for your friendship. Without your assistance, my own lack of confidence would have sabotaged my efforts to return to Meg's side.

We have made our home in Rome with Sig. Costanzi, a wealthy and powerful patron of the arts. I am composing for his opera. Several minor pieces have also been purchased by aficionados in the city for other stages, and I've completed sonatas and concertos for the Mondatti and other important families. In addition I have had the immense pleasure of writing the arrangements for several perfor-mances at the Teatro Argentina.

Don Marcelo, Sig. Costanzi, has allowed me to assist him in the design and construction of a new opera house—it will be on a scale grander than any of the existing opera houses in Italy or France—and I have already succeeded in making additions and modifications to the original plans so as to create a series of underground chambers that I may call my own. There are catacombs and natural tunnels that interlace under the ancient heart of the city, and I have drafted the plans that will connect the theater to one which leads to the river at the southern edge of the city, as well as another that extends in an opposite direction. Don Marcelo is frankly puzzled by my insistence in creating this subterranean labyrinth. Anyone who understands my history should not be surprised. Ever since I left the Opera Populaire, I have felt at risk. Now I will have a sanctuary. God willing, I will never be forced to bury myself again in an underground kingdom, but the existence of the secret vaults gives me enormous reassurance.

Lucianna, I am finally able to make a contribution to the world through my music. I have a life. Without you, this would not have been possible. I don't believe I ever told you why I so willingly accepted Ponzio Fiortino's invitation to come to his estate. There were two compelling reasons. The first was you. I could not abandon you to your husband's cruelty. When you met me in the stable that night so long ago, you spoke to me as a woman speaks to a man. I had little experience in such matters. The few I had had were devastating except, of course, my experience with Meg. Your attentions were a revelation to me. That a woman—who did not even know me—could treat me as if I were a man like any other man gave me hope that I could make a life with Meg. I will always treasure what you gave me. I accused you of using me, of betraying me, but I have reconsidered my sojourn at the Fiortino estate and ask you to forgive me for being cruel and insensitive to your plight.

The other compelling reason I accepted Ponzio's invitation was that Sabia, a seer at the fair, read my palm when I first came upon them, intending to cast my lot with theirs. She told me that I had begun in darkness and would end in darkness. Before she finished my reading, however, she glimpsed one hopeful sign, a light. I saw that light in you. My earliest memories as a child were those of living in my own filth in a cage at a traveling fair. I was an exhibit. My handler who, unbeknownst to me, was also my father beat me and treated me like a dumb beast. He made his living from my suffering and humiliation. Returning to work in a traveling fair was my own form of self destruction. You saved me from myself. You showed me another path instead of leaving me to the path my father had laid before me. You were the light Sabia had foreseen. You also led me back to Meg.

We have a second child, Laurette, named for my mother. This time I was with Meg throughout her confinement. I tried to make up for my absence when she carried my son. I insisted she share with me, as much as she might, her experience of holding our child in her body, and I refused to be sent from the room when our babe was about to be born. I have never been so frightened or so awestruck in my life. Nor could I believe the joy I felt when Laurette was finally born. I held her moments after she was delivered. I placed her in Meg's arms. I was so sure that Meg was in danger of dying! I had never understood the courage and strength a woman needed to bear a child. How strong your sex is!

Perhaps the length of this letter will make up for the fact that it is long overdue. Please forgive my silence. I wasn't sure that you wished to hear from me. It was only when I chanced to meet Signore Da Luca at one of the benefits for the opera that I felt I could write you as a friend. I normally avoid all such social events, but on this occasion I was discovered returning late from the construction site and couldn't get away without at least greeting Don Marcelo's guests. As you may recall Don Marcelo has opened his home and his heart to me and my family. He treats me in all respects like a son, and I sense that my regard and affection for him is what a son should feel for a father. Don Pietro Da Luca mentioned that you were happily settled at the estate and that several honorable gentlemen in the area were actively courting you. This gave me the courage to sit and compose this letter. I fervently desire your happiness, and I know from experience that we are not meant to live in solitude. You must reach out, Lucianna, and find someone with whom to share your life.

Accept these words as an expression of my friendship. Do not hesitate to call on me if you are ever in need.

Your humble servant and most sincere friend,

Erik

Meg and Erik had settled in under Sig. Costanzi's protection. Don Marcelo and Erik worked well into the night going over the plans for the premiere opera house of Rome as they continued to operate the more modest Teatro Argentina. When not with Meg, Erik could be found at the Teatro Argentina or with his mentor and patron at the construction site. It seemed to Meg that Erik barely slept. He robbed the night, while Meg slept, to work on his music. No matter the situation at the construction site, Erik would return home in the late afternoon and spend the remaining hours of the day with his wife and son. Meg, on the other hand, slept longer and longer during her pregnancy and woke by late morning to join her mother, Madeleine, in the library or in the garden with François.

At first Erik was uncomfortable around his former protector, Madeleine. Their new relationship struck them both as strange. Erik was unable to think of Madeleine as a mother-in-law. She was only a few years older than he was. But that was not the only obstacle that confronted them. When Madeleine joined the family in the sitting room in the evening, Erik would find some excuse to retire early or he would go to the piano to play. On the latter occasions, he would become so absorbed in the music that Meg and her mother could chat with each other or play card games without fear of disturbing him.

But no matter how much the women would intend to ignore Erik, the music would draw their attention time and time again to his corner of the room. Cards would lie unshuffled, uncounted. Their stories would remain unfinished. The book would lie open on their laps as they listened to his latest composition taking form. Inevitably when his fingers lay still on the keys, he would only then become aware of the women's rapt attention. It never failed to surprise and embarrass him. Meg's open adulation always gratified him, but Madeleine's reaction was always indecipherable to him. He didn't trust her praise, yet he recognized that he sincerely wished for it. It reminded him of his devotion to her when she rescued him from the cage at the fair and hid him in the underground vaults of the Opera Populaire.

After Laurette was born, Madeleine dedicated herself heart and soul to her grandchildren, in particular the newborn infant. François was growing fast and required only minimal supervision. The presence of an infant gave Madeleine a crucial role in the family. She was so smitten by the child that she wouldn't allow anyone but Meg to answer her cries even in the middle of the night. After several nights of interrupted sleep, Meg allowed her mother to make her bed in the nursery and asked her to bring Laurette to her when she woke to feed. The first night the infant woke in the middle of the wee hours of the morning as she usually did. Madeleine lifted her from the cradle and came to the master bedroom. She was on the verge of knocking when Erik opened the door. He, too, had heard the babe cry out. Embarrassed by the unexpected encounter, the two of them stood looking at each other while Laurette fussed in Madeleine's arms. Erik stepped aside and allowed Madeleine to bring the infant to Meg who lay groggy, barely awake, in the bed.

Erik told Madeleine that he would return his daughter to the nursery after she had fed. Perhaps half an hour later, he carried the baby into the nursery where Madeleine had lain down again on the cot by the cradle. He had meant to steal in and leave without disturbing Madeleine's sleep, but as he laid the sleeping infant in the cradle and turned to go he realized his mother-in-law was awake and watching him silently from her bed.

It had been years since they had been alone together, and in the time since Madeleine had joined them, she and Erik had exchanged only the most superficial words. Now in the dimly lit room, all the unspoken words weighed heavily between them. Erik sensed that only Meg connected and made their cohabitation bearable. Madeleine must have felt the coolness in Erik's manner. She admitted to herself that she had done little to repair the damage between them. Perhaps it was Laurette, the little angel, whose arrival even more than François's convinced Madeleine that Erik was an inextricable part of her daughter's life.

She had done everything she could to protect Meg and that had meant—years ago—finding a way to separate Erik from her daughter. Her efforts had been unsuccessful. Whatever Erik was, he was her daughter's lover and husband and the father of her grandchildren. He was no longer the poor soul hidden in the cellars of the opera house.

Before Erik reached the door to leave, Madeleine called to him to stay. He reluctantly paused, his hand on the doorknob, and waited for her to speak. She called to him the way she used to at the Opera Populaire when she brought news or supplies that he needed. He stood so still, so tense that she thought he would refuse to listen to her, but she steeled herself for his anger and spoke about the wall that had grown between them. He listened quietly as she explained how frightened she had been when she discovered him in Meg's dressing room, the two of them naked and asleep in each other's arms. She reminded him that he had been obsessed with Christine, and that she could only believe he was using Meg vilely when he made love to her. She realized later that no matter what she did to protect Meg from him, it wasn't going to work because Meg loved him.

Erik still didn't move or speak. It was as if he were waiting to hear something she hadn't yet said. She had betrayed him to Inspector Leroux. Without her assistance, the police would never have found Erik in his underground sanctuary, would never have beaten him and dragged him to prison. He would not have been tortured and displayed before the mob in the courtroom and condemned to be hanged. He had trusted her, depended on her, loved her in his own ignorant way.

She seemed poised to continue, but Erik interrupted, "Madeleine, do you know what you meant to me? How much I …? I adored you." He spoke in a rushed whisper as if fearing he wouldn't be able to finish before his lungs would collapse. The words were so soft that Madeleine wasn't sure she had heard correctly.

Defensively she confronted him, "Put yourself in my place. What would you have done?"

Erik turned aggressively toward the reclining woman and growled in response, "I would have given anything to be in your place, or in anyone else's place for that matter, rather than the one I was condemned to!"

"I tried to protect you!" Even as she said it, she knew it was ridiculous. Perhaps everything she had done up to that fatal act when she entered Inspector Leroux's office had been meant to protect the strange creature she had rescued in a moment of pity. But she was unable to convince even herself that her betrayal of Erik to the police was anything but an act of destruction, a sacrifice at best. She had consciously decided to sacrifice Erik to save Meg.

"I had no one! I believed you felt something for me, something stronger than pity. All those years, Madeleine, and you never knew me!" Erik tried to keep the tears out of his voice, but the anger was fast supplanted by the memory of betrayal. It was irrational, he knew. She had regretted informing Inspector Leroux of his secret rooms. He had recognized her shame and her plea for forgiveness during the trial when she was forced to testify against him. But the pain he had suffered when Madeleine's name was forever linked to betrayal still gnawed at his soul and mocked his continued need for her love.

She was so hurt by his accusation, as well as by his confession of love, that she burst into tears. Erik didn't move for several moments. He listened to her cry. He stood by her cot debating what to do. Madeleine looked up into his face, and there she saw that he, too, was fighting back tears. His eyes had always been so stirring. He was afraid to reach out to her so she reached out to him instead. The moment he saw her opened hand raised in his direction, he grasped it in his own and sank beside her on the bed. They embraced one another wordlessly. She was surprised at the size and strength of him, for he seemed still that young boy she had taken by the hand and pulled to safety through the dark streets of Paris.

My husband's estate loomed out of the fog like a gravestone. Everything about it reminded me of Ponzio Fiortino and his cruel games. Everything reminded me of what I had lost, Erik. I had lived a nightmare while Ponzio was alive. He had brought me to this prison, an unwilling bride. I could have forgiven him, perhaps eventually loved him, if he had forced my father to allow our marriage because he loved me. But he never loved me, and only briefly did he desire me. He was constitutionally incapable of love. His greatest joy was my pain and mortification. That he beat me was endurable. What I could not bear was the humiliation, the debauchery, his pleasure at my pain and the pain of others.

Erik saved me from my torment. He also taught me to love and to experience pleasure—a pleasure clean and bountiful from giving and receiving pleasure. He was the only man who could see my pain and was brave and strong enough to confront Ponzio and set me free.

Now I was free, but my freedom was empty because I was heartsick without Erik. How could he have risked his life to save me and yet not love me? I had to leave him in his wife's arms.

I vowed to put my life back together.

He had.

Nevertheless, I felt stifled inside the walls of the Fiortino estate, so many scenes of violence and lust, such ugliness and betrayal. Those who had known my husband eschewed me. Those who had always turned their backs on my husband did not rush to embrace me now. Only a handful of adventurous suitors—more enamored of my financial situation than of my character or beauty—presented their cards at my door. Few members of society called upon me, and mostly out of duty or for the sake of propriety.

Rome beckoned to me, offering a new set of acquaintances and social connections. And of course there was Erik.

For Lucianna, Rome offered her the chance to be near Erik. Unfortunately, she rarely came into contact with him in spite of his success and renown in the artistic community.

The opera scene was accustomed to Erik's eccentricities and even enjoyed them. Erik, without meaning to, had become the toast of Rome. His mysterious aloofness enhanced his popularity. Everyone who was anyone ostentatiously subscribed to the Teatro dell'Opera and refused to miss an opening night or the soirées hosted at the opera house or at Sig. Costanzi's elegant mansion. They all hoped to glimpse the artistic genius whose vision was celebrated throughout the country.

Lucianna understood well that Erik's reclusiveness alone didn't explain the intensity of the attraction he held for the public. He made for a dramatic and striking appearance. There were rumors about his penchant for the mask. All the women—and many of the men—were strangely drawn to him. He was an imposing, regal figure of a man—tall, graceful, well proportioned, strong, with broad shoulders, narrow waist, slim hips, and long legs. He also carried himself as if somehow untouched by his surroundings. Most who had or pretended to have exchanged a handful of words with him reported that he spoke only rarely and that his eyes—a deep, dark green that sometimes looked black—would fix on you as if he were examining your very soul. Even the boldest who assailed him retreated hastily, feeling naked under his dark and piercing stare. Lucianna had long ago fallen under his spell.

Only during the opera's hiatus did Lucianna reside at the gloomy Fiortino estate near the Adriatic. Otherwise she preferred Rome. She had reserved a box at the Teatro dell'Opera, and she never missed an opening night performance. Upon arriving in Rome at the beginning of the season, she would send her card without fail to Sig. Marcelo Costanzi's mansion to announce her return. She occupied the same apartments each season in a fashionable section of Rome, not far from the theater district. Within the day, Sig. Costanzi would send her his regards and request her presence at a dinner party at his home.

She knew Erik rarely attended such parties, but he was always present at this welcoming dinner for Lucianna. She treasured these moments. His smile when they greeted one another warmed her heart for she knew it meant he still held some affection for her. Meg was always gracious and sweet, but Lucianna understood the guarded reserve that lay barely hidden under the surface of Meg's hospitality. Lucianna had made no secret of her love for Erik, and had bowed out reluctantly when Meg and Erik were reconciled.

Sig. Costanzi invited only a handful of the most select gentry in Rome on these rare occasions in part to introduce Lucianna into society and in part to limit Erik's exposure. Erik would rather not be present at these social gatherings, so his willingness to attend when she was one of the invited guests touched her deeply.

This contact—always guarded and in public—was all she had a claim to now. It was not enough; she yearned to share a few intimate moments with Erik. These might have been arranged—away from Meg's watchful gaze and away from the others—if Erik had wished to speak with her alone, but he clearly did not. Lucianna understood what this meant and respected his desire that no intimacy take place between them. She would have to be content with friendship. To comfort herself she took every opportunity she could to see him at the opera, to know him through his work, and to glimpse him in those public moments when his patron and mentor, Sig. Marcelo Costanzi, encouraged him to step forth and receive the well-deserved accolades of the spectators.

Upon his release from prison, Giovanni Cimino meant to return to his family home just outside Pianosa only long enough to strip and burn his clothes, exchanging these for the elegant wardrobe his mother had spent months preparing for him. The discarded items he had thrown to the floor reminded him of defeat and imprisonment, humiliation and punishment. Turning a deaf ear to his mother's pleas that he remain at home with her and his father, Giovanni sent his valet to make arrangements for new accommodations in the heart of Rome where he intended to give himself over to a life of luxury and debauchery until the memory of the wasted years he had spent in a prison cell was thoroughly erased.

The first night of his return, he spurred his horse into town and emptied his purse on the counter before climbing the stairs to a series of doors where he expected to find the petite figure of Amalia. He opened the door only to find a large-boned dark haired beauty with the look of a demon on her face lying semi-clothed upon the rumpled bed sheets. Her dark red lips spread in a lewd smile as she saw Giovanni's tall frame and broad shoulders fill the doorway. She ran her gaze appreciatively over the dark hair falling across his forehead, his dark-rimmed eyes narrowing at her in surprise. Momentarily disappointed, he considered returning to the desk to demand the whereabouts of the small blond whore he had always preferred, but years he had spent confined in the company of other prisoners had whetted his appetite to a fevered pitch. He kicked the door shut with the heel of his boot.

Several hours later he emerged much more subdued than when he had arrived. He flexed his knuckles and glanced at the bruises along their ridge. It had been worth it after all. The dark haired Amazon had resisted his blows much longer than Amalia ever could have. He didn't even mind the slight bruise on his chin the bitch had left when she tried to defend herself.

Two days later the arrangements were made, and Giovanni set off for Rome turning his back on Pianosa and his family. He had had plenty of time to decide on the plan of action he now set in motion. The first step was to leave Pianosa. He was adamant that he would not stay in his hometown and face those who had witnessed his humiliation at the hands of Meg Giry's husband, the man who wore a mask to cover his hideous face.

Meg and her husband had purchased the vineyards and orchards that Giovanni had always had his eye on. No one else in the region had the resources to buy the property, so Giovanni felt no urgency to close the deal. Then all of a sudden a foreign lawyer completed the transaction and sold it to other foreigners. He was furious to find the land stolen out from under his nose. But then the new owners arrived, Meg and her strange husband Erik. No sooner had word gone round of their arrival than another wave of rumors circulated that the husband had abandoned the wife.

Giovanni smirked at the French tart's misfortunes. What did he care about her marital problems? And then he saw her. He was on his way to the club when she stepped out from the carriage. He hadn't thought that she would be so young nor so beautiful. She was small and graceful, slim and lithe, with large doe-like eyes, a soft rosette of a mouth, a long delicate neck, and milky skin. Several weeks passed and no one had any idea of the fate of her husband. Slowly the horizon brightened. Not only would he obtain the lands he wanted, but he would happily wed the beauty that went with them.

It was not easy to woo an abandoned wife who still clung to the hope that her errant husband might return. Worse yet was the task of seducing one who was with child! So he waited until the child was born and a reasonable amount of time had passed. The whole town adopted Meg. Everywhere Giovanni went—all the social events of the year—she was there. The women pitied her, and the men admired her. Both bachelors and married men began to insinuate themselves into the exiled French Madonna's company. Soon they all forgot about her mad husband. Word went round that eventually she'd be able to set aside her vows and marry again. The married men contemplated taking her as a mistress. Already married, her honor was not so precarious as it would have been otherwise. Biding his time, Giovanni nevertheless discouraged any legitimate rivals and placed himself at the head of the list of suitable matches. He even began to attend mass regularly since she did so with her old servant, Annetta, and her little prince, François. He had to admit that the boy was sweet. As long as she gave him his own children, he'd allow her to keep the other husband's child.

The father remained a mystery. All Meg would confess to Giovanni was that he was obliged to wear a mask due to a disfigurement, and that he was deeply troubled by a painful past. They had met in Paris where she danced in the opera ballet company, and he had been a musician. Giovanni could find out nothing else. Unlike previous paramours, Meg was unwilling to share intimate details, nor could he fan her emotions into anger against her husband and learn what he wanted by that means.

No one expected her husband ever to return.

After nearly two years of bending his knee, restraining his natural passions, and playing the gallant lover to that blonde minx, Giovanni had finally seen her begin to warm to him. His patience was fast slipping away when Erik returned. All those years wasted! And any tender feelings Meg had felt for him were but nothing compared to the warmth of her renewed affection for the tall, dark stranger whose features lay hidden behind a mask.

It made him mad with jealousy and envy. Worse. It cut his vanity to the quick. He knew well that he was handsome; he had yet to fail to seduce any young woman he'd set his cap for. He had congratulated himself that Meg was falling in love with him, but when he saw her with her prodigal husband, he realized how feeble was her regard for him. It was like comparing a candle to the sun. How she clung to Erik. How she lit from within, a fire that only the masked man could spark in her.

Erik's return had ruined Giovanni's plans and made him the laughingstock of Pianosa! He wanted revenge. Something she had said about their departure from Paris gave him the idea that Erik and Meg's flight from their home was due to some misfortune, perhaps a scandal or worse. So Giovanni investigated and came across the lurid accounts of the murders at the Opera Populaire in 1870. Once he got his hands on a copy of the gazette reporting on the trial of the Opera Ghost—also known as the Phantom of the Opera—it was too much of a coincidence that both the criminal in the account and the man married to Meg wore a mask to hide a disfigurement. Meg had also admitted they were both from the same world, the same opera house where the crimes of the Phantom had occurred. He was amazed to think that the man Meg swooned over was a murderer! According to the same accounts, the Phantom had been hanged and buried just days before Meg and Erik arrived on the doorstep of their new villa and grounds.

Any entanglement with the law would surely frighten the monster off again and leave Meg in Giovanni's capable hands. What could be easier to mimic than a man whose features were disguised behind a mask? It had not been difficult to pilfer one of his rival's masks, and the only other decision was the target of the crime.

Signora Tedesco was the richest and most ostentatious dowager in Pianosa. She wasn't dressed if she didn't have several pounds of gold and silver chain and jewels hanging on her wrists, neck, and ears. Since Giovanni was approximately the same size as Erik, it was delightfully easy to glide past Signora Tedesco, disguised in cape and mask under the protection of a waning moon, and rip the family heirloom from her neck, wobbling several of her double chins and bringing an apoplectic gasp to her mouth. Everyone saw the mask, and they were convinced Erik had stolen the necklace.

Erik fled as Giovanni had expected. It would have been perfect if he had not returned, but he came back and caught Giovanni trying—in an ill-advised and drunken moment—to sneak into Meg's bedchamber to wreak his own private revenge on her for his frustrated courtship. Meg was not unprotected. Enraged, Erik held the young Italian by the heels over the balcony, threatening to drop him to the paving stones below if he didn't confess his role in the robbery of the diamond necklace. Fearing for his life, Giovanni confessed his guilt and was sent to jail for three years. It was only because his family was respected and of some importance that the sentence was so light.

Now he was free. He'd not stay in Pianosa where everyone knew his story. Besides, he had heard that Erik and Meg had left the manor and taken up residence in Rome. That's where he would go as well to settle old scores.

he sweeps his large, square hands over my body, his fingers heavy on my breasts, I feel the weight of his shadow and inhale his smell of cedar and grass and the pungent smell of musk, his breath rushes over my skin and I taste berries and part my lips and sigh for him, his eyes darkly green want me, the dark brow of his forehead furrows in concentration as his pulse accelerates, mine responds in kind, he brushes the auburn strands of my hair from my shoulder and lowers his mouth to my neck, his tongue traces the salty track of a rivulet of sweat that has trickled down my throat, I feel his mouth kiss and suck at my throat and I lick my dried lips sensing his before they are lowered to press against mine, our flesh slick, soft and yielding, merges and I taste him salty and sweet, wet and hard and thrusting inside my mouth, he moans and his voice is low and harsh like the deep note of a cello, the vibrations course across my body like a million finger tips dancing along my skin, his body tense hovers over mine, we are naked and I wrench my mouth from his and through the wound call his name, Erik, I arch my body toward his, my hand brushes the side of his face, my skin rasps against the barbs of dark stubble, I move my hands along his back hoping to press him into me, they glide down the slope to the valley and up across his buttocks, firm and rounded, the muscles flat and taut along the sides, I spread my legs and bend my knees to thrust my hips up to nuzzle against him, to catch him like a vice and swallow him whole, I feel him, hard and weeping between my legs, slip inside and his pressure rend me asunder, and I feel …

The dream. Again the dream leaves me exhausted, panting and empty. A sick loneliness holds me in its fist. I have slung the blankets to the floor and am twisted in the sheets. A sheen of sweat cold in the early morning chill covers the exposed skin of my body. In the course of the dream, I had lifted my gown above my waist and away from my breasts so that Erik could take me unhindered by the cloth. The sunlight strips away the last remnants of the dream, and I bite the fleshy side of my hand to keep from crying.

Meg watched Erik and Lucianna talking in the corner of the salon. They were a striking couple, he tall and broad-shouldered and dark, she only slightly shorter than he with deep blood-red hair coiled and captured against its will and pinned to her head. The coiffure allowed the admiration of her fine, white neck and sloping shoulders. Suddenly Erik shifted uncomfortably from one foot to another and turned slightly away from the bustle of the room and toward the veranda windows. Lucianna, at the same moment, bowed her head as if to examine her hands, one of which held a glass of brandy, the other unnecessarily smoothing the skirt of her gown. Meg ignored the chatter and agitation of the other guests in tight, intimate groupings scattered round the room. At times one of the twenty to thirty invited friends would cross her line of vision erasing completely the figures of her husband and his former lover.

Meg bit her lip nervously as she recalled the history Erik and Lucianna Fiortino shared. Adulterer! That was what the auburn-haired Amazon was! Of course, so was Erik, but Meg brushed that aside as irrelevant. He had come home to her after an absence of nearly three years! He had left the arms of this stunning woman to come back to her bed, and she was glad of it, proud of it, and jealous of it. She would brook no infidelities now. She had forgiven Erik, but she would make sure it didn't happen again!

After she momentarily lost sight of them, she was relieved to see Erik bow slightly toward Lucianna who in turn curtsied attractively, tilting her head slightly to one side. God, the woman was beautiful!

Smoothly, Meg made her way across the room, following Erik. He had come to greet the guests, had supped with them, but only minutes after everyone had retired to after-dinner conversation and drinks in the parlor he had meant to sneak away. He had stopped only briefly to converse with Lucianna. As far as Meg could tell, they had not touched, not even the brief formal touch of hands in greeting. But no matter how brief the conversation, it had struck Meg as intimate, charged with a tension that was both dangerous and seductive. Several times, as she wove her way among the guests, Meg lost sight of her husband as he strode quickly out of the parlor. Her dancer's body served her well as she negotiated the labyrinth of the parlor enclaves to follow Erik outside through the hallway and eventually into the library.

Finally in the dim light and soothing stillness of the library, she paused and watched her husband as he stood staring into the fire. The only sounds in the room were the crackling of fire and wood. In the distance, Meg could hear Sig. Costanzi's voice above the crowd encouraging a few of the party to gather round the piano as someone played a selection of popular tunes from the night's performance. Erik turned as he heard Meg step forward into the room.

"Lucianna?" he whispered before he saw that it was Meg.

Meg froze to the spot. What had been the tone of that utterance? Was it surprise? Or was it the greeting a man gives to his clandestine lover as she steals upon him in a dimly lit room?

The light shone on Meg's face, darkening her eyes, sketching her mouth, drawing lines down her body accenting the bounteous curves of her breast and the narrowness of her waist. Erik turned back toward the fire. His expression was hidden from her.

Perplexed and annoyed, she held her ground, waiting for him to speak, to make clear what he was thinking. He finally spoke, but he kept his back toward her. "I thought it might be Lucianna."

"Obviously," Meg responded in a dry, clipped tone. Had they arranged an assignation that she now interrupted? She crossed her arms under her breasts and pursed her lips into a small pout. If she had been a large woman, she would have forced him to turn to her and explain. She might have slapped him, lashed out at him in her frustration and anger. But she wasn't tall and imposing. He would easily capture her hands before she could strike him.

He stiffened at her tone and slowly turned to face her. "Come here."

"No."

"Come here, Meg," he repeated, his tone low and ominous.

She held her breath, swallowing the sharp reply she wanted to spit at him. Something in his posture stopped her. She slowly approached. The light from the fire lit the uncovered side of his face. He scowled down at her, but undaunted she returned his gaze.

Without a word, he caressed the back of her head. His hand firmly lodged at the base of her skull, he pulled her forward. Bending over her, he brought his lips to hers. Her body melted into his as his other arm wrapped around her lower back, settling at the rise of her buttocks. She was still angry, still upset, still worried, but she was unable to resist him. She savored the familiar taste of him along with a hint of brandy. She felt a tense urgency in his embrace that surprised her, a need she found suspicious but exhilarating, until she remembered he had last been with Lucianna.

Unexpectedly, Erik felt her suddenly push away from him. He released her immediately but stared at her, annoyed that she had broken the moment.

"What is it?" he asked harshly. It vexed him that she bore this useless jealousy. He had returned to her; he shouldn't need to prove his love to her. "You're being unreasonable. I look on Lucianna as a friend, nothing more."

"Why did you call out her name when you heard me come in? You were expecting her!" Why was she torturing herself? She didn't want to know the answer if it was the one she thought it was!

"I wasn't 'expecting' her in the way you mean it. I feared it was she."

Meg kept silent, waiting for Erik to explain. Instead he stretched out his hand to take her again. She stepped back, beyond his reach. He narrowed his eyes and clenched his jaw tight in anger at her rejection. The two of them stood as if measuring one another before the first blow.

"You little fool!" he hissed and raised a clenched fist for emphasis.

"You wouldn't dare!" Meg took the gesture as an excuse to challenge him. She had seen Erik violent, dangerously and frightfully violent, with others, and she, too, had been able to infuriate him to the point of madness. But he never raised an angry hand to her except as a warning. Even when she struck him repeatedly and threatened to claw his eyes out, he would not return the blows. He would take her anger for a while and then wrap his arms around her, pinning her arms to her side, in order to restrain her until her anger or her strength were spent.

He took one large step toward her and grabbed her once more in his arms. He held her in an implacable embrace.

"Let me go!" Meg squirmed against his restraints. His eyes darted angrily at her, but he wouldn't release her.

"Not until you ask me to forgive you!"

"Forgive? Are you as mad as you are ugly?"

"If I'm mad, it's because you've made me so," he returned and squeezed her just a bit more tightly until she emitted an involuntary gasp. Then he relaxed his hold slightly. "Tell me that you are sorry that you doubted me. Tell me that you know that I would never touch another woman. That you're the only woman that I desire!"

Meg felt pierced by his eyes.

"I came back to you! I could have left with Lucianna. She wanted me, still wants me, and I've slept in her bed. I know how passionate and skilled a lover she can be."

Meg stopped struggling, caught frozen by his eyes. Her lips trembled, and tears welled up as she listened.

Erik's face was close enough to hers that he felt the warmth rise from the blush that covered her fair skin. He felt drawn to her mouth, but he would not stop. "I made love to her many times at her estate. I … I even did so once in Pianosa." His gaze faltered momentarily as he heard Meg's sharp intake of air and felt her body shudder with pain. "I had watched you and Giovanni in the garden and was consumed by the need for you. I was wracked by jealousy. She came to me, and I didn't resist."

Suddenly he released her.

"Forgive me, Meg."

Without his support, she almost crumpled to the ground. He leaned in toward her, his hands still by his side. His eyes were averted, and he waited for her to lash out at him for this new confession. Meg had known about the relationship between Lucianna and Erik, but it had ended before Erik left the Fiortino estate to come home. She didn't know that her husband had made love to Lucianna while he watched and waited for his moment to make his return known. She raised her clenched fist to hit him, but left it hanging in the air. She couldn't hurt him! She loved him with all her soul, and now she must accept that he had found pleasure in the arms of this other woman even when he professed that he loved only her!

Erik took Meg's raised hand and brought it gently, softly to his lips.

"Meg, you are my light, my soul. Yours is the only body that I have loved! No one touched me. No one wanted to touch me. When you followed me into the underground vaults, I was in search of death. I had nothing, no life, only an aching desire that was destroying me. My body was my enemy. You touched me. You gave me tenderness and returned my passion, and I found myself. I don't want Lucianna. I love her as a friend, and it breaks my heart that she desires me. But she's no threat to you, my love."

Meg wrapped her arms tightly around Erik. "I'm sorry I doubted you. I love you, Erik. I love you so terribly much that sometimes I think you and I are one soul. If ever I lost you, I would lose myself."

"My silly song bird! My canary!" Erik murmured in between kisses. "Come." Without another word, he led her by the hand through the adjoining compartments until they reached the servants' quarters and the back staircase that led to the upper chambers of the estate. He led her directly to their room where they undressed and fell into each others arms.

Erik glimpsed the malevolent face of a ghost from his recent past. Giovanni sneered as he pushed the door closed and barred it from the other side. Immediately Erik smelled burning wood, heard the crackle of flames searing and devouring the walls, felt the heat seep through the fissures and rise from the dark corner of the room toward the ceiling. Glancing around, he estimated the time it would take for barrels, crates, fabric, papier-mâché, and panels to catch and consume themselves in the blaze.

Erik didn't fear his own death. Little did Giovanni know—that was the face he had spied before the door came slamming shut—that Erik had designed the underground chambers and further modified them secretly to match in many ways his sanctuary at the Opera Populaire. Hidden doors, secret traps, corridors and passageways linked the compartments to multiple escape routes. He could and would easily escape the fire Giovanni had foolishly set. It was the rising panic in human voices just above him in the dressing rooms and backstage halls that filled him with dread and purpose. Climbing to the next story through one of his secret pathways and stairs, Erik saw the reason for the panic. The opera house was not deserted. Several of the cast and stage crew had lingered in the west wing, and the fire had predictably risen and engulfed these rooms trapping the inhabitants in a corner of the operatic maze.

Quickly Erik gathered those who were not yet overcome by the thickening folds of smoke and, wrapping cloaks, wall hangings, and other articles of the actors' wardrobe around them, sent them through a secret passageway leading tortuously to a natural grotto whose mouth opened onto the west bank of the river well away from the opera district and the fire. Once these could see their way clear, Erik returned to assist others who had been unable to move on their own. Several times he had returned, his handkerchief tied over his mouth, to drag an unconscious victim from the corridor or from one of several rooms. The fire had advanced rapidly. Under his foot he could tell that the entire structure of the floor was about to crumble. He turned to leave when he noticed a bulk crammed in under a stairway which had partially collapsed. He had heard just minutes before the crash of timbers. The man may yet live. Crawling along the floor where the air was still breathable, Erik went to the bulk and pushed the timbers to the side. He protected his hands as best he could with the thick fabric of his coat. Finally he managed to free the man's body and without regard for the possible additional injury he might do him he pulled the man's arms until he felt some resistance give way. Placing his shoulders against the massive frame of the staircase, Erik pushed the debris up and out of the way as he pulled the man from the last barrier. Once freed from the debris, Erik could see the bulk was a young man, nearly his own size. The face barely visible in the smoke seemed to be unscathed by the flames, but it was bloody from the scrape of wood or metal across one cheek near his jawbone. Erik couldn't help but pause as he recognized the fool who had meant to murder him, Giovanni. Caught in his own snare! He hesitated only a second—it did occur to him that he might abandon the scoundrel to his fate—before hoisting the prone body over his back and shoulders and scrambling for safety. Several minutes later he deposited Giovanni's body—whether alive or not he couldn't be sure—on the edge of the grotto where the others were recovering from smoke and fire.

He could not be sure no one else remained trapped behind. He judged he might yet go back once more to see. He would also try to salvage the valise he kept with him at all times—his music lay inside. Although his eyes watered profusely, and he coughed convulsively, spitting up black spume from the smoke, he reentered the labyrinth.

The rooms were aglow with riotous flames, and he realized the fire was progressing more rapidly than he had calculated. No one could survive that cauldron! The fire was moving downward as well as laterally now. He dropped to the next floor below the dressing chambers, to the room where he had gone to meet the mysterious author of a note he had received earlier that day. Now he understood who had written it and why he had sent it. The revenge Giovanni sought struck Erik as disproportionate to the wrong—monstrous in its possible consequences.

This room was also in flames and a narrow passageway was the only path Erik could safely traverse to reach his valise. This miraculously had not yet been touched by the flames. As he dropped to hands and knees to crawl to the spot where the valise lay, he heard an ominous clap of noise as if it were thunder. As Erik grabbed the valise, the boards above and below him suddenly gave way, and he fell through to several levels below. Fragments of flooring toppled over him. Part of a burning post landed on Erik's back and rolled to the side. An unidentifiable chunk of walling glanced off the back of his head leaving a weeping gash. Erik was struck unconscious by the falling debris and lay sprawled upon the stone of a natural cave. Here the fire could get no purchase and gradually spent its effort and died. The smoke rose away from Erik. Above him, the world was an inferno that was eventually contained by the volunteers who rushed to the scene to fight it. Several chambers on two separate floors were destroyed, but the grandest opera house in Rome, in the entire country, would survive.

Having roused himself, Erik crawled blindly forward. He was not unconscious, but neither was he lucid. Blinding white pain made thought impossible.

He drove himself, pulled himself forward, not towards anything, but simply away from certain death. The stone floor cooled the fever along the side of his head and soothed the lacerations and burns on his hands. He dragged one leg which was perhaps broken from the weight of the beam that had fallen across his body. He forced himself to breathe in spite of the overwhelming sensation of broken ribs and choked lungs. He pulled himself oblivious to all but the need to remain in motion until he felt the sweet breeze of fresh air and sensed the open vault of the night sky above him, and there he welcomed the black coolness of night. It invaded his body, his mind, leaving him charred and hollow, but alive.

CHAPTER 3

❀

Through a Glass Darkly

For now we see through a glass, darkly, but
then face to face: now I know in part; but then
shall I know even as also I am known.

1 Corinthians 12 King James Bible

*blackness, heat, unbearable heat, a sound like thunder, hundreds of thunderclaps,
the crash of falling objects, pain licking across my back, a searing brand, the
weight of centuries, impossible to breathe the liquid hot air, smoke filling my
mouth, my nose, my eyes stinging, red-tinged blackness through tightly squeezed
eyelids, unable to move, unable to open my eyes*

"They say that a fire broke out in the storage rooms. Several people have
managed to escape through an underground tunnel."

"Did they say anything about Erik, I mean, Sig. Costanzi, the younger one?
Has he been accounted for?"

"No, signora. Unfortunately, Sig. Marcelo Costanzi arrived shortly after the
survivors were discovered on the west bank several meters from the opera
house. He has given up hope of finding Don Erik."

Luigi had been a retainer at the Fiortino estate since well before Don Ponzio
returned home one day with his reluctant bride, a beautiful, tall, auburn
haired woman of nineteen whose name was Lucianna. He vividly recalled a
couple of years later the arrival of the strange masked man his master had
invited who would change everything, putting Don Ponzio's reign of debauchery and violence to an end and rescuing Donna Lucianna from her loveless
marriage. The servant knew it was not his place to comment on his mistress's
concern for the gentleman, but all of the servants who lived at the Fiortino

estate were well aware of the debt Donna Lucianna owed Don Erik. There had been a duel, and the masked man had vanquished Don Ponzio, ridding them all of a tyrant. Luigi withdrew discreetly pretending not to see the look of sorrow on his mistress's face.

Lucianna choked back her tears as she watched the gradual disappearance of the remaining bursts of flame from the opera house. She had just enjoyed the premiere of *Don Giovanni*, an opera under Erik's artistic direction, and spent a fruitless hour exchanging congratulations with cast members and patrons of the opera in the vain hope Erik would make one of his infrequent appearances.

Tonight she left the opera house after waiting for nearly an hour to see if Erik might appear at the after-performance reception. Sig. Costanzi had taken pity on her and approached to say that Erik had gone to the storage rooms and would probably leave without coming by the reception. He squeezed her hand in the sweet, familiar way he had with those, like Lucianna, who were younger than he. She accepted his touch as it was meant, as a kind and compassionate gesture from a man old enough to be her grandfather. She blushed, knowing that Erik had probably confided to his protector the essential details of their relationship when he was estranged from Meg and a guest and victim of Lucianna's sadistic husband. She could tell from the old gentleman's behavior toward her that Erik had forgiven her many errors and cast her only in a favorable light in his account of those months he spent at the Fiortino estate.

Now she sat looking out her carriage window toward the destruction in the distance and grieving for the one man whom she had loved. Erik had been in the storage rooms underneath the backstage dressing rooms. A fire had broken out in that wing of the opera house. He was not among the survivors!

She sat crying softly for some time. The survivors had been found several meters from the opening of a natural cave. They had evidently escaped or been helped to escape through the underground tunnel system Erik had designed. Erik was the only one who knew these passages! He had written once to her about the construction of the Teatro dell'Opera. She remembered his mentioning the vaults, the recently installed panels, the various exit paths he had constructed himself. One of these tunnels opened on the southern slope of the hill, some distance from the Teatro, but she recalled there had been others. It suddenly occurred to her that there was a chance Erik survived the fire. Indeed she was sure that the survivors had made it out with his help. If one exit had become blocked and he could not get out, there was at least one other that he might have taken.

"Luigi, quick. Take me around the river path! We'll start where the survivors were found and continue clockwise until we make a complete circuit. He may still be alive!"

Luigi instructed the driver, and they set out slowly following a path many meters distant from the opera house and the surrounding buildings. Here the buildings came to an abrupt end due to the natural boundary of an escarpment and a river that twisted along the basin. After an hour and two complete circuits, they had found nothing. Lucianna refused to listen to Luigi who suggested that there was nothing to find. Instead she urged him to hire several men to assist in the search on foot along the slope descending toward the river. The path skirted the edge of the district and could not abut the river due to the irregular terrain. The ground was steep, broken by several rocky ledges. Lucianna insisted that they must continue the search on foot in spite of poor visibility and unsafe conditions.

Luigi had managed to enlist several men who combed the area, their lanterns swaying in the darkness. Lucianna could not bear to sit in the carriage waiting. She took a lantern and joined the search. If the moon hadn't risen, casting its ghostly light along the side of the hill, she would never have seen him. What remained of his white shirt caught the light from the moon; otherwise the man was shrouded in darkness and she might have passed within an arm's length of him and not seen him. She called to Luigi and, without waiting for the others to join them, she climbed down the precarious path to the ledge where he lay prone, his legs still hidden just inside the cave opening. She knelt beside him and called to him. Drawing up beside her, Luigi bent and carefully turned the body over.

"Does he live?" she pleaded.

Luigi searched the man's body for some sign of life. Finally, he felt a pulse in Erik's throat. "Yes, signora. His pulse is regular, but faint."

screams, loud and frightened, men's and women's voices, blackness and pain as if my body had no skin, as if my body were flayed and rubbed against roughly hewn stone, as if there were nothing but pain, the inside of my brain presses against my skull clawing against bone to escape, the screams are louder and louder in my ears, inside my head, I can't breathe, I can't open my eyes, heat swirls around me, heat fans across my flayed skin, stabs at my pores, eats my eyes, licks my back until I imagine flames in the form of rabid wolves biting and gnawing at my limbs, one digs away into the soft flesh of my belly, screams, my own, screams of others, the crack of wood, of bones, of skull, the fall, the press of the entire vault of heaven smashes me, ribs groan, lungs unable to take in the searing smoke, eyes watering and stinging, lids thinned and transparent vulnerable to the flash of the firebrand, and I feel death laughing behind me, I see death touching my legs, rubbing his white sepulcher bones up along my thighs, the crushing of bones, the skull's gaping jaw grins at me as I drag my legs along the stone floor, as I grab with my elbows, claw with my broken fingernails a purchase beyond myself and pull my body and the entire weight of the world that has crashed down upon me, I gasp, I feel blood, my blood, cold! running down my face, my body is heat, my body is melting, my body is pain and death and I scrape the skin from my arms, I claw at the rock surface and pull away from the death's head, the pain is with me, I drag the pain with me, it is in me so deep now that I cannot slough it off, I cannot pull out from underneath it, I take it with me, it is me

Black soot covers his clothes and face, the palms of his hands are red with blood, his mask gone, lost somewhere in the underground inferno of the opera house. As the men carry him toward the sofa, I glimpse a wicked tongue of raw, burned flesh lashed across his back, from shoulder to shoulder. Carefully, carefully, the men lay him on the green and gold fabric of the sofa; I cringe as his weight rests against the rough material, and once more utter a brief prayer of gratitude that Erik is insensible. Carefully I cradle his head in my lap brushing the ash from his hair, tenderly examining his smudged face; tears from swollen eyes have left tracks in the soot that covers him. His lips are parted, and his teeth shine in the dark visage. Slowly I rise from the sofa and lower his head to the cushion. I ask Luigi to turn him gently. The back of his shirt has been burned away except for a fragment blackened and apparently melted into the skin along the soft plane between his shoulder blades. I find angry welts left from falling debris and fire. We turn him gently to rest on his side. I begin to cut the clothes from his torso methodically. Along his chest are bruises, cuts, and minor burns. Suddenly I notice my blood soaked skirt. Quickly I examine his head and find an open gash across the back of his skull which rests against the pillow; a steady flow of blood spreads along the heavy damask and slowly soaks into the cloth. All that I've seen till now seems insignificant compared to this angry, gaping wound. I take the wet cloth from the basin Gretta has brought filled with warm, soapy water and gently clean the wound. The blood flows more quickly as I clear the dirt from the gash in Erik's scalp. To stanch the flow, I take a dry cloth and press it firmly against the weeping wound. I tell Gretta to hold it while I continue to cut his clothes away and wipe his body.

Before the doctor enters, I wonder whether to hide Erik's face and conclude that I should not hamper the physician's examination. The doctor asks me to wait outside the room in spite of the fact that I am the one who has stripped Erik, cleaned and covered him with a light blanket. Reluctant to interfere with his immediate treatment, I step out to the parlor where Luigi waits.

"The fire is out."

"Did you speak with Sig. Costanzi?"

"I was unable to speak with him. He had already returned to his estate. I spoke with some of the bystanders at the scene of the fire. Don Erik is credited with saving those who survived. The last time he was seen he was returning to the opera house. Everyone has given him up for dead."

I stood looking at Luigi as the full meaning of these words unfolded for me. They believed he was dead! Thankfully, I knew Meg was in France visiting with friends. But someone would eventually send word to her. Sig. Costanzi must be distraught.

"Did you not go to Sig. Costanzi's estate?"

"I did, signora. You instructed me to contact Sig. Costanzi. I tried to do so at the site of the fire. I went from there to his residence. I was told that Sig. Costanzi is not accepting visits of any kind except those of his physician. It seems that he has taken to his bed."

"Well, thank you, Luigi. We'll have to wait. Perhaps it's for the best. What good would it do to raise hopes if Erik were to die now?" I smiled weakly at Luigi, but found it difficult to take my eyes off the closed parlor doors.

After what seemed an eternity, the doors opened. I rushed in and went directly to Erik's side. He breathed still. His head had been bandaged, as had his eyes! A quick glance gave me some idea as to the extent of his injuries. Yet I insisted the doctor give me a detailed account of his condition. He wasn't accustomed to being interrogated by a young woman and reluctantly answered my questions. When he saw I would not desist until fully satisfied, he sighed and returned to Erik's prostrate body to point out the major issues of concern.

"The side of the face, of course, is a previous disfigurement and therefore of no concern in this case. He has suffered some burns, mostly superficial with the exception of a nasty burn across the back which you will have to tend very diligently to avoid infection. That one will most probably leave a scar, whether or not it festers. His eyes are inflamed, severely irritated from smoke and heat. I'm leaving this salve to be applied every four hours day and night inside, under the lids. We'll have to wait to see if there's scarring that could lead to blindness. The leg was wrenched, and I fear some tendons were pulled if not torn. I've splinted the entire limb. Keep him off it until I tell you otherwise. Four ribs along his left side are badly bruised—a miracle they weren't broken—and I've bound them to make his breathing easier. He has probably inhaled a great deal of smoke, and if he regains consciousness he'll have fits of coughing and choking. It will not be pleasant given the condition of his ribs. Let's see what else before I get to the real concern." He stopped and glanced across Erik's body as if checking off a mental inventory of problems until he finally seemed satisfied and turned his eyes again toward me.

"Well, he's pretty badly bruised all over, but that is the least of our worries. You can use the lineament liberally as long as you don't move him too much. It's the head wound that concerns me. It's quite bad. I've seen no sign of his coming to. But there are signs that he's in severe distress, and there's a good chance, Signora Fiortino, that your husband may not recover. I'm very sorry."

Erik might die! "What can we do?" I grabbed the physician's sleeve as he reached the door.

"Nothing, signora. Pray. Tend to the other injuries in case your husband does wake up. That's all we can do." As gruff as he seemed, the doctor gently pried my fingers from his coat sleeve and quietly left me alone with Erik. My husband, he had said.

I sat on the floor beside Erik and took his bandaged hand in mine. Dear, dearest husband, my dearest Erik! If only you were! Of course the physician had assumed we were married. A woman in my station would never have attended, as I had, to a man who wasn't her husband. What was I to do? Who should I call upon? Meg was out of the country. Even if I sent one of my servants to fetch her back, it would take days, and Erik might be dead well before then. Sig. Costanzi refuses to receive anyone. I'm the only one, Erik. I won't let you die alone, my love.

Erik's lips were parched. He stretched and broke the taut skin as he opened his mouth. His tongue flicked over the opened fissures and tasted salty, metallic blood. Someone was moving around him, but he couldn't see. He heard a moan; it came from his own throat. Suddenly aware of pain radiating from all parts simultaneously, he jerked as if to rise only to find the pain intensify to an unbearable pitch. He was incapable of movement.

Why couldn't he open his eyes? What had happened?

As he thought to raise his hands to his face, he heard her voice and felt her bend over him. He sensed her solidity as it approached his body. She smelled of lilacs and soap. A soft hand brushed against his cheek. "You're safe. Don't move," she urged, sweetly, concern palpable in each breath from her mouth. He felt that, too. He willed himself to trust the voice, the breath, the smell, the presence. He waited for her to speak again, to tell him he was dead, to comfort him in his damned state. For surely this much pain must be the consequence of hell itself. He thought he remembered the smell of charred flesh and the searing heat of hell fire. The deep intake of air set off a chain of coughs, and the spasmodic movement of his chest directed the formerly diffused pain to his ribs and across his temples. He choked and coughed as he gasped from it.

Again the voice, "Here, drink this, Erik. It will help."

Her hands—cool and soft—assisted him. The edge of the cup touched his swollen lips. The cool, sharp taste of water and honey poured into his hot mouth and slid down his raw throat. He felt it course down to his stomach.

"Erik," she had said. Erik? She was talking to him, and she called him Erik. He tried to remember the man to whom the name belonged. Who was Erik? Who was he? There was nothing, no sound, no answer to this question. Inside his mind he raced back and forth only to find the memory of waking to the taste of blood on his cracked lips.

She bent close to him. There was something wrapped around his eyes. But he could sense her body and hear the swish of her skirt against the bed. He turned his ears toward her and listened to her whisper to someone in the room. Another series of coughs crashed through his body. Her hand wiped his mouth.

He waited to hear her voice again, the beautiful calm voice of his angel.

"Aren't these hopeful signs, Doctor?"

"Possibly, signora. But we must be patient and cautious in our optimism. If he lives, there may still be serious problems."

"What problems? Will he be blind?"

"His eyes have improved, but there is a chance that he may have impaired vision. I'm still more concerned by the blow to the skull."

Lucianna could tell the doctor was not forthcoming. He scowled as he inspected the gash in Erik's scalp. Finally he turned to ask her a question. "Has he spoken? Has he shown that he recognizes where he is, who you are?"

"No, but he did wake up, as I told you before. That must indicate something." She waited hopefully, anxious for the doctor to reassure her.

"Of course, it does."

"Then what are you really saying? What do you think might be the problem?"

"Since you insist, signora. A severe head injury can lead to many subsequent problems. Some patients with severe brain trauma remain alive but in a vegetative state, neither alive nor dead, at times seeming to react to their surroundings but most of the time oblivious as if in a perpetual sleep. Or they might wake up and suffer brain damage leading to many problems including amnesia, personality disorders, retardation. You understand?"

Lucianna answered faintly, "I see."

"In brief, Signora Fiortino," continued the squat burly man, "we must wait until he is fully conscious and responsive to see what his true condition is, and even then we can't be sure that down the road there might not be a problem. I've known patients to wake up perfectly normal, go about their lives as if nothing had happened, and then suddenly drop dead in the middle of their soup."

Lucianna followed the doctor to the door. Only when she was sure that he had passed through the passageway and out the front door to the street did she crumple to the ground, her fist wedged deep between her teeth to keep from sobbing out loud.

Hands are tugging at my head. I stifle the groan in my throat. Voices swirl around me, voices other than my angel's. I smell the dark scent of a man, wool coat and cigar, as well as other things that I can't name. Why can't I see? A gauze-filtered light grows as layers of cloth are stripped from my face, and I feel my eyelids twitch. I try to open them, but they are glued shut. I want to rub them, to clean the viscous matter from my eyes. I lift my hands to do so, but they're heavy and someone forces them down. I blink repeatedly. The silhouette of a woman against a cream colored background grows larger until it bends toward me. Lilacs and a hint of soap come with it. It's my angel, my comforter, my protector.

Hands are on my body; hands pull and push me. I try to resist, but my limbs are heavy and won't respond.

I cry out to the shadows, to the hands, to stop, to leave me alone!

"Erik, it's all right. We need to move you. It will only take a moment." Her voice reassures me. Again she calls me by a name that I don't recognize. I try to think of my name. Nothing. I try to find my angel's shape, but my face is turned into the wall, a wall of softness; I make out a hint of green against creamy gold or light brown. I smell fabric, I think. How do I know the smells of these things? I try to speak, but my throat tightens painfully. My body convulses, and I emit deep, raspy coughs. I struggle to breathe between spasms. I feel the spittle fly from my mouth. The muscles along my stomach ache. A sharp pain stabs my side with each explosion of air that bursts from my lungs, and I imagine the red lining of my viscera breaking loose and flying from my mouth with each new wave of coughing.

Someone holds my head. Someone runs a cool, moist cloth over my face. Someone—the voice—makes low, soothing noises by my ear. I pray she doesn't go away. I pray she'll stay by me until the hands are done, until the pain stops, until the spasms quiet.

"Gretta, you're a wonder!"

"Prego, Donna Lucianna."

"I sometimes think you have more skills at healing than our physician. The salve has really calmed his cough, and he's resting much more easily now."

Gretta smiled at her mistress, pleased to have her talents recognized. "Would you like me to bathe him for you, signora?" When Lucianna arrived at the Fiortino estate, Gretta became her personal maid. The broad-hipped and muscular Gretta looked as if she should work in the field or kitchen—work requiring both stamina and strength—but she had a gentle touch and soon revealed her knowledge of medicinal plants. Lucianna had taken an instant liking to her, and Gretta felt a doglike loyalty to her mistress even when she disagreed with her.

"No, I'll do it." Lucianna didn't worry that Gretta would find this improper. Gretta had aided Lucianna, several years ago, when Erik was Don Ponzio Fiortino's guest at the estate. It was Gretta who provided the potion that drugged Erik, making him pliant but unaware so that Lucianna could seduce him. Ponzio had wanted an heir. Lucianna had decided that Erik should father the child. But Lucianna's seduction of Erik had been a mistake. Not only did she not conceive, but she found herself falling in love with Erik.

So it was that Gretta understood how important Erik was to her mistress, and it didn't surprise her that Donna Lucianna cared for him personally. She also knew that it would be pointless for her to ask her mistress why Don Erik had not been taken immediately to his family.

Erik had been moved to a bedroom, and he lay propped on his uninjured side, off the nasty burn between his shoulder blades and off the bruised ribs. Gretta had fixed the bed so that Erik's torso was slightly elevated, and together with the strong smelling salve this had made Erik's breathing easier.

"Do you think he'll be all right, Gretta?" Lucianna asked with a childlike plea for comfort in her voice.

"Signora, he's a big, strong uomo. Hard head, strong bones. He heals fast. Look at these cuts, signora. They've already done so!" Gretta patted her mistress's hand familiarly and smiled as reassuringly as she could. Before she left, when Lucianna couldn't see her, her smile fell away. Her mistress so loved this man who didn't belong to her! Gretta, too, worried about the blow he had received to the head. And what of his woman and his children? He'd chosen a different life. If he recovered, surely he'd go back to them, leaving her mistress devastated once more.

When Gretta closed the door behind her, Lucianna began to wash Erik gently, section by section. She first washed his face, carefully around the gauze bandages so as to keep them dry. She moistened his full, red lips with a clean cloth dipped in clear, cool water. Laying it aside she bent toward him. She ran her finger over his lips. They were slightly parted, and she felt his breath flow across her skin. She took her finger away and saw a hint of tongue, lying like a sleeping dog in his home, and the white glint of his teeth. Irresistibly she felt drawn to his mouth. Her lips settled softly over his, and her tongue teased gently inside the warm, moist opening. Her heart leapt when she felt his tongue respond to her tentative greeting. She drew back to look at him. He closed his mouth and swallowed, and the lips parted again. He sighed deeply, but otherwise didn't stir. Lucianna's lips still retained the ghost of his kiss.

In the first few days Sig. Costanzi had gone to his room and instructed his servants that he would see no one. He immediately fell ill, and his personal physician was called in to examine him. For the next several days he was confined to his bed under his doctor's orders.

No one had found any signs of Erik's body in the charred remains of the underground structure. The building was inspected and found to be safe. The chambers destroyed belonged to an addition that was separate from the foundation itself. Sig. Costanzi would have to have some of the construction replaced, but the opera house itself had been salvaged.

A week after the fire, Sig. Costanzi met with his associates to discuss the results of the inspection. The search for Erik's remains had ceased after the first forty-eight hours. Sig. Costanzi knew that he must come to grips with the situation; he had waited too long to inform Meg of Erik's tragic death.

As he sat at his writing table, his fingers trembled. The paper lay before him, and with a heavy heart he began to compose the letter. He decided, after several failed attempts, that he couldn't address the letter directly to Meg. He must enlist the Count de Chagny's aid in breaking the tragic news to her. This was something she should not read in a letter. She needed someone to tell her who could study her reaction and fit the telling to the situation.

Lucianna woke to see Erik staring into her face. Startled she jerked her head back onto the pillow a few inches farther away from Erik.

He still stared through filmy green eyes. The doctor had removed the bandages, pleased with the way the eyes were healing. They were no longer swollen, and he was hopeful that the man would recover at least partial vision.

Lucianna saw the strained expression as Erik tried to speak. He was awake! He was conscious! He must be shocked and puzzled to find her by his side, in the bed, lying next to him. She blushed a red more vivid than the scarlet of her hair as she realized she had lain down beside him in her chemise, tired and hot, in the summer heat.

Before she thought to rise from the bed, his voice stopped her.

A raspy, hoarse sound erupted from his mouth. "Tell me," he began, but closed his eyes as he swallowed painfully to moisten his raw throat. "I can't ... I don't remember." His effort set off a series of coughs. She drew near enough to place her arm behind him and softly rub his back, carefully avoiding the burn.

"There was a fire, Erik," she began to explain, but he shook his head impatiently and brought his bandaged hand to her face as if to place his fingers on her lips. Carefully, he whispered, his eyes urgently searching hers, "No. Before. Nothing. I don't know."

Understanding dawned slowly on Lucianna. She recognized confusion and pain, entreaty and hope, in his intent gaze as he waited for her to respond.

"Erik, do you remember me?"

Again he swallowed audibly before opening his mouth to speak. "Wife?"

What did he mean?

"Meg? Do you remember Meg?" she asked.

A puzzled scowl crossed his face, then a look of pain. He shook his head only slightly, very carefully. "Who am I?"

"But you remember your wife?"

Again he shook his head, but he pointed his bandaged hand toward Lucianna's breast. "Don't remember you. Heard Doctor. It's all gone." The panic slowly rising in Erik's mind took over as he tried to explain the empty blackness that swallowed everything except the experience of waking in these apartments a few days ago. Tears welled up in his eyes and spilled down his cheeks, but he bit his lip to muffle the sounds pushing against his throat.

Lucianna realized that Erik woke with only one piece of knowledge. He must have heard the physician refer to him as her husband. She had not thought to correct the physician. Each time Erik woke—even briefly—it had been she whom he found by his side. Even now she lay beside him as only a lover would. He did not remember her or anyone! He had learned—been told—that she was his wife, and he had accepted that piece of information as the truth and clung to it now as the only certainty against a vast emptiness that was his past. His memory had been burned away in the fire.

She leaned forward and kissed him sweetly on the lips. She kissed his eyes, his cheek, and kissed his tears away. She whispered to him that she loved him and was thankful that he'd come back to her. Everything would be all right, she cooed to him as she pressed him ever so gently against her bosom.

"You want me to return to Sig. Costanzi's, signora?"

"Yes. Leave this note for him with my respects. Hurry back. We have much to do."

My esteemed Sig. Costanzi,

Please accept my heartfelt condolences on the tragic death of your son, Don Erik. I am deeply saddened at the horrible accident in the Teatro dell'Opera. I will write personally to his family to express my condolences to them. As you know, Erik and I were old friends. I haven't the desire to stay in Rome under these circumstances. I can't imagine the opera season without Erik. I intend to leave immediately for my estates in the east. Please forgive that I do not take leave of you in person. I understand that you have been indisposed and have received few, if any, visitors.

I remain your humble friend and servant,

Signora Lucianna Fiortino

The journey had been long and painful, but they had finally settled their trunks in the airy rooms of the seaside manor. Erik suffered tremendous knocks and jolts on the arduous trip across land from Rome in spite of the special coach hired by Lucianna. The sea passage to the island in the Adriatic had been easier on his wounds, but the waves of nausea from seasickness left him weak and despondent. On the island it was warm and sunny so Lucianna gave orders that the windows be left open and that Erik be dressed in a light night shirt. At last he lay on clean soft bedding, motionless and safe, with a warm salty breeze playing across his skin.

He slept the first entire day and night after their arrival, exhausted from the constant jarring on the road and the virulent bout of illness at sea. Late in the morning of the next day, however, he woke to birds singing and the view of an expanse of green-blue grass that fell away in the distance to the sea. He felt giddy as he admired the sheen of emerald and blue-green water and the endless horizon. He fought a sensation of falling, his hand clutching the edge of the mattress tightly as if to keep himself from plummeting into the limitless space of sky and water at the edge of the grounds below. Little by little he quelled the wave of irrational fear—a desire to close the windows and barricade the door. He was safe. There was nothing to fear. He gave himself over to the appreciation of the strange, new landscape—the colors, the clean smell of air, the warm caress of a gentle breeze.

He heard the door open behind him. Her footsteps. His wife. He admired her as she came round to greet him. He lay propped on his side to keep the pressure off the healing ribs and the worst of the burns along his back. Her beauty shocked him anew each time he saw her. He had to remind himself that this tall, auburn-haired beauty was his wife. He strained to remember her, anything, but the effort slammed his mind against a white wall of pain. She spoke to him; he had nothing to say. There was only emptiness and questions, a deluge of questions whose answers might fill the void that was his past.

She had already explained that he had been injured in a fire that broke out in the opera house where they had watched a performance of *Don Giovanni*. He already knew from the doctor's comments that he was her husband. Lucianna mentioned the estates in the east, a few miles from the Adriatic, and a summer manor on an island off the coast. She avoided his other questions saying that the doctor recommended waiting to see if the memories would come back on their own. He had been too weak to protest, too much in pain to insist.

Now he felt stronger, more lucid than he had been during the first fortnight of his life, for he felt that he had been reborn in a macabre sense when he woke in pain and without a past.

The only bandages that remained on his body were the ones that protected his hands. Lucianna had removed all the others. His palms itched miserably, and he wanted the use of his fingers. He tired of being fed, washed, dressed by others. Even the basic needs of relieving himself in the chamber pot required the intrusion of another!

She placed the scissors, gauze, salve, and strips of cloth on the table next to the bed. His hands were to be cleaned and dressed again in fresh gauze and wraps. He waited as she tended to him, growing more and more annoyed. She unwrapped the hands and applied a salve to the few remaining sores. He could see that they were nearly healed. There was no need to bind them. He flexed his fingers gingerly. As she reached for the clean, white strips of cloth, Erik pulled his hands away from her and scowled. She didn't insist.

She returned the strips of cloth to the table and picked up the bowl of porridge. She brought the spoon to his mouth, but he turned away, his lips pressed tightly shut. "I wish to feed myself."

Lucianna returned the spoon to the bowl. "It's one thing to stain the coverlet with the ointment from your hands, but I can't abide the mess you'll make eating while lying on your side in the bed!"

"Then have Luigi come and help me to the chair. I'm tired of lying in bed."

She began to protest, but Erik cut her short. "Call for Luigi or I'll get up without his help."

When she saw him try to swing his legs off the side of the bed, she relented once more and called for his valet. Once he was dressed and seated in a chair facing the open window, he insisted on being left alone.

Erik took two bites of porridge before the trembling of his hand became too severe and he had to sit back and rest. It took several spells of eating and resting before he managed to consume a good portion of his breakfast. Clearly he would have to build up his strength. He was heartened by the fact that he no longer had fits of choking. His lungs seemed to have cleared. His eyes, too, were clearer, and it was only when he first woke that they were filmy. He would have thought Lucianna would be pleased by his rapid recovery, but surprisingly she seemed quiet and tense as he shared each new sign of returning health.

Behind him, the door opened again. This time the sound was lighter. He turned only slightly in his chair and called out to see who it was.

"Signora sent me to fan away the flies," came the soft voice of a young girl.

The wound on his back was exposed. Pillows propped behind him on the over-stuffed, high-back chair kept the wound away from the fabric. The exposed tender flesh was likely to attract flies in the warm air. The girl came to the side of the chair and began to agitate a large palm fan when she stopped dead in her tracks with a shocked expression on her face. Erik had been about to ask her name when he saw her dismay. As suddenly as it had appeared, the reaction was wiped from her face, but not before Erik had noticed. Puzzled he turned to look out the window. Perhaps she was squeamish and the burn along his back had surprised her. But she wasn't looking at his back; she had glanced at his face. Icy fingers of doubt ran up his spine as he wondered if there was something wrong. He knew that there were some cuts and bruises on his face, but thankfully it had escaped the flames. Slowly as if to wipe the hair from his eyes he brought his recently liberated hand to his brow.

He felt the raised skin of a small cut along the forehead as his fingers glided surreptitiously over the left side of his face. He tried to remember the portrait that Lucianna had shown him with pride. It was a portrait of him that she had painted for their first anniversary. Gliding across the lower part of his face, across his cheek, he felt the stubble of a yet unshaven jaw. As his fingers crossed over his chin and the edge of his lips to the other cheek, he stopped. His pulse sped dramatically, and a shock ran along his fingers through his arms down to the pit of his stomach where the burden of recently eaten porridge churned violently. He swallowed the sour, burning reflux and willed himself to take deep, slow breaths before continuing. Edging away in the chair from the spot where the pretty girl—whose eyes were now trained on the floor—stood fanning away the flies from his wounds, Erik forced his trembling fingers to move across a rough and ragged landscape that was supposed to be a face. This was not the image in his portrait!

The door opened behind them, and Erik lowered his hand to his lap as if caught in some vile and secretive act. He heard Lucianna approach but kept his eyes fixed on a corner of the bedroom away from her. He couldn't look at her, not yet. He needed time to rearrange and compose the broken fragments of his face.

"Are you hot? You look flushed." There was no revulsion in her voice, only concern. "Natala, come forward a bit so the air circulates better."

"No," he said a little too quickly, a little too loudly.

Lucianna stared at him, confused, waiting for an explanation that didn't come.

"All right. Would you like some juice? Perhaps a cider? I could have …"

"No. I don't want anything but for everyone to leave me alone!" His color had deepened to a scarlet, and Lucianna saw his chest heave in agitation.

"We'll leave you for a while. Natala, come."

He waited until the two women had left, until the door settled audibly into place. He waited until the soft footsteps faded completely and counted under his breath the steps it might take to descend the large staircase in the foyer, to walk across the way and enter one of several front rooms of the manor house. Then he waited even longer for his courage to return to him. He glanced round the room searching for some object, a mirror, in which he could see what sat upon his face like an unwelcome guest. There was no mirror on the bedside table.

Fearfully he raised his hand again to the traitorous side of his face. There was no pain along the alien surface, yet he could feel the rough turn of his fingers over the welts and bumps, a swatch of scars zigzagged from the top of his lip to the edge of his hairline above his forehead. The skin puckered around his eye. It was his flesh, his skin, his jagged and irregular surface that he felt.

There was a wardrobe along the opposite side of the room. Perhaps on the inside panel of one of its doors would be a mirror. But the distance between him and the wardrobe might as well have been the distance between the manor house and Rome!

It was not until several days later that Erik trusted himself to stand and make his way to the wardrobe. His leg was still splinted, but he had been doing what he could to strengthen his arms and build his stamina when Lucianna was not in the room. He sensed that he needed to do this without her knowledge, that she would not be pleased to see him improve so rapidly. She seemed to like his dependence on her and thwarted, when possible, any sign of independence from him. Lucianna tended to his every need. Only when she was exhausted did Gretta or Luigi take her place. The young girl who had attended him before, a girl with large eyes and a few blond curls that escaped her cap, never returned. It grieved him that she might have refused to come back, frightened by his appearance.

He had asked Luigi to help him to the simple chair away from the window, half the distance to the wardrobe. He had explained that he was chilled by the breeze in the morning, but wanted to sit up. Luigi improvised a cushion for his leg to keep it elevated. Soon he hoped the splint would be removed so that he might bend his knee and start to walk on crutches. Since they had left Rome, there had been no doctor to visit, and Erik wondered again if Lucianna was somehow hoping to keep him an invalid under her constant care.

Erik lowered his splinted leg to the floor and braced himself on the arms of the simple wooden chair. He easily raised himself to a standing position. Careful to avoid putting pressure on the wounded leg, he grabbed the table and made his way gingerly across the back wall of the room. He had studied the pathway as if it were a map and had decided beforehand where he would find support. He needed to pause every couple of steps to catch his breath. It was more taxing than he had thought it would be. He had time. Lucianna wasn't expected for at least an hour or more. And fortunately no one else was encouraged to come into the sick room.

Of course this was a waste of time if the wardrobe had no mirror. In that case, he'd have to risk confronting Lucianna. Why didn't he just ask her what was wrong with his face? Perhaps she was accustomed to the disfigurement. Perhaps it didn't occur to her that he had forgotten his own face along with every other memory from before the fire. Perhaps. Then he should simply talk with her. But he couldn't. He didn't even want to think about his face. He needed to see it first. He couldn't postpone the shock of seeing himself for the first time any longer.

He was panting and sweating profusely when he found himself standing before the closed doors of the wardrobe. He paused long enough to catch his breath and slow the rapid beating of his heart. His hand reached for the door, but he couldn't make himself grasp the handle. Panic threatened to overwhelm him as he wondered what it would be like to see something in the mirror that he didn't recognize as himself. What if he couldn't come to terms with the face in the mirror? Would he be forced to live forever in this room, seeing only a handful of people, fleeing from mirrors and reflecting ponds, terrified to see his image in their surfaces?

It had to be now. He wouldn't have enough strength to attempt this again for several hours, perhaps even days. His hand squeezed the handle and turned it downwards. The door unlatched smoothly and on its own began to swing open. In the blackness of the interior hung men's clothes waiting for him to return to a normal life. That was heartening! He spied out of the corner of his eye the silver cold gleam of the inside of the door panel. As he had thought, it was a full-length mirror, and in its surface he saw reflected a monster.

She found him sitting on the floor. The wardrobe door was askew. His splinted leg stuck out in front of him along the carpet. He braced himself with his hand pressed against the floor. He held his face buried in the palm of the other hand. A soft keening sound rose from him, and she approached slowly and cautiously until she was close enough to see him shudder. He let her hug him against her skirt. She waited for him to speak, which he did after a few minutes.

He didn't mention his face. He told her that he would need Luigi's assistance to reach the bed.

She saw the edge of the mirror inside the wardrobe. In the angle, she could see his down-turned face. Reaching across Erik, she pushed the door closed until the latch clicked in place.

"I'll call him. I'll be right back."

When she returned, he had composed himself as best he could, although signs of his distress were still apparent.

"Erik, I didn't realize you weren't aware of …" her voice faded out as she saw him turn his face quickly away from her. "It was a hunting accident several years ago."

How could an accident cause the disfigurement he saw in the mirror?

What happened the other day must not happen again! Lucianna assembled the staff. She walked down the line of servants, from those who worked the grounds to those who attended to her own personal needs. She had been careless to send a young girl in to Erik without having prepared her.

She had invented a story to explain his disfigurement, and the servants must act as if they had long become used to seeing their master's scars.

Anyone who could not control their reaction would be dismissed.

She had begun with the accident, the one that took half his face away, and found him so thirsty for stories that she couldn't stop. How could she imagine the emptiness, the loss he must feel, waking to find all that he had been blighted and swept away? He hadn't even known which question to ask first, so he settled on naming the absence itself. He could not remember anything before the fire, and even this was intuited, more than remembered, from the pain, the wounds, the seared flesh and smoke-clogged lungs. No image of the underground rooms, no lingering sound of frightened voices he had saved, no shock from the fall of burning wood around him. Only in dreams. Only then, perhaps, did his body recall the danger of that conflagration and the proximity of death. She saw him twitch in his sleep, writhe like a martyr on the spit, heard his exertions and cries of frustration as his nerves and muscles relived his desperate efforts to drag himself from the heat, smoke, and flames, out from underneath the debris that had buried him. But when he woke, his eyes, at first pained and frightened by dream images, would clear and fill with puzzled emptiness, the void of a mind that protected by locking the door to all that had ever been.

Who am I? she had asked.

She was his wife, he answered before she could tell him the truth. The one fact he gave her as proof of his solidity, his existence. Lucianna heard the lie, knew it to be a lie, a misunderstanding at best. He had awoken, hollow and desperate for meaning, for life, demanding to be filled with images, words, thoughts, memories.

Sig. Costanzi had played an inadvertent role in the story as well. He had written it down and passed it on to Meg. Erik's death murmured among the survivors was inscribed in the official account, was now part of the record. Everyone knew Erik was dead! *She* had not proclaimed him dead! She had fought to save him, *had* saved him. She willed him into existence from the ashes of his past. Her desire had named him. He wasn't who he had been. He was hers.

But if he were no longer Erik Costanzi, who was he?

She would have preferred to start afresh and let him unfold. He would gather his memories as he made them from this moment on, with her. His first memories would be of pain, but they would also be of her. He had said to her that whenever he woke, she was there. Inextricably woven into his pain and his new life was her love for him, her constancy, her tender mercies. Yet he wanted more, something before the pain and loss. He demanded that she share the story that was "theirs." If she were his wife, then her memories must in part be his, and he would have them.

She wanted to give him a gift. She could not take the disfigurement away. But she could erase what was already gone: his torment, the rejection, the lonely and wicked childhood, the violent and fraught history of his obsession. She could tell the story, and it could be filled with light instead of darkness, love instead of solitude; it could be the story of a man who was whole. She would tell a fairy tale, a love story.

Once upon a time ... But she didn't use these words, only thought them in the sigh before she began.

CHAPTER 4

❀

Once Upon a Time

And the silken sad uncertain rustling of
each purple curtain
Thrilled me—filled me with fantastic terrors
never felt before;
So that now, to still the beating of my
heart, I stood repeating
`'Tis some visitor entreating entrance at
my chamber door
Some late visitor entreating entrance at
my chamber door;
This it is, and nothing more,'

"The Raven," Edgar Allan Poe

You walk across the room with feline grace, barely nodding your head at the pleasantries flung your way. Your dark hair is combed back from your face with the exception of a wayward lock that hangs over one of your arched eyebrows. You take a glass of punch from the tray of a passing servant and eye the color suspiciously. After one sip, you return it to another tray carried by a different servant in his rounds, a look of disgust on your face. From inside your coat pocket you withdraw a slim silver flask, unscrew the lid, and raise it to your lips. An old dowager at your elbow catches you in the act and scowls scandalously, but you offer her the flask with a sardonic smile and slightly bow before she quickly walks away making sharp clucking sounds under her fan. I see the chuckle in your chest and a flash of white teeth between two dark, full lips.

I lose sight of you for I've promised this dance to Lord Campolieto, and he has swept me along the dance floor in a series of turns and twists leaving you on the other side of the ballroom. When the music finally stops, I have completely lost my bearings and have no idea of the whereabouts of that tall, striking gentleman who stood nearly a head above the rest. But as I turn away from Lord Campolieto, I find myself the object of the mysterious gentleman's gaze. You stand directly in my path, barring my way, a warm smile twists the corners of your mouth. You have the audacity to stare into my eyes for one moment and the next to run your gaze down my body as if examining a breed mare for your stable. My chest rises in alarm, and I feel the blood pulse hot under my skin as your eyes linger with evident delight on my breasts, fall to my hips, and climb once more, moist and piercing, to my face. Your lips have parted, and I see your tongue flick across the edges of your teeth. I feel as if I might faint, but your hand has come forward and trapped mine in its grip. It disappears completely in your large, square hold.

"May I?" you have asked, and I frown momentarily trying to understand your request. But you don't wait for my answer. Your other hand has landed firmly on the side of my waist, and between the two they have maneuvered me onto the dance floor for the waltz. I have no choice but to follow your unspoken instructions, responding to the movements of your body, the sway of your narrow hips, the bend of your knee, the power of your thighs, the guide of your broad shoulders, and the arch of your arms. Your hands move me as if I were a child. I look into the dark green of your eyes which have grown serious. They hold me, unblinking as if an invisible filament were cast from them and into mine. The music ends too soon, and the two hands have suddenly left. Their absence leaves me adrift on an unsteady sea. You bow. Your eyes still fix on me firmly, a lighthouse upon the breakers. But you back away, and I have floated off to open water.

Suddenly I am surrounded by potential suitors. A young inconsequential man, for you have transformed the other bachelors into lackluster parodies, asks for the next dance. I totter slightly on unsteady feet. You have gone, allowing the crowd to swallow you whole while I sink into the maelstrom of the dance floor.

I hear the whispers among the guests. You are the only son of Signore Tiberio Fiortino. Both of your parents are deceased, and you are the lord of an estate in the east. You are a rogue who spent much of your youth in Paris carousing and gambling. Your Italian is deliciously flavored with a foreign lilt you have picked up in France. Your parents had wished you to marry, but you were reluctant. The whispers say that you have finally decided to fulfill your promise to them and are in search of a wife. The young unmarried women hold their breath as you pass, praying you'll exchange a few words with them, praying to be asked for a turn on the dance floor. More audacious ones pull at their bodices and lift their breasts to show off their abundance of flesh. They flutter their fans seductively as they stroll around the rim of the dance floor across your path as if to hawk their wares.

In need of a bit of air myself, I come upon you once more near the veranda windows as one buxom beauty glides before you. I note your eyes dart with a connoisseur's appreciation over her décolletage. Your tongue flicks across your lower lip, but you turn away from her and scan the dance floor as if looking for someone. The buxom signorina fans herself in agitation seeing that she has lost your interest. Embarrassed by her failure, she rapidly retreats into the arms of a gallant officer who can't believe his good fortune. Your gaze eventually circles round to intercept mine, and I gasp as if we have touched in that moment. Although I, too, feel embarrassed, except in my case by the surfeit of your attention, I can't look away.

You approach, and I begin to tremble. You place your hand familiarly on my elbow and guide me through the veranda doors to the garden, and I know that I am lost.

"We were married a month later, and you brought me home to the Fiortino estate. We spent our days hunting, riding, reading, and our nights in those pursuits in which newlyweds are wont to engage. You managed the estate, the tenants—through your overseer—and tended personally to your favorite horses. I took on the running of the house, dealt with the servants, nurtured my plants in the greenhouse. We were very fortunate in our happiness until one day, when you were out hunting, there was an accident. I never understood exactly what had happened, but they carried you back, your face a mass of blood and torn tissue along one side. The doctor cleaned your wounds and sutured them as best he could."

Erik shifted uneasily in the chair. He brought his hand up unconsciously to his face, but pulled it down to rest in his lap when he realized he had done so.

Carefully, she began to spin out the web in another direction, one that she hoped would draw his mind away from the deformity. "We tired of the estate. You didn't like living there. So we began to spend more and more time between this manor house and our apartments in Rome. Living by the sea seemed to revive you tremendously, and we were quite happy. We bought a small sailboat and sailed around the island, exploring the coves and bays. I taught you to fish!"

"How long have we been married?" Erik interrupted. Lucianna had gotten carried away by her fantasy and resented the interruption. She was relieved that he hadn't asked about the hunting accident, but she was reluctant to flesh out the story. Details such as the one Erik wanted to know didn't concern her. She had been obliged to use some facts from her actual marriage to hide Erik's identity and to give him a new one. She was Signora Fiortino, so Erik must, to a certain extent, walk in her dead husband's footsteps. He had to be Sig. Fiortino, Erik Fiortino. She had been on her way to marry Ponzio when she first met Erik a number of years ago. The closer to the truth, the better, so she answered, using her own marriage as the model. "Nearly six years."

She resumed her story, but Erik interrupted yet again. "Why haven't we any children?" She couldn't read his tone of voice. Nevertheless, she understood that the question was swollen with meaning. She pursed her lips in frustration. This was not part of the story she wanted to tell. She wanted to recreate him and to give him a glorious, happy past, one without tears, without sadness. But, of course he would wonder. A marriage without issue, what could it mean? If the lovers were indeed in love, why wouldn't their union be blessed?

Lucianna thought about the two stone markers in the cemetery on the estate. They had never seen the light of day, nor taken a first breath. They had died before they lived, but she wept for them, small miracles who had died in her womb. They were her babes. Would she have Erik share in their loss? Would she force him to assume Don Ponzio's debt?

"We lost two children," she whispered.

Never having known the experience, Erik didn't remember their loss. He watched her for clues as to the way he should feel.

He had lost his parents, had no other relatives apparently, and had fathered a son and a daughter, who were now dead. A sinking sensation in his gut mourned the lack of them, if not their loss.

How had he consoled Lucianna? What words had he used or had it been a touch, the silent speech of flesh on flesh? Had he cried or had he steeled himself to the death of the innocents, the death of his blood? How old had each one been? Why had they died? When Lucianna spoke of the children's deaths, she had refused to look at him. She didn't want to speak of them. Not to him. He saw her lower lip tremble, and he grew embarrassed that he was observing her. He was removed from her tragedy; a wide chasm lay between him and his lost children. Perhaps if he were to know more of them and of what had occurred, they would be real, not floating ghosts before his imagination.

Quickly he looked again at Lucianna, her hair, the blue-green ocean depths of her eyes, her strawberry burnt lips, the tall sleekness of her frame, the slight tilt of her head when she questioned him. The unshakeable fear that she, too, was but a ghostly presence forced him to keep his eyes on her, watching for signs that she might disappear, and to reach his hand across the space that separated them and touch her.

Lucianna started at the unexpected touch, its gentle but substantial weight, on her knee. Misconstruing her reaction, Erik withdrew his hand, shifted awkwardly in his chair, and pretended to inspect the light scarring of his palms.

She was his wife, and she had lovingly tended to him. But was it only duty that kept her by his side? She had married him when he was handsome, whole, uninjured. She had told the story of their first encounter with all the delight of a young maiden. The man she fell in love with was not the one who sat examining his scars. Bitterness flooded him as he remembered the reflection in the wardrobe mirror. "I thought you knew," he had heard her say, referring to the hideous disarray of his features. After the hunting accident, had she regretted her eagerness to marry him? Two dead children! Were they conceived before he lost half his face? Did, could Lucianna feel the same passion for him that she described having felt for the handsome stranger?

Erik glanced again at his unremembered wife and felt the unwanted stirrings of desire. He had healed. Much of his strength had returned, and with it came the insistent needs of the flesh. The splint had been removed from his leg, and he was walking around the grounds slowly and with the aid of a crutch. In the bedroom, Lucianna encouraged him to rise from the bed using her as a support. She would wedge herself under his arm and have him lean heavily into her. Her nearness stirred him. Her closeness, the solidity of her body, made him want to hold her and make love to her. She lay next to him at night, and Erik gathered himself into a motionless entity shipwrecked on his own island, separate and insensible to her presence until she would fall asleep. Only then would he shake the tension from his limbs and turn quietly sometimes to his side and look at her lying in lace upon the mattress, soft and alluring. But mostly he avoided the temptation. She was his wife, but he had no way of knowing if she'd welcome his touch. Now he sat near her in the bedroom, listening to her tell their story in which she described a man she passionately adored. Yet Erik could not see himself in that man!

Lucianna sat indecisive. It had been the first time Erik had spontaneously touched her, and she had somehow displeased him or given him the wrong impression. He sat, his face turned away from hers. She knew it made him uncomfortable for her to look at him. She had found him in anguish, collapsed on the floor, having seen himself in the mirror, hiding his disfigured face behind the palm of his hand. He had forgotten even what he looked like, and all that he had seen was the portrait she had painted of him. Erik thought that the handsome face in the portrait was his, but it had been meant to depict his inner beauty, and for this she had imagined and painted what his face might have looked like if there were no scars or disfigurement. She had tried to console him the day she found him on the floor before the wardrobe mirror, but he wouldn't let her speak. He still refused to talk of it.

She stood and took a short step towards him. He froze in his chair as he saw her bend over him. He felt the fabric of her skirts against his thigh. If he moved his leg away from her, it would draw attention to the contact she had made. So he didn't move, hoping to ignore the sensation. He forced himself to face her. She smiled. Before he looked away, she bent to kiss him.

He recalled other moments during the painful first days when she had tenderly kissed him, but this was not a tender kiss of pity. She pressed her lips hard against his mouth and pushed her tongue eagerly over it. In response he parted his lips and accepted her, enjoying her sweet carnality. His own tongue glided over hers, darting back and forth several times, tasting and feeling the soft rasp, the hard glint of teeth, the pliable flesh behind her lips. His hands grasped her around the waist and pulled her down. Her hip sank into his lap, and his body reacted immediately to her weight.

God knew he wanted her! Yet he suddenly shifted her away from the evidence of his arousal and gently urged her to stand. Lucianna, her face flushed and her breathing rapid and shallow, hesitated momentarily, but did as he asked.

"I'm tired. I think I should lie down now." There was no mistaking the meaning of his statement. Whatever passion she had awoken in him she now saw dampened. The cause of his coolness was impossible for her to know, but her intuition told her that it was a willful resistance on his part.

If she had asked him, he wouldn't have been able to tell her. In his own mind, he grappled with the confusion. Why shouldn't they resume their conjugal relations? They were married, and she had told him that they had been in love. But although he found his need of her compelling, the closer their bodies were, the more aware of the distance between their souls. He wasn't even sure that "souls" was the proper choice of word to describe the vacancy that threatened to overwhelm him when he drew her into his arms. He didn't trust her or he didn't trust himself. Something was wrong, horribly wrong. Perhaps it was the amnesia. Perhaps it was also the painful encounter with his face in the mirror. In time it would be better.

She was hurt, he could tell. She hid it well, always worried for him more than for herself, but he was beginning to understand her. She had helped him to bed and was now sitting on the edge of the mattress, opening her nightly creams and preparing to come to sleep. The scarlet blush had cooled to a pale pink, but she was mentally licking her wounds. He struggled to think of something to say to her, to lessen the feeling of rejection. "Lucianna?"

She looked up from her evening ritual of creams. She was rubbing the white lotion over her long, shapely legs. With visible effort she smiled at Erik and asked him if he needed anything.

For one moment, he wanted to respond that he wanted her, but swallowed the words and the desire as best he could. If she loved him, she would want him to be truthful and sincere with her. "It isn't that I don't desire you. I do. I ache for you. But I can't ... It doesn't seem right."

Her hands stopped, suspended in mid-act as she rubbed the lotion into the skin along her inner thigh. She waited for him to explain.

Reluctantly, Erik understood she would remain silent until he finished. "You know me, but I don't know you. If I take you now, it won't be the way it should be."

"But I've tried to tell you as much as I can about you, about us, about the past."

"I don't know the man you describe! He's not me!"

The look of horror on his wife's face startled him. In a feeble, hoarse whisper she asked, "But how?"

Erik didn't hear her words. He pressed on to explain before the words that had formed in his mind faded.

"No, you must listen to me. I'm not accusing you of lying. How could I? It's just that I don't recognize myself in the man you describe. You speak to me of my past, but it's not real. Not to me. I'm a stranger even to myself." His tone was harsh from his own frustration. He would not look at her. He concentrated on the words he needed to explain himself. He was relieved that she didn't move, didn't try to stop him. He forced himself to speak more gently to her. He did not want to hurt her. "I need time. I can't touch you when I feel this ... this void inside."

When she didn't speak, he risked a glance at her.

He saw her shudder, but her shoulders and back relaxed somewhat. He saw that her cheek was damp, and realized she was crying. He reached out to her and brought her down on to the bed and embraced her. He held her until she fell asleep. Perhaps this is how it should begin.

Erik was out of sorts. Lucianna had spent the morning involved with the servants and sundry domestic chores. His recovery had left him with an excess of energy that no matter what he did he couldn't discharge. He spent several hours in the stable, eventually discarding his fine coat, vest, and shirt to work alongside the stable hands. He could tell they thought it queer for the lord to dirty his hands with the muck of the stalls, but he was tired of the passivity that had plagued him for weeks. He tended several of the animals, combing and wiping them down. He let the boys shovel out the dung, but happily took up the pitchfork to haul the dry straw and spread it about the dirt floor.

After he worked up a healthy sweat, he decided that he would take the white stocking stallion out to ride bareback around the grounds. Erik assumed he had always been a good horseman, and he hoped the horse remembered the fact. The stable hand had cautioned him that Diavolo Rosso tended to fidget and test his rider. Evidently the only one who could ride him was Lucianna. She knew to take a firm hand to him. Erik judged that he wouldn't have a horse in his stable that he himself, as master, couldn't handle. So, no matter how badly trained the animal, he intended to ride him.

As he led Diavolo out to the path, he saw Lucianna pressed against the upstairs window of their room. He waved up to her and decided to ignore the worried expression on her face and the frantic agitation of her arms. "We're going to take a ride to the edge of the grounds so that I can get a good look at the beach," he informed the horse. As he prepared to mount, Erik lowered his head to the reddish-black shoulder of the princely beast and rubbed his cheek along the twitching muscles. The horse reared his head as if to protest and snorted through his nose, but otherwise he stood still and waited to see what his master was about to do.

"Get used to me. You don't smell so good yourself." Erik took a handful of the mane and pulled himself up onto the animal's back. Immediately Diavolo reared in protest, but Erik dug his knees and heels into the animal and commanded him forward. The two of them careened down the grassy pasture that lay before the manor on a direct path to the cliff beyond. It seemed as if Diavolo were prepared to fling himself and his rider over the ledge just in order to make the point that Erik was not in charge. Erik had other ideas and pulled the horse's head sharply to the side, nearly forcing them both to the ground.

They stopped just feet from the ragged edge of the cliff overlooking the sandy beach below. Diavolo snorted and bared his teeth as if to protest his master's treatment, but Erik didn't care if the horse complained as long as he obeyed.

"You thought you were a devil, did you?" Exhilarated from the contest of wills and the pounding race across the sloping grounds, Erik patted the horse affectionately on the neck. "Well, you might as well know that I'm a blacker devil than you ever hope to be." Diavolo snorted, tossed his head, and pawed the ground as if unconvinced.

Below them lay a white sand beach and a quarter-moon shaped cove surrounded by boulders. Lucianna had said that the water was shallow for a good long stretch when the tide was out, as it now was, and you could walk far out toward open water and collect sea shells along the way. On the other hand, if the winds were blowing just right and there was a squall, the view of the crashing surf was exhilarating to behold and the water dangerous. At the moment, the waves were coming in gentle and capping close to the beach. The breeze was laden with moisture, and Erik sat on the grass and contemplated the view. An annoying dull pain hammered behind his eyes, and he noticed the light change and darken over the landscape. At first he thought it was clouds, but when he looked up to the sky it was clear.

The pain grew worse, and he bent his head down into his chest as flashes of light erupted in his mind. The images that sped by were fragmented and clipped. He couldn't make them out. Sounds like piano chords and someone's face kept reappearing. He caught just the barest glance at a woman, but he couldn't recognize her. As suddenly as the pain had come, it ended and with it went the images. He breathed deeply, trying to recall the content of those images, convinced that they were flashes from his wounded memory. Though he had not been able to make sense of them, he was eerily sure that he had been remembering a woman.

Behind him he heard the approach of a rider. Lucianna reined her gray up beside Diavolo who bit peevishly at the mare's haunches when her mistress dismounted. The mare was startled and reared to the side, knocking Lucianna down to the ground. Erik ran to her side and pulled her to a safe distance away from the frightened mare.

"Are you all right?"

"Yes, I'm fine. Just ripped my skirt a bit."

Erik noticed that she had not changed to her usual riding habit, but had rushed out in the same dress she had put on in the morning. She had wisely donned riding boots, but otherwise she was not equipped for a vigorous jaunt on the grounds.

"You thought I couldn't handle the stallion, didn't you?" Erik asked.

Lucianna couldn't be sure whether his tone was laced with an edge of bitterness or sarcasm. Perhaps it was both, for his mouth turned up only slightly on one side as he helped her dust off her skirts.

In the next moment, Erik walked over to the mare and calmed her down. He brought her to Lucianna, well away from Diavolo who, content with himself, nibbled at the grass and wild parsley. Then he strode directly over to Diavolo. He took a fistful of the horse's mane to get his attention. Diavolo tried to shake his master's hand free, but Erik placed his strong, large hands on either side of the horse's cheeks and brought the animal's muzzle up to within an inch of his own face. Holding the massive head firmly in both his hands, he pressed his face against the hard bone separating the animal's eye and spoke in a low rumble. The horse tried to lift his head away from Erik, but couldn't. Erik held on to him until he was sure the horse had gotten the message.

When Erik released him, Diavolo reared his head for show and neighed sullenly, but he stood still as Erik mounted him and turned him toward a distant woods.

"Let's take a ride around the grounds toward the forest, shall we?" He felt good out in the clear, fresh air with a rebellious horse to distract him from his problems. He also enjoyed the sense of being in charge. He wanted Lucianna to understand that he was well and that he didn't need to be smothered by her protection.

He watched her mount gracefully in spite of the abundant material of her dress. He admired the stretch of slender leg that he glimpsed as she adjusted herself in the side saddle. As usual it sent a quiver of desire through his body. He thought again about the headache and accompanying vision and wished that the woman he had seen were his wife, but she wasn't.

the blinding light washed the world away in one bolt and shards of razor images cut across the back of my eyes bleeding through my wounds and filling my mouth, my throat, my ears, flashes of brocade curtains and gilt statues, cedar and oak beams, the hint of naked flesh, music, a music that composed itself slowly into a melody, her blond hair loose across her shoulders, a smile, one eye from the profile of a delicate face, behind her a shadow, a shadow whose hand caresses her arm, the pain obliterates the here and now, the then and there, as well, the pain lashes across like a paint brush leaving an angry swatch of white light that swallows everything in its wake, a voice, sweet and pure, sings to me, I know she is singing to me, and it is the voice of the woman I see each time the pain returns, I welcome the pain to see her face, but it gives me only the shards of her reflection in a broken mirror, I feel the edges of the glass cut me, the blood flows from the mirror obliterating the sweet vision of the angel, it flows over her eyes and across a small red mouth, the walls fall in around me, I glimpse the walls of a cavern, a grotto, the smell of water and moss puts its wet fingers up my nostrils and I swallow the smell like a glutton, the coolness of stone wraps around and blunts the pain that cuts, dulls the sharp edges, she hovers over me, I lie below her, the shadow weeps for her? for me? she lets her long blond hair fall over me …

"Where is he?" Lucianna didn't like losing track of Erik's whereabouts. She told herself that it was because she was concerned for him. On several occasions she had seen him pause in the middle of an activity, turn deathly white, squeeze his eyes closed, and bring his fist to his forehead. He was experiencing pain of some sort, and she was sure that it was a result of the head injury he suffered in the fire. Thankfully these episodes were brief; he would soon open his eyes, take several gulps of air, and rapidly recover without any apparent ill effect. But she knew that it wasn't the headaches alone that concerned her. She wanted to be with him. She wanted to break through his reserve and to bring him closer to her. Each night they slept in the same bed, but he made it clear that he had no intention of resuming conjugal relations. She was becoming impatient. She wanted him more than she could bear. To have him near and not to touch him or be touched by him was torture.

The young girl that had once been sent to their bedroom to fan away insects was watering the plants in the downstairs rooms as Lucianna passed. She stopped the girl, who blanched as the mistress came up behind her, and asked where the master might be. The servant—Lucianna recalled that her name was Natala—twisted a stray bit of her blond hair nervously between her fingers and said she had seen Master Fiortino a while ago. He had been going from room to room. She pointed in the direction that she had last seen him.

"What on earth was he doing?" Lucianna hadn't really directed the question to the young girl, but to herself.

"He seemed to be searching for something."

"Well. Go on, then." She dismissed Natala. Going from room to room, Lucianna wondered what Erik was up to. Then it came to her! It couldn't be! She went directly to the back rooms where she had told the servants to move the piano. She feared that his attraction to music was so great that it might spark his memory. She walked more quickly the closer she got to the room. She swung open the door, and there on the piano bench sat Erik.

He wasn't playing. The keys were uncovered, and one of his hands was lightly poised over the keyboard while the other was pressed against his forehead. She recognized the signs. He was fighting off the headache.

"Erik?" she whispered.

He stiffened but kept his back to her.

"Are you all right?"

Instead of answering, he directed a question to her. "I played, didn't I?"

Lucianna considered lying. She feared the great black beast with the black and white teeth that Erik adored. It was so much a part of who he had been before he became hers. If he played the notes, would it all come back to him? Would he remember that he belonged to Meg, to the world of opera, that he had children of his own who mourned his loss. Guilt tugged at her breast, and she caught a gasp in her throat, tasting bitterness in the back of her mouth. She knew they suffered; they grieved for his loss. But she had not taken his memory from him! It had been fate. Fate had delivered him into her hands. She couldn't give him back, not now!

Erik glanced curiously over his shoulder at her silence. Gathering her courage about her like a cloak, she smiled gaily at him and came to sit beside him on the piano bench. She took his hand in hers and brought the fingers to her lips, kissing each one in turn. He knit his brow puzzled by her behavior but waited and watched her patiently.

"Yes, you played. And very well. In fact, you composed music as well." She met his gaze directly. "Why don't you play something now?"

She felt cornered. When she looked into his eyes, she realized she had made the right decision. He had already known the answer to his question. He simply wanted her to confirm what he sensed to be the case.

Again his fingers hovered over the keyboard. Shyly he glanced again at Lucianna. She was touched by his hesitation. It was as if he were worried that he wouldn't meet her expectation of him. There was also a childlike pleasure barely hidden in his earnest look. Then he laid his fingers on the keys and gently began to stroke the ivories. Lucianna felt a thrill run along her throat as if his hands had glided along her naked flesh from her face to the rise of her bosom. In her deepest secret places, his fingers seemed to stroke and delve with each note of music that he teased from the piano. Unable to bear it any longer, she brought her hand down upon the back of his in mid-note. Annoyed he glared at her, but the rapid heave of her bosom struck him in the same instant that a bolt of sensation rose from her hand to his. She moved into the circle of his arms and embraced him hungrily. Her lips pressed against his surprised mouth, seeking to melt inside his. Erik responded by returning her kisses, folding her onto his lap, and sliding his hand from the swell of her hips along the side of her body to her breasts. No one would disturb them, Lucianna was sure. She broke away from his hold and stood. The piano forgotten, Erik reached out for her, but she stepped outside the circle of his arms. Her eyes never leaving his, she backed her way to the sofa. In the thrall of passion, Erik followed.

"Evil, that's the only word for him. I had cause, on more than one occasion, to be in the hallway outside their bedchamber door. He had to be doing something foul to Donna Lucianna for her to cry out in such pain. I know for a fact that he beat her regular and other things I won't say. The marks were under her clothes where we couldn't see. He didn't let up even when the mistress was with child! I'm sure that's what made her lose the babies. With his fists! I saw the bed linen."

Erik froze, his hand on the door, sickened by what he was inadvertently hearing. Beyond the door were the servants' quarters. He was on his way to the stables, and had thought to take a shortcut through the backrooms. He meant to ask the cook for a lunch on the way out. Before he could open the door, the cook's voice stopped him. She was talking with someone. He now recognized the deep, educated voice of his manservant, Luigi, who entered the conversation.

"The mistress was not the only woman Master Fiortino mistreated. You remember Pia. He took a special interest in her."

"Yes, I remember. She disappeared one night, didn't she? I suppose she went back home. She'd told me that he …" Here the cook had lowered her voice conspiratorially, and Erik could not make out the words.

"Well, it doesn't surprise me." Although Erik could hear shock in Luigi's voice. "I had to take care of his menagerie in the cellar. He kept all kinds of bizarre things down there."

"If he weren't rich and powerful, I think the magistrate would have carried him off to prison."

Confused and shamed by what he had heard, Erik's knuckles shone white as his hand clutched at the doorknob. Sadism, adultery, debauchery. Appalled, Erik pulled his hand free and slowly backed away from the door as if it were alive and slimy.

Perhaps this is why Lucianna's story seems to belong to someone else. She lied. There is an ugly secret she is hiding from me, and this is it. I was a monster. I brought about the death of our children! But why would she care for me? How could she stand to touch me, to be near me? She desires me in spite of what I was. Of what I am? Does she think that I'm different now? Am I?

He searched inside his soul, and wondered if he could do the cruel things the servants had accused him of. He understood the allure of power, but the pleasure of inflicting pain was repugnant. Had he enjoyed inflicting pain on Lucianna? He thought of her beautiful, soft body and tried to imagine, in the heat of sexual desire, lashing it with a whip or striking her with his fists. The image sickened him. *No, I don't desire to hurt her.*

Had the fire changed him? Or had he been the gallant lover she imagined when they first met and had something happened to scar his soul and to turn him into the monster the servants knew? They had been married for some time. Had the first few years been good? Had he changed at some moment in their marriage? Why and when?

My face! There had been an accident. I came home with half of my face mangled. Did it drive me to strike out in rage at everything around me? Could I not bear to be reminded of what I had lost? Whatever was beautiful and whole mocked me. I gave myself over to disgust and sought my consolation in destruction. Was that why I became a monster?

He ran from the house, from those who knew what he was.

no memory, no past, no sins, no crimes, they had happened to someone else, another's hand had committed them, my soul blackened by cruelty had been cauterized by fire, the pain that woke me ripped me from myself, alive again but for a handful of months I am not who I was, will not be what I had been, could this not end it? could I live from this moment and be forgiven my past, my sins, my crimes? could I pray that my past remain hidden from me? the headaches, like harsh, unmerciful judges, threaten to bring the weight of the past crashing down on me, will it open the door and let the spider fingers of my past depravity come seize me again? would I awaken to blood and semen and pain? lusting after Lucianna's agony? thirsting to drink her blood, to smear myself with her pain, and writhe in ecstasy at her tortured soul? God help me! I had wanted to remember, I suspected she was holding back my true nature, the report of my history, but she was protecting me from myself, protecting herself from me, protecting the world from my evil, but the image of the blond girl beckons to me, calls to me, and I feel compelled to seek her out, she warms me, calms me, wraps her arms around me and protects me, the shadow behind her caresses my cheek, my fair angel offers rest, she offers, what does she offer? why am I drawn to her? who is she? I ache to know her, to touch her, there's no desire for blood and pain in my body when, golden, she comes to me, her voice is music, my ears tremble, my fingers yearn to touch her, to touch the keys of the piano, when I sit at the black and white keys I feel her behind me, she puts a small, delicate hand on my shoulder, she bends into me, her hips pressing into my back, her breasts soft and warm against the scar between my shoulder blades, if I turn, will she smile at me? will her heart-shaped face bend to kiss me? why is it her that I dream of and not my wife? why do the flashes of memory always bring me to her blond tresses, her slim waist, her lithe body, the body of a dancer, the voice of an angel?

Erik watched as the young servant girl watered the spider plant hanging in the corner of the salon. She kept her hair pinned and covered by a white bonnet, like the other servants in the manor. But he recalled the blond strand that escaped one day, the day she came to scare the insects from the oozing wound on his back, the day he raised his unencumbered fingers to his face and felt the incongruous weave of angry tissue. He had heard Gretta call the girl by name. What had it been? Natala.

Natala stretched the watering can high above her head and poked the curved spout into the hanging plant. As she tilted the pot, she lifted up on tip toe and craned her neck back as if to spy over the rim of the planter. The unusual tilt of her head brought into relief the long curve of her tender throat. Erik shifted uncomfortably at the piano, ashamed by his unabashed arousal. His pulse sped up perceptibly as he stared at the profile of the girl's body, her small breasts, the depression of her belly, the imagined generosity of her hips hidden under billowing skirts.

His fingers faltered as he played. Hearing the unexpected discord, Natala glanced in his direction. Immediately she looked away.

Reminded of his disfigurement, Erik lowered his eyes to the keyboard. More forcefully than was required, his fingers resumed their exercise on the keys. Was it only because a servant should not look directly into her master's eyes? Or was it the hideousness of his face? *Of course, fool!* How long had it taken Lucianna to learn to look upon her husband's face without showing revulsion? Perhaps that was why he had exacted revenge on Lucianna's flesh. There were many and diverse forms of revenge.

How long had Natala been with the Fiortinos? Did the girl fear him? Was she the one in his flashes of memory? He glanced up again at the servant as she threaded her way around the plants that festooned the large windows. He stripped her mentally and held her next to the ghost images of his past. Could she be the one he longed for? Had they been lovers? Or had she been his victim, too?

Disturbed by his own thoughts, he brought the lid down too sharply, too suddenly over the keyboard. Natala let out a sharp cry at the unexpected noise. In that instant, they both looked at each other, each surprised by the other. She bowed her head and set off toward the door, the watering can, empty, held at an awkward angle. He opened his mouth to call to her. He turned on the bench to follow her departing shape to the door. His heart ached with confusion. But he let her pass through the door without calling, without following.

When she had gone, he scowled at his hands. He inspected the large square plane, the slight distortion of his knuckles and then turned the palms up and studied the tracery of white scars left from the fire. Impotent, he closed them into fists and pressed them to his thighs.

He couldn't ask Lucianna about the girl. He couldn't mention the flashes of images from his past, the phantoms from his headaches. He couldn't tell her that he imagined her auburn hair a bright gold when they lay in bed at night.

All day long he looked for the golden girl. He skulked around the parlor, the conservatory, the rooms close to the servants' quarters, the passageway outside the kitchen and pantries. Gretta on more than one occasion nearly bumped into him as she went about her duties, begging his pardon and asking if he was in need of anything. Puzzled, she watched him walk hastily away from the back rooms and toward the parlor as if he had mistaken his way and had just found the path.

Later that evening Lucianna retired early to bed, smiling seductively at him. He assured her that he would follow soon. He wished to read for a bit longer. Lucianna was about to change her mind and say that she would wait for him, but he insisted that she go on to their room. He didn't want her to wait up for him tonight. He saw the peevish look of disappointment cross her face. She quickly disguised it and forced a smile of compliance in its place. Before she left him, she gave him a soft, lingering kiss that he accepted passively. He knew he should try to meet her desire with the same degree of fervency, but he simply couldn't. Disgruntled with his own lack of finesse, he felt incapable of masking his true feelings. He tried, but he couldn't love her.

Lucianna swept from the room, her skirts rustling about her like faithful dogs. Erik waited, the book forgotten in his lap, until he was sure she must be ensconced in their bedroom. The entire day he had been obsessed. It wasn't a plan, but a driving desire. He had purposefully refrained from thinking it through. He rose from the chaise and left the room. Instead of climbing the stairs to the bedchamber, he went directly to the back of the house beyond the music room to the stairway that led down to the kitchen, the larder, and eventually to the staff dining room and up to the attic rooms where the servants slept. He paused only long enough to question his resolve one last time before he began to ascend the narrow wooden staircase. At the top, he stopped again, this time confused and annoyed. He had no idea where she was! Which would her room be? Then from one of the rooms came a small and mousy-haired girl who worked in the kitchen. He placed his hand quickly over her mouth when he saw that she was about to scream from the fright he had given her. Her eyes stared up at his face, his horrible face, with wide-eyed terror, yet she knew he was the master and understood that she must obey him.

"Where is the girl they call Natala?" he whispered pitilessly close to her face, knowing that she was repulsed by him.

She pointed toward the bedroom doors down the hall. He released her slowly, ready to place his hand over her mouth again should she start to scream. "The third from the end, sir." She had summoned enough courage to curtsy briskly after he had released her.

"Not a word," Erik growled at her. He felt evil, powerful, and without mercy. It was a strangely familiar sensation, much easier to bear than the shame and confusion that had recently taken root in his soul. The mousy servant girl must have sensed it, too, for she shrank from him, backing away and entering her own chamber again. He was aroused even before he reached the door. His muscles tensed and tightened, and every nerve in his body jerked alive, as if wires would spring forward from his flesh and ensnare the young blond angel. How old could she be? Sixteen? Seventeen? No more than that.

Without knocking, he opened the door. On the far bed sat another servant, but he disregarded her completely. Natala sat on the other, her hairbrush suddenly trapped in the curls of her long blond hair. He felt the air sucked from his lungs as he saw the previously imprisoned tresses, free and floating like seaweed in the calm waters of the bay. He jerked his head at the roommate who rose from the bed and slipped quietly by him out into the hallway.

Erik let her pass. Then he braced his hands against the door jamb on either side, blocking the path. He stared at the girl, Natala. He said her name over and over in his mind, willing it to become a part of his memory.

Without a word, the girl lowered the hairbrush to the side table and laid her hands, palms up, in her lap. Her waist-long hair streamed forward, dropping gently like a curtain over the sides of her face. She bowed her head as if upon the executioner's stone, waiting for the axe to fall.

Silence. Several moments seemed to pass, and nothing happened. Natala looked up at the doorway. He had gone.

She was not the one. She could not have been the golden angel. She would have opened her arms to me, the woman in my dreams, in my broken-glass memories. The blond hair that caresses me in those moments belongs to a woman, not a child.

"Come," he said as he grabbed Lucianna by her elbow. Taking large strides, he dragged her back toward the music room. For every step he took, Lucianna took two.

He released her only when they were at the piano. He sat and played several measures of music from sheets that he had filled. A quill rested carelessly on the top of the piano, ink dripping onto the polished surface. Lucianna noticed the wadded sheets of previously rejected scores strewn haphazardly about the room.

Without looking at her, he pointed to the lyrics beneath each measure on the score and began to play. "Third measure. Quarter note." He played several notes and abruptly stopped. His head jerked in her direction. "Sing!" he demanded.

Lucianna jumped at the sharpness of his tone. She glanced from him to the score and back again. "But, Erik, I don't sing," she confessed. "That is to say, I don't sing opera."

When she saw his look, the words died in her throat.

"Don't be absurd. Sing!"

He played the measures again and pointed with his chin to the music. Taking a deep breath, Lucianna gave it her best effort. She sang the first three words. Erik crashed his fingers angrily down on the keyboard and rose so quickly from the piano that the bench toppled noisily over on its side.

For a moment, she was truly frightened by him. He clenched his teeth and glared at her, his body tilted dangerously close to hers, his hands balled into fists. She swallowed loudly and tried to explain again that her voice was not suitable for opera. It was a nice voice, but it was not remarkable. Like most people, she sang light tunes, but nothing more.

His fists lost their power. Bit by bit the hands relaxed, and the fingers simply curled into a soft hook. He stepped slowly away from the piano. She cautiously drew up beside him and stretched out her hand to touch his shoulder. Before the gesture could be completed, he left the room. Lucianna watched him go, her hand suspended in empty air.

my heart races with the stallion's, we won't look back, I won't let her stop me, she races behind me, her blond hair caught in the wind, she cries for me, her voice echoes strangely as if she doesn't sing alone, she knows my name and calls me and I feel drawn to her, but I cannot find the way to her, I see no other path, she mocks me, she is a phantom, she can't save me, I thought she was Lucianna, but hers is not the voice, I thought she was Natala, but she's only a child, my angel taunts me, tricks me with false promises, empty gestures of love and comfort, the black void lies behind and in front of me, I can't remain in this limbo any longer, I dig my heels into Diavolo and know that I am cutting him with my boot, his ruddy black coat glistens with blood and sweat, my own skin tingles with coldness as the wind whips round me, the edge of the cliff rushes up to us, it will be quick, the giddy swirl in my gut, the disorienting suspension, then the clutch of the ground reaching up to us, will my blond angel prove her love for me? will she die with me? will she go that far? does she love me enough to wrap her arms around me as I crash against the shore below?

The fire had died down to smoldering embers giving off waves of heat but little or no light. He had come to the bedroom, and now he sat, his back to Lucianna, on the edge of the bed. He stooped to remove his boots. Lucianna wondered at the lateness of his return. He smelled of horse and dung. A strong musk rising from his body clung to him.

She hadn't seen him since he stormed out of the music room. *Leave him be. He's angry and frustrated. He thought I could sing like Meg. He needs time.* When she sat alone and supped, she reassured herself, as her ears strained to hear his footsteps. *It will be all right. He's working off his anger. He's confused.* As she rubbed the creams along her arms and legs, she reasoned, *Music was his life, his refuge, the source of everything he held dear.* Then she sobbed, *And he knows that I've never been part of that world.*

She wondered if she should send someone to search for him. Maybe he had fallen; perhaps he lay injured somewhere on the grounds unable to call for help, too far for anyone to hear him. The stable boy reported seeing him ride off on Diavolo like a madman. Of course the boy was clever enough not to say it just that way, but Lucianna could read his frightened, excited eyes. She couldn't think what to do. He'd resent it dearly if she sent someone after him. She had resolved to wait. Fate had brought him to her thrice already—once at the stable on the road to her wedding, once at the fair, and once when he died in the fire. It would bring him back again.

He threw his shirt to the floor and unfastened his breeches. Naked he stood quiet by the bed. His uneasy silence—except for a low, hoarse, rasping sound deep in his throat—unnerved Lucianna as she lay, feigning sleep. The low rasp grew louder erupting into stuttering, pitiful sobs. His body folded in upon itself, and he buckled to his knees beside the bed, his face wedged between his hands pressed against the edge of the mattress.

Lucianna reached out and touched his shoulder. Startled, he jerked away from her. The sounds were swallowed whole as he took several gulps of air. Quickly he rose from the floor.

"Erik, I was worried. I'm sorry I can't …"

It wasn't a kiss. It was his mouth pressed hard against hers, but it wasn't a kiss. His hands tore the blankets from her and lifted her gown. They pulled and bent her to his will. His body lay upon hers. She brought her arms around him, feeling the healed scar along his back, trying to calm him, to soothe him, to make his savage, desperate taking of her body an act of love. It was not love; it was something else. She was unprepared for his roughness, his hard, glass-edged pain; it shocked her. But she held to him tightly. She met his force with her own. She kissed and bit at his throat. She buried her fingers in his flesh. He held her tightly in his grasp, pinning her to the bed like a desiccated butterfly in a collection box. Breathless and startled, Lucianna felt wave after wave of pleasure ripple through her own body. He spread her arms and legs beneath him and lifted his chest above her to thrust his hips between her thighs. She angled her hips to ease him deeper inside. He groaned as flesh ground and slapped against flesh. She pulled at him as the pleasure roiled through her stomach, along her thighs, deep within her sex. With a savage cry he finished. Wide-eyed and trembling, she watched him collapse slowly upon her. She felt his heartbeat pounding against her chest. Gently he rolled away from her. She followed to lie in the crux of his arm.

Neither spoke for some time. She thought he must have fallen asleep until she heard him whisper, "I'm sorry, Luci. Can you forgive me?"

It was not a kiss; it was something else. She would be bruised and sore in the morning, but she answered, "It's all right. I needed you, too."

His face turned to hers. She could only see the glint of his eyes as he looked at her. "I know what I've done to you. How can you stand to be near me?"

"What? Erik, what do you mean?" The cold bones of a skeleton reached inside her chest, clutched her heart, and began to squeeze without pity.

He told her what he had overheard the servants saying. He told her how he had stalked the poor servant girl, chasing a ghost. She felt the cold numb her limbs, creep up her thighs and belly to her breasts and throat. She heard Ponzio laughing at her from the dark corners of the room. No, no, no, no, no, her mind protested. Erik continued to speak, to confess, seeking absolution for crimes that belonged to another, to her husband, to the monster from which Erik had saved her.

"Luci, our children, my children! I killed them! I don't think there can be forgiveness for such a thing!"

"Erik," she said, but the words turned to ash in her mouth. How could she relieve him of this burden? How could she wash the stain from the weave she had fashioned for him? What life had she given him? "It wasn't you. You're not the same man. You've … you've changed, my love."

"Have I?" Doubt was eating away at him. "Does it matter that I don't remember?"

His music. It had saved him before. She had tried to keep it from him. She understood now that she had been wrong to do so. He must have it. She was not enough. She had wanted to protect him by rewriting his past. She thought the story she told him would heal his soul, free him from the burden of his scarred childhood, the loneliness and anger would have no hold on him. But linking his story to her own had created a new horror. Ponzio Fiortino's ghost haunted and distorted her re-creation of Erik. Only the music was pure; only it could save him from this new threat. Only the music could show him the beauty of his soul.

"I tried to ride Diavolo over the cliff." The tears had faded from his voice. He confessed this in a flat, toneless murmur. He had tried to kill himself. He had wanted to die. The life she had given him was slowly, mercilessly draining the life from him. The horse had bucked at the last minute, throwing Erik from the saddle, refusing to jump into the blackness beyond the cliff's edge.

Lucianna drove her fist into her mouth to keep from sobbing out loud. He held her absently.

Lucianna encouraged him to compose. She explained to him that she had kept him from the music because she worried that the burns on his palms had robbed him of the ability to play. She thought he had forgotten his love of music with all the other things he had forgotten.

Erik seemed relieved by the new revelation, the modifications of the story line. But he didn't ask about the beautiful, blond woman who sang for him, the one he glimpsed in his dreams.

Within the month he had completed an opera. He had been forced to sing all the parts himself or to imagine them in the voices of others. He was pleased with the work. The world surrounding him—including Lucianna—had ceased to exist for the time that he had been working. He locked himself away for days on end, even slept most nights on the sofa in the music room. Now it was finished. He eagerly called Lucianna to the music room and played it through from beginning to end. She sat beside him, watching the score as he played and sang. The arias that were meant for the soprano he could not sing, but he had Lucianna speak the words. It pained him to have her speak them, but it was worse to hear her untrained voice attempt singing them.

Lucianna was awed. At the end, the sounds still ringing in the twilit room, she sat next to Erik, unable to speak. Tears blinded her eyes. It was beautiful. Until this moment, Erik had been unabashedly delighted, confident in his own genius. Suddenly he sat, shyly regarding Lucianna, anxious for her to speak, to say something about the music, the story, the tones, the contrasting styles. She slid closer to him and kissed him tenderly on the cheek and softly told him that it was beautiful.

For several days afterwards, Lucianna and he spent their time together. They went on picnics, bathed together in the cove, rode around the grounds, explored the forest beyond, read to each other in the late afternoons. Only toward evening would Erik slip into the music room and pass a few hours reviewing the opera, perhaps to assure himself that his appraisal of its worth was correct. For several days, Lucianna was enraptured by his joy.

Then one afternoon he burst into the library where she was reading. He held something out excitedly for her to see. In his upturned hand, like a gift, lay a silken cream-colored mask. She stared at it appalled as if it were something gruesome and alive.

"What is this for?" she asked, careful to control the rising bile in her throat.

"Isn't it obvious? It's a mask." He looked away from her to hide his annoyance. "You don't expect me to go out in public looking the way I do, do you?"

He put on the mask, brushing his hair out of the way—he had not yet tied the long brown strands back—and waited for Lucianna's reaction.

"You don't need one."

Removing the mask, he studied her face to see if she were serious. "Luci, I've seen some of the staff turn away when I enter a room unexpectedly." He bit back the sarcasm in his tone. "They're good—actually they're quite kind—to ignore it, but my face is … It's even difficult for me at times to look at." He grew pensive and quiet as he fingered the soft ridges of the mask. "It may not be significant to you, but to others … I have to be realistic." Recovering some of his previous enthusiasm, he argued, "It's completely impossible for me to go about the streets of Rome looking as if …"

"Rome?" interrupted Lucianna, the dread making her shrill.

Erik stopped cold and dared her to continue. As he loomed over her, it was as if she didn't know him. Her mouth was so dry that she couldn't swallow.

He put the mask back on, covering all but his dark-green eyes and the lower part of his jaw. "Yes, Rome." Serious and commanding, his words left no room for argument. What did she expect? The opera was complete. He was not asking Lucianna, but informing her of his intentions. "I'm taking my opera to Rome. I will have it staged."

CHAPTER 5

❈

The Mask

The sailor dream'd of tossing on the flood:
The soldier of his laurels grown in blood:
The lover of the beauty that he knew
Must yet dissolve to dusty residue:
The merchant and the miser of his bags
Of finger'd gold; the beggar of his rags:
And all this stage of earth on which we seem
Such busy actors, and the parts we play'd,
Substantial as the shadow of a shade,
And Dreaming but a dream within a dream!

Life Is a Dream, Pedro Calderón de la Barca

Sig. Costanzi had made sure that the rooms were prepared for Meg, her mother, and the children. He had, on his own accord, sorted through the general objects in the bedchamber in order to remove any obvious reminder of Erik, thinking, mistakenly as it would turn out, that Meg would be relieved to find them put away. He had also made provisions for the nearby chambers to be made ready for Meg's guests, the Count and Countess de Chagny and their children. He was delighted that his house was to be filled with children, and pleased that Meg thought of his manor as home.

Although she understood, when she entered her bedchamber, that his intentions had been charitable, she was heartbroken and frantic as she searched the room and saw no sign of Erik. She immediately went to Marcelo, finding him in the library conversing in low serious tones with Raoul, and interrupted them both unceremoniously.

"Where are they?" Her voice was loud and harsh in the deep, cavernous room lined with books and manuscripts. One entire side of the room was filled from ceiling to floor with leather bound musical scores.

Raoul and Don Marcelo stood, their mouths agape at the urgency in Meg's demand.

"I want every last thing put back! I want them put back now! You had no right, no right. They're his!" She shifted nervously from one foot to another, like a small child considering running from certain punishment, and pointed at her benefactor, her raised finger punctuating each word through her tears.

Don Marcelo went quickly to Meg and put his arms around her. "Meg, please forgive me. I thought it would ease your suffering. I'm so sorry."

"I want them back. I want … I want … back." She sought his eyes, a lost and sorrowful incredulity fixed in her own hopeless gaze.

"I will have them put back immediately. I promise, Meg. Please, my dear, don't, don't cry." He patted her back tenderly.

Raoul indicated that he would retire. He intended to go in search of his wife, thinking she would be able to comfort Meg better than either he or Don Marcelo might. By the time Christine had laid Erica in her bassinet with the nanny in attendance and gone down the stairs to the library, Meg had cried all she could cry. Christine came into the room her arms opened wide, and Meg slipped away from Don Marcelo and anchored herself against her friend's breast. Christine rocked her gently back and forth for a moment and then led her from the room.

A little while later a maid came to Christine's room, where the two women had taken refuge, and informed Donna Meg that the objects had been restored to their proper places. Meg led Christine, who followed dutifully, to the bed-chamber she had shared with Erik. She went immediately to the dressing table and lifted the brush and comb from the polished oak surface. Inspecting them, she frowned to find they had been cleaned. There were no stray hairs trapped among their bristles. She replaced them on the table and went to the wash-stand where Erik was wont to shave. His straight razor was safely closed and placed beside the basin.

Christine watched her friend, fascinated by the rites of mourning she was performing. She herself swallowed hard in an attempt to dislodge a knot that had formed in her throat. She glanced around the room, imagining Erik involved in the same morning preparations she watched Raoul undergo each day. She could almost hear his feet as he walked to the basin to shave, see his broad back as he bent over to wash the lather from his face. A movement near the bed dispelled the illusion, and Christine saw Meg cautiously pick up a small notebook that lay on the bedside table.

"This was Erik's. He said it was for odds and ends, ideas for operas, fanciful thoughts, private thoughts. I picked it up one day, and he took it from me and said I shouldn't read it. He said it would be embarrassing. I asked him, 'Embarrassing for whom? You or me?' And he said, 'Perhaps for both of us.'" She held it close to her as if it were a piece of him. "Should I read it, do you think?"

"I don't know. Well, yes. I should think that it doesn't matter now. I mean it can't embarrass him, and it might **give** you some comfort."

"I'll read it later, shall I? When I'm alone?"

"Yes, Meg. When you're alone."

"The Teatro dell'Opera is doing quite well. The structural damage was minor, and we missed only the one season. In part, I have Erik to thank for that. He had reinforced the structure, the supporting walls and beams, when he made the modifications he wanted. The subterranean rooms and corridors were almost separate constructions, connected, but independently supported. We opened just days ago with the same slate, basically, as last season's. We're dedicating the entire run to Erik."

"I still have trouble thinking of Erik as a successful businessman. He was so ..." Raoul searched for the right word.

"So what? So disfigured? So mad?"

"No. Actually, that's not what I meant. I was thinking of how isolated he had always been. I'm amazed he could function in the real world. You didn't know what he was like, or what his world was like. For the first thirty or thirty-five years of his life—I never really knew his age—he lived as a freak in a traveling fair and then in an invented world underground. He had no idea how to live in the real world."

"Perhaps not. It cost him dearly, living in the 'real' world. He did well, but I could see the effort. There were times that he ran, simply ran, from everything. If he hadn't been able to run to Meg or to hide away days on end in those underground vaults, I think he would have died." Don Marcelo poured Raoul another glass of sherry. "I hope you like it. It comes from the vineyards in Spain."

"Yes, it's quite nice. I must have some of our Bordeaux sent to you when we return. I believe you'd enjoy it."

"So kind." Don Marcelo took some moments to study Raoul as he sipped his sherry. "You are, you know."

Raoul raised his eyebrows in confusion at Don Marcelo's remark. "What?"

"Kind. Erik told me that, after me, you were the kindest man he had ever known."

Raoul felt the heat rise in his face, and he turned a bright red. He was dumbfounded that Erik would have made such a statement.

"He said that you tried hard to be firm and cruel with him, but that cruelty was not in you. He said that when you hurt him, it was always inadvertently."

"Why would he say that?" Raoul sat forward in his chair, the sherry forgotten.

"He had quite a few confusing feelings toward you. I didn't understand some of them, even after he tried to explain them to me on several occasions. You see, after Meg and he came to live with me, he felt he wanted to understand himself better. He thought if he could understand his past and why he had done the things he did, he would be a better person for it. I asked him what he would like to be, who would he like to be. He thought for a long time and said that he'd like to be like you."

Raoul raised his eyebrows in surprise. He felt moved and puzzled. Embarrassed, he looked away from Don Marcelo toward the windows. The sun had set, and the last rays of orange light were filtering through the window. The fabric on the sofa was warm where the light struck.

"He told me," and here Don Marcelo chuckled lightly, "that should we meet again—you and I—I was to beg your pardon for speaking to you so harshly the last time we met."

Raoul remembered how he had come to Rome to inform Erik that he planned to save Meg and the boy. He intended to take them back to Paris to live with him and Christine. Uncomfortably, he recalled the devastated look on Erik's face when he thought he'd never see Meg or François again. He certainly didn't think Erik had considered him kind at that moment. Don Marcelo had railed at the count for his lack of compassion.

"He forgave you. He realized that you were concerned for Meg and the child and that you thought life with him would be untenable." Don Marcelo looked into the swirling deep purple of his sherry, and his tone grew sad. "Unfortunately I think for Meg, life without him may be untenable."

The two sat for some time silent. Eventually, as the darkness spread through the room, Don Marcelo called for the servant to light the gas lamps. Once the servant left, Don Marcelo forced himself to dispel the gloom that hovered over the two men's minds as well.

"I've heard that there's a new opera at one of the smaller venues in town that everyone is talking about. It's rather good according to an old friend of mine who went to a performance last week. Would you like to see it?"

"I'd love to. Do you think we can convince Meg to come?"

"I'm hoping that you or your wife will be able to convince her. She's wasting away. Erik would never forgive us if we were to let her languish. You know he had great faith in you. Said you were tenacious and stubborn, almost as tenacious and stubborn as he. A rare thing, a compliment from Erik."

Erik insisted on having his opera staged. Lucianna suggested Milan. She also convinced Erik that he should use a pseudonym to protect the family name. He chose Henri Fournier. As Henri Fournier, Erik drafted a letter to the manager of the Teatro alla Scala requesting an appointment. In the missive, he included one of the arias as an example of his composition. A reply arrived within the fortnight agreeing enthusiastically to a meeting with the composer. The seaside manor was temporarily closed, and a lovely villa near Milan was rented and equipped for the season.

On the date of the appointment, Erik was making preparations for the meeting when Lucianna suggested that she act as his agent. He had put on the mask and was examining himself in the mirror. For days Lucianna had been trying to come up with convincing arguments to keep Erik out of the public eye.

"Don't be silly, Luci. Who better than the composer to sell the composition?"

"Well, of course, you're right. And the mask does do a fairly good job of hiding your disfigurement."

Aware of the insinuation of doubt in Lucianna's voice, Erik cautiously searched Lucianna's eyes. He turned again to study himself in the mirror.

"It's just that it's hard to ignore a man who wears a mask. It makes one curious. It might distract from the purpose of the appointment, which is after all your music, not your face." She tried to sound light, but she could tell the effect her words were having on him.

The nervous excitement drained away. In its stead crept indecision, anxiety, doubt.

"Whereas I can take your composition as your representative. There will be no awkward false modesty. I can praise the work to the heavens. He's already interested or he wouldn't have granted the interview."

Erik sat and listened with a grim expression. Lucianna hesitated for one moment when she saw the way he looked at her. A grim premonition gripped her heart. *He fears to look upon himself. He looks to me to tell him he's not hideous, and I corroborate his worst fears. He thinks that it's I who feels revulsion. He thinks it is my rejection!* But there was no way around it, no way she could avoid hurting him. She must keep him hidden; he must not become a public figure.

"I'll wait for your return," he said.

Relieved, she turned to leave. Before she closed the door behind her, she saw Erik take the hand mirror and turn it face down on the dresser. Her heart tightened in pain.

Fournier's opera was the talk of the season in Milan. The second letter from the owners of the Teatro Regio in Rome was opened by Erik before Lucianna managed to intercept it. The owners again requested permission to perform Sig. Henri Fournier's opera later in the season and asked him to come to Rome as their special guest. Erik sat to write his enthusiastic response immediately. He barked orders to Luigi to find apartments in Rome and make preparations for the journey. Lucianna wrung her hands, unable to stop the events as they spiraled out of her control.

Erik's notebook lay on Meg's lap for a long time before she dared open it. Everyone was in bed. She had retired several hours ago. She had heard the men's heavy footsteps in the hall as they, too, went to their rooms. She ran her fingers lightly over the cover pretending to trace the path of his fingers. She suddenly felt it naughty to read his private thoughts. Would they shock her? Would she think she never really knew him? No, that could not be. She began to read.

the second act is all wrong. need to start with the aria and then have the soldier enter, duet follows, ending needs to be stronger.

François has tricked me once more. Little devil. I told him to stay out of my papers, the song is not finished, and he's already played it twice and improved it! Damn. have to put his name on the next opera, I'm sure.

Laurette lay in my arms today like a perfect angel and then puked all over me. I could abide that except that it made me want to retch along with her. How do women deal with so much spitting up and mess? Meg had pity on me and cleaned her up. She deposited her, clean and in a fresh napkin, in my arms once more as if she were the gazette and went off to do something. I stared at the bundle of pink blankets for several moments fearing she'd explode, but she slept. She had just been at Meg's breast, and she kept making little sucking movements with her lips. She smelled of milk and something sour that wasn't all that unpleasant. I didn't realize until Meg came and scooped her out of my arms again, this time as if she were a bundle of dirty clothes, that nearly two hours had gone by. I followed her to her nursery and snuck in after Meg left. I couldn't take my eyes off her. Then she woke up and cried. The nanny wasn't anywhere to be found. I think she's nipping the brandy! I picked my daughter up and held her, but she fretted so until she found my finger and took it in her mouth and sucked away at it. I took her to Meg, because I could tell that Laurette was fast learning that she can get no milk from my pinkie finger, no matter how hard she sucks.

Meg was sleeping. She must have been very tired. She left her bodice unfastened. Her breasts, exposed to the breeze that was thankfully blowing through the half-drawn curtains, were spotted with milk. I couldn't breathe for several moments watching her. She is so beautiful. I sometimes feel her beauty as a sharp pain. It is intense like my music. I hear a melody. Her body is becoming music. I have to …

I completed the first measures.

I wish Lucianna would desist. She stirs something in me that I don't like. I know her in a way that is uncomfortable. It feels like we are naked when we're together. I try to avoid being alone with her. She comes each season, and each season she's as beautiful as that night so many years ago when she came upon me in the stable. She was so wild, like an unbroken horse. Meg is jealous. I rather enjoy that she is. She gets this wonderful crimson splotch on each of her cheeks. I find her exciting when she's angry or upset. If only Lucianna could find someone else to love! God, she's clever. She can't help but tease me.

must buy more of the gold leaf for the final scene. tell sig. Bianchi the key is all wrong for the tenor. not that changing it will help him that much. he's atrocious. I've told Marcelo to fire him, but we've no replacement so I'll have to rewrite the damn score so he can hit the notes and hope for the best. she's good though. I'm surprised because she doesn't look as if she would have that resonance to her voice, no one can sing better than my canary though.

no more sausage ravioli ever ever again feel nauseous

Damn Meg. She butchered the solo, butchered it! If she won't practice it won't get better. Laurette can sit in a basket downstairs in the piano room as well as in her nursery!

Fired the nanny. she guzzled a whole bottle of Marcelo's favorite brandy.

François's tutor is beside himself. He says François is the naughtiest child he's ever tutored. I had to scold him. Hated it. I hate scolding him. When he looks frightened it frightens me. I asked Meg to talk to him, but she says it's my duty as a father. A father's duty? What do I know about a father's duty? I thought immediately of the way my father would strike me repeatedly on my back and legs with a cane or how he flayed me with the whip! Of course I know Meg didn't have that in mind! I don't know if François knows how much I love him. I talk to him as if he were a stranger sometimes. I can hear myself. I cringe as I do it, but I don't know how else to speak with him. I think he likes it sometimes, though. I think it makes him feel adult and serious. The tutor is an idiot. He should know how to interest a child. He's boring. I almost fall asleep just looking at him! His voice has the range of a duck! How can François sit in the study and listen to the duck quack on and on about geographical borders or the purchase of linen at such and such a price and for such and such an amount? Sometimes I think I should simply apprentice François to me in the opera house. He'll learn business, architecture, music, and so on. As long as he can read and write, the rest he can learn on his own! Meg disagrees. She insists we retain a tutor. I told her she better look for one that doesn't put everyone to sleep just by walking into the room.

Meg has missed her courses two months now. If it's a girl, I wonder what she'll wish to call her? If a boy? I know that I don't want her to give him my name.

Meg brought her hand quickly to her mouth to stop the startled cry she felt imminent upon reading this last entry. She didn't realize that he was keeping watch over her menstrual cycle. What else had he noticed that he didn't write down in his little book? She remembered the time. She was only nursing Laurette at night, and she had missed several cycles. She had indeed thought she might be with child again. Then finally she experienced a very heavy flow with severe cramping. It was so early that it wouldn't be apparent if she miscarried the child. But for weeks afterwards she was depressed. She remembered now his gentle kindnesses during that time. She hadn't realized that he knew. She thought it silly to share with him since she wasn't sure anything had actually taken root inside her womb. She told him she felt ill, although she manifested no outward symptoms other than fatigue and low spirits. He insisted she rest. He brought fruits and flowers to her in bed. She recalled hoping he would not wish to make love for a while, but hadn't said anything to him. Yet he had not pressed her to make love but had lain with her like a brother for several weeks until, feeling restored, she turned to him and made her desires clear. Then he had made love to her with a sweet gentleness that amazed her as if his only concern was her pleasure. He had known! He had shared her grief without betraying her privacy.

She continued reading the little book. Some entries were nearly illegible. Many were lists of chores or purchases to be made for home or for the opera house. A few musical entries were peppered throughout, even a drawing or two. One in particular moved her. It was a pencil sketch of her nursing Laurette. He had captured the molded way that a baby's body is indistinguishable from a mother's. Arms, breasts, baby wrapped around each other like the spirals of a clock spring. She skimmed the entries, pausing at those that reached out to her, rereading others.

Madeleine and I spoke last night. We should have spoken ages ago. I didn't realize I was still angry with her. She cried. I made her cry! How could I do that to her? She held me. She put her arms around me and held me! I didn't know how much I needed her to do this. It's still painful to think about those days when I was alone. I can't think about it. I …

Meg bought me a new cravat. I'll wear it tomorrow to the reception. I can't leave until the clock strikes 10:30. Meg tells me she will castrate me if I leave before that. I can always hide for ten to fifteen minute stretches. The rules are that I can't leave the premises, not that I can't sneak out of the room!

I try not to think about it. I'm amazed that I go through the greater part of the day without any thought of it. The banker from Milan, Sig. what-ever-it-

was, hasn't even seen my face. "Hideous." That's a favorite word. I don't listen, I don't hear. But last night I let my guard down. The whispers were too many to ignore and I couldn't help but hear them. I thought he was talking about my opera. Why is it that they have to talk about my face? Why are they curious about ugliness like mine? Why aren't they attracted to great beauty, like Meg's face or the face of my children. They are so beautiful that it makes me cry. These men, and the women do it too, wait for the moment I'm out of earshot and they bring their faces together and whisper in thrilled exhilaration that behind my mask I'm "hideous."

I wanted to rip my mask off and give them a real fright! As if they were so handsome! Sig. banker is a hideous little toad with eyes that pop out of a sallow complexion. And the Weird sisters, God I can't and don't wish to remember any of their names, have more warts on their faces than most witches in the Grimm tales. And they say I'm ugly? Well, I am. I wish I weren't. I wish I were handsome. Silly that someone like me is vain! Meg isn't vain, and she has every right to be. Perhaps only the ugly are vain? Meg will run her fingers over my deformity and smile at me. I don't understand. Yet I know she's sincere. I sometimes want to crawl behind her eyes and look at myself to see myself as she sees me. Or even Christine. I know Christine looked at me as if … well, I don't know how she saw me, but it wasn't the way old toadstool sees me. Raoul sees me as I am. It's curious to think about it. He does see me as I am, deformed and hideous, but he regards me as if that's simply what I am. He used to be appalled by me, frightened by me, even sickened. I think he sees me now the way one sees someone with a nose that is too big or with a very weak chin or a head that is too big or eyes that are crossed or bad teeth. I wish I only had a nose that was crooked. My son's beauty takes my breath away. Meg says he has my beauty. I know she's wrong. He may resemble me a great deal, but there is a lot of Meg in his face. The combination is amazing. I do feel somehow vindicated when I look upon him. He is my seed. How could something so hideous, like me, make something so beautiful, like him?

Lucianna has gone too far.

the tenor will destroy me! he sings like a giraffe with its neck caught in a vice. god save us from him!

Laurette shall certainly be a great singer. She wails, and the walls shake!

I heard many wonderful comments about the staging of the opera. They particularly liked the faux garden. Must say something to Thérese. Several of the young men were trying to sing the love song to a particularly pretty brunette. Of course, they got it all wrong. I went to the piano to play it for them. The next thing I knew several voices were shouting for me to sing it. I wanted to escape, but Meg came and restrained me by putting her hand down on my shoulder. As I began to rise, she pushed me down as hard as she could without making it obvious. I thought I might make a scene, but I had drunk several glasses of champagne and decided that I would throw caution to the wind and sing for them. When I finished, I was embarrassed to hear absolute silence in the room. I was about to flee in shame when they began to stamp their feet. Then they broke out with a shower of bravos. I don't know which was worse! thinking I had made a fool of myself or being the toast of the party. I bowed quickly and walked as rapidly as I could in a dignified manner out of the room. Later when Meg found me hidden in the upstairs dressing room, she laughed at me. She doesn't understand how raw my emotions are. I am at their mercy, and I can't be sure that they won't rip my skin from my body. Every look, every word they say is like a knife blade raked across my flesh. She'll never understand. It doesn't matter if they applaud or if they jeer, it pains me to the depth of my soul!

Meg placed a marker in the page and closed the notebook. She couldn't read anymore tonight. She was having trouble seeing the letters because she had begun to cry. She mustn't let her tears fall on the paper for the ink would surely run.

"What the devil is going on?" Raoul grappled with the strange confusion of limbs rolling about the floor. He finally managed to grab the edge of François's coat and had picked out his own son's leg in the jumble and pulled both in opposite directions. Slowly and unwillingly the knot seemed to untangle, and two sullen, angry boys were extricated from the fight. "Answer me!"

François's eye was already turning a dark purple, and Raoul noticed that Victor's nose was bleeding and his lip was slightly swollen on one side. They had always gotten along so well!

François glowered at Victor who tried to kick at François in spite of the fact that his father held him at arm's length. Neither boy looked at Raoul and neither spoke up. Madeleine stood in the doorway, appalled.

"I may not be able to force François to obey me, but you have no choice," he addressed his son. "You're the older and should take responsibility for what's happened. We are also guests."

"That's not fair. He hit me. He balled up his fist and hit me straight in the face!"

François glared at the other boy. Raoul couldn't help but see the resemblance to Erik in the child's intent silence. His lips were pursed, and his fists were clenched at his side.

"Madeleine, could you take Victor to the library? I'll speak with him there, later." Madeleine took Victor by the hand and led him out. Before she closed the door behind them, she stole a sympathetic look at François. It wasn't like him to fight.

The room was the children's room. Toys lined the walls and spaces had been designated for certain kinds of activities. Raoul took one of the several chairs from the table where paints and drawing materials were neatly displayed. He sat facing the silent and angry boy. He was used to dealing with his own children and didn't know François well enough to guess the exact tact he should take. But he knew that silence might best be met with more silence, so he folded his arms on his chest and sat watching François fume. Gradually the boy shifted his weight from one foot to the next and looked away from his "uncle." It amused Raoul that the boy still remained silent. He was definitely resolved that Raoul would have to break the ice.

It struck him suddenly that the child had returned home, and his father was not here to greet him. His father was dead. "You miss him, don't you, François?" he asked gently.

François turned his head farther in the direction of the windows and away from Raoul in an effort to disguise the tremble of his lower lip. From his lip the shudder seemed to spread to his shoulders. Raoul reached out and grabbed the boy roughly and squeezed him against his chest. The tightness of the embrace allowed the boy to hold on to the man and to sob without any thought of restraint. Raoul held him for quite some time until he felt the sobs fade. He released François from the embrace and gave him a handkerchief to wipe his nose and eyes. Placing his hands firmly on the boy's shoulders, he looked him directly in the eyes and asked him for an explanation. "I've never seen you do anything violent. Your grand-maman says you don't fight. Why did you hit Victor?"

"He said …" François stopped and looked worriedly at Raoul.

"Yes?" said Raoul encouragingly.

"He said that you said something about my father." The boy's voice faltered as he finished. Then he blurted out with angry determination, "You called my father a monster." The boy felt betrayed. Clearly he assumed the duty of defending his father against such calumny.

Raoul groaned audibly and shrank back in the chair. He studied the dark eyes so like Erik's, the well-formed mouth, what would become a strong jaw and chin, the broad forehead, and straight nose. A handsome boy, a proud and brave boy, protective of a father whose vulnerability he had already sensed.

"François, can you forgive me?"

The dark intensity lifted in the child's eyes, replaced by surprise.

"I spoke ill of your father in anger and before I came to know him better. I'll speak with Victor."

François looked sheepishly up at the man and whispered, "I heard my father say you were an idiot once."

"Well, you see? Sometimes we say things we don't mean."

"I think he meant it," replied the boy innocently.

Raoul chuckled briefly before continuing. "Oh, I see. Well. We all have our faults, don't we?"

"I suppose so," smiled François.

"Do you think you and Victor can forgive one another and shake hands and be friends?"

"Like you and father did?"

"Yes. Like your father and I did."

François hesitated only a moment and nodded his agreement.

"I'll have a chat with Victor. Shall I?"

"Thank you, Uncle. May I go now? It's past lunch."

Meg began to bleed very badly. She's also in great pain; the cramping is brutal. There's no child. I heard her crying when I passed the door. I don't know why she hasn't spoken to me about it. I won't say anything unless she does.

She's still in mourning. I wish she'd let me bring a doctor to examine her, but she insists that it was her normal time.

someone's been in the storage rooms. it's as if they've been looking for something. I told Marcelo, and he insists everyone has been told not to go beyond the storage room marked "D."

For some time now I've had the feeling that someone is following me. I can't think who it might be. The wine glasses have arrived. They're exquisite. I'm sure Marcelo will adore them.

Sig. Valerio is quite pleasant. I played several hands of whist with him and Sig. Beauchamp and Sig. Conti. The other two are asses, but Sig. Valerio has a sharp wit. We discussed the sad condition of several of the great architectural wonders in the city, and he is heading a committee to pressure for wise restoration. We were talking architecture, and he asked me to be on the committee. I thought he was trying to insult me at first, a joke at my expense, but he was deadly serious. Of course, I declined, although as an afterthought I offered my services as a consultant. Valerio suggested we have a cognac sometime after a performance. Won 5,000 lira. Beauchamp is particularly bad at whist.

finally the new tutor has arrived. seems much more interesting than the last one. he knows the difference between a major scale and a minor scale, has a nice voice, but can't play the piano worth a damn even though he thinks he can, and understands the basic elements of architecture. and of course he has all the other subjects under control such as math and drawing and so on, his sketches were respectable. he's an athletic looking fellow and believes children should be outside for a certain number of hours involved in physical activity. I think I agree, having had to make do with a very different kind of education than the one he proposes. I like the idea of François out in the fresh air! I wonder if this tutor will be able to instruct Laurette as well?

the kitchen maid Madeleine assigned to the nursery for the short term is working out nicely as nanny, she doesn't like brandy, thank God, and she genuinely dotes on Laurette. I suggested to Meg we keep her.

our anniversary is coming and I have the perfect gift. I'll hide it in the secret panel of the wardrobe. she'll never find it.

Meg realized that their anniversary was six weeks after she had left to be with Christine. He was already dead by then. He had bought her a gift and hidden it away before she left for Paris.

She placed the book down, careful not to lose her place, although there were few entries left, and went to inspect the wardrobe. She removed the clothes and began feeling along the back wall of the wardrobe until she realized that there was something strange about the bottom that she had never noticed. It was higher than it needed to be! The clothes had nearly touched the floor, leaving barely any room for shoes or other articles. Examining the base of the wardrobe, she found a handle so clever that it lay flat within a groove of the wood, invisible to the naked eye. A section of the flooring lifted out of its place and inside the dark enclosure she found several strange objects. There was a lady's fan, a rosary, several scrolls of sketches he had made of Christine and of sets Meg remembered from different operas performed years ago at the Opera Populaire, a lock of blond hair she recognized as her own, a book of poems, and a box wrapped in silver and gold ribbons.

This she removed and brought to the bed. She unwrapped the bows carefully, almost regretting having to disturb the gift that Erik had made for her. He had been thinking of her, had selected a gift, had it wrapped, and hid it away thinking to bring it forth when they were together again.

She wiped her face with the back of her sleeve, tried to blink the tears away so that she would be able to see, and gently opened the box. Inside she found a pearl necklace with a gold clasp and two pearl drop earrings. As she lifted the strand from the box, her fingers trembled.

"Pearls are for tears, Erik. Didn't you know?"

Later that night, Meg opened the notebook again. She felt as if he were still with her as she read the awkwardly penned entries. Madeleine had taught Erik to write, but he was older than most children when he learned. His penmanship never attained the elegance of those schooled from an earlier age.

I dreamed of Christine last night.

"Christine?" Meg barely whispered the name out loud. She took several deep breaths before she took up the notebook and began to read the entry again.

I dreamed of Christine last night. It was a disturbing dream. It was the last time we were alone together, when little Raoul had drowned and she seemed dead to the world. I brought her down to my rooms under the streets of Paris. I kept her there for nearly two weeks. The dream was almost like a memory, but at one point it diverged completely from what actually happened. Is it true that we have no control over our dreams? Philosophers have meditated on the meaning of dreams for centuries. Does anyone really understand them? I have given up any claim to Christine. I have pledged my heart willingly to Meg. Yet in the dream Christine asked to stay with me. She asked me to lie with her, and I did. I felt the old stirrings of love and passion for her. I woke drenched in sweat, my heart was pounding, and I think Meg thought I was having a nightmare. I immediately made love to her. I was so aroused and ashamed. I feel as if I've been unfaithful to Meg.

"Damn you, Erik!" she exclaimed, her face scarlet and her blood pounding in her temples. She threw the notebook across the room where it struck the wall and landed open, its pages bent. "Always Christine!" She sank into the bed and hugged herself in self pity as she tried to figure out which night it might have been. Which night had he awoken from a terrible "nightmare" to reach out to her and make love? There was not just one night. It happened from time to time. It was not unusual for him to thrash in bed as if pursued by the hounds of hell or to whimper in pain or sorrow. Most of the time, he didn't wake. She would edge closer in the bed until they lay side to side or she would wrap her arms around him, pressing her body along his back until the sobs or the shudders passed and once again he would relax into a calm sleep. But there had been other violent, frightful nights that he awoke, not knowing where he was, and clung to her. Only after making love would they both sink mercifully back into the blankness of sleep.

She thought she remembered the night. There was a dream he had, not long before she left for Paris, in which he seemed anxious, but not terrified. He woke disoriented, but once his eyes locked on her lying beside him in the bed, she sensed only his arousal. Was it she or Christine that he embraced? She thought back to the incident. He was greedy in his passion at first, but eventually he became attentive to her, to her needs. He kissed her repeatedly at the mole that lay at the base of her throat. He had often told her that it was her mole—now she self consciously worried the brown fleshy tip just above the depression between her collar bones—that gave her identity away to him when long ago they made love in her dressing room. That had been the second time they had made love. The first had been the time she and Christine wore the same disguise at the Carnival ball in the De Chagny manor, and he had thought she was Christine.

Relieved, she realized that he might have awoken excited by Christine's image in his dream, but it was she that he had made love to, not Christine. And he had known the difference.

Regretting her anger, she flew from the bed to the spot where the notebook had landed awkwardly and stooped to lift it. From the pages fell a folded piece of paper, whose writing she did not recognized. It was a note, not a formal letter, addressed to Sig. Erik Giry. No one in Rome would refer to Erik by that name. Giry had been her surname. When Sig. Costanzi conferred his family name on Erik, Meg legally assumed, as Erik's legitimate wife, the Costanzi name as well. She unfolded the paper and read.

> *If you have any regard for your wife's reputation, meet me in the storage room below the backstage after the performance. We have unsettled business, you and I. Do not tell anyone or you will regret it, but not as much as the Giry whore will.*

She didn't recognize the hand, but she had an awful feeling she recognized the hateful tone. But surely he was still in prison! And even if he had been released, he wouldn't be foolish enough to follow them to Rome, would he? Could he want revenge so badly?

She folded the note carefully and placed it inside the notebook. She resolved to read further. Perhaps Erik had commented on the note somewhere in the notebook. There was no indication of the date of the meeting. It may not have coincided with the fire at all. Erik might have met Giovanni, and that had been the end of it. Even as she tried to convince herself, she was filled with dread.

I know someone has been in the storage rooms and someone tried to force one of the trap doors to the lower floors. I found the marks of a chisel in the wood frame. I don't want anyone down there! Those are my rooms!

I asked Marcelo last night if he ever dreamed of other women when he was married. I had wanted to ask him for days, but felt embarrassed to do so. He asked me if I had had such dreams. I thought it foolish to lie so I gave him only the barest details of the dream I had had of Christine. He said that he loved his wife more than anyone in the world, and that was why he had never remarried. Then he said that he had dreamed of other women. I asked him if he dreamed of being with them in compromising circumstances? He understood my drift immediately, which reassured me somewhat. He said that it was perfectly normal. He had torrid dreams of sultry seduction with real and imaginary women while married to his wife and after her death they still plagued him. He asked me if I would wish the dream real if that were possi-

ble. I thought about it. After all it was something in my past, not my present, which I think makes it a bit different from the type of dream Marcelo was thinking of. Would I wish to have had Christine? Yes. I think I wish I had one such memory. Would I wish to take her now? No. I would not. Our time has passed.

Raoul would never have invited us to come if Christine were not in grave peril. I have to let Meg go. I don't want to. I won't rest until she's back. What will I do?

Meg scanned through the last few entries describing the preparations for departure. But she couldn't resist lingering over one that spoke of his loneliness and desire for his family's speedy return. Then she found what she was looking for.

it must be Giovanni, the petulant tone gives him away. he was released several months ago, no one in Pianosa has seen him since the first few days after his release, seems he wanted to make a new life in Rome like I did! somehow he's gotten access to the underground rooms, he's probably the one who's been following me. clever, I'll give him that. tonight I'll have to meet him to see what he's scheming.

For her sake and for the sake of the family name, Erik allowed Lucianna to handle the details at the Teatro Regio. Her cousin, Don Carlo, would present himself, when and if needed, to the public as the composer, Henri Fournier. Erik was allowed a glimpse of him only briefly—a young dandy who stared at him fearfully from the foyer as Lucianna hurriedly dismissed him. *That worm is to stand in for me?* Erik chafed at the precautions Lucianna insisted were necessary.

Erik looked for his mask and did not find it on the table where he had left it. Below waited the barouche to take them to a narrow causeway next to the opera where the manager had arranged for him and Lucianna to enter and leave quietly, unseen. Lucianna helped him search the room for the missing mask but to no avail. Surely it had fallen to the floor and had been mistakenly swept up by one of the maids, suggested Lucianna. At any rate, there was no time to do anything about it. She went to instruct the driver that they would not be going, but Erik stepped in front of her and prevented her from calling for the servant. He would go, with or without the mask.

Don Carlo accepted the accolades meant for Erik. He took several bows at the opening night performance while Erik seethed, hidden, in the box seats especially picked out by Lucianna and the manager. They sat in the back of the box protected both by the angle and the heavy tapestry hangings along the sides. Now that the performance had ended and most of the audience had made their way out of the auditorium, Luigi escorted Erik and Lucianna from the box into the narrow hallway that would lead to the alternative exit. The manager had requested meeting the real genius of the opera and, in spite of Lucianna's objections, was coming from the opposite direction toward them, his hand already raised to take Erik's. Under the circumstances, Erik was loath to meet anyone. Without the mask, he had settled for hiding his face behind the high, stiff collar of his frock coat and the low brim of a large hat. He had no intention of letting the little man see his deformity. Lucianna was right; he wasn't brave enough to have his unfortunate appearance heralded to the world—even at the price of his artistic recognition.

Just as he was about to turn and follow Luigi, Erik glimpsed a commotion at the foot of the marble staircase. A crowd had gathered round several other spectators who were attempting to depart. The excited murmurs suggested it was a matter of some celebrity. His eyes lit upon a small figure of a woman—those around her were keeping the enthusiastic crowd at bay—who graciously bowed her head and smiled as she made her way to the door. Something about her tugged at Erik making it impossible to take his eyes from her. From this distance, he could not make out her features, only the outline of her body, her graceful carriage and gestures, her long blond hair pulled high into an elaborate coif. Above the general murmur of her admirers, the name was barely intelligible, Signora Costanzi.

In the next instant, Erik's attention was drawn away from the scene below to the sharp cry from the opposite direction. Before him stood the startled, gaping manager. In his trance-like perusal of the scene in the foyer, Erik had lifted his face away from the stiff collar, exposing a portion of his face. Coming upon his new composer suddenly and understanding the brief pause to be an invitation at last to approach and meet the eccentric artist, the manager had drawn near enough to see Erik's face. Lucianna grabbed Erik's arm yet again to pull him away. This time he turned eagerly to follow and to escape the horrified look of revulsion on the other man's face.

Later in the barouche, Lucianna took Erik's hand in hers and tenderly told him not to worry about the manager's reaction. She muttered some vague words of comfort, but Erik wasn't thinking about the manager, his thoughts returned repeatedly to the beautiful, graceful figure of the signora in the foyer of the theater. He read the gazettes; he knew the name. She was the diva from the Teatro dell'Opera. She was said to be the loveliest and most talented woman gracing the opera stage in Rome, if not in the entire country. He must hear her sing.

CHAPTER 6

❀

A Stranger

I have been a stranger in a strange land.

Exodus, King James Bible

"I thought the second act was amazing. Everything came together so well, the voices, the motifs." Sig. Costanzi had nothing but praise for the opera they had just seen at the Teatro Regio. Raoul and he had discussed the music, the setting, the story the entire ride home. Christine and Meg had been silent, politely listening and nodding in the pauses left by the two men.

Madeleine was waiting for them when they came into the downstairs parlor for a touch of brandy. She had declined Don Marcelo's kind invitation to accompany them to the opera, preferring to stay with the children. Even so, she looked forward to hearing about this new opera composed by a completely unknown artist. As they entered the parlor, she immediately noted the troubled looks on Meg's and Christine's faces.

"Was it not a good performance?" she asked.

"Not a good performance?" repeated Sig. Costanzi, scandalized. "Well, to be brutally honest, Donna Madeleine, the performances were competent. The Teatro Regio's opera singers are good, but not as good as mine." He smiled sweetly at Meg as the prime example of the merits of his company in comparison with Montenegro's.

Meg, distracted, barely acknowledged her patron's praise.

Raoul poured the brandy and handed one to Madeleine.

"It's the opera itself that's remarkable. Far better than most of the material we've seen in Paris. Everyone's talking about this Fournier."

"Fournier?"

"The composer. He's an eccentric that no one's ever heard of before. He did come out and take a bow after the performance. Rather young. I expected him to be a more mature man."

"Something isn't right about all this," said Meg. Her eyes looked past them as if they were invisible.

Christine sensed that they had both come away with similar reactions to the opera. Emboldened by Meg's remark, she said, "I know it's impossible, but …"

"But what?" urged Meg, eagerly grasping her friend's hand. "You felt it, too, didn't you, Christine?"

"What on earth are you two talking about?" laughed Madeleine. She stopped laughing when she glanced at Raoul and Don Marcelo. They had sobered and were intently waiting for Christine to finish.

Embarrassed, Christine lowered her gaze to her lap and remained silent.

"Well, what was it about? What was the story?" Madeleine broke the preternatural silence that had taken hold of all of them.

"A reworking of Odysseus's return from the Trojan war, if you ask me," offered Raoul. "Two lovers are parted by war. He's severely wounded and has to fight to return home. Once back he finds his fiancée beset by suitors, in particular one who is quite a scoundrel."

"He's been very badly wounded, and he fears that she …" Meg's voice trailed off into silence.

Raoul waited for Meg to complete her statement, but she stared out through the darkened window seemingly lost in her own thoughts. When she began to speak again, it was as if she were speaking only to herself. "She thinks Etienne's dead and mourns him. He comes back only to find that everyone believes he's dead, including the heroine, Marietta. He's disappointed that she can't sense that he's still alive and struggling to return to her. The hero sings of betrayal; she sings a song in which she remembers their love. Marietta has no intention of accepting the scoundrel's proposal, but he intends to dishonor her to force her to marry him. The third act belongs initially to the scoundrel who has found out Etienne is alive and yet intends to press Marietta into marriage anyway. He plots to murder Etienne. Maddened by jealousy, Etienne kills the scoundrel, but Marietta doesn't recognize that it's Etienne. She stabs him in the back. Only when he sings to her does she recognize him. He dies in her arms."

When Meg didn't continue, Marcelo added, "The song of their leave-taking at the beginning of the opera and the song she sings at the end of Act I when she's told he's been killed are hauntingly beautiful. The other highlight for me was the duet in Act II. It's a duet, but they don't know the other one is singing.

Etienne sings of anger and betrayal while Marietta tells of a dream in which she relives her love for Etienne. You'd think it impossible, but Fournier brings the two together in spite of the difference in mood and tempo. Amazing! The finale when he dies in her arms is a duet that brought tears to everyone's eyes!" Don Marcelo was clearly affected by the music even more than the story itself.

"He's scarred, horribly disfigured. She doesn't even recognize him until he sings to her." Meg's statement disconcerted Raoul and the others. Only Christine seemed to understand her logic. "Don't you see? It's uncanny."

Catching her drift, Raoul blurted out, "You can't be serious." He was incredulous, but he quickly subdued his voice, softening it as he added, "Meg, it's understandable that you'd feel the tragedy of loss to be …"

"No! It's more than that!"

"Let her finish, Raoul," joined in Christine as if she and Meg had rehearsed their statements before. How this could have been, though, mystified the men since the women had been silent the whole ride home.

"The music, it bears his signature. There are motifs similar to those in *Don Juan Triumphant*. Surely you heard them? He favors certain chords. It's subtle. I think only someone like me, or Christine, who has studied under him, would hear it, but the opera … It's Erik's! I sense it. It was as if he … As if …" She couldn't go on.

Christine looked to Raoul, panic in her eyes. "It's true, Raoul. It's as if he had reached out from the grave."

Meg shook her head excitedly. "Grave? What do you mean? There's nothing supernatural about this. He must have written it. Don't you see? Erik must be alive."

"But why would he allow us to think he was dead? It doesn't make sense." Raoul was fast becoming impatient. He didn't like to think it, but it had been a disastrous idea to take Meg to an opera, especially this particular opera. It was true—even he could see it—there were too many elements in the story that coincided with Erik's and Meg's experiences. He was sure that Don Marcelo felt it, too.

"They never found him, did they? There's no body. There aren't even any bones in the crypt you had built for him, are there Marcelo?" Meg needed to convince herself as much as she needed to convince her friends. If they could be convinced, then perhaps there was some hope that Erik was alive.

Don Marcelo didn't have time to reply.

"He was in the opera house. He was in the labyrinth that he had designed and constructed. He has always been a genius at escape. He went one last time back into the burning building. And ..." Meg had risen to pace the room while she argued through the idea and its contradictions. Suddenly she dropped heavily onto the sofa next to Christine. Evidently the connection between the two women had finally been severed, for Christine was puzzled as she watched Meg grow deathly pale.

"What is it, Meg?" she asked, solicitously.

"The lover came back wounded," she quietly murmured. "The fire. Could he have been even more ...?" The thought died unspoken on her lips as she imagined Erik alive, covered by flames, tortured and burned hideously. Had the flames consumed his entire body? Was he so disfigured that he preferred she think him dead rather than have her see him again?

Raoul saw Meg pitch forward and ran to catch her before she hit the ground. Madeleine and Christine followed him as he carried her to her bed-chamber. The women stayed behind and put her to bed. Raoul returned to the parlor where Don Marcelo sipped gloomily at another snifter of brandy. He nodded toward the bottle on the table, and Raoul declined the invitation in favor of a bottle of scotch from which he poured himself a liberal shot. He drained it before he spoke again.

"I think I'll pay a visit to the manager of the Teatro Regio tomorrow. I'd like to arrange for a meeting with the composer."

on the stage the tenor sings of his battles and of the wounds he has received, he sings of the joy he felt thinking of returning to his lover's arms, his voice is like honey, it drips from his mouth and slips over the edges of the stage, deepens and strengthens into the low vibrations of a baritone, he is broad in the shoulders, his profile strong, his long straight nose, his broad back, the narrow hips, the firm muscles and slim legs in tight leggings, I want to sing to him, I come out onto the stage and I sing to him my song of waiting, my song of patience, my song of endur-ing love, he doesn't believe me, he steps back, he keeps his back to me, he starts to leave, I cry and run to him, I reach out and place my hand on his shoulder and he turns toward me, his mask has fallen, his face is gone! it is blackened and melted into a twisted lump of flesh in which blind eyes stare, his lips have been burned away and his teeth mock me with a skeletal grin, I scream and the stage falls away into a fiery pit and it's Erik, my Erik, he is trapped under burning wood, he cries out in such agony for me to help him, I can't reach him, my tears fall on his burn-ing body and sizzle in a whirl of steam, his pain undiminished, my sorrow without end, he keeps falling away from me

Lucianna insisted that Erik remain in the apartments. At night, on occasion, she would suggest they take a ride through the streets of Rome to watch the crowds, but not once did they stop the barouche to join the festivities. Although this was far better than remaining trapped in the apartments, it irked Erik. A prisoner, he could not see beyond the bars. At least on the island, he could walk about the grounds; there were activities that he enjoyed. There he had not missed the society of his fellow creatures. There were servants bustling about; he could overhear their banter and watch them go about their chores. He imagined their lives going on at their own pace with sorrows and joys that were common to all men. In the echo of their struggles, he felt less alone. He had established a sort of camaraderie with those who worked in the stable. Here in Rome he was surrounded by thousands of people, but he had never felt so lonely. His separation and his isolation were painfully obvious to him. He had contact only with Lucianna and Luigi. The other servants were distant, occupied with their own duties.

The night they went to the opera opened his eyes to a need that he barely knew he had. He asked Lucianna if they might go again, to see another opera, to see a play, to go to a concert, or visit a museum, to be immersed in the sound of a multitude of heartbeats. She invented reasons that they should not go out. Unspoken behind these excuses, he understood that he was not to be seen. Luci was ashamed of being seen with a freak!

He would be the first to confess that his deformity was repulsive. And yet, on the island, he had gone about without a mask, only sometimes aware of the way others saw him. The stable workers quickly got used to him. They didn't stare at him after the first few days. Rarely did they look him in the face when they spoke. Usually they kept their eyes averted. This strategy didn't bother him. It was less painful than the appalled stares of the few kitchen servants who remained hidden away in the servants' quarters, venturing out into the main rooms of the house only on special errands, and therefore unprepared to come upon him. Lucianna never said it, but everything she did told him that he would be rejected in Rome if anyone were to see his face.

He hadn't been so naïve that he thought he should go out into the streets of Rome without a mask. He had already purchased one for such occasions, a mask that would cover most of his face, the one that had mysteriously disappeared just moments before they were to leave for the opening night performance of his opera. It was never found. Not a word was said about it. Erik waited and watched Lucianna, more and more resentful of her protection. A week after the opening night, Erik stated that he would like a new mask. Would

Lucianna pick one out for him? When she returned, after spending the after-noon shopping, he asked if she had found one. Flustered, she pretended to have completely forgotten, but she assured him that she'd purchase one the next time she found herself at the shops. That day didn't come. Erik waited and watched, and he never mentioned the mask again. It was too plain that Lucianna didn't want him to have a mask. She didn't want him out and about in the streets of Rome, not without her, not alone and free to do as he pleased.

Erik was surprised when Lucianna invited the diva and the musical director from the Teatro Regio to dine with them in their apartments. The two artists were from France and had come to Italy specifically invited for the season. They were, for this reason, new to the opera scene in Italy. Erik could tell that Lucianna arranged the dinner party to quell his increasing anxiety and satisfy his desire for the company of others. He wasn't to go out into the world, but she would bring a piece of the world to him. The morning of the dinner party she spread before him a selection of masks from which she hoped he'd find one to his liking. There was no question that he would hide his face. Of course, as much as it bothered Erik, he had himself decided that he would prefer to wear a mask than allow strangers to see his face. Even so, it confirmed his own worst fears: he was too hideous to be accepted in society. He felt somewhat mollified by Lucianna's efforts to entertain him, and he began to think that he was selfish to complain when she was trying to protect him from the cruelty of others.

He enjoyed the dinner with Mlle. Valmont and M. Lambert. They spoke of Paris and the opera scene. They were also very pleased with his opera and enjoyed discussing the fine points of the compositions themselves. Mlle. Val-mont was beautiful and tactful. He felt her gaze fall on him when he wasn't looking, but she refrained from asking about the mask.

After they departed, Lucianna retired immediately. He stayed behind for a moment to finish his drink. When he entered her bedroom, she was in her bedclothes and brushing her long auburn hair at the vanity. Her hair flowed like liquid flame down her back shimmering in the soft light. The servants had prepared the fire, and its light shown on her as if she were copper plated, just a lesser hue from the same palette as her hair. The folds of the lace skirt of her dressing gown fell away from her leg. The skin of her thigh glistened in the orange and butter light. His eyes followed a trail ascending from her naked foot along the tight muscle of her calf and over the swell of her thigh to the edging of lace on her gown.

She saw the way he was watching her and put her brush down on the table. It had been a long time since he had shared her bed. Neither could say when the estrangement had begun, but it had taken a firm hold of them both.

Watching her in the light of the fire, he wanted her. He imagined himself taking her up in his arms and laying her down on the rug before the fire and licking the reflections of the flames along her body. He saw the fire kindled in her eyes. But he couldn't force himself to step forward into the room. He burned for her, wanted her auburn hair to lash him like the fire itself. He remembered the pain of it, the real pain, and squeezed his eyes to dispel the image of the two of them engulfed in flames. A knot twisted inside his gut, and he sensed fear rising in his body as he suffered from the desire of her. She was the fire itself, and as it seemed to call out to him, he knew it was deadly. He mumbled a brief goodnight, backed out of the bedroom, and went quickly down the hall to his own room.

That night he dreamed of making love, but it wasn't Lucianna's scorching body that he held. It was the soft, cool light of the other's golden body. Her blond hair ran across him like soothing balm. Her touch didn't burn but healed the pain in his body. He woke feeling oddly out of place. Eventually he recognized his surroundings and sank back onto the pillows feeling empty and hopeless. He must escape the fire! He must!

"How did you get your hands on the hit of the season, Sig. Rossi?" It had taken some time to get the appointment to speak with the manager of the Teatro Regio. In the end, Raoul had to invent another reason for the interview in lieu of the actual one. Thinking that Raoul wished to invest in the theater, the manager had been only too happy to receive the count in his offices.

"Oh, you mean *The Stranger*?" Sig. Rossi coughed reflexively into his hand and scowled at the turn of conversation.

"Yes. We're interested in offering the composer a commission."

"A commission?"

"Yes," said Raoul patiently. "We'd like to meet the composer and commission a work for the next season."

"The composer?"

Raoul was aware that the manager's idiotic responses were an unsuccessful attempt to stall for time. Obviously uncomfortable with the present line of questioning, the manager had uncrossed his legs, shifted several times in his chair, and crossed them again as he continued to cough and repeat the question just asked.

"Do you know how I can contact him?"

"Contact him?"

"Yes! Damn it, man! Can't you answer a straight question?" Raoul had lost any patience he had ever had with the silly little man. "Clearly you're under some instruction that his identity or whereabouts be kept confidential. But we're talking business here, signore."

Seeing the hesitancy, Raoul took advantage of the opening. "Of course, you'd gain as well. After all you discovered him. You'd be given a very generous commission for acting on our behalf with Sig. Fournier."

"Oh?" The little man sat bolt upright and gave Raoul his eager attention. Then just as quickly as he had sat up, he wilted in the chair, his thoughts turned inward. "Well, it would be difficult. He's … an odd one, he is. We received the score after some correspondence back and forth. I've no idea where he is now. He left Rome almost immediately after the opening night. He said *he*'d contact *us*."

"What address do you have from the correspondence?"

"Well, that's no help either, you see. The packet he sent was brought by a courier who returned within the week for our reply. He's very eccentric. Doesn't want anyone to see him or know who he is."

"He didn't seem so retiring when he took his bows on opening night."

"Oh! Well that wasn't him, you see." The smile of complicity dropped from Sig. Rossi's face as he realized he had said more than he was supposed to. Hurrying to rectify his mistake, he added, "Of course you're a gentleman, and this is only between you and me! It's part of the deal Fournier struck."

"You have my assurance that this news will only be given to those directly involved."

The manager furrowed his brow, trying to figure out if Raoul's statement complied with the spirit of his request for discretion. Resigned to trust the gentleman, he decided to share what little he did know of Sig. Fournier. "The fellow who took Fournier's bows was a fake. Fournier wants to remain hidden, and I can guess why!"

Raoul could barely control his breathing as his pulse accelerated in anticipation of what the manager was hinting at. "What exactly do you mean? Did you ever actually meet the composer?"

"Well, yes, in a way. I couldn't restrain myself. Opening night he was in a boxed seat well out of the view of the auditorium. As he was leaving, I came to congratulate him personally. He was covered from head to toe. A large hat and high stiff collar hid his face. But when I came upon him I must have taken him unawares, and he raised his face to look at me. Well, what I saw!" Here the little man shook his head sadly and paused for dramatic effect. "He was terribly scarred!"

Raoul asked him to repeat the story several times before he accepted that he had heard it correctly. It was too much of a coincidence. It had to be Erik.

"And you have no idea of where he might have gone?"

"No, I don't know anything about either of them."

"Either of them? You mean Fournier and the man who took his bows?"

"No, I mean the composer or his wife."

"His wife, did you say?"

"Oh, yes. He was accompanied by his wife. From what I understand, they're inseparable."

Meg had been shocked when Raoul told her what he had gleaned from Sig. Rossi. It had to have been Erik. But they had no idea where he might have gone. Raoul held back the existence of a "wife." First, he thought Meg wouldn't be able to bear it. Second, he believed the manager might be mistaken as to the true nature of the relationship between Erik and the woman who accompanied him. He felt he knew Erik well enough to doubt that he would have taken another woman as a wife. He truly loved Meg, Raoul was certain. There must be some other explanation. Perhaps the woman assisted him, as Madeleine had for so many years at the Opera Populaire.

Meg had asked Raoul about the scarring. Was it from the fire? This he couldn't say for the manager had gotten only a brief glimpse of Erik's face and couldn't recall if it was the entire face or only a portion of the face that he saw. All he could attest to, without doubt, was seeing the scar itself. So he might have been further disfigured by the fire and unable to face Meg. It was a viable explanation for his persistent absence.

Raoul promised he'd continue looking for Erik, but both he and Don Marcelo were concerned for Meg's state of mind. To calm their anxiety, she informed them that she intended to proceed with her original plan to star in the next performance of Gounod's *Faust* in which she was to assume the role of Margarita. Rehearsals were to begin the next day. Not only would it keep her busy, it would also bring her out into the public view and to Erik's attention if he were to return to Rome. Surely he would come see her, even if it had to be from afar. At any rate, she resolved that each performance she gave would be for Erik and for Erik alone.

"Where are you going?" Lucianna's voice was sharp and surprised. She was nervous and out of sorts. She had tried to convince Erik that they should return to the island. The opera was in its fourth week and promised to have a successful run. Don Carlo had left shortly after the premiere, so everyone believed Henri Fournier had left Rome.

Erik didn't want to leave Rome, not yet. "I won't be home for the rest of the day." Without another word, he closed the door behind him.

It had taken days of planning. Luigi could not be included in the scheme—his loyalty to Lucianna was unquestionable. So Erik had asked for a servant of his own that he could send on errands. At first Luigi insisted that he himself would be happy to go for whatever Erik needed. But Erik sent him on so many errands—in search of concoctions from the apothecary, drafting supplies, gazettes, staff paper for his compositions, new ink and quills, and special polish for the piano—that within the week Luigi had hired a young boy from the streets who would report directly to the master. Once Erik enlisted the boy, Mario, by promises of generous remuneration, he set in place the elements of his plan.

Ten days later, he sent the boy to hire the services of a driver to take him to the Teatro dell'Opera. Rehearsals were underway for the next performance of *Faust*. The star of the performance was to be none other than Signora Costanzi, the same blond-haired beauty that he had glimpsed several weeks ago at the opening of his own opera at the Teatro Regio. He had tried to forget that image, but it had converged with his dream of the golden angel.

Money greased many a rusty hinge, including the doors to the backstage at the Teatro dell'Opera. Hidden, off stage, Erik had a clear view of the rehearsal. He waited, listening with half his attention to the set designer confer with scene shifters while he watched the ballet stretch and limber up in the center of the stage. The orchestra tuned and rehearsed several troublesome sections of the score. Erik was distracted more than once by an odd catch in the musical director's voice as he scolded one of the violinists for missing his cue, coming in just a half beat too late. Although he anxiously anticipated the diva's arrival, he became fascinated by the general preparations leading to their culmination in the performance. He was watching a particularly graceful dancer in the ballet execute several difficult pirouettes when *her* voice—the diva's voice—broke into his reverie and drew his attention to the far side of the stage. It was Signora Costanzi, the same beautiful chanteuse he had seen leave the Teatro Regio—surrounded by admirers—after the performance of his opera, *The Stranger*.

A tall, handsome man was speaking to her in a familiar manner. When he said her name, it was with a French lilt. He called her "Meg." She placed her hand on his arm and smiled farewell before he left. Erik fought the sinking sensation of hopelessness and dispelled the image of the man from his mind. He was here to see her, to hear her voice, listen to her sing. He had no other aspirations.

She was smaller and more delicate than he had thought. The top of her head would barely reach his chest. Her hair was pinned up, away from her long neck and sculpted shoulders, awaiting the wig that would turn her golden curls into brown braids. She was in full make up which accentuated her large brown eyes, making them even more vivid and alive than they would normally appear. As the director cleared the dancers from center stage and consulted in hushed tones with the conductor, Erik watched the diva find her mark. All were silent; everyone's attention was focused on the diva. Like Margarita, she was dressed as a simple country maiden. Erik swallowed the hard lump that had gathered in his throat. Aware that his heart was pounding, he wondered that it was not heard in the silence preceding the first notes of the piece.

When she began to sing, he forced himself to stifle the gasp that shook him. The crystal of her voice cut deliciously to the depths of him. He felt deep misery and profound joy indistinguishably mixed. Why did she so unman him? His eyes were blurred by unshed tears. He had dreamed her, yet she existed! Though his dreams had allowed him to glimpse her imperfectly—the turn of her thigh, the flowing tresses of her blond hair, a glint of fawn-like eye—he was sure that this woman was the angel that haunted his dreams. Her voice reached some buried corner of his being, and suddenly he realized how desperately unhappy and lonely he had been. He had felt nothing like this in his current life. Whatever happiness he had enjoyed with Lucianna was a pale, forced imitation of the pure joy that now overwhelmed him.

Erik withdrew when Meg Costanzi left the stage. He stood back among the curtains, surrounded by their purple darkness, willing himself to breathe. His head began to throb with that familiar insistency that he no longer resisted. He waited patiently for the pain; it seemed the only thing that convinced him that he lived. Until he saw her. Until he heard her sing. He felt as if he had lain asleep in a long dream, and only this woman could wake him. He must be mad! He squeezed his fists to his temples and fought the growing panic. He was powerless to control his delirium! Could he remain hidden, woven like a black thread among the regal strands of the curtain? He would hang in the fabric and listen to her and never leave. If only he could be near her, silent and unseen, he could content himself with that!

The clatter of feet, the sound of chains and pulleys, and the scrape of scenery and props along the floor grew faint. He felt she must have retired by now. He sent his mind through the amphitheater, the backstage rooms, the stage itself, but could find no hint of her. His heart sank with her absence. He straightened himself and sighed. Then he stepped out of the heavy folds of the curtains to return to his apartments. Lucianna would be waiting.

Erik called for his servant, Mario. The boy was short for his age. Bad nutrition had stunted his growth, but the constant dangers of life on the streets had sharpened his mind and honed his reflexes. Erik smiled to himself when the boy darted an apprehensive look down the hallway—on the lookout, he supposed, for Lucianna—before he approached Erik in the study.

"Maestro?" Once he had come upon his master playing the piano and writing down the notes on his special paper, the boy insisted on calling him "maestro." "You called for me?"

"Yes, Mario. Come here." He smiled and beckoned for the boy to come to his side.

"You know the Florist's shop down Treveli way?" The boy merely nodded. "Take this and go there. Tell the Florist to send a dozen roses of the deepest crimson to Signora Costanzi at the Teatro dell'Opera and to include this card. Each day I will give you a new card, and I wish you to do the same thing and give the Florist the same instructions. Is that understood?"

The boy could barely be older than ten or eleven, but he smiled coyly and asked, "You will make love to the beautiful lady at the opera? Si, signore?"

The child meant no harm, but Erik stiffened momentarily in disapproval. He scowled at Mario. "Keep your tongue inside your mouth if you can't avoid such impertinences. I do not, as you say, make love to her. I admire her talent." Mario's face dutifully assumed a mask of blankness at his master's admonition. Erik softened his own expression and reached out to the boy in a gesture of kindness. Suddenly he felt a deep sadness that he didn't understand. At the last moment, he brought his hand down without touching the child and, waving it lightly in the air, pretended that he meant to dismiss him. He had come to depend on Mario's clever resourcefulness. He was a servant, no different from the others who worked, in the main, silently and invisibly around him. And yet he felt a tenderness toward the child. When Luigi brought Mario to him the first day, he had been revolted by the child's dirty face, tangle of greasy black curls, and ragged clothes. Amid the filth, however, shone clear and sharp a pair of deep blue eyes. Erik wore his mask only when he left the apartment. So he studied the child's reaction to his naked face carefully. The boy looked at him with interest but without revulsion. His sweet and innocent acceptance of the disfigurement tore at Erik's heart. He ordered him cleaned, dressed, and fed. Through Luigi, Erik verified that the child did indeed live by his wits, alone, without any known blood relatives. From that day on, Erik resolved that he would always protect the child, and he would find some way to give him a better future than he would have had on the streets.

Mario could tell that his master was not truly angry with him. He kept his face carefully blank until he reached the study door, then looked back at Erik over his shoulder, and quipped, "Si, signore. She's very beautiful. If you don't make love to her, then perhaps I will?" With this, he grinned impishly from ear to ear and ran from the apartment.

Lucianna nearly collided with the boy on her way into the study. He paused only a moment to bow awkwardly at his master's wife before speeding away. "That child, Erik, has no manners. If he's a servant, he should act like one." In spite of the severity of her words, Erik knew that she often looked wistfully at the child. He sensed that she, too, was drawn to him by some instinct sorely ungratified. "He sleeps in the kitchen by the stove like a dog."

Erik had arranged for a simple bed in an alcove off the kitchen proper, but Mario took the blankets and slept where he wanted. On more than one occasion, Erik had ventured to check on him and picked him up off the floor himself and carried him to the bed. But Mario explained that he liked to be near the stove for the warmth and that the smell of baked bread gave him good dreams. For one who ate the scraps left by the passersby in the avenues and boulevards of a great city, the aroma of fresh bread was a more powerful talisman than any soft cot tucked away in a corner. Erik, of course, could not remember having passed a hungry day in his life, but he instinctively understood the child's reasoning. A whiff of buttered bread suddenly seemed like the richest gift in the world to Erik. He shook off a feeling of hopeless hunger and longing with difficulty.

"Let him be, Luci. He's lived most of his life on his own terms."

"Yes, he's a wild thing, isn't he?"

Erik didn't remark on her tone; it seemed as if she were talking of something else only tangentially related to the boy. She came and sat beside the piano where Erik was working, his hands stained with ink, indigo fingerprints smeared in overlapping patterns across the ivory keys. She listened while he played melodies that were unconnected, single petals plucked from the same flower. She knew he'd slowly reconstruct the flower petal by petal, choosing this one for its color, another for its texture, still another for the fragrance it exuded, and only when the pattern was established would he take it whole and offer it for its beauty. She loved his fingers while he played. Each note she felt on her body as if he touched her, played her, as if she were his composition. She shook the thought from her mind. Silly to wish to be an opera in order to see passion and love in his eyes.

She had tried anger and tears to no avail, so she was careful to watch her tone when she asked him if he was going out again in the afternoon. He didn't stop playing, but she heard the tempo shift abruptly.

"Yes," he finally answered, his tone level and calm.

Lucianna quelled a sudden flare of anger and waited until she could speak again without strong emotion. She was losing him. Music had been only the beginning. Now he was fighting to establish a life without her. "May I ask where you're going? I might wish to accompany you."

This time his fingers stopped coldly on the keys, and Erik looked at her intently before responding. His green eyes were guarded. His brow cast a dark shadow over their brilliance making them appear black. She wasn't sure if she saw anger or caution in those eyes. His tone was strained, yet calm. "No. It doesn't concern you."

Her anger burst, red hot and searing. "What do you mean, it doesn't concern me? I'm your wife! How dare you. How dare you! You'd be dead, if it weren't for me!" If she hadn't said the latter, he might have felt shame. Calling him to his duty was within her rights. Erik detested his infidelities to her. They had shared a life, even if he couldn't remember it. He had robbed her of two children, had refused her the joy of motherhood. She was chained to him as surely as he was chained to her. But when she demanded he bend his knee for obligation in payment for his life, the enormity of his enslavement overwhelmed him. His only recourse was flight!

He closed the piano, willed himself to be silent, and rose to go. Lucianna stood, too, and viciously slapped him across his face. Her breast heaving she waited for his reaction, expecting him to lash out at her, hoping he would raise his hand to her so that she could fight him, tear at him, and replace the impotence with pain. To feel his blow across her face would at least have been to feel him. If she couldn't have his love, she'd have his rage. She couldn't bear his indifference, his benign neglect. He curled his fingers into fists and kept his face turned away from her as if her assault had permanently set his position.

The blow had stung deeply, more deeply than the surface of his skin. With the sharp tingle of her open palm's imprint still on his cheek, he felt her frustration, her anger, the betrayal that ate away at her.

He raised his hand, the fist now relaxed, with spread fingers. She flinched involuntarily, but he placed his hand tenderly on her face and brought her mouth up to his. His lips, dry and pressed closed, barely brushed her swollen, blood-red lips. He whispered, his mouth still close to hers, his eyes earnestly seeking hers, "Forgive me, Luci."

For a moment, she thought she understood his words, but in the next she stifled a moan. He dropped his hand from her face and walked out of the room. Moments later he called Luigi to send for the driver. She sat and listened to his footsteps as he readied himself in the other room, as he left the apartment, as he went down the stairs to the waiting barouche.

She knew where he'd go. Luigi had followed one day, on her orders, and informed her that Signore Fiortino was last seen entering the Teatro dell'Opera by a side door. Luigi had waited for well over an hour before Sig. Fiortino left by the same door and returned to the apartments.

He had found Meg.

She had received the flowers everyday for more than a week. Each time she came into her dressing room, her heart would race with mad joy to find the dozen roses and each day a new note signed, "a Stranger." This afternoon was no exception. On a small table next to the full-length mirror mounted on the back wall of her dressing room, a fresh bouquet of roses awaited her.

The first day the bouquets began to appear, she had thought the roses might be from Christine and Raoul or from Don Marcelo. But when she read the card, she knew they must have come from Erik.

> *To Signora Costanzi, with humble regards from a most fervent admirer.*
> *Your obedient servant, a Stranger.*

The handwriting was the same as the awkward scrawls in his notebook. And then, as further proof of the identity of her admirer, there were the flowers themselves.

Erik had always had a penchant for roses. To him they embodied passion and perfection. Years ago at the Opera Populaire, he would send Christine, then his protégée, one perfect rose, the thorns removed by hand, a black ribbon tied around its stem. For this reason, Meg had preferred other flowers. So it puzzled her that he would send her roses.

Casting aside her own reservations, she gathered the recently delivered bouquet to her face and rubbed her cheeks along the soft petals. She drank their fragrance, intoxicated by its richness. What matter that they had been Christine's flowers? They were *his* flowers, the expression of his yearning for beauty, for love. He was out there somewhere, wounded and afraid to come home.

Raoul had not been able to find out anything more about Fournier. The composer supposedly had left Rome ages ago now. No one could convince Meg that he had actually gone. Fournier was none other than Erik. Even Raoul agreed that this was indeed the case. Erik had reached out to her. He wanted to come home, but something was preventing him. Even the opera he had written was a cry to Meg, his message to her, telling her not to mourn, that he was alive, that he was afraid to return. Its tragic denouement troubled her. She might understand it as a sign of his fear. She refused to see it as a prophecy of the end of their love or the impossibility of their reunion. Now the roses. The signature on the cards—a Stranger—was from the title of the opera he had written. Why would he call himself a stranger to her? What could have happened after the fire?

She had kept his cards locked in the drawer of her dressing table. Now she unlocked the drawer and read each one in turn. Each succeeding note burned her hand with an ever increasing heat. Then she opened the delicate envelope that accompanied the new bouquet of roses. She took out the card and read.

> *To my Diva, Would you were so. I become emboldened to tell you my most wretched desire. I listen to you sing your passion and maddened I find I pretend it is to me you sing. Forgive your slave, a Stranger.*

He hears her sing! He must be somewhere in the theater during her rehearsals. That was the only explanation. *How can he be so close and not come to me? To think, he's here, somewhere in the opera house, listening to me. He speaks of his most wretched desire. My Erik, my love, is here!* Trembling, she took a rose from the bouquet. She would hold it next to her heart while she sang, and he would know that she *did* sing for him, for him alone.

I scanned the auditorium, searching for him. I wouldn't see him if he were hidden in the dark recesses of the boxed seats. The best I could hope for was to see some indirect sign of his presence, a shadow cast against the wall, the opening edge of a door barely visible from the stage, the fluttering of curtains. I held the rose so tightly that the juice from its stem was wet against my palm. Maestro Bianchi was pleased with the duet. He had kissed me on both cheeks and told me to go rest. Before I left the stage I looked one more time around the expansive amphitheater where, in less than a week, five hundred souls would take their seats for the space of more than three hours to thrill to the story of the man who sold his soul for knowledge. I felt sorely tempted myself to make a similar bargain with the devil if he would promise to tell me where I could find my love.

I heaved a sigh, not having found anything remotely significant, and directed my steps toward the backstage dressing rooms. In the time my heart beat once, I saw a flash of whiteness in the dark shadows surrounding the curtains which were drawn to the sides, off stage. The glimpse of alabaster recalled to me the satin finish of a mask. Aware that I was vulnerable to chimera of dubious origins, I walked hurriedly toward the darkness where for a brief instant I had seen the ghostly white. Someone had just passed by for the curtains swayed and fluttered to and fro from his passing. My heart in my throat, undecided as to whether I should call out to him or not, I ran in his wake. Freed from the velvet forest of the curtains, I looked around me to find that he had disappeared. Then I heard it, the sound of a door closing softly. He had left by the side exit we used to avoid the crowds. Someone was calling for me from the area of the stage, but I hurried on to the door. Opening it, I stepped out into the alleyway and caught sight of a tall man, austerely dressed, as he climbed into a barouche. As he turned to sit, I saw the mask! It was Erik. The moment he stepped inside, the driver urged the horses on, and the barouche set off down the alleyway toward the street. I was about to run toward him—there was still perhaps time to stop him, to call to Erik—when out of the corner of my eye I saw, hidden in one of the doorways, a woman that I thought I recognized. She hadn't seen me, her eyes were on the barouche, and I reached her before she managed to leave. It was Lucianna!

"Why are you here?" I asked her. Her face was a ghastly color as if she were sunk in turmoil. Clearly, she was spying on Erik. As the barouche started down the street, her servant approached and asked if he should follow Sig. Fiortino. I could hardly believe my ears. The man had referred to Erik with Lucianna's dead husband's name. A dawning suspicion was too incredible for me to accept. I grabbed her sleeve, making it impossible for her to retire without causing a scandal. "What's going on? What has happened to Erik?" I didn't ask, but demanded, that she explain.

She could not pretend that it wasn't Erik that I had just seen. Nor could she hide the fact that she, too, knew it was he and was, for some reason, following my husband and calling him by her dead husband's name. I thought I might have to drag it out of her. Her face was ashen, and she seemed to consider breaking away from me and fleeing.

"For pity's sake, Lucianna, say something. I thought he had died!" I tried to keep the despair from my voice. The carriage was gone. Lucianna's servant had taken off in its wake. She knew what had happened. She must tell me.

"Erik barely escaped the fire," she began. "He was gravely injured. His mind was erased. He has no memory of you."

I stood transfixed waiting for her to go on.

"You don't exist for him," she said, her voice stronger, more confident. "I've brought him back to health and have taken care of him. He thinks that he's my husband. I've given him a new life."

"But you can't. He has a life. A life with me and with his children. Where has he gone? I must talk with him." I turned, prepared to run out into the street.

Frantically, she grabbed hold of my arm so that I couldn't get away. There was a mad intensity to her eyes. "He has no memory! Even if you were to tell him that you're his wife, he wouldn't understand it. He won't be able to feel it! You can't just show up and tell him that the only thing he knows is a lie, for he has nothing else to fall back on."

I couldn't believe she was asking me to stand aside and allow her to have him. Then she squeezed my arms with both her hands and coldly told me that the shock might drive him insane or kill him. "Think, Meg. Surely if his mind were strong enough to remember you, he would have already done so. The first moment he saw you it should have come back to him. But his mind isn't strong enough. When I found him, he was nearly dead. The doctor told me that he wouldn't regain consciousness and that he would die. When he did wake up, there was nothing but pain and emptiness in his mind. He wouldn't let me leave the room for fear that the blackness would eat him alive. You can't risk it, Meg. You can't be so selfish."

"I have to do something. I can't act as if he's dead."

"Why not? Why not if it will allow him a new life? He's not the same man you knew, Meg. He walks around our apartments without a mask. He allows the servants to see him. He only wears it when he is faced with strangers." Then she added coldly, "Strangers like you, Meg."

If she hadn't been holding me firmly in her grasp, I thought that I might have crumpled to the ground. But I wouldn't let her see my weakness. As if I were on stage, I forced my limbs into the straight, erect pose of a ballerina.

"He has a son and a daughter who think he's dead! I must bring him back to them!"

"He'll be an empty shell of what he was. You'll kill him! You'll rip the world that I've created for him out from under him."

"Lies! You've given him lies."

"Lies? Yes, but doesn't he deserve something better than the truth life has given him? Meg, in my world he is not a monster. I gave him a past in which he was handsome, whole, unblemished. He grew up with loving parents, was educated in the finest schools, is the lord of vast estates. His disfigurement was caused by an unfortunate accident. It is not who he is. What will *you* tell him of his past, Meg? When he remembers nothing, will you tell him that he was raised in a cage at a fair? What memories can you bring him? What pain do you want him to recover? Can you bear to force him to relive the loneliness, the rage, the violence? Tell him, if you dare, that he was deformed since birth, cursed by God, unloved, that he lived like a madman underground for years, that he murdered, that he …"

"Stop it! Stop it!" I cried. I placed my hands over my ears and shut my eyes so I would not have to see her cruel mouth speaking to me. He didn't remember me! It was all gone—our life together and with it all the horrid pain he had endured. He hadn't stayed away because he had been burned horribly and feared to show himself to me. He wasn't my Erik anymore. Even so I still loved him. I lowered my hands from my ears and pretended to a calm I didn't feel. Determined to know the extent of his injuries, I asked, "Was he badly burned in the fire?"

She understood me immediately. "Yes. There are scars. It isn't because of the injuries that he doesn't show himself to you, Meg. He doesn't know you. He can't trust you. He trusts only me."

But he hadn't stayed away. He was the stranger who sent me roses and wrote of wretched desire, who stood in the shadows and listened to me sing of imagined loves and losses. He had been drawn to me as I had always been drawn to him.

"Where are you staying?" I asked, too tired to continue fighting her, unwilling to let her know that she had not convinced me to surrender.

"Meg, I beg you to give him this chance to start afresh."

She had called me selfish. Was I? She had given him a chance to start afresh, a new identity that severed his connection to the Phantom, to those mad years living like a ghost under the weight of Paris. How could I tell him that he had killed? Would he even believe me?

"I won't come," I said, "but I want to know where you're staying. I want to know what he's doing, how he is. I can't just let him disappear again."

She hesitated, weighing her options. If she refused to grant me even this modest request, she must know that I would track her down and subsequently find Erik. I knew his name now. It would just be a matter of time before I found them both. On the other hand, if she agreed to allow me a modest connection to Erik's life, perhaps she could buy herself some time. I, too, needed time.

I must think this through. Lucianna was right. If he had indeed forgotten his past life with me, I couldn't go to him and tell him that he was my husband. I couldn't, I realized, tell him what traumas he had suffered. It didn't matter that he had led a happy life with me and our children since coming to Rome. It would be a tale whose telling would risk portraying him as a monster. And with no memory of his desire for redemption and love, even if I told him that he regretted his past actions, he would be overwhelmed by the account of a life of misfortune and violence. I had to find some other way to bring him home, for he must come home.

Masking my true resolve with every skill my training on the stage had afforded, I repeated, "I promise I won't tell him who he really is. But you must tell me where the two of you are living. You must share something of him with me."

Reluctantly, she agreed.

Meg Costanzi, the prima donna of the Teatro dell'Opera, stopped in the middle of the aria, apologizing for an error she had made. Behind Erik came a noise as if someone were quietly approaching him. The fine hairs on the back of his neck rose, and he turned around quickly to see a large, dark-haired young man with handsome features marred only by a jagged scar that ran from his brow across one cheek. The man was standing within an arm's length, but he froze when he saw Erik's puzzled expression. There was an odd look on the young man's face, and Erik assumed he came to see what a strange masked man was doing backstage. His clothes suggested he was a gentleman, not a staff member at the opera. Perhaps he was a patron.

Erik bowed slightly and explained that Paolo knew he was there. Thinking this sufficient explanation, he turned his back on the young man—even though it was with some misgiving—to watch Meg's rehearsal. His ears twitched with atavistic tension, listening for the young man's retreat, but instead he heard the stranger draw up beside him, after a momentary hesitation, to observe the diva's performance.

"Sir, have we met?" asked Erik, annoyed, realizing the intruder had no intention of departing.

This brought a wide grin to the young man's face. Erik had no idea of why his question would amuse the young dandy so, but it gave him time to study the man's face. He was handsome in spite of the jagged scar. This struck Erik as ironic. Of course the young man's scar was nothing as compared to the deformity Erik hid under his mask. Finally the man managed to control his surprise sufficiently to reply.

"Evidently not. Excuse me, signore, for my impertinence. I took you for … someone else. Signore Cimino, Giovanni Cimino, at your service, signore." Giovanni offered his hand to Erik who cautiously accepted it.

When Erik did not proffer his own name, but kept his gaze riveted on the stage in an obvious sign of dismissal, Giovanni whispered conspiratorially in his ear, "She's lovely, isn't she? Ripe, you know."

Erik repressed a wave of disgust as he sensed Giovanni's implied intimacy with Meg Costanzi. Roughly he moved away from the enforced proximity between them. "Signore, I'd advise you to speak with respect."

"Oh, of course. I didn't mean any disrespect. I just noticed your … interest … in Signora Costanzi." He waited for Erik to respond, but Erik resolved to ignore him.

"I can't believe it!" Giovanni muttered to himself, but Erik glanced at him, confused, out of the corner of his eye. "May I ask your name, Signore?"

"Fiortino, Erik Fiortino, if you insist."

"Please accept my apologies, Signore Fiortino. I really don't mean to cast any aspersions on Signora Costanzi. I just meant that she is a … widow."

That caught his attention, Giovanni saw.

"She's absolutely charming, isn't she? I understand why you come to her defense. I, too, sneak in from time to time to listen to her. Are you an opera buff? Have you seen the latest at the Teatro Argentina? Maybe we could go together some evening?" Giovanni reached inside his vest and pulled out an embossed card and held it out to Erik. Erik took the card coldly and stuffed it away without examining it into one of his side pockets. Giovanni examined the mask Erik wore. He lowered his head slightly as if embarrassed. Then he spoke again, but his voice was devoid of the self confidence and irony of just moments ago. "I've considered wearing a mask myself."

Erik reluctantly examined him. Giovanni unnecessarily ran his index finger along the seam of the scar tissue that traversed his face. "Accident. I'm still not used to it. People ... stare ... they ... have trouble ... getting beyond it. I suppose that's why she fascinates me. Such beauty is almost sinful, don't you think?"

Erik studied him for a moment. When he spoke again, his voice had softened. "It's an unfortunate scar, but it hasn't destroyed your looks. In spite of it, you have a comely face."

"You're kind, too kind. But most people aren't as kind as you are, signore. Can you imagine a beauty like that letting a man like me—one with such an obvious flaw—make love to her? I think not. That's why I hang back, like you signore, feeding off her image."

Erik had difficulty reading the young man's tone. There was a touch of sarcasm in his conversation, and his smile struck Erik as insincere. He wished the young man would go away. He wanted nothing more than to watch and listen to Meg. With Giovanni by his side, he felt embarrassed to give himself over to his fantasy. He wanted to imagine himself, on the stage, singing with her. He wanted to take her by the hand and sweep her off her feet and escape with her to some secret chamber away from prying eyes. Today she held his rose in her hand. She brought it to her cheeks and then held it over her heart. She was singing for him!

Giovanni stayed the full hour until Erik, finally resigned to his presence, turned regretfully from the stage to leave. The young man followed on his heels to the alleyway where Erik's driver awaited his departure.

"Could you possibly give me a ride, Don Erik?"

Wondering if he would ever rid himself of the other's attention, Erik agreed to take him where he needed to go.

"Do you have some time? I know a place. It's out of the way, very comfortable and very, very friendly where the likes of us are always welcome."

"The likes of us?" Erik asked, suspiciously.

Giovanni smiled and pointed at his scar. "No one minds it there as long as you've got money."

He thought of returning to the apartments where he would undoubtedly find Lucianna waiting for him— angry or worried or hurt. Beautiful as she was, he had absolutely no desire to be with her. Why couldn't he love her?

When he woke in such pain with no memory of who he was, it was her presence alone that kept him from going mad. He recalled with shame how he cried for her to stay with him, not to leave him alone, for whenever she left the room he felt the blackness of the void threaten to swallow him whole. Yet he couldn't love her. Even the desire for her body was no longer compelling. She could, he realized with a sinking feeling of self-loathing, be any woman and evoke the same carnal passion, the same animal stirrings in him. He had been a cruel and evil man. He didn't want to be that man, but he couldn't avoid being cruel to Lucianna. He could more easily make love to a total stranger than to Lucianna, for her desires went far beyond those of the flesh. What she needed from him was exactly what he couldn't give her.

Erik had no acquaintances of his own in Rome. Giovanni could show him around the city. Something about the young man made Erik hesitant. He was dissolute, maybe even dangerous. The way he spoke of Meg indicated that, as refined as he might wish to appear, he was not a true gentleman. But then again, Erik had excelled at debauchery in his previous life; he was evidently no stranger to the kind of world Giovanni lived in. Why not take his pleasure as he may? What else was there? Erik thought of Meg singing on the stage. She had no idea who he was. If she did know him, would she be offended by his attentions? What did he have to offer her? Why would she even look at him? Giovanni was right about the face. What would a beauty like Meg think if she saw him without his mask? If Giovanni felt despised because of a single scar, what hope did Erik Fiortino have of Meg's favor? All he could hope for was that Meg would kiss the petals of his roses.

"Give the driver the directions."

"Excellent! You'll like it, you'll see." Giovanni, delighted, chuckled as he gave the driver the instructions.

Erik fought the impulse to shiver.

Erik awoke tangled in the naked limbs of strangers. The room danced before his eyes in a fuzzy white cloud. Besides the reek of his sweat, Erik smelled the lingering smoke of the opium pipes, strong liquor, the musky scent of naked bodies, and a dizzying hint of blood. His stomach threatened to spasm again, but he swallowed several times to keep from retching. He was naked, and across his body and next to him in the bed were the naked bodies of several others. Giovanni's arm lay limp across Erik's stomach, the young man's torso pressed warm and intimate against Erik's thigh. The prostitute slept heavily between Erik's legs and across his groin; her head had slid off to the side and rested among the covers. From the other side of Giovanni came a moan. The other prostitute lay half buried under Giovanni. Desperately, Erik pushed at the foreign limbs and pulled his body out from the heap to fall to the floor. He had lost his mask somewhere in the room. The clothes lay jumbled in piles, having landed wherever they had been tossed as the four of them undressed the night before.

His head swam as he searched through the wreckage and began to dress. He heard the rustle of bedclothes as the others stirred. He must get out! He couldn't bear facing them.

His legs wobbled unsteadily as he climbed down the stairs. The tavern was quiet. It was nearly two in the afternoon and the regulars had not yet arrived. The bartender saluted him with a lascivious grin and asked if he needed a stout drink to get him on his way. Erik waved the offer aside and asked for a carriage to take him home. The heavy set man eyed him suspiciously and told him that the young fellow had said that he would pay. Erik stiffened and asked, with an edge of irony in his voice, the price for the entertainment. Told the cost, Erik threw several coins, more than enough to pay, on the dirty counter and left the establishment.

Lucianna as usual was waiting in the study. When she heard him enter, she came to greet him. She gasped when she saw the state of his clothing. His eyes were bloodshot, and he walked hunched over as if his body were a burden he was forced to carry.

"Can I help? Are you all right?" She stepped forward, her hands outstretched toward him.

"Don't touch me!" he growled at her through clenched teeth. He brought his hands up to stop her and edged away along the wall. "Luigi," he shouted down the hallway. He couldn't recognize the harsh sounds as his own voice.

Immediately Luigi came to the front entrance.

"Prepare a bath."

Erik stumbled to his room and slammed the door behind him.

Later when he had eased himself into the hot, soapy water he allowed himself to breathe deeply and consciously tried to relax his bunched muscles. He felt the water ease the rawness he felt. His body ached, but the evidence of his night of debauchery was more than sore muscles. He felt torn and lacerated from the violence of the orgy. It had all come back to him in the coach on the way to the apartment. He had gotten horribly drunk. Giovanni gave him a pipe of opium and encouraged him to take it in deeply. Erik had heard of opium dreams, but he had never taken the drug. The idea of losing oneself in its clutches had disquieted him. But last night, fired on by Giovanni, Erik had done a great many things he had never done before, as far as his memory served him.

Lucianna entered the room softly and quietly came to his side. He covered his face with his hands and groaned pitiably. "Please, Luci. Don't. Don't touch me. Not now. Please, leave me alone. I don't want anyone to touch me."

"What happened, Erik?"

He didn't answer. She could tell he was upset, struggling to calm himself. She touched his shoulder tenderly, but he flinched at the touch and shrank further into the warm water. Eventually, he lay back and steadied his voice to speak to her. "I'll be all right. Leave me now. I'll be all right. We'll talk later."

Only slightly reassured, Lucianna left him.

Erik rinsed his skin of the residue of the sweat from other bodies. He sank under the water and soaked the feel of Giovanni's hands off his flesh. He rubbed the prostitutes' mouths from his body, and he scrubbed them away as best he could, leaving his skin raw and sore but clean.

CHAPTER 7

❀

Among the Dead

Whither is thy beloved gone, O thou fairest among women? whither is thy beloved turned aside? that we may seek him with thee.

Song of Solomon, King James Bible

Erik's notebook gave me the idea. I wonder if there are others hidden away somewhere? He hid things, even a few of his musical compositions were stored between rare volumes of philosophy or art in Marcelo's library. I saw him searching for the right place and watched him as he tucked them high on a shelf where their edges wouldn't be visible. I'd forgotten about them. What made them objects of worth that he would protect from others' curiosity? The next chance I get I'll get them down. Christine regularly writes in a diary. She says it keeps the cobwebs from taking over her mind. It clears and orders the daily muddle.

*He didn't send the roses today! Does Lucianna know that he sends me roses? Has she confronted him and demanded that he not come to watch the rehearsals? Is that why the roses have stopped coming and I no longer sense his presence? His flirtation with infidelity has been squelched. That would make me the jilted lover, wouldn't it? Would that it had gone that far! I miss him so terribly I could cry tears of blood. He was there in the theater—I know—because he wanted **me**.*

Does he touch her the way he used to touch me? He had learned to play me well. He knew the secret chords humming under the surface of my skin, the flats and sharps of belly and breasts, and just the stroke to make me play. He knew to flick his tongue under the curve of my jaw and to exhale warmly and softly by my lips so I could taste him breathe. His breath was so sweet! Does he play another song for her? Does she make him stretch his fingers wide and abrade her keys? Does she moan and writhe under his careful rhythm?

Will this help? Will imagining him making love to my enemy bring me comfort? Why do I torture myself? I drop the quill on the blotting paper and pace furiously round the room. These wild fancies do not console me, and they certainly do not put things in order! I cannot think. I feel ravished, abused, torn and left bleeding!

He lives. Damn him! Damn him! He lives! Can nothing kill him? I might have gotten used to his being dead! I could have worn my widow's weeds and dried up and blown away with the last scorching breeze of summer. Or I might have learned to love again, not nearly so well, but well enough. And then I would lie down someday and die, and he would be there waiting for me! At least I could have hung on to that hope. My days would be filled with unsullied memories. I would relive those frightening days when I followed him, a deranged killer, the Phantom, to his gloomy lair. Face to face with a madman, I stood my ground. Under the streets of Paris, alone, with a stranger, someone I truly didn't know. He might have broken my neck, crushed my throat, with one hand! His eyes were dark and fevered. He stared at me with such angry despair. If he hadn't fallen gravely ill, might he have murdered me?

I thought about this for several minutes before continuing to write. I'm sure he wouldn't have harmed me. He knew who I was. As surely as he had watched Christine grow up in the opera dormitories, he had also watched me. Not with the same intensity certainly, but he had brought me dancing shoes and other signs of his favor. He carved a ballerina from cedar that I cherished for years until one day it must have fallen from my pocket and gotten lost.

I loved you, Erik. I love you still. Forgive me. It was wrong and foolish to be angry with you. You have no memory of what we've lost, you and I. I should cross out those angry words, but I won't. Here I should be honest and write whatever comes into my head. I'm ashamed I blamed you for what has happened. You saved lives. You were brave. You were nearly killed in the fire. She says she saved you, and for that I should be forever grateful to her. But I can't be. I loathe her! I wish she were dead. There, I've said or written it! I wish I had the strength and the resolve to challenge her to a duel. Would that I were a man! I would fight her for you, Erik. I'm filled with such a rage. I would cut out her heart in the market place and drink her blood. But would you come willingly to me if I did so? If only you remembered us! I would fight her regardless of the cost. She says you have no memory of us, not of me or of our children. How could you forget François and

Laurette? I'm more a stranger now than when I followed you like a love-sick puppy that night and you told me to go away.

Oh God, please make him come back to me! He didn't come to hear me sing today. Nor did he send the roses! She's keeping him from me. Even if it never amounts to more, I want him to come hear me. I could make that sufficient reason to go on. Without even that, without him, knowing that he lives, I don't think I can bear it. If it weren't for our children, I think I'd do something desperate.

The roses are back! The same bouquet, but there's no card! I searched for him at the rehearsal, but I couldn't see any sign of his presence. Something tells me he didn't come again today. But the roses must be a good sign. He hasn't forgotten me completely. Not yet.

More roses. Erik still doesn't come. It's been several days now. Is he ill? I've told Raoul, Christine, and Marcelo about my encounter with Lucianna. Raoul went into a fit of anger saying he'd have her arrested as a lunatic if not a criminal. She's robbed his identity, he said, when I asked him the charges he'd bring. Fraud was another word he threw about like an unsheathed sword. It took all of us to restrain and calm him. It pleased me to see him thrash about the parlor ready to go to my defense and to rescue Erik. I cried from joy. I don't feel so alone with my friends around me. Of course I knew they would comfort me, but Raoul was upset not only for me, but for Erik. It's so strange to think that Raoul would fight for Erik, that he would come to his aid. He thinks I should simply go to Lucianna's apartments and claim Erik as my husband. It was very difficult for me to explain to him why my hands are tied.

Christine understands. She helped me explain it to Raoul. Erik's past has been wiped away, and he has been forced to reconstruct his world yet again. Raoul doesn't see that Erik is freed from the memory of how he was abused as a child; nor does he have to carry the burden of his loneliness in the bowels of the opera house. Years of pain and anger have been erased. Unfortunately, along with his sufferings and crimes went all that we shared. All our happiness, gone!

It was hard for me to share my plan with my friends. It sounds so outrageous even to me, but I have the right to do what I can to restore my children's father and my husband. We're still married before God and man. If he is at all attracted to me, I will use his attraction to my advantage. To put it bluntly, I will seduce my husband! I will live as his mistress, if I must, and call our children "bastards." I will take him away from Lucianna Fiortino and pray that eventually his desire turn into love and that our love be so strong that I can risk telling him the truth.

But can I ever tell him the truth?

Raoul says that he will tell Erik if I can't. I made him promise he wouldn't do anything without my consent. He doesn't see that the "past" Lucianna has invented for Erik may be superior to the truth. Of course Raoul argues that the truth is always superior to a lie. Perhaps. I don't know.

Roses. No card. No Erik.

Lucianna agreed to meet briefly in a café near the Teatro dell'Opera. She insisted that Erik is happy. I bit my lip and listened as she went on and on about the months they spent at one of her island residences: morning horseback rides and evening dips in the warm waters of a cove. She had enough sense to refrain from giving more detail. I tasted blood, but I didn't interrupt. I was too greedy to hear her speak of him, even if it were lies. She said he's working on another opera as if this proved his contentment. I almost blurted out that he wrote Don Juan Triumphant in the throes of the deepest sorrow and rage.

"What am I to tell his children?" I asked her.

She had the decency to blush. Eventually she said that it was time for her to go. But before she left, she cautioned me to keep my distance. It took everything in me to keep from slapping her. He was drawn to my talent, she said. As if I meant nothing more to him!

"Does he love you?" I asked.

Lucianna is not a good liar. She said yes, but I saw it in her eyes, in the fleeting moment when she was struck dumb by my question.

"I'll take him away from here," she warned me.

Does she have that much power over him? I can't imagine Erik would let her control his life. Although I think it a hollow threat, her warning brings me misgivings.

Several days have gone by—more than a week now—and the roses arrive anonymously each day. Raoul spoke with the new man who was hired just over a month ago to attend the backstage door, Paolo. He has been letting Erik in during the rehearsals. Evidently Erik has bribed him well. After some persuasion we've enlisted Paolo's help to watch for Erik, should he return. As I suspected, he says Erik hasn't come for well over a week.

If he doesn't return soon, I'll do something desperate.

No word from Lucianna. No sign of Erik.

Raoul has an idea. Since Erik has no memory of the past, he won't recognize Raoul either. We know where Erik is—as a matter of fact Raoul confessed that he's had someone watching Lucianna's apartment day and night for some time now—and he intends to find a way to be introduced to Erik. Very few visitors are admitted to the Fiortino's. The detective hired by Raoul mentions a young man who came several times but was never admitted. Then there was a visit from two artists—Mlle. Valmont and M. Lambert—from the Teatro Regio. Raoul will convince Mlle. Valmont to allow him to accompany her on a surprise visit to Lucianna and Erik.

Erik has not left the apartment. Is he ill or is she keeping him prisoner?

Erik and Lucianna had come to uneasy terms. It had been difficult for both of them. The morning Erik stumbled in with the smell of sex and strong drink on his disheveled and soiled clothes, she marked something drastically wrong with him. Although he promised they would talk later, he locked himself away for two days. During those two days, Lucianna heard him pace back and forth, making an awful noise—fighting some unseen demon—when he wasn't evidently asleep. Several times she considered having Luigi break down the door or send for a doctor. Sometimes she heard sounds of distress emanating from his room, sometimes it sounded as if he were breaking the furniture apart by dashing it against the wall.

He finally emerged from his room. She was relieved to see he had shaved, and his clothes were fresh and neatly arranged. He wore only a simple shirt, his vest, and breeches. He had not placed his boots where Luigi could get them, so they were badly in need of polishing. Otherwise, he seemed recovered from whatever bout of insanity had attacked him.

They retired to the parlor after a light breakfast, and Lucianna sat on the divan, silent and anxious. The early morning sun flooded the room with light, but she shivered at Erik's tense silence. He stood looking out the window, his body unnaturally still, for a long time before he addressed her.

"We have to talk." He was having difficulty returning her gaze.

Her heart sank. She could tell from his bearing that this conversation could not but bring her pain. She didn't respond. She waited for him to break her heart. It was after all his, and he could do with it what he would.

He cleared his throat nervously before he spoke again. "Luci, I owe you the rights of obligation as your husband. Even more, I know how you've cared for me since my accident. Actually my debt evidently goes back even farther to the accident that mutilated my face. You might have left me then." The color rose deep scarlet in his face, and he looked abashedly at his boots unable to continue for several moments. "I remember nothing, as you know, of my past deeds. You've tried to protect me, but the truth will out. Did I ever love you?"

His question shocked her. She hadn't expected it. He asked it with a calm tenderness that suggested his doubt and his hope that he had once loved her. She couldn't answer. She was overwhelmed by tears. He sat down next to her on the divan. His arm encircled her shoulders and drew her near.

"Forgive me, Luci. Please," he whispered. When her tears subsided, he went on as if it were a duty he must discharge. He was trying to be gentle. He was loath to hurt her, but it must be done. "If I did love you, I must have stopped at some point. I could not have been such a monster to you if I had loved you. I know what I did, what I was like. I overheard the servants talking one day. I can't repeat the vile things I learned, things that they had seen me do. Even if they exaggerated, the least truth in their accounts would suffice to damn me." He paused, perhaps to collect his thoughts. "I don't love you, Luci. I think sometimes that I hate you. Don't cry, please. It's only because it angers me that you demand my love and I can't respond in kind so I begin to resent you. I don't want us to live locked in a marriage in which I will surely end up hating you and you will come to despise me."

"I could never hate you," she cried.

His tone cooled slightly and his spine visibly stiffened, but he tried to recover his previous composure. He wanted somehow to avoid the inevitable tragedy he saw before them. "No, you mustn't love me. I'm not worthy of such self-sacrifice. We're married, but I beg you to release me from the obligations of a husband. I beg you. I'm willing to live with you and care for you, as a brother, as a friend."

She jerked away from him and stood panting in outrage. Her tears had vanished. She stared at him as if she could kill. "What? Like a brother? I don't want your brotherly care, your brotherly love, your flaccid embraces and dry kisses and sweet smiles and pats on the hand! I want you, Erik! Heart, body, and soul!"

All the color drained from his face. He gazed up at her from the divan, fearing he was doomed to failure. This must be his penance for past crimes!

"You're my husband. Mine! Where were you the other night? You were with her! You were with Meg, weren't you?" She was wild with rage, insane with jealousy. Her hair, pinned loosely off her neck, began to shake free of its restraints and to fly about her face and shoulders in swirling waves. In Erik's mind, they were flames that flickered and crackled round her head. She was raving about adultery. Erik felt his chest tighten. Instead of Meg, he envisioned naked limbs rubbing and pulling at him, the smell of opium thick and pungent in the air, the mad laughter of a painted mouth, muscles taut and quivering. He felt his breakfast heave in the pit of his stomach and wanted to crawl into some deep, dark, dank hole in the ground where the light of day would never warm him again. Her voice cut his eardrums like strident chords, like the sound of a knife across a violin string, like a hammer beating against the piano keys.

"You lust for her. I feel it in your touch. I see it in your eyes. You leave my bed to crawl into the wings of the opera house to watch that ..."

"Shut up!" he screamed at her. He hadn't realized his fist was raised until it swung forward toward her face. He just managed to stop its descent when he saw the look of triumph in her eyes! He forced his voice to quiet. "Don't speak of her again! Don't even say her name or I will ..." He wanted to say he would kill her. It sprang full blown into his mind. He might be capable of such violence. He was capable of much that surprised him. Giovanni had shown him. Lucianna was still instructing him on the limits of his soul.

He wouldn't say more than he had already. He had tried to give their relationship a new direction, but it was not meant to be. She rejected his friendship, his gratitude, loyalty. He had resolved to live celibate, to be a good husband in all ways but the most important one. He knew he couldn't hope to love her. He loved someone else. He loved his angel. He loved the little chanteuse, and he would go to his grave loving her. He had betrayed them both. He had awoken in the mire of bodies and known that he could waste the years away in the empty pleasures and depravity of the flesh. His body was capable of great pleasure, but he awoke appalled and sickened, for it was a soul-less body that he dragged from the heap of naked limbs. A knife had sundered him in two. He felt that the wound might never heal.

He would not come to her bed again. It had been weeks since he had. But must he give up Meg? Was he capable of slavish fidelity to Lucianna?

He hadn't returned to the opera house to listen to Meg. He was too ashamed, as if he trailed behind him a cloud of contamination that would surely poison the air of the theater. He had been a fool to skulk in the shadows, spying on the diva. Better to cut the limb from his body. He'd not return.

Erik had been puzzled when Mlle. Valmont came to visit accompanied by a stranger, a French count with an interest in opera no less. This wasn't an arrangement made by Lucianna. Erik saw her tense and tight-lipped greeting as she offered the two guests a seat. It seemed she recognized the Count de Chagny's name, but she said nothing to indicate that they had ever met.

The count spoke intelligently about music. Erik was surprised to find that the Frenchman knew he was the composer of *The Stranger*. Mlle. Valmont must have let slip the secret. It pleased Erik that the count knew. It pleased him even more when Raoul—who insisted Erik address him by his first name—invited himself to dinner the next evening.

The dinner party was like a reprieve for Erik. In the company of the count, he relaxed in a way he had not for days. Raoul wedged himself between Erik and Lucianna like a protective wall. After dinner the count suggested they take a stroll through the park not far from the apartment. Erik hadn't so much as set foot in the park due to Lucianna's imaginary fetters. The idea of walking along the path surrounded by trees and flower gardens, nymphs and fountains delighted him. Lucianna too abruptly begged off complaining of a headache. Erik was sure her excuse was meant to include him. But he quickly seized the opportunity to kiss her sweetly on the forehead, recommend that she retire early, and accept Raoul's invitation to accompany him alone to the park.

Lucianna had no gracious way of preventing Erik from going, so the men left. The night air was refreshing, cool. They walked the short distance to the park and started down one of its many twisting paths. The conversation, like the banter during dinner, was friendly and light. They commented on the architectural wonders of the city, the landscaping of the public gardens, the history and grandeur of Rome. Raoul feigned dismay that Erik had seen so few of the major monuments of the city.

"Speaking of beauty, you must have been to a performance at the Teatro dell'Opera?"

"Yes. I mean no."

"Well, which is it, man?"

"I've taken time to see the edifice. I've yet to see an actual performance." Erik felt a twinge of pain as his thoughts flew unintentionally to Meg. He tried to dispel the effects her image had on him. Suddenly, he wanted Raoul to go away and leave him to his imagination. He wanted to sink down onto the grass itself to cool the feverish heat that he felt rising along his body. It had become more and more difficult to avoid thinking of her.

"Well, you really must come with me to the opening night gala of *Faust*. I have a box. Signora Costanzi is singing and …"

It struck Erik why Raoul had seemed familiar. He was the tall man Erik had seen speaking to Meg at the Teatro dell'Opera. He had called her by her given name. She had placed her hand lightly on his sleeve before he left her on the stage.

"How do you know her?" Erik interrupted unceremoniously. He stopped on the path and forced Raoul to stop as well. His tone, formerly jovial, was harsh, suspicious.

Raoul studied Erik in the dim glow of the gaslight. He considered lying, but he reasoned that Erik must know already that he knew Meg. If he lied, he'd have no chance to enter into Erik's confidence again. "Why, yes, I do know the diva. She and my wife are close friends. I've known Meg, I mean Signora Costanzi, for years."

Erik didn't consider this answer sufficient. He spoke in the same tone, low and gravelly. "How well do you know her, sir?" Raoul caught the Biblical inflection Erik had given the word "know." He understood finally what he meant by the term.

Very quietly and clearly he answered, "She's a dear friend. I have great respect for her." Reluctantly Raoul realized that he had an opportunity to further Meg's plan—as unwise as it might be. "I'm worried about her."

Erik's harsh tone was replaced by one of concern. "Is she ill? Is there something wrong?"

"No, she's perfectly fine. That is she suffers no ill health. It's that she's lonely. She lost her husband some time ago now." They had resumed their stroll. Raoul was careful to glance at Erik out of the corner of his eye to judge his reaction before going on. "Lately she's been receiving notes from a secret admirer. I've noticed a change in her. She seems less depressed." Again he stopped, for Erik had suddenly remained behind him, fixed to the path. "Well, I shouldn't speak of it. It's actually rather personal. I just hope the man is not toying with her."

"I see," responded Erik noncommittally.

"He sends her a gorgeous bouquet of roses every day."

"Does she like them?" Erik no longer sounded impersonal.

"Quite."

Unexpectedly Raoul saw Erik's face transform. His mask covered all but his eyes and mouth. But these were enough to send shivers up Raoul's spine. Erik's eyes grew fierce, and he clenched his teeth in a grimace. Behind Raoul came a silky, sarcastic voice. When he turned, he came face to face with someone he recognized with some difficulty. He had only seen him on two occasions.

Once, when the young Italian had stolen into Meg's bedchamber meaning to rape her, they had fought. The young man had stabbed Raoul before Erik burst into the room and finally subdued the cad. The other time Raoul testified against the same young man in court. Briefly he wondered how Giovanni Cimino had gotten the scar that ran across his face.

"Well, are you out for an evening stroll or would you both like to accompany me to Roderigo's Tavern? You enjoyed yourself, didn't you, Erik, the last time we were there?"

Before Raoul could speak, Erik pushed him to the side and approached Giovanni.

"Leave me alone, Sig. Cimino."

"What? Such formality? After our intimacies, Erik, it seems so insincere."

Raoul noted how Erik stiffened at Giovanni's allusions. What sort of relationship now existed between these two men? Erik was clearly unaware of the danger he was in. While Erik didn't remember Giovanni, it was obvious that Giovanni had not forgotten his own desire for revenge. It was also certain that Giovanni, like Raoul, was using Erik's amnesia to his own advantage.

Quietly Erik insisted, "Go away. Leave me alone. I want nothing more to do with you."

Giovanni laughed sardonically, but bowed as if to comply with Erik's wishes. As if trying to recall a familiar face, he stared at the man who accompanied Erik. He'd remember, or he'd find out sooner or later who he was. But for now Giovanni turned and walked away into the night.

Erik was visibly upset. He seemed torn between choices equally repugnant, unable to move. Raoul waited. Hesitantly he placed his hand on Erik's shoulder. Erik jerked away from Raoul's touch as if it burned. His eyes were startled, haunted. Then he turned and marched back to the apartment.

Raoul has been in the apartment. He says Erik is well, but he was very subdued. He can't see any visible scarring from the fire except along the palms of his hands. Erik wears a full mask when there are guests. The only portion of his face that Raoul could see was from the mouth to the chin. This seems to have escaped the flames. I'm relieved to know this, but who knows what scars he may be hiding.

Lucianna was furious, but her hands were tied. She had no idea Mlle. Valmont was bringing a guest. Evidently M. Lambert was busy and couldn't come. And now she can't really tell Erik why she doesn't wish the Count de Chagny to visit. Raoul is so clever. He said he wanted to commission an opera. At first Erik didn't seem interested at all. But after Raoul described the lamentable state of opera in

Paris this past year, Erik appeared to be intrigued. Raoul had the nerve to invite himself to return tomorrow (Lucianna certainly wasn't going to offer the invitation). He can be very forceful and shameless, says Christine, when he wants something. I think she was talking about more than dinner invitations! I had to smile—my first smile in days—when she blushed. I told her that Erik and Raoul may be more alike than either of them like to think. For the first time I feel some hope!

Giovanni is back. Raoul ran into him last night in the park when he and Erik were strolling after dinner. He didn't recognize Raoul. It was dark, and Giovanni had had little contact with him. But Raoul said it was very strange. Erik reacted angrily when Giovanni stepped into their path, as if Erik remembered him, but Raoul thinks that his reaction seemed to have arisen from some new and fresher grievance! He also said that Giovanni has a long, jagged scar that runs from the brow near his left eye and along his cheek. We speculated that it might be a souvenir from prison.

It can't mean anything good that Giovanni is here in Rome. I've such misgivings. He obviously has been persecuting Erik. Raoul insists that he won't let me go anywhere without a vigilant chaperone. He intends to escort me to my rehearsals and remain to be sure I get home safely.

I fear more for Erik's sake than for my own. He doesn't know who Giovanni is.

Opening night is only a few days away. I'm having a devil of a time concentrating. The roses mock me from the table! I begin to loathe their heady perfume.

Raoul tells me to be patient.

It's not lack of patience; it's fear. What if he's changed so much that he's nothing like my Erik? Is that possible? I confided my fears to Christine. She and I had talked once before about a similar idea. Wouldn't it be wonderful if Erik had not been born disfigured? What if his life had been filled with love and happiness? It was idle speculation, we thought at the time. But all his past has been forgotten. Lucianna has told him beautiful lies. He thinks he is a different man. Is he? I had told Christine that I loved him just the way he was. I would not want anything to be different about him. I feel so selfish to have wished him no escape from the horrors of his past! Christine soothed me and told me that he is still my Erik or he wouldn't be spying on me at the opera.

I was amazed for a moment when she said this. It suddenly struck me that she had inadvertently reminded me of his obsession with her! We laughed uneasily. Yet it does seem to bear some resemblance to those mad days when he spied on

Christine. She was his pupil, and he had fallen in love with her. Yes, there is some ironic similarity between his behavior then and now. He spies on the object of his desire. But this time the diva is waiting for him with open arms, and there is no rival standing in the wings. He can have his way with me if he wants. I fervently pray that he wants to have his way with me.

Raoul sent his card the next day only to find it returned almost immediately. He fumed! He hadn't come this far to be thwarted now. The encounter with Giovanni had been unfortunate. He felt Erik had begun to relax with him. Now, he couldn't tell what was going on.

He saw a young curly-haired boy rush down from Erik's rooms and out into the street. Before he got away, Raoul called to him.

"Do you work for the Fiortinos?"

The boy eyed him suspiciously. "I don't work for them." Seeing Raoul's disappointment, the boy added, "I work for the maestro."

"Don Erik, you mean?"

The boy nodded proudly. "I must go. He's in great pain. I'm to buy him some powders for the headache."

"Wait!" The boy saw the coin in Raoul's hand and drew closer to inspect it. "I want you to take this to your maestro." Next to the coin, Raoul produced a folded slip of paper. "It's all right. I'm a friend."

"How can I trust you? That other one said he was a friend, too. But I know what he is."

"Who are you talking about?"

The boy made the sound of a knife cutting across his face and traced a scar from his brow down to his cheek. "That one. I carried a note from him to my maestro once. I thought he'd fall, he trembled so. He was sick and angry all at the same time. He told me not to talk to the man and to stay very far away from him."

"I'm not like the man with the scar. You give your maestro this note. Trust me. His reaction will not be like the one you saw before. I promise he'll be pleased." Raoul's voice inspired the boy with trust. He believed the finely dressed man. His face was pleasant, and his eyes were kind. He could tell that Raoul's intentions were to help Erik.

The boy took the note and folded it several times so that it fit in his secret pocket. Then he eyed the bright coin Raoul still held. Raoul flicked it into the air where the child snatched it easily. He nodded a quick thanks and ran toward the apothecary.

Raoul waited until the child returned. He waved as the boy glanced his way and watched as he ducked into the apartment building. Several moments passed. Then the boy emerged and looked around to see if anyone was watching before he ran across the street to where Raoul sat in his carriage waiting. He handed him a folded piece of paper and the same coin Raoul had given him previously. By way of explanation, the boy shrugged and said his maestro was generous enough to him, and no one needed to pay him to do his bidding.

Raoul smiled and thanked him.

"If ever you want to send another note, my maestro says to call for me, Mario. Have your driver ask for me. He can say he has a package to deliver. But be sure he has something for me to take up, even if it's a box of quills or some of that special paper Maestro uses to compose. And he told me I was to speak to you with respect and should call you 'signore.' So I'm sorry I didn't say 'signore,' signore." Raoul laughed as the boy grinned and ran back toward the apartment. "Ciao, signore," he called back over his shoulder.

Quickly, Raoul opened the note and read:

∽

Dear Raoul,

I am pleased that you addressed me simply as Erik and take the liberty of following suit in my address to you. I feared that the encounter in the park might have persuaded you to withdraw your kind invitation. After all we are known by the acquaintances that we keep, and as you'll appreciate, the young man does not bode well for my character. Let me say that I would gladly rid myself of his acquaintance if I could.

My little monkey, Mario, whom I hold closer to my heart than a mere servant, will happily send word to me if you wish to contact me without the mediation of my dear wife. She fears that distractions will take me away from my composition. But let us not talk of a wife's mistaken care. Nor would I wish to speak of the young man in the park.

I would give my soul to hear Signora Costanzi sing in Faust. If you will promise to refrain from asking about the unfortunate encounter and my atrocious behavior in the park, I would most gladly accept your invitation to the Teatro dell'Opera. Let us meet just outside the theater at quarter to the hour?

Erik

Raoul folded the paper and put it in his pocket. He wouldn't bring up the subject of Giovanni unless Erik did first. But there was no promise stated or implied that would keep him from investigating further. He would find out where the man was staying and have a frank talk with him. He wondered if that was the man Meg had thought followed her on a couple of occasions. Raoul had assumed it was Erik, but perhaps it wasn't. She'd be frightened if she thought that Giovanni wanted revenge and that he was toying with Erik. But there was no doubt that Giovanni was plotting something. They should all be on their guard just in case.

he's out there in the audience, he'll be listening to me sing, box 5 Raoul said, his ironic choice, Erik had always kept box 5 at the Opera Populaire for himself alone, tonight I will give the performance of my life and I will sing for Erik

I turned my eyes away, embarrassed to watch him. We were close enough to the stage to see the hint of perspiration stain the costumes of the dancers and to see real tears in Meg's eyes. Erik followed Meg's every move. His body would bend forward toward the stage if she turned even slightly away from our direction as if he could physically follow her. Every emotion on stage I could see reflected in his eyes and in the posture of his body. He forgot I was with him or he might have been more guarded in his responses. I don't think he could control them. His desire for her was palpable. I had to look away.

During the intermission he slumped in his chair, exhausted, as if he had been part of the performance himself. I attempted to make small talk with him, but he answered only superficially. He seemed to have disappeared into the story. Suddenly he turned to me and complained with unchecked impatience that intermissions were too long. His eyes remained fixed on the closed curtain of the stage.

When the play ended, there was a standing ovation. The curtain rose and fell no fewer than six times. Erik applauded as did everyone, but quietly. He seemed drugged. He stared as before down at Meg, who I noticed looked in our direction more frequently than she should have. When the curtain fell for the final time, I turned to leave the box. Behind me, I heard Erik groan as if in pain. I looked over my shoulder and saw he had crumpled in his chair, his head in his hands. He was rocking back and forth, struggling with an uncontrollable emotion.

"Erik, are you all right? Are you ill?" I knew better than to touch him, but I drew close so that he could reach out to me if he needed to. He didn't answer, but the moaning stopped.

Slowly he lifted his head from his hands and looked out toward the empty stage. The curtain had been drawn. The auditorium was swiftly emptying, and a few of the staff had emerged to sweep up the programs and other items left casually behind on the seats and floor. He pivoted in his seat, his back to me. I could see him fidget with his mask. He coughed several times and, I assumed from his movements, brought his mask back in place. Then he rose from the seat.

We didn't speak until we reached the corridor that circled the auditorium. Erik started down the hallway toward the exit, but I dared to touch his sleeve to stop him. He didn't pull away from me, but he frowned as he stared at my hand.

"I thought you might like to meet the diva."

His mouth slowly parted, and I could hear his breathing accelerate. It was as if he were about to bolt and flee. Then he looked so intently at me that I felt his gaze as a physical touch. There was an intimacy in his look that struck me. I wasn't sure what it meant until he spoke. "You would introduce me to her? I could meet her?" I could tell that he avoided saying her name, Signora Costanzi being too cold and Meg being too familiar. Then he seemed to doubt. "She couldn't possibly want to meet me."

I was about to protest when he interrupted me. "What is she like? Can we go somewhere where we can talk? I want you to tell me about her. I want to know everything. Is she kind? Is she …?" I think he would have gone on asking questions, without allowing me a moment to respond, if it hadn't been for someone coming down the hall from the opposite direction. When Erik saw the figure approach, he drew his large brimmed hat down to shade his mask and remained silent. The figure descended the stairs well before he reached the spot where we stood.

I took the moment to persuade Erik to come with me to Meg's room. "Erik, I promised I'd stop by her dressing room to congratulate her after the performance. She'll never forgive me if I don't come by." In point of fact, she was waiting for Erik. She'd never forgive me if I came empty handed.

His eyes have this incredible facility to change in an instant. From the moist softness of yearning they now hardened to a diamond sharpness that threatened to cut into my very soul. His lips pursed tightly together, and I could swear that he grew several inches taller than he had been just moments before. He towered over me ominously.

"Exactly what is your relationship with Signora Costanzi? You said she's a friend of your wife. I see that the countess does not accompany you, signore."

Understanding the drift of his words, I was taken off guard and stuttered my amazed reply. "I ... I ... my relationship ... sir ... you risk offending me ... is exactly what I said it was. Meg's a friend, nothing more. I didn't invite my wife because I thought you might be more comfortable if it were only the two of us." I could see he wasn't quite convinced. "I swear to you, Erik. I happen to love my wife. I'm very fortunate, because I struggled a good deal to win her. I wasn't the only man who loved her."

I clenched my jaw firmly shut for I was dangerously close to revealing our past rivalry. It was strange to be explaining to Erik that I loved Christine. Who wouldn't love her? Erik had certainly loved her once himself. He released me from his uncomfortable scrutiny at last and sighed in deep thought. He glanced down the hall toward the stairs that would lead him out into the streets, then behind us toward the backstage and Meg.

"Why are you hesitant?"

"Because ... because ... I can't ... explain. I'm sorry."

"Well, what shall we do, Erik? Eventually they're going to throw us out. We will certainly be in the way."

"Of course." Finally he smiled. The tension drained away. He had made his decision. "Please, Raoul, I would be honored to meet Signora Costanzi."

Amazed I watched him do what he had always done. He assumed the role the present performance required of him. He donned the confidence of a gentleman admirer just as easily as if it were his cloak. It was as if even his body had changed. His expression, as hidden as it was by the mask, exuded an assurance and tranquility that I knew he didn't have. He followed me back to the dressing rooms to meet his wife.

Raoul led the way through the corridors behind the stage to the newly refurbished dressing rooms. He glanced behind to assure himself that Erik was indeed following. It surprised him how silently he walked. He was a large man, taller than Raoul, broader in the shoulder, yet he had a light step like a cat's. Erik's face, mostly hidden by the mask, revealed little of his mood. However, Raoul had come to realize that this very lack of obvious emotion indicated an intense effort to disguise his anxiety. Raoul wondered if at the last moment Erik might panic, bolt, and flee.

They came upon Meg's door. Raoul waited for Erik to draw up next to him. He gave him an encouraging smile and raised his hand to rap softly at the door. Before his knuckles touched the wood, Erik's hand grabbed his wrist and pulled it away.

"She's expecting only you, isn't she?"

"No, I mentioned that I would be accompanied tonight. She's expecting to meet you."

"Did you tell her …" He paused, swallowed audibly, and continued in a whisper, "Did you mention the mask?" This was the first indication Erik had given him that he was in the slightest way self-conscious about his appearance. Since the first visit at Lucianna's, Erik had made no reference to the mask he wore, or given any explanation of its use, or taken note of the curious looks of his guests.

"As a matter of fact, I did mention it. I hope you don't mind."

Obviously relieved, Erik replied in a sigh, "No, I don't mind. It will avoid … startling her."

Raoul thought it best not to hesitate any longer and quickly rapped several times on the door.

Erik could hear the rustle of fabric and faint tap of her heels as she approached the door. In French, from the other side, came her voice asking if it was Raoul. Raoul's answer was also in French. The warm sounds flooded over Erik like a long forgotten song.

The door opened, and there she was, closer than she had ever been to him. She had changed into a casual dress of cream tinted satin with a pattern of wild flowers. Her hair was loosely pinned in ringlets that crowned her heart-shaped face with a golden light. Erik's mouth was dry as if packed with cotton. He had not heard Raoul make the introductions. She was looking up at him with large, soft brown eyes in expectation. He dropped his gaze reluctantly from her face to see a delicate, graceful hand raised for him to take. He had removed his gloves and had not had the chance to put them on again. He hesitated before he reached out to touch her hand. It disappeared inside his, a large square hand, and he bent and barely brushed her fingers with his lips.

He heard himself answer her easily in a deep murmur of French. "Je suis tres enchanté, madame, de faire votre connaissance."

"I'm delighted, M. Fiortino, that your French is so fluent. You have a wonderful accent. One would think you were born speaking it. Please do come in." Meg had steeled herself for this moment. She fought the desire to throw herself into his arms never to release him again. His nearness intoxicated her, but she reminded herself that she was an actress as well as a chanteuse. She had to be careful. She couldn't succumb to him before he'd even begun an assault.

Raoul did not take a seat. In the next moment, he made some excuse and withdrew from the dressing room, leaving Erik, in shock, alone with Meg. The two of them passed a charged moment waiting to see who would be first to speak. Beyond Meg, Erik's eyes were drawn to a huge bouquet of crimson roses, so dark that the edges of their petals looked black. Mario! He had told the boy that he would no longer send the flowers, but Mario had, on his own initiative, ordered that they continue to be delivered to Meg's dressing room.

"Do you enjoy the roses, Mme. Costanzi?" He nodded his head only slightly in their direction. "They seem to occupy a prominent place among the others." Indeed there were various other bouquets left haphazardly in corners and on side tables, some grander and many gaudier than his bouquet of roses.

Would he admit that he was her secret admirer? Should she let on that she suspected? "Yes, they are spectacular, don't you agree, Monsieur?" She was heartened that he continued to speak to her in the intimacy of their native language instead of the acquired Italian. "Lately, my admirer has become shy. He used to write the loveliest notes, but the past fortnight the roses arrive silent. Why would an admirer suddenly grow so quiet, do you think? As a man, perhaps you might help me understand. Does his interest wane?"

He felt flushed with the joy that she had received his roses and his notes with such pleasure, but the question came dangerously close to those reasons that nearly made this meeting impossible. She demanded an answer, and he couldn't lie to her. "Perhaps he feels unworthy."

Meg's brow furrowed slightly at his response. What had happened to daunt him so? His reticence was not due to lack of interest, but to some sense of his own lack of merit. Lucianna had bragged that she had given him a new life, one in which he enjoyed the full range of power, without guilt, without restraints. This didn't seem to be borne out by the hesitant lover who sat stiffly across from her.

"It takes courage to love, doesn't it, monsieur?"

"Please, call me Erik."

"Then you must call me Meg."

"No, I couldn't."

"Why not?"

He stared at her, incapable of speech. Finally he murmured, "You are a famous prima donna of the opera."

"I'm also a woman." She felt her pulse quicken, and the words came out with a slight tremble. She felt the blood rise to her cheeks. She must change the course of the conversation or she would melt at his feet. "You have a secret, Erik. Don't worry. It's a wonderful secret, but Raoul has given it away. You are the puppet master, and the man who said he was Henri Fournier is the puppet. You're the genius behind the hit of the season, *The Stranger*. Without composers like you, there would be no prima donnas like me."

"The public is easily entertained, madame. Whatever worth the composition has is due to the artists who interpret it."

"False modesty does not suit you, Erik. And I insist you call me Meg."

"If you insist. Meg." The intimacy of speaking her name, the closeness of her body, the fragrance of soaps mixed with the lingering musk of her own sweat threatened to overwhelm his senses. He waited, again, hoping to hear her voice. It mattered little the words, he wanted to watch her lips and tongue make the sounds, to catch the vibrations of her throat as she spoke.

"How did you come up with the story, Erik?" The question interrupted the pleasure of listening and watching her, and he looked at her as if he had not understood a word she'd said. "The story? What was your inspiration?"

"I don't know. It just flowed." His hands were unconsciously moving as if lightly tracing the notes on the piano. When he saw that her eyes had focused on them, in particular on the burn scars of his palms, he dropped them to his lap and folded one hand inside the other.

He hides them from me. He holds them like scared prey in his lap. "I'm sorry. I didn't mean to stare," Meg rushed to assure him. She couldn't let him flee, not now!

"No, there's no need for you to apologize," he answered in a low whisper, his eyes cast aside so as not to look at her.

"You were talking about the story of your opera, *The Stranger*. It must have had some significance for you?" Anything to divert his thoughts from the scars.

"Significance? For me personally, you mean?" Was his look wary all of a sudden? "Aren't we all strangers?"

"Some of us are, perhaps," she said wistfully, her eyes burning with the threat of tears. "Some of us are fortunate to find a companion with whom we are no longer strangers."

"Your voice, Meg, I can't explain it. It touches me in a way that I find …" He had shifted to the edge of his chair and was looking intensely into her eyes when he stopped.

"Familiar?"

It wasn't the word he was looking for. The words he wanted to say were shocking, inappropriate, extreme. He wanted to describe to her how aroused, how excited, how desperate and sad and happy her voice made him feel. He wanted to take her in his arms and smother her with his body. He wanted her to tell him that she sang only for him. He wanted to possess her beyond death, make her his God, and pray to her. He would obey whatever she asked of him, even if it brought him to hell itself. And he felt shocked and confused that she should make him feel this way. Familiar? It was such a calm, safe word. Yet it hinted at an intimacy between them that Erik believed real!

He rose suddenly from his chair and took a step toward her with his hand held out in farewell. "I'll take my leave of you, now, madame. I mean, Meg." His formal voice softened with the sound of her name on his tongue. "May I call again?"

She stifled her desire to beg him to stay with her. She desperately wanted to invite him to her bed! But she smiled pleasantly—warmly, she hoped—and placed her hand softly in his. "I would very much like that, Erik."

He brought her fingers to his lips again, but this time his lips felt moist and heavy on her skin. They lingered, and she felt his breath roll across her hand, warm and intimate like the heat of the noon-day sun on a summer's day. His eyes rose to catch hers for one instant, and she saw the recognition of her desire in them before he turned to leave. At the door, his hand clutching the knob, he turned his head only slightly in her direction. "I think your roses will not be silent tomorrow, Meg." Then he left.

> *To Meg, Forgive my previous silence. It was the awe that you inspired that robbed me of speech. Your performance in Faust has so affected me that I can't imagine music without hearing your voice. I would be honored if you would consent to allow me to visit again sometime. Your most obedient servant, Erik.*

"Why would you think the story had any personal significance for me? Doesn't art take on a life of its own? Do all stories simply reveal the life experience of the author?"

"Certainly there is such a thing as the imagination. I know the story isn't your autobiography, but surely we respond to those aspects of art that speak to us personally?"

He walked along, deep in thought. She was very near him, but they were not touching. Their conversation had been safe, but suddenly Erik feared they were dangerously close to terrain he had carefully skirted all evening. *Fear.* He took a deep breath and let it out slowly. His throat constricted making it difficult to talk. He didn't want to talk about his fear. Confessions and confidences would reveal too much.

Meg didn't ask the question he knew she wanted to ask. He was grateful. He felt raw and vulnerable. The least word, especially from her, could wound him now. Even a glance in her direction struck him as a risk. How was she looking at him? What was it that she saw when she looked at him? What did she think of the mask he wore? Did she believe it was an affectation? Did she have any idea how aware he was that it stood between them?

Yet she seemed to enjoy his company.

"Have you been alone for a long while, Meg?" He was thinking of her husband. She never spoke of him. Of course, there was much in his own life that they hadn't yet discussed. She hadn't asked if he was married, and he had not been forthcoming. Did it matter? He fooled himself that it didn't. He was smitten with her, but he assumed she was out of his reach. He hadn't planned to meet her. He would have been content, he lied to himself, to stand in the wings, hidden, to watch and listen to her.

"It's been too long."

"A woman of your passions should not be alone."

"I don't wish to be alone, but there are some things worse than being alone."

Would she want to be with him? If she saw his face, if she knew what he had done, what he was capable of, would she be here, now, walking in the park with him? He felt despondent. They had come to an impasse. She would soon demand to know more about him. She was alone and should not be. He should step aside and let her get on with her own life. He was risking her reputation and any chance of happiness through a suitable match.

"Erik, come with me. I have something I want you to see." She pulled at his sleeve like a child with a delightful secret to share.

The driver was waiting outside the theater as usual to take Meg home. Erik had dismissed his and told him to return at a predetermined hour. He would most likely come within the hour, but he would certainly wait until Erik was ready. Meg pulled him behind her into the carriage. They settled back as the driver urged the horses on. Where was she taking him? They sat in the darkness, the light from the gaslights along the avenue flashed rhythmically across her face as they left the theater district and approached the large mansions that lined the way. Erik watched the route they took, mentally committing it to memory should he ever need to retrace its path. The driver drew up before an austere mansion. Meg edged forward in her seat. She had been nervously silent the entire ride. Erik had refrained from speaking, intrigued by her silence. Before the driver could descend, Erik opened the door and assisted Meg in climbing down from the enclosure. She hesitated for a moment, asked the driver to wait for Erik's return, and led the way to the door. There the doorman had been watching vigilantly for Signora Costanzi's return. Meg brought her fingers to her lips in a quick signal for the servant to keep his tongue. He bowed in greeting to the mistress of the house and disguised his momentary impulse to greet the master as well.

Meg discarded her gloves and cloak, indicating Erik should do the same. She took him to the bottom step of the grand staircase where she paused. A blush of red had painted her cheeks, and Erik felt suddenly uncomfortable. She was leading him to the private quarters of the household. In spite of its inappropriateness, she beckoned him to follow quietly behind her. At the top of the landing, Erik felt his heart pounding in his chest as if he were a thief sneaking about the mansion in search of hidden jewels. Meg unexpectedly took his hand and pulled him more earnestly down the hall to one of many doors. She held her fingers to her lips in a sign of silence and carefully opened the door. Inside there was a dim glow from a lamp in the corner of the room. In spite of this light it took Erik several moments to adjust to the gloom and to make out the two beds at the far end of the room. In them he could see two piles of blankets. One of the blankets moved. Meg tiptoed forward and waved for him to approach. He was very quiet on his feet, and he was beside her before she realized he was there. She smiled up at him as she drew the covers down enough for Erik to see the face of a small boy in deep sleep. He lay with his mouth slightly open, his features relaxed, a tangle of black curls falling across his forehead. Erik felt Meg's love as if it were waves of warmth rising from burning coals. He looked from the boy's face to hers and saw only a slight resemblance. He must resemble his father. Before he could take his eyes off the beauty of the boy, she had tugged at his sleeve and brought him round to the other bed. Now he could see that pillows had been arranged along both edges of the bed to serve as a barrier. In the middle cosseted, safe and secure, was a very small child, a girl. She was sleeping on her back, her legs akimbo, one arm leaning on one of the pillows by her side, the other bent, her thumb securely lodged in her mouth. A tight knot suddenly twisted his heart, and he gasped at the tenderness he felt toward the child. Meg had not released his hand. The touch was intimate even though her complete attention seemed riveted on the child. At that moment, Meg brought his hand to her chest and pressed it tightly to her bosom. Then she released it, still tingling from her touch, turned, and led him from the room.

They didn't speak until they arrived at the bottom of the stairs. She stood looking at him intently as if she expected something from him. He assayed to quell the intense ache that had arisen in the moment she pressed his hand to her chest. Confused, he felt he must leave. He had expected almost anything except this glimpse into her heart. She had brought him to gaze upon her sleeping babes, and he felt as if she had bared her very soul to him. Yet he didn't know how he was supposed to react. He had no gift of equal worth he could give her.

He muttered that he must be going. She asked if he might stay just a while longer, but he thanked her and repeated that he must leave. "They're beautiful, Meg. I don't think I've ever seen anything more beautiful than the two of them." She smiled proud in her love, but something wistful passed into her expression. He sought her hand to take his leave. He held it, studied her long, delicate fingers, and slowly brought her hand to his lips to kiss. At the last moment, he dared turn her hand and kiss the soft tender flesh of her palm. If she were about to speak, she decided against it.

He wanted to remember the way she was looking at this moment for the rest of his life. To remember that he had been a part of it.

It was foolish, but I thought perhaps the sight of François and Laurette might jar his memory. For a moment I thought it had. He was amazed by their beauty. I could tell he was genuinely touched. Something pulled at him, for he left me rather abruptly, but I sensed he didn't really wish to leave me. How much longer can this go on? I can't bear being near him and yet unable to touch him, really touch him, the way a woman needs to touch a man. He asked me how long I have been alone. I wanted to respond to him that he should better ask how long it has been since he's held me in his arms, since he's made love to me.

"What? The evening has hardly begun, and she's kicked you out?" Giovanni stepped out of the shadows and blocked Erik's way to the door of the apartment building. The driver had already retired.

"Get out of my way." Erik could smell the stale smoke and liquor on Giovanni's breath. He wanted to back away, but wouldn't give the young rake that satisfaction. They stood only a hand's width from each other.

"You've not been very courteous, Erik. I thought we were friends. After all we shared." Giovanni raised a finger and slid it slowly down the side of Erik's mask. The significance of the touch was not lost on Erik.

"Get out of my way, or I will hurt you." His voice was low and even, but the tension was unmistakable. The dim light of the street reflected off the pupils of Erik's eyes and the surface of his teeth which he held in a tight grimace.

Giovanni looked down the street, pretending that he had heard someone approach so that he could step away from Erik, just beyond his reach. "We're men of the world, Erik. I ask your pardon if I misunderstood your inclinations. Please, accept my humble apology." The young man bowed low, his eyes trained on Erik the whole while. "Can we be friends?"

"I sincerely doubt it," Erik said as he started again toward the door.

"Come have one drink with me. Just to prove there are no hard feelings? I know an establishment not far from here. We could walk and chat. It's perfectly respectable, not at all as fun as Roderigo's."

Erik considered the young dandy. He understood the bravado that a man would assume when the world had beaten him down. He could forgive that Giovanni was cruel and sadistic as long as he didn't take his aggression out on someone who was not a willing victim. But he didn't want to be a part of it. Something about the scarred man recalled to him his own sins. Giovanni had come around every couple of days. It was beginning to be awkward and annoying. Perhaps, if he went now with the rake, they could part on civil terms and he'd be rid of his association.

The establishment was an opium den hidden amid respectable shops and businesses several streets away from the apartment. Erik would never had known of its existence, but Giovanni followed the labyrinthine path easily to its door. Giovanni offered Erik a pipe which he took grudgingly, inhaling the sickly sweet smoke shallowly and infrequently. He wanted to stay as clear headed as he could without abstaining completely. No one in the dark room would have felt at ease if he hadn't accepted at least a modest toke on the pipe. Giovanni talked about the women he had known, describing in lurid detail both their charms and their flaws. He invited Erik to share his experiences, but to no avail. Erik sat sullenly listening and responding, if at all, in terse one word answers.

"Now I do remember meeting Signora Costanzi. Of course, that was a long time ago, and she wasn't a famous opera star then." Erik shifted nervously at the mention of Meg. He was about to tell Giovanni to refrain from talking about her when the young man's voice suddenly changed and became serious and urgent. "If you want her, take her." Erik blinked trying to clear his stinging eyes of the pungent smoke that surrounded them. He couldn't have heard him correctly. "If you want her, take her. Believe me, she wants you. She's handing herself on a silver platter to you, and you've been acting the fool around her. She's a diva. She works in the opera. God, Erik, how long do you think you can hold her interest? If you don't make a move soon, she's going to get bored. There are plenty of admirers she can turn to."

Erik's mouth fell open. He wanted to leave, but the floor was sliding back and forth under him and he couldn't quite steady himself.

"Don't you want her, Erik?"

Yes, a voice ripped through his mind in spite of the fog that was wrapping itself around him. *Yes, I want her. I want to take her and mark her as mine! I feel like dying when I'm not with her.*

"You think she won't want you if she sees your face? Well, there was a time when she looked at me the way she looks at you now. Ask her!"

Giovanni and Meg? No, that was impossible. Giovanni sneered at him, laughed. "Erik, you're so blind. Has she told you about her husband? You think that's the only man she's had? If she's mourning, why is she flaunting herself on the stage for all of us to see? The way you feel when she comes near you? How many other men do you think feel the same way when they see her make love to the tenor on the stage? You're a fool if you don't grab her now. She's ripe, Erik, ripe like a persimmon, round and heavy with nectar, waiting for you to take her and squeeze her dry. That's what all those theater and opera people want. Well, I'm sure that your gallant courtship will give her years of pleasant memories to share with the other men in her life."

Erik shoved himself off the cushions. Stumbling, he searched for the door. He managed to find the exit, leaving Giovanni behind in a drug-induced dream. His hand raised to steady himself from time to time against the wall of the buildings, Erik groped his way along the streets to the apartment. By the time he arrived some of the effects of the opium had begun to dissipate.

He entered without waking Lucianna. Luigi lit a lamp and followed him to his room. Erik dismissed him and undressed quickly and lay down in the cool bed. He was acting like a silly love-sick swain from a Romantic ballad. Meg wasn't a young maiden. She was a mature woman, still young, but not so naive. She had been married, was now a widow. She had to have guessed that he was married and that he couldn't offer her marriage. Yet she consented to meet him in her dressing room, late and alone. He was in love with her. He wasn't dally-ing with her. If she agreed to live with him, if she agreed to be his mistress, he would take care of her, he'd give her the world. He couldn't marry her, but if she would love him and be faithful to him, it could almost be as if they were married. If he didn't make love to her, would she grow tired of these chaste encounters? Would she look to someone else for passion? Was that all she wanted from him? He thought of the way she looked at him, the daring neckline of the gown she had worn tonight, the times she had softly touched him. Yes, he felt her desire; it fueled his own to fever pitch. Why shouldn't he respond to her?

Would she consent to be his mistress? He wondered if he were capable of asking her such a question. Things could not continue long as they were. He felt her impatience, her curiosity in the way her eyes strayed to the scars the fire had left on his hands, the way they lingered on his mask when she thought he was unaware. Would he be able to remove his mask? And how would she react when she saw his face? Surely she would be shocked and revolted. Could he bear to watch her desire for him wither?

They had met, many times before, on starlit nights and walked along deserted streets, long after the performance, long after the carriages had clanged their way homeward, when the lone figure of a patrolling officer passed from building to building vigilantly checking the locks, when the city sounds had at last given way to the roar of crickets, the scurry of animals breaking through the hedges, the swoop of an owl and the startled cry of the hare.

Tonight they had dined in her dressing room and had spoken softly, taking refuge in the strange silences that grew between them. Erik had arrived late, mumbling an apology, unable to meet her gaze. He hesitated before he took her hand and lifted it to his lips, letting them linger for an instant longer than usual before he released it. Meg checked the urge to ask him what the matter was. He'd tell her in his own time. He had always been like that. It would only drive him further into the silence if she were to pry.

After they had dined—Meg was painfully aware that they had barely touched—Erik suggested, as he had on previous occasions, that they step out for a walk. This, too, had become a comfortable ritual between them. Years ago, before he lost his memory, it had taken Meg much to convince Erik that he was safe to leave his cellar rooms under the Teatro dell'Opera. However, his new identity had appeared to instill in him a restlessness and feeling of claustrophobia hitherto unknown to Meg. He would not linger after dinner in her dressing room. She took his arm as they left the theater.

Tonight they didn't cross the way and head toward the central plaza and the parks. He gently turned her in the opposite direction, and they walked in silence for nearly half an hour before their destination loomed before them. He had guided her to a small chapel next to which was an wrought iron gate that opened upon a cemetery. She stopped and pulled on his arm to stop him as well.

"Why here?" She felt cold and unsettled. This was more macabre than Romantic to her sensibilities, especially given the raw wound of her recent mourning for him.

"You're not afraid of the dead, are you?" He pushed the gate open which was not locked. "They can't harm us, and no one will bother us."

Was there a touch of sadness in his voice?

"We could have stayed in my room and been quite undisturbed."

He didn't answer her, nor did he look away. He seemed to consider saying something but changed his mind and guided her through the gate, closing it softly behind them. "Over there is a small clearing. The moon will be high, and we can sit and talk."

"Erik, you're scaring me." She held back, and he pulled her forcefully along. "Erik, please. Can we go back? Why are you acting so strangely?"

She saw his shoulders slump and his head lower. He had pulled out ahead of her, resolutely holding her hand firmly in his to bring her behind. Unexpectedly, he released her hand. She nearly tumbled back but caught herself before she fell. "If you must, go." He was breathing heavily, taking short shallow breaths. He kept his back to her.

Confused, she made no move to leave. Instead she called to him. "I don't want to. But you're frightening me. What's the matter?"

"Very well. This is, I suppose, just as good a place as any." He beckoned to her to sit on one of the tombs that they had approached. She hesitated only a moment, then sat on the marble ledge of a high rectangular slab.

He didn't sit. He drew close to her and lifted his hand as if to touch her hair. She closed her eyes, lifted her face toward him, eagerly anticipating his touch. It didn't come. When she opened her eyes, he had again drawn away and had turned his back to her. Something clutched at her heart. Something was terribly wrong!

"I have to leave, Meg." Were those tears she heard in his voice? "I won't be able to see you again." This time she was sure she had heard the catch in his voice. A hard wet intake of breath, a shuddering exhale followed.

"I don't understand. Why? Where are you going?" What were the correct words to use now? What could hold him to her? Why didn't he feel the inexorable tie that linked her heart to his?

"You must be aware that I haven't made any declaration of intentions to you." The tears were gone. There was, instead, a cool matter-of-fact dryness to the formula he was using to break her heart. "I'm a married man. This flirtation has gotten out of hand, I'm afraid. It's gone further than I had purposed. If we stop now …" There it was! The catch in his voice, the proof that this was hurting him almost as much as it was her! "I believe we've managed to be discreet."

"No! This is not right! We've done nothing we should be ashamed of, Erik."

"If we don't stop now, we shall."

The face that turned toward hers was unreadable. The mask shown with reflected light, and Meg could not make out his eyes in the contrasting depths of shadow.

"Even so!" She had begun to cry freely, heedless of her pride.

"Would you want me to make you my mistress? You have children. You must love them. If you aren't concerned for your own future, think of theirs!"

"But this is wrong, Erik. We have every right to be together."

"I can't do that to you, Meg! I can't. I love you too much."

He brushed quickly by her and headed toward the gate. He would leave her. She hurried behind him, running to catch up to him. When she finally reached him, she threw her arms around his waist. She knotted her fist inside her other hand to lock him in an unyielding embrace. She pressed her body against his back, squeezed her eyes shut against the tears, and told him she wouldn't let him go!

He felt her arms, tight silken threads, binding him. Her body had never been this close to his. His heart was seized with a pain so deep he knew it would never heal. How could he leave her? She had become the voice inside his head. He didn't know in what part of his soul she lodged; there was no limb he could hack off to rid himself of her. She would be a constant loss inside him. But he couldn't make her his mistress. Giovanni's leering face loomed over him, *Take her. She's ripe.* He wanted to, felt it as a need so demanding that he thought he might die without her, but the thought of ruining her reputation, of her name bandied about in the mouths of miscreants like Giovanni, the situation she would find herself in should he die before her, the fate that would hound her children—their children should there be any—tortured him. He wouldn't do that to her! It had all been so useless, so destructive!

They had been discreet. There may have been rumors, but there was no damage that time wouldn't heal. Should this go any further the harm would be irreparable.

He forced her hands apart. Summoning every last shred of courage in his body, he assumed an impassive face and turned to confront her once more. "Meg, my wife and I are returning home tomorrow. I won't ... we won't see each other again."

"Erik, stop!" Meg grabbed at his hand. "We haven't even ... We've barely kissed! Give me this night!"

Would he trust her? If he spent just one night with her, surely he wouldn't be able to leave her. The same thoughts were battling in his mind. However there were other thoughts that also tumbled across his mind, the remembrance of the terrible vision in the mirror, the way the young girl who fanned the insects away from his open wound had looked at him, the sickening thought that perhaps showing Meg would be the best way to sever her desire for him! *If she sees what I look like, she won't be so eager to have me come to her bed!*

They stepped into each other's arms. Erik bent and kissed Meg gently on the lips. He opened his eyes and searched hers, wondering if it was love he saw painfully luminescent in their depths.

"Ssshhh," he whispered, placing a trembling finger on her lips. Then he slipped away from her. He stood transfixed by moonlight. Then he lifted his hand to his mask and raised it from his face.

A look of shock crossed her face. She brought her hand to her mouth, and she broke out into tears.

A fist of ice came crashing down on his heart. He turned and ran from the graveyard.

he ran! he ran before I could say anything, before I could take him in my arms and kiss his face, kiss his beautiful face, explain to him that my tears were of joy, of relief that he hadn't been touched by the fire, that God had been merciful and not destroyed the rest of his face, I had been so afraid that he was injured from the accident and that he would have to bear the burden of complete disfigurement, but his face was the face I had grown to love, the face that was sadly tortured and wonderfully handsome, his angel and demon visage, the one that he had begun to accept when the accident happened, the one that I had prayed he still had, but he saw me gasp and saw my tears and he ran, it took me several minutes to under-stand that he ran from me in horror, in pain, that he had misunderstood my tears and my surprise, oh God, how can I explain it to him? he doesn't remember me and he thinks that I've never seen his face, he thinks that I'm repulsed by his face, and he has tried to be noble and to save me from the gossip, to protect my reputation and the future of our children—mine and his—but he doesn't know that he has every right to lie with me, that we are and will always be man and wife, no matter what Lucianna has done or told him and no matter how unfaithful he has been with her! duty and honor have won over love and desire, but I might still have called him back to me had I controlled myself, if I had steeled my heart to quell my emotions, if I had calmly waited for him to speak, when he unmasked and I found my Erik had come home to me, had I thought about how he would understand my amazement, it didn't occur to me that he would feel it as a sign of my revulsion, now I don't know what I can do, if I write to him will he believe me? or will he believe that I write to him out of pity? I must find a way to reach him

Lucianna heard him enter. He didn't retire to his room. She heard him walking about in the parlor. She thought she heard the sound of bottles. He was drinking. There was something wrong, she could sense it. She rose and put on her morning dress. She quietly walked to the parlor. The door was ajar, and through the narrow opening she could spy him. He sat, close to the fire, with a bottle of whiskey in one hand, a glass in the other. He had drained a shot and was pouring the next. He had taken off his coat and thrown it to the ground, loosened his collar, and thrown the cravat into the fire where it was smoldering in the flames. His mask was nowhere to be seen. His hair was disheveled, and his white shirt was soaked in sweat and sticking to his chest. The ravages of strong emotion had left their mark on his features. His eyes were bloodshot, swollen. He stared into the fire, unblinkingly. Perhaps it was the effect of the flickering light, but he wore the look of the damned.

She stepped back and considered what she should do. She had resigned herself to his anger and antipathy. She had steeled herself to go through the paces of everyday life beside him, like a shadow and fellow prisoner, ignoring his rejection of her. She had vowed never to let him go, to be cruel in her vengeance for his failure to return her love. But she hadn't yet prepared herself to face his sorrow! He had made her cry until she thought she would cry tears of blood! She should be immune to his suffering, yet she was not.

She slipped into the parlor. He glanced at her and looked away into the flames. She took her seat beside him. He had avoided her touch before as if it burned. So she hesitated to reach out her hand towards him. Her fingers barely grazed the fabric of his collar, lightly settling like a moth, then quickly flitting away. Just as quickly and as unexpectedly, Erik turned and buried his face in her lap. She stroked his hair silently, afraid to disturb the moment. He lay in her lap, his hands gently holding on to her as if she might float away from him. He eventually calmed. When he didn't speak, she asked him if he'd lost his mask. He nodded.

A glancing pain surprised her. It was his, but she had felt it nonetheless. Something awful had happened tonight, something between Erik and Meg. She was perplexed. He had lost the mask; he had removed it sometime in the evening. But Meg wouldn't have rejected him! Her hands squeezed his shoulder tightly against the thought. Yet he was here, with her, seeking comfort from a great disappointment. But was he home for good?

"Erik, have you come home?"

He heard the unspoken half of the question, "To stay?" He pressed himself hard into her body. This was the woman he had married. Her fate was bound to his until death itself. He must try to find some way to live the rest of his life. He didn't wish to be alone. Luci loved him. Perhaps no one else ever could.

"Luci, you said my parents loved me." He tried to form the question rumbling inside him. "How old was I, exactly, when they died?"

"Why do you ask?" she asked. She had tried to avoid details that she might later jumble or forget.

"It doesn't matter. I just wondered if they died when I was young. Meg took me to see her children one night. I saw them sleeping. They've lost a father." Luci's hand stopped its rhythmic stroke. She listened intently to what he was not saying, what he couldn't possibly know. Was he mourning his own loss to them? She fought the sharp edge of guilt when she thought of Erik's son and daughter. He rose softly from her embrace and walked away from her examination of him. He wiped his face roughly with his hands and went to pour another drink. Lucianna stayed his hand before he could raise the glass to his lips.

"Not that way, Erik. That's the coward's way."

For a moment, he looked angry. Then he placed the glass down next to the bottle. "Was it worse when I drank?"

Luci momentarily didn't understand his question. Then she remembered that she had unwittingly forced him to assume Don Ponzio's history when she called him husband and gave him the Fiortino surname. She answered ambiguously, "Drink changes some people."

"Do you mean," Erik asked, a note of hope in his voice, "that it was when I was drinking that I did those things …?" The words, the exact words, choked him; he pushed them away for they came wrapped in images of blood and violence, of the death of innocents, the perverted twisting and marring of flesh. "If that's the case, then I can swear never to drink." The night he spent at Roderigo's came flashing back across his memory. He didn't have to be a monster. He could trap it, seal it in a bottle, keep himself safe from the monster.

"Erik, did you do something tonight that made you think about your past?" He wouldn't, couldn't, have hurt Meg. But he was acting so strangely Luci didn't understand what was going through his mind.

He stiffened at the thought of Meg. It all came back in a rush to him, and he knew he'd have to act upon his decision. To save Meg. To let her have a life. To guard her children from the consequences of shame, scandal, and dishonor. He'd not make the woman he loved a whore!

"We're leaving tomorrow. I've already spoken with Luigi."

"Leaving?" She'd misunderstood. He was upset because he dreaded telling her that he was running off with Meg?

He must have seen the disconcerted look on Lucianna's face. "You and I are returning home." He chose the word, "home," purposefully. He must get used to it. He would make his mind accept that home was with Lucianna, his future was with Lucianna, any hope for happiness or comfort was with … He would need to discipline himself. Perhaps over time it would be true. If he said it enough, if he forced his thoughts enough, they would bend, they must, and take the shape he willed them to take.

"You and I?" She considered this for a moment. He had come back to her. But if it were so, it wasn't by his choice alone. It was because he couldn't go with Meg. "Erik, if you've come back, it must be to me." Her voice was cold and firm.

He met her eyes and understood the challenge she was making. She wouldn't accept him on just any terms. Her eyes blazed with jealous anger, righteous revenge. He'd need to bow to her demands. He had known that, too. He was prepared to agree to her stipulations. If he had no life without Meg, it mattered little the blood Lucianna would squeeze from him.

"You must come back to me as a real husband, Erik."

He couldn't sustain her gaze. It burned his eyes. He looked away, his heart pounding, but he answered calmly in resignation, "I know that."

She waited for him to say it. She wanted it perfectly understood between them. She wouldn't live with him like a brother, nor like a friend.

Her silence pushed him to it. He resisted only slightly. "I'll come back. You are my wife."

"Swear to me. Swear that you'll keep to my bed and no other!"

He clenched his jaw tightly but refrained from answering in anger. "I swear. I swear to anything you want." The desperation of his act began to sink in for him. He had given up any hope of being with Meg. He was raw and bleeding inside. Like a demented demon Lucianna—all fire and darkness—wrenched from him the words that would forever cut his soul in two! Desperately he repeated, "I swear!"

Satisfied, Lucianna reached out and took his hand. "Come with me, Erik. It's late. You're tired." She gently led him to her bedroom. At the door, she felt his reluctance. She paused and considered. She could be merciful. She had time now. The rest of their lives. She dropped his hand and kissed him softly on the lips. "Go. Go sleep." She went inside and closed the door, leaving him in the hallway. She'd give him this one night to grieve. Tomorrow would be soon enough.

He's gone! She's taken him, and I'll never see him again. I asked Raoul to go talk with him the very next morning. I begged him to explain, to bring him to me so that I could explain. He had run off so quickly, I couldn't tell him that I was crying from relief. I was sure that he had been burned in the fire. I thought his whole face might be disfigured. When he took the mask off, I was overwhelmed by my emotions. But he's so misunderstood. I found the mask in the street just outside the graveyard and no sign of Erik at all.

Raoul went, but said there's no one in the apartment. He found the owner who said Lucianna and Erik departed today. They've given up the rooms without notice. They left instructions for their possessions to be sent afterwards. Raoul said that there was some talk of a manor on an island off the coast of the Adriatic. That's where she took him after the fire! I've begged Raoul to do something. Even the boy is gone. Supposedly Erik and Lucianna took him with the other servants.

Later in the morning a messenger brought me a note. It was from Erik.

✿

Dearest Signora Costanzi,

My wife and I have decided to retire from society to our manor house in the east. I have enjoyed the privilege of sharing many pleasant moments in your company. We will always share our love of music. I hope to hear you again some day on the stage, perhaps in an opera of my own composition. Please know that it is duty that takes me away from Rome, for I feel that my greatest happiness has been here in this city. My deepest regards, from your obedient servant,

Sig. Erik Fiortino

Such a formal letter. Raoul received a letter, too, in which he was perhaps a little more open. He doesn't want us to follow him. He explained that he had decided before we met last night that he was going to take his leave of me. He doesn't want to put my reputation into jeopardy. How can I fight his sense of duty?

Raoul doesn't know what we should do. Erik made it clear in the letter that this is what he wants. That may be true, but he's acting under false premises. He thinks he's protecting me!

I had come so close to telling François and Laurette that their father was still alive. It had only been a horrible mistake. I fear Laurette is so young that she's begun to forget Erik. François has gotten wind of some of what's been happening, but he doesn't have the courage to ask me. We've kept him away from the theater, but I found him standing outside the library one night after Raoul, Christine, Marcelo, Maman, and I were talking about Erik. I don't know what to do!

CHAPTER 8

⚜

To Sleep, Perchance to Dream

Suddenly an old man came drifting
Toward us in a boat, his hair white with
decades.
"Woe to you," he began shouting,

Give up all hope of heaven, you depraved
shades:
I come to lead you to that other shore
Where fire and ice abound, and dark pervades.

The Divine Comedy, Inferno, Dante Alighieri

She appeared in his dreams, uninvited. She sang to him and reached out to him from the darkness. Buried in a pine box, it was her face that he first saw when the lid was pulled away. She lay naked in his arms in a thousand different ways. He watched her nurse her baby girl. He found her near a piano, singing. He caught her sneaking through his papers, reading his compositions, humming the melody, and hiding the sheets behind her skirts at the sound of his entrance. She danced in his arms, dressed like an executed queen, and led him to a secret room where they made love. She cried in a garden for him. He couldn't check the rush of images, the dream of Meg, no matter how many times he went to sleep holding Lucianna and willing himself to dream of her. It was Meg's face, Meg's body and laugh and touch and voice and tears and ecstasy that vanquished his will and erased Lucianna from his mind and soul. So he tried to remember the scene in the cemetery and as he lay in that semi-conscious state of half sleep when we still have some control over our escaping thoughts, he forced himself to see, over and over again, her look of horror when she saw his unmasked face. Even this wasn't enough to dispel her power over his dreams. So he imagined the scene again with alternative endings:

her laughing at him, running from him in terror, screaming at him to go away, calling him a monster, begging him not to hurt her. If he could imagine her cruel or repulsed by him, surely he would stop wanting her, dreaming of her, waking in a sweat, aroused by her. A nagging doubt pursued him into wakefulness. What if he hadn't run away from her in the cemetery? He had given her no warning, no preparation for what she was to see. Would her initial reaction have given way to acceptance? And if it had, did it mean that she could bear to look at him and that she would look at him with the same love and desire she had before? Would he have been content with her friendship, if love and desire had died along with all hope that night among the dead? Lucianna had never looked at him in that way. She loved him. Meg had not loved him. And even so, even after he had put Meg on trial, judged her, and sentenced her to oblivion, she still haunted his dreams and filled his waking moments with longing.

He woke to the smell of salt water. He sat up, careful not to wake her. In the morning light he examined the teeth marks she had left on his arm. He rubbed his hand over the others she had made last night on his neck and shoulders. He hadn't complained. He was used to her violent possession of his body. He understood why she did it. The pain made him look at her, planted him in the here and now, forced him to see with whom he was making love. "See me," she demanded, fighting against the ghost that lay in the bed between them.

He had done everything he could to exorcise Meg. He had clamped his teeth on his tongue, drawing salty blood, to stop her name before it rose from his throat even while he screamed it inside his mind. He tried to focus on Lucianna instead of closing his eyes to imagine Meg. He tried, but again and again he'd drift away from her. This was by far the most painful aspect of their love making—far worse than the passionate kisses, her teeth on his skin, nails sunk into his flesh. Eventually he'd succeed in making Lucianna forget her vigilance, by softly stroking and gently possessing her. Only then could he close his eyes and give in to the rising excitement, the ardor, in their bodies. He tried to keep his mind on the language of touch, on some dark, imageless center of sensation, but inevitably when the flood of intense pleasure washed over him, obliterating Lucianna completely from his mind, it was Meg's face he saw, her name that was confused with his inward cry of passion. Then he would sink beside his wife, his eyes tightly shut, laboring to control his breathing, to fight the rise of desperation and pain, holding to that other moment of intense release and abandon, putting off the time when Lucianna would again claim him, bringing him back to her. Inwardly mourning his loss, he would still feel a tenderness for the woman—the flesh and blood woman whose body he could touch and hold without imagining it—that lay sated in his arms. Slowly he'd whisper goodbye to Meg and smile sadly at Lucianna. Eventually, he prayed, eventually his wife might wash away his longing for the other woman.

As his weight lifted from the mattress, Lucianna rolled toward him and stretched luxuriously against the wrinkled sheet. She loved watching him rise, naked, gathering himself afresh to face the morning. She ran her hand over her body, glorying in its hum of satisfaction while she watched Erik pull on his breeches, pour water into the basin, and splash his face in preparation to shave. She had told him Luigi would be happy to shave him if he liked, but Erik waved the suggestion away. He was uncomfortable having a personal manservant, insisted on dressing himself, even when doing so might take longer.

She noticed Erik stretching stiff muscles and recalled his gasp of pain the night before when she bit him hard enough to draw blood. He had jerked his arm away from her mouth, and for a moment she thought he might strike her. He took her savagely, and she responded in kind. She thought, in satisfaction, that she had angered him more than hurt him. Again she vowed to herself to control the urge to punish him. She broke it regularly but expected that in time her anger would fade and she'd come to trust him.

She had purposefully put temptation in his path. Natala, the little scullery maid that had once drawn Erik's attention due to her slight resemblance to Meg, was promoted to upstairs maid assuring that Erik and she would cross paths occasionally. Lucianna had been pleased to note that Erik cast only a curious glance in her direction the first time Natala entered to bring fresh linen for the bed. After that, he seemed to ignore her completely. He was keeping his promise. And if all went well, soon she'd be able to seal their relationship with a bond that would surely bring her his love.

"Would you like to go down to the water today? We could bathe."

He dried his face, grimacing at his reflection in the small shaving mirror, as he thought about the excursion. He had hoped to lock himself away in the music room to play and to compose. However in the last month or so since their return to the island, he hadn't been able to write. Nothing came to him except the repeated sounds of a lament he'd already written which at the last moment he cut from his opera, *The Stranger*. Lacking inspiration, he agreed to Lucianna's plans. If she didn't mind his silences, he rather enjoyed accompanying her on these outings. He became uncomfortable only when she seemed bent on making him join in on long, involved discussions.

"We'll get a picnic lunch from the kitchen and walk down the cliff path if that's all right with you?"

Erik looked over his shoulder at his wife. She sat up in the bed, the sheet barely draped around her chest, the swell of her breasts evident; her dark auburn hair, alive, stroking her white skin, seemed to move of its own volition. He felt her beauty awaken drowsy desire. He was tempted to undress and pull her sheet from her and take her in his arms, but on his terms, forcing her to yield to him. Arousal stirred him, but when the maid knocked softly at the door with a breakfast tray, he brushed the desire aside, puzzled and unsettled by its unexpected urgency.

They agreed to meet later in the mid afternoon to go to the beach.

In the meantime, Erik wandered about the house unable to settle on any gainful employment of his time. He thought that sooner or later he'd need to play a more active role as lord of several estates to make sure his properties were being well managed and the tenants prosperous and content. But he had no talent, he feared, at administration. He was a musician, and the other work struck him as tedious. He was somewhat more enthusiastic about his plans to redesign the manor. He didn't like the current layout of rooms and felt it would improve with a grander entrance, a solarium, and certainly the music room was woefully inadequate to his needs.

Finally the hour struck that they had agreed to go to the beach. They rode to the cliff path, hobbled the horses, although Erik joked that it would hardly be a loss if Diavolo Rosso wandered too close to the cliff edge and fell to his death on the rocks below. Both Lucianna and Erik had worked up a sweat by the time they reached the beach. They changed in the bathhouses constructed for the season and walked out into the surf. Erik wasn't a confident swimmer, but Lucianna was actually quite proficient at several strokes, in spite of the ballooning garments she was forced by propriety to wear. Erik tentatively stretched out and floated, enjoying the feel of the water. The waves began to pick up some force, and it became more difficult for Erik to lie back on the surface of the water. Nor could he see Lucianna who had gone out beyond the breakers to swim. Each time he searched for her on the horizon a wave would come crashing into his face. An unexpectedly high wave knocked him off his feet. Suddenly under the water, everything was muffled; a hum, low and deep, surrounded him. Momentarily, he couldn't tell which way lay the surface of the water. The tow dragged him, making it hard to regain his footing. When he finally stood, gasping for air, he looked around him, unable to see Lucianna at all. Another wave came crashing into him. This time he let it wash over him, pulling at his body in its unforgiving embrace. He searched the horizon for her. Lucianna was nowhere to be seen. Panic threatened him. He pushed himself out farther past the breakers until the sandy bottom gave way. He didn't like being this far from the shore, but he continued to swim awkwardly out toward the widening expanse of the cove. He paused long enough to call out her name. Hearing no response, he screamed it frantically out against the wind! Then he thought he saw her. She lay, farther out, in the water. She bobbed in and out of view with the rise and fall of the sea. He made his way to her, risking exhaustion, and grabbed her by the arm. She lifted her face startled, struggling to get away from him, until she saw that it was he and not some denizen of the deep that had seized her.

"I thought you'd drowned," he managed to yell above the sound of the sea. His fear had given way to anger. He was having difficulty keeping his head above the waves that were picking up in speed and volume.

She wanted to laugh, but she saw the genuine concern in his eyes. She turned to swim in toward the shore. Erik followed. Sluggishly, they walked out from the waves onto the sandy beach where Erik fell to his knees, sucking at the air. The salt water dripped from his hair obscuring his expression. Lucianna dropped to his side and was about to say something when he grabbed her roughly around the waist trapping both her arms tightly against her sides. He kissed her violently, pressing his mouth against hers. They both tasted the brackish water and smelled the fear and longing.

Without a word, he lifted her and carried her to the blanket they had spread in the shelter of the rocks. He placed her there, on the pebbly sand, and fell heavily on top of her. The wet clothes between them felt cold and spongy. His fingers worked expertly to find the opening in the garments, and then he took her. She gasped with the ferocious seizure of her body, his chest crushed the air from her lungs, and she thought she was drowning on land under the waves of his passion. She wrapped her limbs around his and trusted him to bring her to shore. The cry in his throat was short and intense, and when she heard it, she felt her body quiver exultantly in his unforgiving grasp. They lay like that until the sun had dried the sea water and sweat on their bodies and their skin began to tighten under the scorched residue of salt.

Even then, Erik held Lucianna.

"I remember," he whispered almost fearfully.

Lucianna held her breath.

"I remember you were fleeing from me or I was chasing after you. You were on a small grey and white mare. You were dressed like a boy." He grew more excited as he saw the gleam of recognition in Lucianna's eyes. "It was dark. I remember you veered off the road and recklessly plunged into the forest. I thought you were going to break your neck! I followed at a gallop in your wake. I came upon you in a small clearing, and the moon shone on your hair—it had come loose from the wind—and it glowed as if the light were coming from its strands. You looked like some pixie or fairy, some magical creature. I remember it, Luci. I remember! Tell me, tell me it's not my imagination. It's not just some dream I've had. It happened, didn't it?"

He could tell from her reaction that it had indeed. It wasn't fancy. It was a memory.

"Did I ... did I act on my desire, Luci? I can't remember beyond the moment I was standing behind you, and you were in the moonlight. The memory came to me when I lost you in the water. It came without warning. And I thought ... I thought I've just remembered her, and now she's lost to me. I thought you'd drowned. And you had just become ... real ... to me." He was choking up and paused to swallow several times before he could go on. "When we got to shore, the memory of my desire hit me like a blow, and I had to have you!"

She held him tightly as he dealt with the strong emotions that were wracking his body. He held her face in his hands, looking at her as if she might disappear and kissing her cheeks and lips, then he pressed her face to his shoulder and hugged her tightly again.

Lucianna felt warmed in his love. What he remembered had been so innocent. Two strangers exchanging a few words, casually flirting in an unexpected encounter in the middle of the night in a stable. He hadn't been able to sleep, nor had she. He was grooming her mare when she stole upon him in the stable. She was struck by the fact that he wore a mask. It seemed a part of him, and she asked no questions, and he offered no explanation. She teased him, invited him for a ride, didn't even know who he was! They cantered out of the village and soon were riding at a gallop down the road. All she wanted was freedom. She was doomed to a loveless marriage with a man whose reputation for cruelty and debauchery was already a legend. One last night of pure abandon with a stranger who wore a mask! When he followed, she felt her blood race and an idea, a daring idea, took hold of her. She wanted this faceless stranger to take her deep into the woods and make love to her. She wanted him, not her future husband, Ponzio Fiortino, to be the first man to touch her. And he *had* followed her—she felt sure he lusted after her—but he never touched her. She supposed that when he left her in the forest, he returned to his room at the inn.

Perhaps he woke Meg in the night when he entered and made love to her instead.

But he remembered part of the event, and it made her real to him in a new way. If he remembered their encounter, would other memories soon come to the surface of his mind? Would he soon remember Meg and who she was? That would mean the end of her own hold over him, unless she found some other way to bind him to her. And miraculously she may already have found it.

After dinner, that evening she told him. She told him that she had not had her courses since they returned to the island. She told him that she was with child.

She's with child, my child, a son or a daughter, I am thrilled and frightened beyond belief, a child, a living soul that is connected invisibly to me and to Lucianna, a soul whose tie to me cannot be taken away, I have never seen such happiness, Lucianna is filled with love, it surrounds her, glows, hums and affects all who come near her, I feel giddy when close to her, she has devoted herself to furnishing a nursery for our child, the child that will comfort her for the loss of the babies that died in her womb, she has sent for the best fabrics, she knits clothes for the baby and shows them to me, they are so small that I think they can't possibly fit, the child can't be so small, can it? I grow strangely shy around her now that I know she carries our child in her body, she chides me that it is well protected, but I worry each time I touch her that I am harming him, I would avoid touching her except that she laughs at me and pulls me to her, she says that I will watch her body change and enjoy it, she doesn't fear me, I thought she might, I thought she'd worry that I would harm her and the child as I did before, the before which I still don't remember, I am quiet when she talks of the future, my mind is constantly drawn back to the black void of my past, I had thought the memories would come quickly after the first one, but nothing, nothing but swirls of chaotic images that have nothing to do with my past and of which I can make no sense at all, if they didn't often include music I would find in them no relationship to my history, the history that Lucianna has told me, in one image that keeps haunting me I am buried alive, but its spell might be traced to horror stories of premature burial such as the one by the American writer Poe, I scream and scream for someone to release me, when I have had this dream it takes Lucianna a long time to convince me that I'm safe, the other dream is stranger still, it seems mundane, I see myself in a room which is not a room but a cave or an underground vault, the sound of water is all around me, candles are lit, I am sitting at an organ in the middle of the cave, I have the strong impression that this is my home, surrounded by mirrors hidden

*behind long, velvet drapes, I am playing, I wear a mask and a dark wig which give
me the appearance of some spectral lord in a gothic romance, a woman stands in
the shadows behind me, it isn't Lucianna, nor is it Meg, she sings and I seem to be
directing her, when this image passes through my mind I feel quite anxious, as if I
were in the wrong place, as if I have forgotten something quite urgent, when will
my true memories come back? will I have to meet my child with this void still in
my mind?*

∾

My dear friend, Erik,

I was puzzled by your precipitous departure and would hope that it is not due to
some urgent and pressing problem. I believe there are matters of some importance that I would like very much to discuss with you. If it were possible for us to
meet again, soon, I feel the meeting would be beneficial to us both.

The season is not the same without you. The Teatro dell'Opera is considering
restaging your opera if Don Marcelo can get the release he needs from Don
Rossi at the Teatro Regio. It is still playing to packed houses, sold out on every
occasion. Are you writing something new?

Forgive the indiscretion, but I would hope that you and I have become friends,
and friends do help one another. I think it is in your best interests to return to
Rome, as soon as you can arrange to do so. Perhaps Signora Fiortino tires of the
society in Rome and would prefer that you alone return? That would allow you to
devote yourself, fulltime, to a lucrative and productive career in the opera. You
may count on me to assist you in any way you see fit. I would be willing to
accompany you to Rome should you wish my company.

Your friend and obedient servant,

Raoul, Count de Chagny

**I have thought that perhaps writing might help me see how unreasonable
my fears are. Lucianna complains of tenderness in her abdomen. She says it's
nothing to be concerned about. But she has lost a good deal of weight. Last
night I was holding her, and I could feel her bones; her ribs and her hip bones
jut out under the skin. I know that this was not the case even as recently as a
few weeks ago! She's sleeping long hours, going to bed early and remaining in
bed until nearly midday. Is this normal? She doesn't look healthy. Her skin
color is sallow. I want to send for a doctor to examine her.**

Raoul writes. He's careful not to mention Meg. I have written him only to tell him I am well. I haven't mentioned the baby. Whatever I write him, I'm sure he will share with Meg. It feels wrong to tell her about the child. I feel ashamed and have no idea why I should feel so.

Since Raoul's letter, I think constantly of Meg. I'm a scoundrel with no possibility of redemption. Lucianna stayed in bed all day. If she recovers from whatever this is, I swear I will find some way to rid myself of these improper longings. I pray each day that my memories return. I'm sure that they will make a great difference in our lives. If I can remember our past together, my love for Lucianna would be real, stronger. More and more I'm convinced that the hunting accident that destroyed half of my face embittered me, changed me, made me hateful and sadistic. I won't let that happen again. I'll recover the love we had before I was mutilated. Meg will be a flight of fancy, an insignificant flirtation. Even as I write this, I know somehow that I'm trying to deceive myself. Meg is more than that, much more.

Luci didn't get up again. I've sent for the doctor. What will I do if anything happens to her?

It's cruel, too cruel. There is no God! There's only death.

I have not had the courage to write for days. She languishes. There is no child. She harbors death in her womb. The doctor says the growth is malignant. It saps her strength, consumes her with each passing day. He offered to tell Luci that she's dying. I told him that the truth should come from me. But I've spent hours in my room, trying to think of the words to tell her. I can do nothing to save her.

Erik gave Luci the medicine. It would ease her pain. She was deathly pale and shivering in spite of the fire blazing in the chimney and the mound of blankets heaped across her body. He had lain next to her on the bed, dozing on occasion, waking whenever she moved or called out.

"Luci, can you take more of the broth?"

"No," she answered in a whisper.

"You need to keep your strength up." He wondered why he would say this. Why delay the inevitable? Watching her body eaten away by the foreign thing growing inside her, Erik now prayed the end would come soon.

"I've lost the baby, haven't I?"

He squeezed his eyes shut against the shock that she had again forgotten that she was dying. He didn't think he could bear to tell her again what he had told her several times over the last week.

He smoothed her dulled hair away from her face. He put his arms around her and drew her close. "Luci," he whispered tenderly in her ear, "there wasn't a baby. It was, is, something else, something wrong. The doctor left medicine to help the pain."

"I'm going to die, aren't I?"

"You're very, very ill, Luci. You must rest."

"Yes. I'll rest."

"Mario, tell the footman to go for the priest."

"Erik, is the baby all right?"

...

...

"Yes, Luci. He's fine."

Erik held her hand and stroked her face. The doctor told him it would be any time now. She had been delirious through the night, but after the priest's visit she seemed more peaceful. All day she had come in and out of consciousness, sometimes making sense, sometimes talking wildly of their child, telling Erik to take care of the baby. He no longer had the strength to explain to her that there was no baby. He assured her that he would take care of everything. Under the influence of the laudanum, she had finally dropped off to a relatively calm sleep and had been that way for a while.

She stirred under his caress and opened her eyes. When she saw Erik by her side, she smiled. She seemed almost lucid. Her hand lifted but fell back onto the covers. "Why are you wearing that mask, Erik? We're home," she chided him.

He had forgotten he wore it. He glanced over his shoulder at the doctor who quietly left the room. Erik took the mask off and laid it on the bed beside Lucianna. "There have been a number of visitors. I thought it best to wear it."

"You shouldn't ever have to." She looked at him so tenderly that he couldn't stop the trembling of his lips. He had walked about the manor in a daze, occupying himself with the business at hand, keeping himself at several removes from the reality of Lucianna's impending death. There had been instructions to be given to the staff, the priest to be sent for, accommodations for him and the doctor. The constant activity surrounding the sickbed had kept him in control, calm and purposeful. Everything to be done was done; there was nothing more to do but wait. He bent his head, crying softly against her hand. Her fingers lightly touched the skin of his face, unconcerned that it was the rough, twisted surface of his disfigurement.

Emotionally exhausted, he could not silence his selfish fear. Who would ever look at him again with love?

Her voice rose barely over a whisper. "You almost died then. You woke and called me your wife." She was talking about the fire. Her eyes lit with a sudden passion. "Erik, what would you do for love? Is there anything that you wouldn't do for love?"

Erik thought of Meg, and his chest tightened. Had his act been an act of love? If he loved her, why had he left her? Should he have forsaken propriety and honor, flaunted the mores of society, and asked her to run away with him? Would she have been able to abandon her children or would she have dragged them down to the gutter with her and her lover? He thought his choice to forsake Meg was the true act of love. That was why he had taken off the mask and shown her his face. Would she have risked everything she had for a man so disfigured that he had to hide behind a mask? Lucianna was watching him closely as if his answer could somehow save her.

"I would do anything to make you well, Luci." He had chosen to return with her to the island. He had found a kind of peace, even love, with her. He had enjoyed the calm of resignation. When he thought she was with child, he had taken it as a sign that he had been right to choose Luci. Now she was dying, and something was tearing inside him. He didn't want her to die. She was the only one who remembered for him!

"Erik, I love you. I've always loved you. Please forgive me. Remember that I love you. Don't hate me." She fell silent, exhausted by the effort, but Erik could see she was troubled. She fought to go on. He bent closer to her and kissed her cheeks. They were cold and clammy. Death had already begun his advance. Before he could pull away, she whispered earnestly, "I was wrong to do it. I know that now. I can't … I don't have the strength. There's no time. You must swear you will bury me next to my children. Take me to the Fiortino mansion. You'll see. You'll know."

Her boney hand clutched the collar of his shirt until he agreed to do as she asked. "Of course. I swear. I'll take you there. You'll rest better next to the children."

"My children, my lost babies." And then she smiled as if at rest. He thought she still spoke softly, but it didn't make sense. "Find the children, Erik, find your babes." She closed her eyes, then, and he could hear her labored breathing. A soft rattling of air in her chest continued for some moments more, and then nothing. There was no sound, no breathing, no heartbeat, but his own.

Luigi had gone before to make the arrangements. The grave was waiting. It had taken two days to transport Lucianna's remains to the Fiortino estate. Erik had traveled with the coffin. Lucianna lay in a closed casket in the parlor. The burial should not be delayed any longer. The funeral must be the next morning. Erik wanted to visit the plot. Tomorrow she'd be laid to rest next to the small graves of Rafael and Sophia. Neither child had seen the light of day or taken a first breath. Both had died in the womb, but she had given them names and held them for a moment before they were again placed in darkness. Erik supposed that he, too, would one day take his place beside them.

The grounds were kept free of weeds, the gravestones cleaned and polished to a glistening, smooth sheen. Luigi had meant to accompany him, but Erik had declined his offer, asking only for some directions on how to find the site. Under a huge elm, he saw the upturned soil from the freshly dug grave. To the side, the children's markers were decorated with lambs and cherubs, their names and the one year—birth and death—carved in the center. Lucianna's gravestone was in place; the stonemason had carved the only missing detail, the year of her death. The one next to hers, of identical size and material, was his. They had both been commissioned years ago, as was the custom, and each one awaited the arrival of the occupant whose name was etched on its surface. Erik felt a morbid fascination with the confrontation of his own marble gravestone and drew near to read the inscription. The stone was elegantly carved with the Fiortino insignia. However, instead of his own name he read, with growing confusion and alarm, the epitaph of another: "Here lie the mortal remains of Ponzio Florencio Fiortino. May his soul find peace." Erik read it over several times as if he could somehow make sense of it. The grave was indeed occupied, for the date of death indicated that the man lying there had been dead these past four years. Who was this man, this Fiortino, who lay in the sepulcher where he should eventually rest?

Erik turned to Lucianna's stone and read there an inscription in the same style. But it, too, mocked him with its cryptic message. Baffled, he staggered away from the gravestones. It made no sense! Yet the stone had been etched years ago. The recently carved date of her death clearly was new—its marks sharp and clean—whereas the rest of the writing in the epitaph was smoothed and weathered by exposure to the elements and the passing of time itself.

Behind him he heard someone approach. It was Luigi who had followed in spite of Erik's instructions.

"What? What in the name of God is the meaning of this?" Erik pointed at the epitaph before him. "It says 'Here lie the mortal remains of Lucianna Maria, Wife of Ponzio Florencio Fiortino.' And this Ponzio Florencio Fiortino, her husband, is buried next to her."

"Signore, she couldn't tell you. She was too weak in the end."

"Tell me what? Why is this man's name inscribed on my gravestone?"

"Because Don Ponzio was her husband."

"Her husband? But I don't understand. She was married before? She was married to someone in my family? She told me I had no siblings, no cousins, no one. It's impossible. Lucianna and I have been married for the last several years."

"No, Signore. Her only husband lies buried there under that gravestone. You're not who you think you are. You were never Signora Fiortino's husband. Nor are you a Fiortino."

Erik stood, slack jawed, staring at the man. "How?"

"You lost your memory in the fire, and Donna Lucianna let you believe …"

Before he could finish, Erik rushed off searching through the graveyard. There was no stone that bore his name. He ran back to Lucianna's and then to the children's markers. They were not his!

As if he were explaining it to himself, Erik muttered, "She was widowed. The date is more than four years old. She gave me *his* name. No, not completely, only the surname which she herself bore. She called me Erik, not Ponzio. She knew my name. She must have known who I was … before the fire."

Luigi silently watched Erik.

"Do you know who I am?"

"No, Signore," he lied. He wanted nothing to do with the fraud his mistress had perpetrated. He would leave the Fiortino estates and seek employment elsewhere just as Gretta had when she saw her mistress take ill.

"My name. Did she ever mention another name for me?" was all that Erik managed to say.

"Erik was the only name I ever heard Donna Lucianna use. You had no other."

"No name?" Erik didn't exist. He had no right to be here. "What else? Do you know anything else about me? About who I was?"

"Nothing, Signore. Donna Lucianna dismissed most of the staff and hired new servants shortly after she reopened the estate a few years ago. What I've told you is all that I know." He pitied the man, but surely he'd eventually find out the truth. If he returned to Rome, he'd be once more among old acquaintances and family.

Nothing! He had nothing! The past was a lie. He had no name, no past.

It took some time before Erik realized Luigi was waiting for his instructions. "After the funeral, I'll be leaving. I'll take Mario with me. A modest sum of money. Nothing else. Would you be kind enough to make the arrangements?" The change in address was not lost on Luigi. Don Erik was not his master. He was not Sig. Fiortino.

"I'm sure Donna Lucianna would want you to have …"

"The properties belonged to him, not to her." He interrupted pointing in the direction of Don Ponzio's gravestone. "He's the one the servants were whispering about. Those were his children?" Erik didn't need Luigi to answer. He already knew the answer. "I'll be in my room. Don't disturb me until it's time for the burial. Have a carriage ready to leave immediately after the service."

In his borrowed room, Erik stood, struggling to breathe. In a low hum, he repeated the name of Ponzio Fiortino, a name belonging to a man he'd never known. Although he faced the open window, the memory of letters carved like a dry wound in glittering marble blotted out the sight of the vineyards, the rolling hills in the distance. Erik ripped open the collar of his shirt, heedless of the spray of buttons that skittered across the floor. Sweat trickled along the sides of his face, pooled at the base of his throat. He stripped the linen shirt, pulling his arms free, and threw it to the floor beside his discarded mask. His chest heaved as he gulped at the air, fought the urge to bash his body against the wall.

A ball, a gala, a dance, they had met. All eyes upon them. Educated in the best of schools. But never a name mentioned. No relatives. No father to call him son, no mother to welcome him. Beloved. Handsome.

The portrait. She had shown him the portrait. He was the man in the painting. That had been his face. But when had she painted him? She must have known him. He had asked her to put the painting away. The handsome face disturbed him, made him feel ugly, inside and out. He couldn't tell why it unsettled him.

His heart raced. It had all been a lie. He was not the man in the portrait. What if the resemblance was just a coincidence? She had told him the figure in the painting was he—unblemished, whole. He had accepted that statement just as he had accepted that his name was Erik Fiortino. *Half truths, like his face.*

She had told him nothing. Each day and each night, a lie. Every touch had been part of a charade, a puppet show, and she had held the strings.

Erik raised his fists to the sides of his face, squeezed his eyes tightly shut. Teeth bared in a painful grimace, he stifled the animal scream surging from deep inside him. Blindly he leaned against the massive wardrobe, pressing his forehead into the wood until the pressure turned to pain and the silent beast inside him backed into its den.

Cedar wood and varnish, the scent wafted up his nostrils in deep and steady waves. The dense anger of taut muscles receded. He opened his eyes. Slowly he braced himself against the smoothed wood and pushed himself back. Polished to a high gloss, the wood grain ran vertically, a path his eye followed, pausing at the darkened knots, the strange striations in the material that had once lived. His hand stroked the surface as if it could soothe a long forgotten pain.

He opened the door of the wardrobe, knowing that inside was a mirror. Warm wood gave way to cold, silvered glass. The room receded in the background, a mocking illusion of depth. Erik could see the reflected image of the door he had locked when he returned from the graves to hide away from the strangers that peopled Lucianna's world. Standing inches from the glass, his figure blotted out everything else. His eyes skimmed over his own image, noted the powerful strength of strained and clenched muscles, the stance of his firmly set feet, the broad scope of his shoulders, the dark hair that shadowed his bare chest. He lingered on the outline of his body until he could resist no longer and let his eyes travel to his unmasked face.

As if he had never seen it before, he grabbed the edge of the door to steady himself. He stepped even closer. His breath fogged the cool surface but did not hide the ugliness he saw reflected back at him. Lies, she had told him lies. The ravaged, misshapen side of his face was not the result of a hunting accident. He had never believed her story. Badly healed flesh did not rise and fall, pucker the skin, drag down the eye. With all the certainty he could muster, he knew that the face that glared at him from the polished glass had always been his. There had been no accident.

What he saw in the mirror—the visage that strangled his heart—was the only truth he had.

The next day Erik lingered at a distance while Lucianna's coffin was lowered into the grave. He ignored the stares of the few who had come to pay their last respects. Lucianna's parents were deceased, and her family had long ago forgotten her. The only relative of the Fiortinos Erik had known was Don Carlo who had conveniently booked passage to Calcutta upon hearing news of Lucianna's death. After the mourners dispersed, Erik went to Lucianna Maria Fiortino's grave. There he placed the single rose he had cut from the garden. On the graves of the children, he laid a handful of wildflowers—sprigs of white lace, buds of pink, drops of yellow tears—he had collected along the way.

Don Marcelo read the note several times, before the words sank in. "Show Don Erik to the parlor. Tell him that I'll join him presently." There was no time to contact the others. Only Madeleine was at home in the garden with the children. He sent for her, passed her the note wordlessly, and led her down to the parlor.

Erik stood examining the piano, his fingers hovering over the immaculate keys. Madeleine couldn't breathe she was so relieved to see he was apparently well. He turned when he heard them enter and bowed low. He was wearing a mask. His coat had been brushed, but it was obvious that he had worn it for several days, perhaps weeks. The cuffs of his shirt were lightly tinged by dust and soot, but his hair, face, and hands had recently been scrubbed clean.

Neither Don Marcelo nor Madeleine remarked on his long absence. Don Marcelo asked Erik to sit and told him he was pleased that he had come to visit.

"Signore Fiortino, I ..." Don Marcelo began to say, but Erik rushed to interrupt him.

"Excuse me, but I beg to correct you, Don Marcelo. I am not Signore Fiortino. I have taken the pseudonym under which I've worked in the past, Henri Fournier; it will serve as well as any other name."

Erik's statement took Don Marcelo by surprise. But when his guest offered no further explanation, the older man proceeded to say in a casual vein, "I hadn't heard of your arrival. Have you and Signora Fiortino returned to your previous apartments?"

"My ... Signora Fiortino has died. I buried her next to her husband four days ago. It's a complicated situation, I'm afraid. I've been traveling ever since. I will get to the point, Don Marcelo. You know my work. I'm in need of a position. Since I've come to realize that I have no legal status—not even a name I can say is mine—I'm basically left without the means to support myself." Until this moment, Erik had maintained eye contact with Don Marcelo, but now his voice faltered, and he lowered his eyes in embarrassment.

Let him think that I was a gigolo, and my mistress's death has justifiably left me in penury.

Madeleine without thinking went to him and placed her hand on his. He looked up in surprise. His eyes were bloodshot, perhaps from fatigue and surely from strong emotion. In their cool green depths, Madeleine saw that he was haunted by loss and disappointment. Erik didn't remove his hand from underneath hers, but he seemed to be fighting to maintain his composure. Don Marcelo waited for him to regain his equanimity and go on. Erik turned his hand slightly so that Madeleine's lay inside his palm. He brought it to his lips and softly kissed it.

"You're very kind, Signora. I'm all right now." Then he straightened his back noticeably so as to address Don Marcelo. "I prefer not to elaborate on my recent or present circumstances. I hope that I may ask you to refrain from delving into the matter. If you have some work that ..."

"Don Erik, it would be my greatest joy to have you join my company at the opera house. I admire your work tremendously and would be glad were you to accept the artistic directorship of the theater."

He had not expected so much from Don Marcelo. At best, he assumed Don Marcelo might advance him some funds against a commission for some minor compositions to be used during the season, perhaps as entertainment during the intermissions. He was stunned by the patron's offer, especially after the scandalous nature of his current situation. He was without connections, had admitted to living with a woman who was not his wife and to having fraudulently presented himself as someone he was not.

"You can't be serious, Don Marcelo."

"I assure you I am."

He would work with Meg. He would be in charge of bringing to the stage an entire opera, have a voice in which works were chosen, the assignment of roles. And not one opera, but a whole series of operas throughout the season. It seemed an incredible dream. And Meg would be the diva. Meg and he would work together. But he would have to live behind the mask. She would know what it hid. Meg would remember seeing behind it. She would look at him and recall his face! He couldn't!

He stood abruptly, apologizing profusely, and headed for the door.

"Don Erik, what is the meaning of this?" Signore Costanzi rose in consternation at Erik's sudden distress.

"Erik, stop!" The familiarity, more than the words themselves, struck him. He had opened the door but turned, undecided, toward Madeleine. He could see that she wanted to help him.

"I would be happy to compose for ... but I ... the directorship would require that I ... It's more than I could ..." He stuttered to a stop, incapable of finding the way to explain his plight. More calmly, he continued, "I don't believe that Signora Costanzi would wish to work with me."

"Might I have something to say about it, Erik?" Meg was pulling off her gloves as she walked through the door that Erik had opened. He forced himself to turn slowly toward her. He hadn't seen her for months except in his dreams. They could do no justice to her true beauty. He bowed, as formally as he had for Don Marcelo and Madeleine, but he studiously kept his eyes averted from her face. She slowed her pace only slightly as she observed him, a warm burning sensation rising along her neck, evident in the ardent blush that stained her cheeks. "I think Marcelo's offer is excellent. I would be honored to work under your musical direction." She paused to hear Erik's response, but when he didn't speak, she continued provocatively, "Unless ..."

Erik's eyes flashed toward hers, waiting for her to explain.

"Unless you think I'm unworthy. I know, as director, the choice is entirely yours. Perhaps you have someone else in mind to lead in the season. A younger, a better singer? I would be willing to step aside, take a lesser role, if that were the case."

She demurred, and Erik knew he was lost. He couldn't walk away from this opportunity any more than he could stop breathing. He recalled her horrified expression upon seeing his disfigurement, yet now she seemed willing and able to control her disgust. He finally managed to find his voice and insist, "Not at all, Signora Costanzi. I can think of no one who could replace you. I simply worried that it might be difficult for you to work with me."

"Difficult? I don't believe so. No, I think we'll get along quite well. After all, we're friends, are we not?" She held his gaze, willing him to say yes.

He fought the urge to give in to hope. "Very well. I accept."

He's come back! But he's changed. He's so thin, and his face looks gaunt, even under the mask. I could see dark circles around his eyes, and he was so tense when I walked into the room that I thought he would rush out past me without even saying a word. But he's all right. He's alive and appears well in spite of these changes. Marcelo told me later the strange things Erik had said. Raoul is looking into the matter. Erik no longer uses Lucianna's name. He is aware that these past months have been a lie, that Lucianna gave him a false identity. But now it's as if he had no identity at all. He's a ghost. He has nothing. He's using the pseudonym, Henri Fournier. It gives him some legal status, some protection.

We will be working together. I will see him every day! But he acts so tentative around me, as if he fears I'll say something to harm him. He hasn't forgiven me. He still hasn't understood my reaction in the cemetery. And whenever I try to talk to him in confidence, he runs away!

He's asked me to find a governess for a young boy, Mario, whom he has rescued from the streets. He has grown fond of him. I nearly cried when he told me this. I wonder how much he misses François and Laurette somewhere deep inside, and this strange, clever boy has found this wound and benefited from it. He seems sweet. Raoul knows him and vouches for him. I could tell that it was hard for Erik to ask for my assistance, and it was only because it is really for the child that he could force himself to do so. I told him that the boy shall be schooled with my (our) own children. He thought to protest, but I insisted. I still have influence with him. I could see that he dared not contradict me when he saw that I was adamant on the subject. I felt better after this episode. It may be silly, but I thought it was a positive sign. He can't be indifferent to me.

We are going to put on Don Juan Triumphant. It was Raoul's and Christine's suggestion. They think that it will jar his memory! I'm very afraid. What memories will it bring back? It was at the premiere of this opera—his own opera—that Christine betrayed him to the authorities on the stage. She unmasked him before the entire auditorium. I can still remember the look on his face, the look of pain and confusion, the hopelessness and the raging anger that took him over. It's the night that he cut loose the ropes that secured the grand chandelier, and its fall killed many innocent people. Raoul reasoned that only something traumatic will break through the barriers his mind has constructed around his own past, his own identity. I thought seeing the children that time as they slept or seeing Maman might spark his memory. And even though I sensed some curiosity, some unexplained sympathy in him, it was not sufficient to recall to him his identity.

Rehearsals have started. He's back in the Teatro dell'Opera. It takes my breath away to see him on the stage. He knows the score backwards and forwards. And why not? It's his composition even if he doesn't remember. Marcelo prepared the company for Erik's arrival. Those who have worked with him before know that he has lost his memory. Sig. Bianchi broke into tears. Evidently he had glimpsed Erik sneaking in to listen to me months ago. The poor man had believed he was either seeing ghosts or losing his mind. He wept from relief. Once Erik arrived, the company was more than willing to take his instructions. By the end of the session, we were all aware of what we needed to do. He is an amazing artist and director.

He is absolutely ruthless! He insisted on a point in the score that I know I had done perfectly! He made me sing it again and again until I was about to walk off the stage and refuse to come back. No one but he can hear the distinction in the note he wanted me to make. It's ludicrous.

He brought the tuning fork within an infinitesimal distance from my ear, struck it, nearly deafening me, and growled in the most irate tone. "This, my dear diva, is the note!"

I could have killed him with my bare hands. I turned on him and sang the most ear-splitting note that any human being could produce—right into his face! I could see his eyes. They glistened with a spiteful pleasure, and he had the nerve to say to me, "That is the note, Signora Costanzi. But now I think we need to work on control."

My heart was beating so frantically that I thought I might pass out. I walked off the stage and went directly to my dressing room. There I cried, loudly and thoroughly. Yet I wasn't angry! On the contrary, I wanted to throw myself in his arms. I wanted him to scream at me again, to shake me until my blood stopped burning in my veins for him! Oh my God, he riles me so!

She took his breath away. He had been discussing the arrangement of the finale with the conductor, Sig. Bianchi, when the tittering among the young girls in the ballet company distracted him. He was about to say something sharp when he saw her among the dancers, many of whom were much younger than she. Several young girls watched admiringly as she executed a series of pirouettes, ending in an Arabesque Allongee whose grace was as much in her exquisite body as in the masterly control of the pose itself. She had, quite brazenly, gathered the skirts of her costume out of her way in order to join the ballet dancers in their exercises. Erik had never seen her dance, didn't know that she had any training or talent in the art, and was struck dumb. Sig. Bianchi was trying to capture his attention, but Erik's eyes were drawn to the gentle arc of her raised arm, *en l'air*, to the expressive positioning of her fingers, as if they were feathers raised in a proud tuft. Her face was in three quarter profile, chin tilted toward some distant dream, and her neck was long and inviting. He felt a shiver run through his body. He had wrinkled the music score in his clenched fists, unaware of the sudden tensing of his muscles.

He mumbled some excuse to Sig. Bianchi and left the stage. He had to get away. He rushed through the wings to the backstage area where he stopped, unable to make up his mind what to do next. So he paced nervously back and forth, trying to dispel the tension that charged through every fiber of his being. Despair, he felt its grip on his mind and heart. Pure despair. How could he continue in her presence when she drove him to distraction and when he had no hope of ever satisfying his need of her? For he did need her! It was almost as if he were ill and she were the only cure. Now that he was so much in her company, he was in constant irritation. The longing he had felt for her when he was with Lucianna, compared to this torture, had been sublime peace. At least then, he blushed to admit, Lucianna gave him solace.

God, he didn't want to think of Lucianna! Whenever he thought of her, his blood boiled. He mourned her and despised her in equal proportions. She had died without ever giving him the key to his past, his true past. She had left him knowing that she had manipulated him, deceived him, and possibly kept him from his true destiny. But even when he tried to hate her, he remembered her on the beach the day she told him they would have a child. No, he couldn't think about that. Nor did he want to remember her face as she lay on her deathbed. He had cried for her. It made him sad and bitter to recall the grief he had felt for his "wife." Thoughts of Lucianna helped him to calm the tumultuous urge that had sent him fleeing from Meg's presence.

Yet he would return to the stage. He wanted the madness! Even as he felt tortured by her, he realized that he could never leave. Each morning he rose, his first thoughts were of the moment when he would be with her. Sundays were the only days that there were no rehearsals and Meg didn't come to the Teatro dell'Opera. He detested them.

"Maestro, are you ill? Shall I run for Signore Costanzi or the count?" Mario tugged unceremoniously at the hem of Erik's coat. Ever since Donna Lucianna had died, Erik had acted strangely, and the boy was constantly worried about him. As the dark-haired boy had circled the corner, looking everywhere for his employer, he noticed Don Erik leaning against the wall. Something was wrong. Mario might have waited for his employer to call for assistance, but his message was too pressing. He must tell him what he'd just seen before it was too late to do anything.

Erik waved the child's concern away. He placed a reassuring hand on the boy's mass of unruly dark curls and attempted a smile. "What is it, Piccolo?" Mario scowled at the pet name; he wasn't that small. But Erik's smile broadened at his annoyance.

"You told me, Maestro, to watch out for that man." Mario made a zigzag gesture across his face to suggest a scar.

Erik's smile faded replaced by a dark intensity. "Giovanni?"

The boy simply nodded. "I followed him. He was watching the rehearsal."

"Are you sure?"

Again Mario nodded. He knew his maestro would want to know.

"Where? Where is he now?" Erik didn't mean to hurt the boy, but he could see from the brief grimace that passed over his face that his grip on the boy's shoulders had been too tight. He released him and slid a hand gently over his cheek before Mario indicated the backstage dressing rooms. "How long?"

"Just now, Maestro." As Erik rushed down the corridor toward the dressing rooms, Mario called quietly after him. "Careful, eh?"

Erik slowed considerably once he drew abreast of the first dressing room door. This one was the tenor's. He heard the man humming the first few bars of his solo. He had once had an excellent voice, but it was showing signs of weakness, especially in the higher ranges. Erik knew the other rooms were empty at the moment since the rest of the cast was on stage; nevertheless he gently opened each door and peered in. A movement down the hall, near Meg's dressing room, caught his eye, and he slipped inside the closest room to watch through the narrow gap as he hid behind the door. It was Giovanni, and he had definitely been in Meg's room.

Erik waited for the young Italian to pass before he slipped out and followed quietly behind him. Giovanni went directly to the stairs and descended to the rooms below. Why would he go there? There was little of market value among the props, bits of scenery, and supplies stored below, nothing that could easily be converted to coin. Erik followed at a distance, never losing sight of Giovanni, who entered several of the storage rooms. Instead of rummaging among the articles stored within, he ran his hands up and down the panels of each wall, pushing against them, running his fingers along the seams. He repeated this process in each of several rooms until he appeared to despair of finding what he was searching for. It seemed as if he were looking for a hidden compartment or a secret doorway. Finally Giovanni made his way back up the stairs, Erik following discreetly, and went quietly down the passageway toward one of the side exits.

Someone was calling for Erik. He hesitated, trying to decide whether to pursue Giovanni out into the street. But he decided he wanted to find out what Giovanni had been doing in Meg's dressing room. He doubled back, ignoring the general confusion on stage as the staff and cast called for him, and went directly to Meg's room. The door was unlocked—he'd speak to her about this—and he slipped in. Careful not to disturb anything, Erik searched the room for something amiss. He hadn't been there since the night before he had left Rome. He and Meg had dined together in this room, and afterwards they had walked to the cemetery. He shook the memory away. This was no time to indulge his self-pity. On the dressing table, he discovered a note addressed to Signora Costanzi in a hand that he thought he recognized, and if he had not, he could easily deduce from whom the note had come. Without hesitation, Erik unfolded the sheet and read.

❧

My dearest Meg,

It has been several years since you and I sat hand in hand in your garden whispering sweetly in each other's ear. Do you remember those trysts? Ah, young love! Does it ever really go away?

In honor of those feelings, I am compelled to do whatever I can to protect you from harm. I know something you should know about your Erik, something that I blush to commit to paper. I can only tell you in person. You should know what kind of man he is.

Meet me in the Piazza del Popolo Monday night at eleven. Be sure to come alone. I've become quite shy in the last several years. You have my word as a gentleman that you will be safe.

Your obedient and ardent admirer,

Giovanni Cimino

Erik sneered at the note. Giovanni's scandalous familiarity and reference to "trysts" infuriated him. He couldn't imagine Meg allowing herself to be wooed by the man. It galled him to think Giovanni might have been correct in suggesting Meg's honor had been tarnished by past indiscretions. He fought the burn of jealousy and shame. It certainly had been indiscreet of her to entertain him as she had on so many nights in her dressing room. Yet he didn't care. He couldn't think ill of her, no matter how brazen she might have been. He would never ask about her past. He loved her, even if she had been wanton.

He had his own demons to fight! He was fairly certain that he knew what Giovanni might tell Meg. But why? What did it matter? There was nothing between them now. He had lost all hope that Meg would return his love that night in the cemetery when they had to part. He had made his choice. And she had seen behind his mask. There was no going back. Even so, Erik felt his blood rise into his face. He couldn't imagine how disgusted Meg would be to hear Giovanni describe the debauchery of the scene at Roderigo's Tavern. It would bring him even lower in her esteem. It would sicken her, perhaps make it impossible for them to work together.

He started to tear the letter, but then he thought it best to leave it for Meg. He would watch over her. If she met Giovanni, she wouldn't be alone. Giovanni could tell her whatever he liked, then it would be over, and he'd have no power over him or Meg. He'd use the venom, and then be forced to skulk away, impotent and harmless. And if there were other motives in luring Meg to a rendezvous, Erik would be there. He wouldn't let anything happen to Meg.

And if she spurned him, then he would find some way to live with that, too.

Mario whispered through the door for Erik. They were looking for him. Erik folded the note and left it prominently displayed before the mirror where he'd found it.

He had nearly reached the stage when Meg found him. She was out of breath and flushed. He assumed it was from the ballet exercises.

"Erik, are you all right?"

"What is this constant preoccupation with the state of my health?" he snapped at her. "Can't a man get away for a few moments of quiet? Between the constant giggling from the chorus, the stamping of the dancers, and the off-key clarinet in the woodwind section of the orchestra, I can't hear myself think!"

Meg pursed her lips tightly shut and glared at him for a full minute. "Well, if it's all a mess, it's your problem, isn't it? You're the director!"

He was angry, so was she. The anger had assailed him the moment he saw her approach, panting, a slight sheen of sweat on her forehead, along the edge of her neckline at her throat, glistening along the swell of her bosom. The costume was daring, cut so low that her breasts were quite evident, and Erik found his eyes inadvertently fixed on her bust. He dragged them away with effort and looked at her face. But then he was transfixed by her lips. They were full and darkly pink, slightly open. He leaned in toward her. When she didn't back away, he found that he had already pressed his lips to hers and was holding her face in both his hands. He was only vaguely aware that she, too, was holding him, her arms wrapped around his waist. He tasted her with his tongue, gently teasing the corner of her lips and prodding them open so that he could slip between her teeth. He couldn't think what she tasted of, but he wanted to drink from her. He was parched, and he could drink from her forever and never have drunk enough.

The approach of Sig. Bianchi broke the moment, and Erik pulled away from Meg. His lips were swollen and throbbed deliciously. He was aroused and pleased to know Meg, too, was excited. She had not pushed him away. She had responded with equal passion to his kiss. He watched, amazed, for her reaction. Would she now regret the momentary lapse? But what he saw on her face was the persistence of the same desire that he felt. How could that be?

"Yes. Yes. I'm coming," he managed to say. He glanced once more at Meg and turned to go when she stopped him with a touch on his arm.

"Come dine at the house with us tomorrow?" Tomorrow would be Sunday. It was the only day he couldn't see Meg. Every other day he was with her, from morning till night, at rehearsals. On Sundays, everyone rested. Everyone but Erik, that is. Sundays for him were agony. Not to see Meg, not to hear her voice. Sundays were painful. Don Marcelo had invited him to dine with them each Sunday since they had begun to work together, but he always declined the invitation. "Please don't say no. I won't accept no. You will, you must come." Her hand had traveled down his sleeve—he was aware of the slightest movement of the fabric against his skin—until her fingers reached the naked skin of his palm. He closed his fingers tenderly over hers, and the sensation was unbearably intimate, almost more intimate than the kiss they had just shared.

"Yes, I'll come," he answered hoarsely, his voice sounding strange even to himself.

"Bring Mario. The children love him."

"Will I see them?" He hadn't seen Meg's children awake, only asleep, or at a distance.

She was suddenly speechless. Erik wondered whether she thought it a bad idea for him and the children to meet properly. His voice was cold when he spoke again. "Of course, perhaps the children should be spared my presence."

Before Meg could say another word, Erik strode off down the passageway to the stage. She could hear the edge in his voice as he barked orders at the company.

CHAPTER 9

✿

Don Juan Triumphant

DON JUAN: ¡Oh! Sí, bellísima Inés
espejo y luz de mis ojos;
escucharme sin enojos,
como lo haces, amor es:
mira aquí a tus plantas, pues,
todo el altivo rigor
de este corazón traidor
que rendirse no creía,
adorando, vida mía,
la esclavitud de tu amor.

Oh, my loveliest Inés
mirror and light of vision,
listen without derision,
as you do so, it's love: yes,
see here at your feet, I confess
all the haughty pride
of this traitorous heart inside
that never thought to yield,
adores you, my life, ah, I feel
the slavery of your love.

Don Juan Tenorio, José Zorrilla, Mayberry and Kline

Erik arrived with a bouquet of mixed spring flowers that he presented to Madeleine, given that she was the senior lady of the house. His fingers ached from the tight grasp in which he had held the flowers the entire ride to Don Marcelo's. As he bowed and offered them, he eased his grip, his fingers numb. A truly stunning woman, Signora Giry hesitated before she took them. In the pause, as he held them forth, he grew uncomfortable under her gaze. But he was touched when he saw how affected she was. She murmured a gracious response and blushed warmly. Her smile did not disguise a slight tremble to her lips. She seemed truly moved by his gesture, and he felt awkward at his own pleasure in her delight with the flowers. His feelings bewildered him. He had barely spoken to Meg's mother. Yet she had shown him kindness. He still remembered the shocking familiarity of her hand as she laid it across his own that first day he had returned to Rome and come to ask for work.

He was nervous at dinner and barely touched the soup. He picked at the next several courses. Out of the corner of his eye, he watched his dinner partners. He hadn't paid much attention to Christine, Raoul's wife. She was beautiful with long brown hair, expressive eyes, a long neck, but she was too thin for his liking. Tonight he felt that she was often staring at him. Of course it must be the mask that intrigued her. It disturbed him that Meg might have described his face to her friend. It somehow didn't bother him in the same way if the gentlemen had been given a description. But Christine's curiosity unsettled him.

When she wasn't staring at him, Erik took the opportunity to study Christine and Raoul together. He liked the way she brightened whenever Raoul spoke to her. He watched Raoul touch his wife in various, small and discreet, ways. His fingers would brush hers when reaching for the spoon, or he would lean his shoulder just enough to graze her arm. There was no doubt in Erik's mind that these tiny considerations were deliberate. He even caught a glimpse of a wry smile both of them shared at once just as the slightest movement of Raoul's body suggested that below the table his thigh, perhaps, or his foot was gently prodding Christine's. As he turned away from the married couple's endearments, his gaze met Meg's. Her eyes were serious and intent on observing him. There was no humor in them, and he was surprised that he thought he saw something else, too, in her look. She was obviously aware that he had been observing Christine and Raoul, and it somehow annoyed her.

A deep, unsettled feeling rose from the pit of his stomach, and he realized that he had heard none of the conversation for the past several minutes. His reactions struck him as irrational, but he couldn't seem to control them. He desperately wanted to leave, and he didn't know why! He feared that he might be sick; he might fall over before he managed to get away. His head had begun to throb, a sure sign of one of the headaches that plagued him more acutely now than ever before. He rose quickly from the table.

The conversations stopped in mid-syllable, and everyone's eyes were on him, including Meg's. He asked to be excused, gave some vague compliment about the meal and the company, and said that he must be going. At that he turned and rushed out through the dining room doors toward the foyer. Before he could get his cloak from the servant, Raoul's hand was on his shoulder.

Raoul refused to let him leave. He led him, instead, to the garden just outside the veranda. "Are you ill?" Erik appreciated Raoul's concern, but he had no idea of how to explain his sudden fit. The initial wave of nausea and panic had receded somewhat but had not altogether gone.

"I just couldn't sit any longer. I suffer from recurring headaches."

"Did we do something to bring it on?"

"No. Not at all. You're ... very ... kind." Erik edged away from Raoul. He brushed his fingers across the blossoms of an azalea. He must control the chaos of emotions that tossed him without mercy from one crest to another. He was drowning in a black sea of emptiness. "You love her, don't you?" he asked, suddenly jealous that Raoul was so firmly anchored to life, his wife so beautiful, guardian of his soul, keeper of memories. Christine and Raoul shared a story. All that Erik had were lies.

Raoul was momentarily taken aback.

"Your wife," Erik clarified. There was a hint of embarrassment in his tone, and he was careful not to look at Raoul directly.

Raoul couldn't help but feel wary. Any interest in Christine on Erik's part was bound to stir up old rancor and anxiety. Was his old obsession for her rearing its nasty head? Cautiously, Raoul answered, "Yes, of course."

"Yes, of course," repeated Erik in a whisper that almost sounded like a lament.

A bit on guard, Raoul studied Erik. He was surprised to realize that he was fond of Erik, of the man Erik had become over time. He wondered how he'd feel if the "old" Erik were to return, the one who was obsessed with Christine, the one who had been his enemy.

The light from the house dimly lit the men from behind. Raoul couldn't see Erik's expression. Each had his back to the French doors that opened onto the veranda. But something told Raoul that he shouldn't interrupt, that he should wait and listen.

"I was thinking of husbands and wives." Erik's voice deepened.

Raoul ignored the tingling sensation at the base of his neck. The night was coming fast, and Raoul fought the urge to slip back into the room behind

them. Lucianna Fiortino rose like a ghost from a crypt in both men's imagination. No one had asked Erik for an explanation, but they had all wondered
what had happened between Lucianna and him in the months they had been
together.

"She's dead. I think I said that, didn't I? She ... she ... didn't deserve to die
... not like that." Erik didn't go on for some time, and Raoul was uncomfortably aware that he was agitated. "She was ... my ... wife. Watching you and
Christine tonight, I thought of ... Luci." He wasn't able to say her name without his voice betraying him.

Raoul turned to see that Meg had stepped out onto the veranda. She lingered near the door, silently listening. With his hand, he cautioned her to stay
back. Agitated by memories of Lucianna's last days, Erik was unaware of Meg's
presence. His head was bent low. "I buried her. She *did* love me. I stayed by her
side, watching her waste away. She was beautiful. And then she was dying. She
told me she was going to have my child. She was wrong. There was something
else growing in her womb, and it killed her."

Raoul drew up beside Erik. He stood next to him in companionable silence
for several moments. The darkness had grown dense, and Raoul could only see
the glint of Erik's eye and the pale glow of the white mask. "It hasn't been long.
It's natural to grieve."

"Grieve?" Erik tensed, his tone a twist of anger and sorrow. "She was all I
had. And so much more died that day." Anger edged sorrow from his voice.
"She took it all with her!"

"I'm sure she'd want you to get on with your life," Raoul argued. It was
something that people said, and Raoul wasn't sure if it pertained or not. But he
had to say something.

"My life? She might as well have dragged me along with her to the grave."
His tone was bitter. "I'm sorry." He shifted away from Raoul, breaking the
former intimacy. A moment passed. When he spoke again, the hard edge of
bitterness had left his voice. The sadness, too, seemed less pronounced.
"Please, forgive me. I'm not yet accustomed to her absence."

Meg stepped back, unnoticed, into the room. It must be frightening to have
no memory, and then to have the identity you assumed was yours taken away
from you. That was why Erik had abandoned the Fiortino name. He knew that
Lucianna had lied to him. But without the lie, he had no identity at all. Meg
kept her hand over her mouth to soften her own ragged breathing until she
was able to compose herself. Then she called out, as if she had just come upon

the two men, to join her and the others in the front parlor for after-dinner drinks.

After a few moments, the men joined Christine, Meg, and Don Marcelo in the parlor. Erik appeared completely composed, as if nothing had happened. Raoul sat beside Christine, smiled at her inquisitive glance, and accepted the glass of sherry the servant offered. Madeleine entered, shortly thereafter, followed by the children. The latter had eaten separately so that the adults could enjoy a peaceful conversation. Now they were ushered in to spend a few minutes with their parents. Among them Erik was surprised and pleased to find Mario. He hadn't seen him in the company of other children, and it touched him to see how young he actually was. On the streets, in the theater, in their apartments, Mario struck one as neither adult nor child, but rather something in between. But here he was smiling from ear to ear, obviously involved in some childish banter with Victor, Christine's oldest boy. Madeleine introduced each of the other children, one by one, to Erik. A little girl, only just younger than Meg's boy, ran to Christine and jumped into her lap.

"This acrobat is Elise." Christine made room for her daughter so that she wouldn't have to move when the nanny placed a sleeping infant in her arms. "And this is our newest addition." Erik strained from his seat to catch a glimpse but could see nothing. A curiously wordless exchange passed between Raoul and his wife. Christine whispered to Elise, who took the baby carefully in her arms, and walked toward the stunned Erik.

"This is my baby sister, Erica. She's almost six months old and too young to play the games I like, but I'm going to take care of her when she's older." The coincidence of her name amused Erik. He looked into the bundle and saw the sweet face of a healthy baby girl sucking fiercely on a thumb.

"She's beautiful," he whispered as if surprised.

"We're so fortunate she's asleep. She's very loud! And she squirms." Elise, already the precocious mother, looked for confirmation from her own mother, who smiled at her in agreement.

Meg had waited for Christine's and Raoul's children to be introduced. Not until Elise had brought her baby sister back to Christine, did Meg come forward with her son.

"This is François." Erik recognized the dark haired boy from the night Meg had brought him to see her children while they slept. He was even more striking than he seemed that night. Awake, his eyes were serious and intense, making him seem older than he was. Erik was puzzled by the boy's insistent gaze. His dark green eyes were unwaveringly focused on Erik.

Erik bowed his head to acknowledge the introduction. "Your mother says you play?"

"Yes ..." the boy stumbled and hesitated as if he had forgotten what to say. "Yes, signore. My father taught me to play."

"Perhaps you can play something for us?"

"Yes, signore." François walked to the piano bench and searched through the music until he found the piece he wanted.

"Before you play, let me introduce your sister. This monkey is Laurette. She walks, but she prefers to climb and hang on me." Meg wasn't sure what would happen. She had explained it all to François, and she knew she could trust him to be careful. But Laurette was too young to understand what had been going on since they left home and went to visit Christine in Paris. She had barely been two when Meg received the letter telling her Erik had died in the fire. It broke her heart, but she thought Laurette might not even remember her father. She unlaced the child's fingers from her hair and unwrapped her arms and legs so that she could put her down in front of Erik.

Erik hadn't expected to come in such close proximity to the children. He had wanted to meet them. After all, since he was invited to dine with the family, he assumed the children formed a part of that same family scene. He had felt hurt that Meg might not wish for her children to meet him.

Laurette was not even three years old, but she curtsied sweetly. Just as in François's case, her unwavering stare unsettled Erik. Then she held her arms out for him to pick her up. For a moment, Erik looked as if he didn't know what she wanted. But Meg gestured for him to lift the little girl up onto his lap, which he did. Laurette immediately rested her body comfortably against his chest and began to fiddle with the buttons on his vest. He held her in the crook of one arm. Her legs dangled over his lap. She stared up at his face, and he felt warm and strange inside.

François had a peculiar look on his face as he watched Erik with his baby sister. Then without preamble he began to play a gavotte.

After he finished the piece, everyone applauded, but it was Erik's reaction that he sought.

Erik had been quite amazed by the boy's expertise. He was young to have such a developed technique, and it was obvious he was highly talented. Erik was aware that, as the director of the opera and as this evening's guest, he was expected to give a professional appraisal of the child's performance, so he said, "Your father taught you well." Suddenly a huge grin spread across the boy's face, and he gave a small, involuntary laugh. Everyone else remained stiffly silent.

"Wait. Listen." Then the boy began to play the piece once again, this time without reading the sheet music. The previous performance had been noteworthy, but the second was amazing, richer and more fluid. Erik noticed the boy took some liberties with a few of the measures, but the effect was delightful.

"Bravo, nicely done," Erik praised him. "You've a fine ear."

"I get it from my father."

"I daresay your mother has something to do with it."

François bowed his head slightly, but answered, "Yes, but my father's a musical genius." Erik was aware the boy had not referred to his father in the past tense. It seemed natural that the child still thought of him in the present. It must be difficult to deal with the death of a parent.

Meg announced that it was time for the children to retire and asked Erik if Mario could spend the night. His impulse was to say no, for he would miss the child's company. It felt strange to think of going home to the apartments without Mario. But he saw the excitement on the boy's face and agreed to let him pass the night with the other children. The adults would probably not retire for several more hours, and it would be a shame to wake Mario for the trip home.

Meg reached for Laurette who, seeing that her mother was about to take her from Erik's arms, screamed at the top of her lungs, shocking no one more than Meg and Erik. She clung to Erik fiercely, her fingers digging deeply into the folds of his coat and vest, her legs kicking blindly at Meg's arms.

"I've never seen her like this." Meg apologized, somewhat surprised. But she recalled a few occasions before the fire when Laurette had been fiercely opposed to leaving her father's arms. "Could you bring her upstairs?"

Erik rose from the sofa with the girl who now, having gotten her way, nestled contentedly in his arms. As he reached the door, he felt the pressure of another's hand on his elbow. It was François who stood at his side, his gaze riveted on Erik's masked face. A strange feeling threatened to choke Erik with emotion. He controlled the urge to wrap his arms around the boy. He looked at Meg and nearly begged to take his leave, for he felt as if there were tears rising to his eyes, and he didn't understand why. The only thing he did know was that he wished with all his heart that these were his children he was taking to their bedroom, and that Meg and he would then retire to their own. If only she were his wife and these, their children! He swallowed several times to control the pressure behind his eyes and throat. He easily held Laurette cradled in one arm and guided François up the stairs with the other.

Laurette was happy only after Erik tucked her into the bed and gave her a kiss. François made do with a pat on the head. But before Meg and Erik could leave, François called from the bed. "Will you please come again?"

"Yes, I'd like that."

"Could you help me with my lessons?"

"You have no teacher?"

Meg interrupted. "He's a terror. We can't keep a teacher more than a month at a time."

"No, I can't help you. Not if you're bad."

François smiled from ear to ear at his father's reply. It reminded him of other times. "I won't be bad. Not if *you* promise to teach me."

"Very well, then. But lessons stop the moment I think you're too stupid to learn."

"Yes, pa...Yes, signore." François turned quickly onto his side and brought the cover over his head.

The error hadn't escaped Erik's attention, but it didn't seem strange that the boy might make such a slip. He must miss his father terribly.

Before retiring again to the parlor, Erik asked to say goodnight to Mario who was in the next room with Victor and Elise.

They joined the others in the parlor soon after. Erik had the strange feeling that the conversation had come to an abrupt hush when Meg and he came into the room. Meg went immediately to the cabinet and poured herself a rather large tumbler of brandy. Erik hadn't yet finished the sherry that he had been sipping. He felt warm and happy, almost foolishly happy.

Raoul and Erik played a game of chess while Don Marcelo entertained the women with stories of debacles from seasons long past at the opera. Erik was aware that Raoul would most likely win in the next five moves no matter what he did to avoid it. The conversation had turned toward discussion of the current production.

"Erik, you've not said much about the opera itself. What do you think of *Don Juan Triumphant*?" Don Marcelo seemed to have asked a question that intrigued the others as well.

"I like the challenges it presents," Erik commented reluctantly. With more interest he added, "I've been meaning to ask you about the composer. I can't find a name anywhere on the composition. I noticed the initials, 'O. G.' Who would he be?"

Meg took a large sip of her brandy and answered before anyone else could, "We don't know who wrote it. It's a mystery."

Erik frowned.

"What is it, Erik?" asked Raoul.

"Nothing," he answered, but he continued to look puzzled. He felt foolish explaining that many of the melodies seemed familiar to him. He would swear that someone had stolen them from him, but he hadn't ever committed them to paper, as far as he could remember. From the first day Don Marcelo had trusted him with the score, he had felt as if he already knew the work intimately. Was it possible that he had been a composer before the fire? Was that a truth among the lies that Lucianna had fed him? Would it be so incredible to think that he was the anonymous O. G.?"

"Is he Italian or French?" Erik asked.

Before she thought about it, Meg answered, "French."

"French," muttered Erik to himself. If he weren't Fiortino, perhaps he wasn't Italian either. He did feel more at ease speaking in French with Meg and the others. Although he had to confess that it seemed equally proper to speak with Don Marcelo in Italian. If he were O. G. and *Don Juan Triumphant* were his original composition, what could the initials stand for? And under what circumstances had he written such an odd piece?

"It's full of ..." He searched fruitlessly for the right words. "I can't explain it, but it is obviously full of anger and defiance, but at the same time it's a story of love."

"Love?" Raoul bit his tongue. He couldn't help but sound sarcastic. As far as he was concerned, the opera was about lust and obsession, not love.

Erik heard the skepticism in Raoul's tone. "You disagree?"

"He wants to possess her. Is it love to drag her to damnation with him?" Christine threw a frightened glance at Raoul, but he refused to be silenced. "If he loved her, he would let her go." Raoul felt the blood drain from his face when he remembered that that was exactly what Erik had finally done. He had released Christine.

"Perhaps you're right. But not completely. He can't help himself." Erik was puzzled by his need to defend the character of Don Juan.

"The sounds are jarring and discordant."

"Not throughout. There are moments of sweetness. There is love in the music, as well as anger and ..." How could one characterize the desperate nature of the climax?

"Madness?" Raoul gave in to a surge of annoyance. Of course Erik would defend the piece. He had written it as the culmination of his declaration of love for Christine!

"If you so dislike the opera, why would you recommend we stage it?" asked Erik, slightly piqued by Raoul's belligerence. Couldn't he see the passion in it? Did he have no regard for the audacity of its art?

Christine couldn't let the two men continue to argue. "It's an incredible piece," she said with conviction. She and Raoul exchanged dark looks. It was clear to everyone that they had touched upon a subject about which they would never agree. Somewhat more softly, as if to dispel the tension in the room, she asked Erik, "You've been through it quite thoroughly by now, haven't you? It's well beyond anything being done today. It's 'modern' and daring."

"Do you think the contemporary audience will understand it?" He stared intently at Christine, sensing that she understood the piece much as he did.

"Does that matter to you?" asked Madeleine.

Strangely enough, it did, but Erik didn't admit it. After all it wasn't his opera. "Of course, as Director, I want it to be successful."

"Most of our seats are bought for the season. That guarantees that we won't lose money on it," assured Don Marcelo.

"I've heard that you were once on the stage, Christine. Why did you leave it?" The room went deadly silent, as if the air had been sucked out all at once and no one could breathe. "I'm sorry. Was that indiscreet of me?"

"No, not at all. I sang for the Opera Populaire in Paris. There was an accident, and the opera house was damaged by fire. No one had the resources to reopen. At that point Raoul and I had decided to marry. I suppose I thought it might be a strain on our marriage if I continued to work." Raoul knew that it had been difficult for Christine to leave the stage. It was the sacrifice she had made to be with him and to get away from Erik.

"Do you still sing?"

"My wife has a lovely voice," Raoul hurried to affirm.

"Would you sing if I played?" Without waiting for her response, Erik went to the piano and chose a light piece that was currently quite popular with the young. He flexed his fingers to limber them. He scanned the piece and knew that the stiffness in some of his fingers would not hinder his playing it well.

Christine glanced at Meg, who kept her eyes deliberately lowered. A blush of dark red was evident on her face. Raoul had started to protest, but Christine quieted him with a gesture. She wished she could catch Meg's eye, but Meg would not look up at any of them.

Erik began to play the piece. Christine stood slightly behind him in order to read the score and follow the notes. Her nearness to him made her tremble softly. He had taught her to sing! He had come to her in the nighttime, invisible, and had sung her to sleep when she cried from loneliness. She had tormented him without ever meaning to and led him to his destruction.

She began to sing, but was overwhelmed by a gush of tears and ran from the room. Erik stopped, disturbed and bewildered by her fit of passion. Raoul apologized, saying something vague about new mothers, and followed quickly after her.

"I'm sorry. I didn't mean to distress her." His usual calm assurance had disappeared. He turned in particular to Meg, hoping for some explanation, but noticed that her eyes were serious and distant. "I meant no harm," he stammered, helpless to understand.

"No harm done, Erik. She was perhaps reminded of another time, another life. She must miss the stage sometimes." Don Marcelo patted Erik on the shoulder as if these things happened all the time. "It had nothing to do with you," he lied.

"Of course. I didn't realize." Suddenly he felt like a stranger. Nothing quite made sense to him. He thought he knew these people, but they had known each other for so many years that they hardly needed to explain themselves to each other. On the other hand, he had known them only briefly. He had no past to share with them except the recent one, and he knew little about theirs. "I think I should be going. Rehearsal is early tomorrow."

He wished he could have had a few moments alone with Meg. The distance he saw in her eyes saddened him; he couldn't think what had darkened her mood. And then there was the note. He was worried about tomorrow evening. He had almost begun to regret not tearing up Giovanni's note. She must have read it, but she hadn't confided in him. He had thought she might trust him with the information. Perhaps she tore it up herself as the ravings of a madman. Whatever the case, he would be with her every single moment tomorrow. She would not meet Giovanni alone, if she were foolish enough to keep the appointment.

He returned to a silent apartment. The servant had long ago retired to his room in the back. Erik wouldn't see him again until the morning. The rooms he had rented upon his return to Rome were much more modest than those he had shared with Lucianna. The one servant Erik had retained was sufficient to his needs. The cook came only twice a day to prepare the meals and did not live on the premises. Erik ate a cold meal in the evening, preferring to have only Mario as company. He had accepted just enough money from Lucianna's estate to pay for his travels and to set up the basic requirements to live like a gentleman, if only modestly.

Without Mario, there was a stillness of things that had taken over the rooms, a hush that was more profound than the absence of sound itself. The chatter and commotion at Don Marcelo's had been, in comparison, deafening. It was as if Erik had been exiled to the desert. He ran his fingers along the strange, impersonal fixtures that surrounded him and felt the shiver of the grave run up his spine. This not belonging, this severed tie chilled him, and he thought of Luci. She had anchored him against the storm of his oblivion. He now felt cast adrift.

He didn't bother to lay his clothes out properly or dust his coat or wipe his boots, much less polish them. He dropped the garments carelessly by the bed and stole between the covers hoping to sleep and dream of the children's voices, Meg, the warm caress of Don Marcelo's household. Mario would always remember this night. He was only a child and had no one but Erik. His childhood had been blighted, scarred by loss, poverty, fear. It pleased Erik to see that Meg was tender with the boy. If all went well, Erik would try to give Mario a future, but he had to find a trade for him or set him up in some kind of business. Mario was a bastard, an orphan. He couldn't have a life like François's, not without a powerful patron.

He gradually drifted to sleep, thinking of Mario, of children, of lost parents. François reminded him of someone. His eyes. François's eyes smiled when he played. He dreamed François was playing the piano. Meg should have lots of children. *Meg sat in a nursing chair, Laurette at her breast. He was drawing them. The charcoal stained his hands, the cuffs of his linen shirt were smudged. He couldn't stop tracing the soft curves of her body and the figure of the child pressed to her bosom. Meg's bodice lay open exposing both her breasts. The charcoal sketch fell from his lap, and he bent to pick it up. It flew away from him, lost among the sawdust and paper along the floor of the cage. His fingers were blackened with charcoal, grease, dirt. The bars felt cold against his bare back. The coolness eased the burning from the lashes. Around him bars. He sang to himself a melody over and over. There were noises outside the tent—the sound of people laughing, talking loudly, milling about. There was a tinny music playing somewhere beyond the tent flap, but that wasn't the melody he repeated in his mind. He tried to drown out the sounds except for those he created, the notes he ordered and purified to crystal. They were crystal notes, and they'd save him, save him from ...*

Erik struggled to consciousness. He woke, afraid to face the monster in the dream. His heart was pounding, and he looked about the room, at first disoriented, afraid he'd find the bars from his dream. It was still dark. The quarter moon had advanced little. He must have fallen off to sleep and had the nightmare almost immediately. He wouldn't be able to sleep now. He lay back and thought of Meg. He thought of the kiss. He couldn't remember the dream—the details had quickly faded when he woke—but he knew she was in it. The images were already gone and left in their wake a driving need to be with someone.

He quickly dressed and knocked on the servant's door. Within the hour he was standing in front of Roderigo's Tavern. He knew that it wasn't unusual for gentlemen to frequent houses of ill repute. Roderigo's establishment, however, was even more degrading than the posh bordellos the gentry normally supported. But then again Erik was not really a gentleman any longer, if ever he had been. The urges that plagued him now were best taken care of in the dark, somewhere on the fringes of society.

He paused and thought of the kiss he had taken in the wings at the Teatro. It wasn't his imagination, was it? Meg had not pushed him away. She *had* kissed him, too. He almost turned to leave, but he couldn't go back to the empty rooms, the cold bed, the gnawing loneliness he felt inside. His whole body was flayed and gutted. He needed to touch someone or his flesh would rot and fall from the bone. Even if he had to pay a woman to lie with him so that for a few hours he would feel human, would feel whole again, so be it.

Erik knew Giovanni was not present. He had described the young man to the driver and sent him in to check. This was, after all, one of his favorite haunts. Unfortunately for Erik, it was the only place of its kind that he knew. But he would not go in if Giovanni were in the bordello.

The tavern still had some customers at the bar or seated at nearby tables, talking loudly and drinking. Others sat silent, weaving over their half-full glasses. A few were asleep, their heads pitched forward onto the table next to empty bottles, upset glasses. A man was stumbling down the stairs trying without success to fix his suspenders over his shoulders. A couple of women sat talking in a corner. They looked up when Erik came into the tavern. Erik felt the tension immediately. The women stared, their conversations forgotten. The proprietor behind the bar held the whiskey he was about to pour in mid air over the empty glass of an old man already too far gone to drink without spilling the contents over himself and the counter.

"You again."

Erik was surprised by the tone of the bartender. He had only come the one time with Giovanni. Perhaps that had been enough to merit the gruff greeting. Instead of responding, Erik placed several coins on the counter. Convinced by the generous payment, the man pointed to the far corner where the prostitutes passed the time until their services were needed.

"Watch the rough stuff this time," he said in warning.

Erik disregarded the remark. He had no intention of harming anyone. Giovanni was the one who had insisted on inflicting pain on the women.

He walked toward the corner of the room determined to take the first woman available, the first hand raised out to him. However, when he drew close enough to actually observe them, he was shocked to see one young woman among them with long blond hair and a body that made his knees immediately turn to water. She reminded him of Meg. He wasn't even aware that he had taken her by the hand until the two of them were mounting the stairs together to one of the available rooms.

Once they found a room, he took the time to study the woman. She was younger than he had thought and for a moment he felt a pang of regret for having chosen her. She removed her dress and stood before him in a simple chemise waiting for his instructions. Erik made no move to undress; he was overcome by sadness. Whatever pleasure he had anticipated seemed beyond his reach.

"You're badly bruised," he remarked upon seeing large contusions along her upper arms that must have been made recently. "Who could do something like that?" He brushed his hand over them lightly.

She raised her eyebrows in surprise at him and backed away outside his reach. "Well, you should know."

He searched her eyes to see if she were drugged or drunk, but her eyes were sharp and clear. "I don't understand."

"Course not, Signore." She smiled sarcastically. Erik thought the expression aged her a good ten years. It erased any illusion he had had of her innocence. Suddenly the excitement that had driven him to this desperate step returned with renewed vigor, and he wanted her. He wanted to disappear for several hours in her arms, forgetting that he had forgotten and that there was ever anything to remember. If he could simply dissolve his being and become sensation, destroy his mind and soul and with them the regret and pain of longing.

He took the girl-woman and kissed her deeply, with lust and need and a desire to obliterate the very skin that separated them. She stood passively, accepting him, a body willing, but not eager to respond. He drew back, aroused, his breathing rapid and shallow with desire, yet hesitant. Her face stared up at him blankly. She was his. He had paid for the privilege. He raised his fingers to his mask. It was his choice, not hers. He had paid for the privilege of her body. He had paid so that she would accept him. He raised the mask away from his face and held it by his side, unable to let it fall completely away from him.

He regretted it the moment he saw the shock in her eyes. He heard her sharp intake of air. She turned her face to the side and looked away from him. His body tensed. He had paid for the privilege. He took several deep breaths to calm himself. As he brought the mask down over his face, his fingers trembled. Then he surprised himself by taking the girl and holding her tightly. His hands spread across her back, and he buried her face against the soft fabric of his vest. Her hair tickled the skin of his neck, and he lightly rested his chin on the top of her head. He didn't attempt to kiss her; nor did he fondle her as she expected he would. Yet he still held her.

When he didn't release her, a soft questioning voice rose between them. "Why'd you take it off? You never take it off."

Erik pushed her gently away, at arm's length, and asked, "What do you mean?"

"You've always kept it on before. You take off every other stitch of clothing but not the mask. Not before now."

Erik looked at the bruises again on the girl's arms. There were others, less recent, that were fading into a greenish yellow on her freckled skin.

"How often have I been here?"

The girl looked at him strangely, studying what she could still see of the face around the edges of the mask. Then her eyes darted toward his hands. "You're not him, are you? I thought your voice was different. And your hands!"

Erik pulled his hands free of her upper arms and closed them in a fist to hide the fading scars of the burn.

"Who? Who did you think I was?" he asked, although he was certain he already knew the answer.

She turned her back to Erik and lifted the chemise. On her back were welts from a strap. "The one that likes to do this." Then she pulled her undergarments down on one hip exposing the fleshy part of her buttock. "Or this." There Erik could make out the initials, "G C," cut into the skin with the sharp point of a knife. They were just beginning to heal. She dropped the chemise down over her body and faced Erik again. She saw clearly now that Erik was not that man. "He comes two or three times a week. He always wears a mask like yours. I'd have sworn you were him."

Erik removed the mask again. This time the girl barely winced at his disfigurement. She was careful to keep her eyes trained on him. With a certain bravado, she said, "I don't mind it so much. If you don't hurt me like he does, I can get used to the other." She took hold of Erik's hand to lead him toward the bed, but Erik withdrew his hand as if her palm had burned it. He stepped away until he felt the door at his back.

He walked out and flew down the stairs. At the bottom of the staircase, he called to the proprietor. All eyes seemed fixed on Erik's face. The proprietor had seen it just once, but it still shocked him into silence.

"Next time you see me here, tell me to remove my mask." He threw some additional money onto the counter. "Mark me, signore. Take my mask off by force, if you have to. But take a good look at the face behind it."

"I don't have to, signore. I know you're not the same man who's been coming round."

"How's that?"

The barman lifted his chin and indicated the girl at the top of the stairs. She had the barest smile of affirmation on her face when the two men looked up at her. "He never left them the way he found them, if you get my drift."

Erik nodded. They both understood each other. With that, Erik left Roderigo's.

Erik had had enough! He had sent the tenor to his dressing room with instructions to nurse his cold. The premiere was fast approaching, and they needed his voice rested and well. Rehearsal was a shambles. The seduction scene was critical, and they had been working on it for the past week. The scene was the moment Inés chooses hell. Don Juan and she are consumed by the flames. Unlike other renditions of the story, in this version, Inés chooses Don Juan. The duet would be the climax of the opera! But Meg wouldn't be able to rehearse the scene without a Don Juan!

Erik called to Raoul who was watching from one of the boxes, commenting from time to time as Erik queried him about the sight lines and acoustics. "Raoul, I want you to stand in for Sig. Tamburo, the tenor." He resolved that he would have to speak with Don Marcelo about replacing him with a new tenor. Tamburo was less and less effective.

Raoul gasped. "What?"

"You know the music. You must have heard it a thousand times by now," Erik replied testily. He had no time to waste on false modesty.

Christine urgently tugged at Raoul's elbow and whispered, "Tell him you can't."

"I can't," he protested, casting a questioning look at his wife.

"I don't expect you to sing like Tamburo, for God's sake."

Christine answered for her husband, "He can't carry a tune. He's actually quite bad." Raoul seemed slightly offended. In point of fact, Christine had told him many times that he had a lovely voice."

Exasperated, Erik cursed under his breath. Everyone else was waiting. It was a full dress rehearsal. Meg was singing wonderfully even if there was no real passion between her and the aging tenor. The scene had to come to life! If they couldn't convince the audience that these two people wanted each other more than life itself, more than salvation, the whole point of the opera would be lost. *That* had been the challenge. It was a love that accepted damnation!

No one knew the part as well as he did—not even Tamburo whose lukewarm delivery had galled Erik since the first day of rehearsal. The tenor was more interested in his solos than this duet, and more willing to exert himself technically instead of dramatically. Meg was incredibly beautiful in the scant dress, ready to meet her demon lover. No one, he was convinced, could sing to her with the passion he felt. For him, it would not be an act. He'd finally be able to tell her how he felt. He could use O. G.'s words and music. His voice was passable, not pure, not polished. The fire had permanently colored it with a low harshness, a husky quality, and he might strain to reach the higher register. What his voice lacked, his passion could compensate. Everyone was waiting for his instructions. He would hold her. She'd sing in his arms. Suddenly he was aware that he was lightheaded. His mouth had gone dry like chalk. He didn't have enough spit to even swallow. Meg was waiting. He was waiting. It was as if time had stopped. He felt almost as if his own heart had suspended its movement and was hovering between beats.

"Maestro Bianchi, I'll stand in. From the entrance." Time resumed. Suddenly everyone was alive and moving, returning to their spots at the top of the scene. Sig. Bianchi waited for Erik to don the cape and to slip behind the curtain. Then the music began. The chorus sang its introduction, and Meg came out to center stage and sat with one rose in her lap. She sang, waiting for her lover. Raoul and Christine watched from the box, their hands tightly clasped as they anticipated Erik's entrance. A shiver of dread ran up Raoul's spine as he recalled seeing Christine on the stage where Meg now sat. Would this be the spark?

The curtain moved aside, and Erik stepped out onto the stage. At least they assumed it must be Erik for the way he moved reminded them of someone else. His voice was not quite the same as the voice Christine remembered; it was deeper, with a sandpaper texture it didn't have before. It was older, more assured, seductive still, perhaps even more so, for it was charged with the masculine threat of an experienced lover. He glided across the stage like a panther stalking his prey. He offered his hand to Meg and pulled her easily to her feet. He sang to her of love and passion, confessed his desire to take her to the depths of hell, and she responded with equal fervor. She vowed that he'd never escape her embrace and that she burned already with his fire. Erik and Meg climbed the wooden parapet constructed over a pit lined with red paper flames. Meeting in the center of the structure, over the pit itself, above the heads of scandalized witnesses, they clung together and sang their vows.

Erik held Meg tightly to him. Her back cradled against his chest, his hand lay pressed against her diaphragm. He could feel the vibrations of her song and suddenly he was breathless, unable to sing, unable to think. He wanted her more than life itself. He closed his eyes, and a searing pain ripped through his mind. He released Meg who, stunned by his unexpected movement, turned to see him crumple to the boards of the parapet in pain.

He saw before him an auditorium filled with strange faces. He hated them. He felt naked and exposed. He was filled with an anger and despair that twisted his gut, sending nothing but sharp stabs of agony throughout his body. He cried out in pain, and she bent toward him. He didn't know who she was! She looked at him as if she wanted to help, but he couldn't look at her. She was in his way. She would burn if she touched him. He was on fire, and the sound of the conflagration had burst his eardrums. He felt wrapped in blood, and cried out again. Not in pain, but in anger and torment!

She betrayed him! She betrayed *him*! He had given her everything, and he had nothing left to give except his pain. She had sucked him dry to the bone, and he wanted to kill. Someone touched him, and he cried out from the touch. No one, no one must ever touch him! No one would ever touch him. He must get away. The lights were cutting into his eyes like knives into his brain. He had loved her! He had given her the only thing he had. He had laid it out on velvet cloth at her feet, his heart still beating, he had ripped it from his chest and laid it out on the velvet cloth, on the velvet cloth at her feet, and at her feet he had bowed his head, and she had crushed his heart under the heel of her foot. He didn't know why she would do this to him. Why to him, her Angel of Music? And after such pain, why was he still breathing?

Raoul ran from the box and onto the stage. Meg knelt by Erik who writhed on the floor of the wooden bridge, trembling and crying and screaming obscenities. His eyes were clenched tightly shut, and his arms were wrapped around his chest and abdomen as if he were in pain. His knees were drawn up tightly against his torso. He pressed his chin down on his knees, his body a rounded mass of pure nerves. The sound coming from his mouth wasn't human. Meg was crying hysterically, calling to Erik over and over, telling him she loved him, she loved him, to please come back. Raoul tried to move her to the side, to see if he might help. But seeing Erik in the throes of madness, he feared there was nothing he could do. Even so, he knelt beside the suffering man and lifted him into a sitting position. Leaning against Raoul's shoulder, Erik opened his eyes for one moment and looked wildly around him. Then he pushed away from Raoul, got to his knees and then to his feet. He ran along the parapet to the spiral staircase and plunged down the steps. Half way down, he came face to face with a startled Christine.

He gasped. The shadow in his dreams. He stared, incredulous, at her face. His hand reached out to touch her brown hair. She was real! The reality of her astounded him. He hadn't seen her before this moment, but he knew her! He knew she had been the one. *She* had betrayed him. She had trampled his heart and brought him out onto the stage before the eyes of the twisted, ugly people who watched him and laughed at his pain. Someone was pursuing him. He heard someone running along the boards above him, calling out a name. "Christine!" Yes, that was her name. Christine, his angel, Christine, his tormentor. He looked into her eyes and remembered. He remembered! And his heart shattered like glass into a million shards. He squeezed past her and fled from the stage. Shadows stood watching him go. They had no faces. No one would ever have a face again.

He ran blindly, looking for a door. Everything was wrong. The door was not where it should be. He pushed against the wall. It didn't budge. He must get away. He must get away! They were coming fast. Where were his secret openings, his sliding panels, his hidden doors? They were coming for him, and they had torches. They would burn him! He couldn't go on. He couldn't run anymore. He pressed himself up against the wall and slumped to the floor exhausted. His eyes burned. He didn't want them to put him in the cage again. They would lock him away in the cage. *Please, let me go down into the cellars! I'll stay there and never come up again.* He'd wall himself away. He'd bury himself deep, so deep that not even *she* would find him. They would search the tunnels, bring their torches to the very corners of his lair. They wouldn't find him. She wouldn't find him. She?

They were behind him now. He heard them pant for he had suddenly stopped crying. But he listened for *her*. She had come, too. He remembered her smile. She cooled his fevered brow with the touch of her hand. She covered him in blond tresses. She pressed his face to her breast, and no one could find him, no one could stare at him. She forced him to live. She dragged him from the brink of madness. He had drowned in it until she came. Meg. The pounding at his temples came more slowly, more softly, dimly now, only a shadow of its former self, and then was gone. He slowly opened his eyes and glanced over his shoulder. There were no torches. He wasn't frightened anymore. They had faces again. Hers was among them. Her face drew near, but he was falling backwards away from her into blackness.

The scene shifter helped Raoul carry Erik to one of the nearby dressing rooms and lay him on a divan. Meg removed the mask and dropped it on the floor. Raoul heard the surprise in the scene shifter's gasp, but the man held his ground in case he was needed. Meg sat beside Erik, stroking his face. She kissed him softly and called to him. At his side, Christine was quietly crying, brushing away the tears discreetly as if no one would notice. Even Raoul felt shaken by old memories. Erik began to stir, moaning low in his throat. When he opened his eyes, he saw only Meg. Everything was jumbled in his mind. He couldn't quite understand why he was in a dressing room. He had the strange feeling that he had been dreaming fitfully for a long time and had awoken in a different room of the house, not in the bed where he had lain down to sleep years and years ago. The dream had been frightening. It must have been a dream. He was with Lucianna Fiortino. She took him away from Meg and from his children. He had lost everything. There had been … a fire. He raised his hands quickly to his face, expecting to see the proof that it was a dream. But along his palms he saw the proof of the nightmare. They were scarred with unnaturally smooth skin as if it had melted and solidified again.

He grabbed Meg and hugged her tightly to his chest. She had been crying. He released her and pushed himself into a position that allowed him to see the others. Christine and Raoul were staring at him, concern obvious on their intent faces. He remembered everything, but it didn't fit together. He had lived too many lives. He felt as if he were naked. The only one he could bear to have see him at this moment was Meg. He clung to her again and whispered against her face, "Please ask them to go."

Meg turned and asked the others to leave them for a while.

Erik lifted his hand to his face and found it bare. The mask was lying on the ground. The blood rushed to his face, and he felt strangely ashamed. Meg saw the gesture and grabbed his hand and squeezed it tightly. "Do you remember now? Do you know who I really am? Who you are?"

Erik's lips began to tremble, and he didn't trust his voice. He nodded his head instead.

"Oh, thank God! I've missed you so terribly, Erik." She hugged him tightly. "Do you remember the fire? Lucianna?"

"Then it's true? It really happened?"

Meg nodded, watching him carefully.

"I didn't know, Meg. I didn't remember. Forgive me." He blushed to recall that he had lived with Lucianna as her husband.

"No, you don't have anything to be ashamed of." She kissed his eyes and his cheeks. She tasted salt, his tears and his sweat.

Erik wanted to squeeze her tightly until her body merged into his. He wanted her to cover him and hide him from the world. His hands ran along her back. He knew she was too small, too delicate to shield him. He felt his hands large and supple, broad and firm against her, and it made him want to hold her and keep her always near. She kissed his cheek, running her soft, swollen lips against even the ugly, rough texture of his shame. He trembled under her touch, her kisses burned, and the pain was exquisite. He wanted to taste her. She lifted his face to hers and brought his mouth to her lips. There she stayed, captured by his yearning desire, pierced by his hungry tongue. She lay, stretching her body out along his, her bosom solidly against his chest. Their breathing fell into the same rhythm. Her hands pulled at his shirt, seeking his flesh as he continued to delve inside her, warm and moist. His hands slid down past her hips and cupped the rounded flesh through the slim layer of her costume and guided her down, hard, against his groin. He didn't know where he found the strength, but he pushed her away only long enough for them to remove their clothes.

His whole body shivered when her naked skin touched his. Even then he waited, lingered, stretched out the moment as long as humanly possible. He wanted to remember her body, inch by inch. He lay to the side of her and bent over her breasts. He lovingly kissed them, pleased that he knew her secrets. He kissed the damp underside of each one and ran his hands the length of her body from the hollow of her armpit to the sloping descent of her belly. With his lips, he gratefully traced the scars, light, almost imperceptible along her abdomen where she had carried their children. He lost himself in the tangle of the dark blond hair between her thighs. Her thighs opened to his hand, and he followed with kisses, dangerous and demanding. Meg felt the spasms of pleasure spread like his fingers, as if they were everywhere at once, along her body. Shuddering, incapable of stifling the cry that surged from the deepest part of her, Meg begged him to take her, but his mouth hungrily said no and kissed the tender flesh behind each knee until his hands had touched every inch of her skin and he knelt finally between her thighs and came forward to rest his weight on his elbows, his lips kissing the base of her throat, licking the ridge of her collar bone to settle lovingly on the brown mole afloat in the sea of cream of her skin. Erik choked back his tears. "It's you, Meg. It's you." His tongue traced circles around the mole, and Meg took his face in both her hands and again forced his mouth to hers.

"Take me. Take me now, Erik!" she insisted, her mouth on his, the words swallowed between them. But Erik still resisted. He held himself urgently pressed against her, but refused to enter.

"Meg, who am I?"

She nearly sobbed with need. "Mine. You're mine. My Erik, my monster, my angel, my poor creature, my glorious love. Have pity. Take me!"

Erik surged forward, meeting equal force from Meg's pinned body. He sank deeply, deeply, again and again, with increasing force and urgency, until he felt his own hands on Meg as if they touched his body, as if Meg had taken root inside him, no boundaries between them. He felt savage and wild. He trapped her gasps of pleasure as if they had come from him. They were locked together in a final burst of pure joy that rippled along the length of them. Eventually they collapsed in each other's embrace, their limbs inextricably linked, their breath the same.

Erik woke feeling Meg stir beneath him. She lay crushed under his weight, and he wondered how she had not suffocated. He rolled slightly to his side, freeing her. As he felt her rise from the divan, he reached for her arm and held her back. She kissed him and told him to sleep. He was safe. He trusted her. He laid his head back on the cushions, exhausted, wishing he could sleep a thousand years. He felt the blanket Meg draped over his body and drifted gratefully off to dreamless sleep.

When he woke, the room was only dimly lit. Someone had left the light burning low in the gas lamp. He was disoriented for a moment. He saw the dressing table and on its surface, propped up against the mirror, his mask. Meg. Yes, he remembered. It was settling slowly, carefully into place. He called out to Meg, but she was gone. Something he needed to remember was hidden from him. He felt it urgent to remember. Meg should be here. She said he was safe. Rising from the divan, he found his clothes neatly laid out for him. Meg's costume from rehearsal hung in the open closet. She had dressed and gone? Having pulled on his stockings, breeches, and boots, he flung his arms into the shirtsleeves without bothering to button the front, opened the door, and called out for Meg with increasing urgency, not caring what others might think.

Christine and Madeleine rushed down the corridor toward him. He closed his shirt and fumbled at the buttons. Madeleine pushed his nervous hands away and fastened each one carefully while he watched her, his eyes moving from her hands to her face and back again. She started to take his sleeve to fix his cuff but he grabbed her hands and brought them to his face. He studied them, rubbed his thumbs along the back of them. He seemed lost in thought and then he kissed each hand, squeezing them tightly against his mouth. Madeleine made a little choked sound, pulled her hands away, wrapped them around his neck, and cried.

"My Madeleine," he whispered as he returned her hug.

Looking past her at Christine, he reached out a hand toward her. Madeleine let go of him and stepped to the side, watching him with concern. Christine stepped forward and took his hand. He didn't embrace her as he had Madeleine. He held her away from himself, tensely and carefully at arm's length. But he spoke tenderly. "Christine. You're well?" Then he added, "Of course, you are. You named her after me?" Christine felt the words trapped in her throat, suddenly overwhelmed by emotion. She couldn't take her eyes from his face! He wasn't wearing the mask! She finally managed to say, "We thought you died in the fire."

He watched her intently. "I did. Many times." Then he asked, the anxiety returning to his voice, "Where is she?"

"She had to go somewhere."

"What time is it?" he insisted.

"A little past eleven. She said that …"

"Did she go alone?"

Christine hurried to assure him, "Raoul followed her. She insisted she was supposed to go alone, but he promised no one would know he was with her. What is it, Erik?"

Erik remembered the urgent thing lurking in the dark. Without answering, he went for his mask and coat and ran from the theater.

Giovanni mad a sadist pretended to be my friend wants to pervert anyone he comes into contact with was there at the Teatro when I went to watch Meg sing already there his leering face drew up next to mine while I watched her he had already been there was following me wanting me to be like him! he whispered like the snake in paradise into my ear telling me to take her to take her as my mistress he laughed and sneered about her said she was wanton like all artists she lived by flaunting herself for the pleasure of men that women didn't understand what was going on in a man's mind while he watched a beautiful woman barely dressed on the stage singing and moving with such freedom playing the innocent or the whore the victim or the tormentor, Meg enjoyed it, reveled in arousing men, she was using me to get what she wanted so I should get what I wanted from her, wives were meant to seal alliances to increase property and guarantee the legal inheritance of property but they weren't made for love they couldn't bear the needs of a real man, a real man had to hunt and tear his prey, that was what Meg was for, take her, tell her she has to submit, she's weak, force yourself on her dominate her she won't be able to resist you, you are the beast the beast that demands satisfaction he poured his foul desires into my ear and I imagined doing those things to Meg and he led me to Roderigo's to show me what a man does and paid for the services of two whores enough to keep them in bed and compliant for the entire night, we sat and drank and smoked opium until my mind was so fogged I wasn't sure if what I was seeing was real or just smoke, Giovanni stripped and when I didn't move he came and tugged at my vest, the buttons on my shirt, I felt his hands on my body, when my clothes lay on the floor, I still felt his hands on my body, then more hands and mouths, several mouths all over me until I thought they were going to bite me and tear large chunks from my flesh and I felt him rip my mask away and throw it to the other side of the world and I sank down onto another body, warm and alive, pleasantly aware that it offered little resistance to my increasing urge to find my own pleasure, and Giovanni was too close, too close to me, his laughter rang in my ears and I felt pleasure and disgust wash over me, I struggled uselessly to move away from him but hands held me in place and I closed my eyes and rode the waves of alternating pain and pleasure, I know I made horrible animal noises and then I felt blood, warm, smelling faintly of copper and feces, and Giovanni was no longer near me I saw him miles and miles away down inside a tunnel his hand moving up and down across someone's naked flesh and blood spreading out over the bed, I rolled away so it wouldn't touch me but it kept coming closer and closer and someone fell against me, heavy, I groaned and then I was somewhere else, somewhere where people were laughing and milling around and there was tinny music, gaily tinkling, but it made me sad and breathless at the same time and then it was morning and I woke to see myself drowned in human flesh and sweat I pulled myself from their bodies holding back the urge to retch I dressed and fled, he wanted to teach me, to show how to touch Meg, and now he wants to talk with her in the middle of the night and alone and I thought he wanted to tell her how sullied I was, about that night at Roderigo's, about the blood and the pain of women, but now I fear he wants more, he means to take her as he took those poor whores to cut and mutilate her and rape her and I can't let that happen, he will not touch her, not Meg, not her, I'll kill him first I'll kill him before I let him touch her like he touched those women like he touched

He was too late! Meg lay on the ground. Erik prayed she was unconscious, not dead. Raoul, saber drawn, was defending himself from the mad onslaught of a tall man wearing a cape similar to the one Erik often wore. His back was to Erik. Even so Erik knew who Raoul's opponent was, and he was sure the man wore a mask as well as the cape. It wouldn't be the first time Giovanni Cimino had impersonated him!

Over Giovanni's shoulder, Raoul saw Erik running hell bent in their direction. Giovanni only became aware of him when he heard a gut-wrenching cry of demonic fury. Raoul had been on the defensive for some time—Giovanni had stabbed him in the arm when Raoul went to Meg's aid—so he was genuinely relieved to see Erik. However, he feared Erik was no match for Giovanni, for Raoul had already had occasion to test both men. Erik's only hope was his unpredictability and his sheer will!

Before Raoul could hail Erik, Giovanni veered to the side and prepared to fight them both. Instead of stopping to assume a pose, to judge his opponent's strategy, Erik swung his sword belligerently at Giovanni. Taken off his guard by Erik's ferocious advance, Giovanni let his sword fall just slightly. Slipping past his adversary's sword, Erik's body slammed into Giovanni's, knocking the wind out of him. Stumbling backward, Giovanni had only enough time to defend himself against the wild thrusts and lunges of Erik's steel. Raoul took a moment to breathe and check on Meg. He approached to join the fight, but Erik growled through clenched teeth for him to stay back.

"Meg?"

"All right," Raoul answered in clipped discourse so as not to distract Erik. All Erik's concentration must be focused on fighting Giovanni.

"Take her. Go!"

Raoul was torn. He was fairly sure that between the two of them they could defeat Giovanni. But if Giovanni unexpectedly killed one of them, the other alone might not succeed. That would leave Meg at the mercy of the madman. Raoul's arm was bleeding, and even though the wound was not mortal, it was seriously weakening him. While Erik fought Giovanni, keeping him at bay, Raoul could get Meg to safety and get help. He had looked about the piazza for signs of life, but it was eerily silent, deserted. The shops had closed long ago. Along the side streets were residences and small businesses. There he might find assistance.

Raoul could see that Erik was still on the attack, but Giovanni was a skilled swordsman. If Raoul left now, he might save Meg, but Erik might die.

At that moment, Erik backed away from Giovanni—out of his immediate range—and took off his mask. He turned toward Raoul. Erik's look was enough to decide him. Raoul lifted Meg, unconscious, into his arms, whispered a farewell to Erik, and rushed toward the closest side street.

When Giovanni saw what Raoul was about to do, he screamed in rage and ran to prevent him from leaving with Meg. Erik's sword intervened and forced him back, giving Raoul the space and time he needed.

"I'm a new man, Giovanni. If you want to imitate me, you'll have to abandon the mask and get a face like this one." Erik smiled mirthlessly at his young nemesis, his teeth shining madly in the dim light of the piazza. "You can't have her! She loves *me*. The mask won't do. You could never give her what she wants, because she wants *me!*"

Giovanni tried to follow Meg and Raoul, but each time he shifted, Erik was there.

Raoul knocked on several doors before he found anyone willing to open for him. On the fourth try, a candle was lit, and an old man called from the other side.

"We need help. I've an injured lady. Please let us in!"

The man hesitated, but Raoul's voice was reassuring. He told the man who he was and that an assault was in progress as they spoke. Eventually the old man cracked open the door. The moment he saw that Raoul indeed was carrying a young woman in his arms, he opened and ushered the two of them into the side parlor. "Get help. Police. A doctor," was all Raoul had the energy to say.

"You're hurt, Signore."

"There's no time. Stay with her. Send someone."

The old man nodded. As Raoul was leaving, he could hear the man rouse the house, calling for his sons to go for the police and the doctor.

Erik had watched Raoul disappear around the corner and counted in his head until he judged there had been enough time for him to get to safety. As long as she was safe! Nothing else mattered. Absolutely nothing. He would send this fiend to hell or die in the attempt. Raoul would protect her. He would take her and the children with him to Paris, and if Giovanni walked away from this fight alive, he still wouldn't have Meg. And if there was an afterlife, Erik would come back and haunt the man's dreams and make his waking life a hell on earth. He vowed this and lunged forward and sliced a small gash on Giovanni's sword hand to seal the vow with the required blood sacrifice. He smiled grimly to himself.

"What ... do you ... think you're doing ... with the mask, ... Giovanni?" He had to watch the young man carefully. Unfortunately their reach was similar—they were approximately the same size—so Erik didn't have the advantage he had over most men. His fencing teacher had enumerated on several occasions the advantages he should use against his opponent. Size was one factor, the specific length of the sword arm, the dexterity of using both his left and his right hands, his agility, his speed, his determination, his ability to take punishment, and his insanity were, not necessarily in that order, his other advantages. Skill was one that the fencing master always left out implying that Erik hadn't attained the level of mastery that he needed. This had the effect of spurring Erik on to learn the finer points of fencing. He had learned and improved greatly since the last time Raoul had seen him with a sword. But Giovanni was younger, and although that never seemed significant before, it might be more important than Erik had thought.

Giovanni pretended not to hear Erik at first, but eventually his egotism won out over his pragmatism. "It's so much easier ... doing what I want ... while hiding behind this mask. Surely you know this, Erik. After all, you've ... murdered and raped."

"In another lifetime, my dear friend, in another lifetime." It was no surprise to Erik that Giovanni knew that he was the Phantom that had haunted the Opera Populaire. He cared little to set the record straight or to give the man excuses for the life he had led. Erik could not undo what had been done.

"Ah, so you've gotten ... your memory back?" Giovanni lunged forward and nearly reached Erik's throat.

"Yes, I'm happy to announce that we're all here! Erik the Phantom ... Erik Costanzi ... Erik Fiortino ... and Henri Fournier. So, mon pauvre ami, you're actually fighting at least ... four men, any of whom is your superior." Erik slowed his steps, brought in his sword, and limited his movements to a small bull's-eye over Giovanni's heart. He felt his breathing relax and time slow. "Why won't you leave us alone? I've done nothing to you."

"Meg chose your ... ugly ... face over mine! I spent ... three years in prison ... because of you! You should ... have stayed away."

"I love my wife. You must learn to lose more graciously, young man."

"Don't condescend to me!" Giovanni was making broader and broader circles with his strokes. Anger was working against him and for Erik. "You should ... have ... burned in that ... fire!"

"I saved your life." Erik spit this out at the man as if it expressed the depths of his disgust.

He felt that Giovanni's rhythm somehow shifted at that moment. Perhaps he hadn't realized that it was Erik who carried him to safety. Perhaps he simply didn't want to be called to accounts.

"I'm going to kill you now, Giovanni." Erik's breathing was so regular and calm that he seemed not to be exerting himself in the least. "It's sad, because I saved you once. If you had any honor, you would have walked away from Meg years ago." Erik stepped forward, driving Giovanni back. "I don't regret having saved you from the fire." He lunged forward. Giovanni swerved to the side at the last moment. Erik was unconcerned. He continued, as if nothing had happened. "Everyone deserves a chance to make amends. But since I saved you, I believe it is my right to kill you now. In the East, they have a saying about such matters." Giovanni was out of breathe. Erik lowered his sword slightly. The two men circled one another, swords raised but quiet. "Your life is my responsibility, and I won't let you do any more harm than the harm you've already done." Erik lifted the sword in his grip and aimed it at Giovanni, his intentions clear. His eyes—two dark green stones—held no hesitation, no doubt.

Giovanni spit out a vicious curse at Erik as he put his energy into a series of thrusts. Erik fended off his advances easily now, stepping aside, easing forward, meeting each thrust with his own blade, biding his time, watching for weakness. His cold and steady eyes never left Giovanni's sword. His concentration was almost diabolical in its calm.

Giovanni, on the other hand, was angry. Those areas of his face not hidden under the mask were flushed dark with blood, and his breathing was harsh and labored.

"Do you ... remember ... Roderigo's, Erik?"

Erik's gaze momentarily lost the sword and lit on the smoothed material of Giovanni's mask. The error unsettled him, but he quickly regained his composure.

"You are no better ... than I am!" Giovanni hissed at him, his mouth uncovered, shocking in its nakedness. Unfortunately he was beginning to sweat profusely, the moisture pooling round his eyes, trapped by the mask. Sweat glistened in the poor light of the piazza, near the corners of his mouth, along the rough texture of his chin.

Erik saw his opening, knowing the move Giovanni was about to make. "There you're mistaken, Monsieur Cimino." Erik's mouth twisted up on one side in a cruel smile. As his opponent shifted his weight from one foot to another, preparing for another assault, Erik switched his sword from his left hand to his right hand. "I'm certainly a better fencer than you are." Erik lunged forward into the opening that Giovanni had unintentionally left for him. The sword plunged into Giovanni's throat, severing the spinal cord. Blood gushed through his opened mouth, his eyes frozen in a look of surprise and horror. Erik pulled the blade from the wound. The man was dead before his body hit the paving stones.

Raoul was followed by two strong young men from a nearby shop. But when he came around the corner he stopped dead in his tracks. Erik had learned his fencing "on stage," following the instructions a fencing master gave to the actors in the opera for those dramatic sword fights feigned before an audience. It was only sheer madness and will that made him dangerous with a sword. He had no real training or skill! However what Raoul saw before him was not what he remembered from years past nor what he had left behind when he took Meg away from the danger.

Giovanni and Erik were calmly—with the deadly certainty of serious and fatal intent—circling one another. Ironically, from a distance, the masked Giovanni was the one who reminded Raoul of the Phantom, while Erik whose disfigurement was barely discernible was the unmasked hero. The two men were otherwise of a piece. He understood why Erik had removed his mask. If he hadn't, it was uncannily as if a man were fighting his mirror image. He wanted no one to confuse him with Giovanni.

The swords met, and the clash was unforgiving and constant. Watching Erik's control of the sword was like seeing a different man. He had never wielded a sword with such grace and accuracy, such conservation of movement and energy. The wildness was gone, replaced by cold calculation and the precision of much practice and study. Giovanni, on the other hand, was tiring. His defense was sloppy. Raoul froze as Giovanni parried several strokes from Erik and countered with a lunge forward. Raoul's attention was so focused on the threat posed by Giovanni that he hadn't noticed Erik's feet, the shift in angle, the toss of the sword from one hand to the other, and the upward thrust as Giovanni left himself unprotected.

The two men were suspended for a moment. So close were they that it seemed almost an embrace. It reminded Raoul of two statues like those which grace so many of the fountains in Rome, this one a depiction of Jacob wrestling the angel or perhaps more fittingly the battle between Michael and Lucifer. Then the tableau was broken. Slowly the one in the mask fell away from Erik's hold to the ground. Erik pulled the sword from his enemy's throat. He stood transfixed, staring at the dead man at his feet.

The danger past, Raoul took his time crossing the width of the piazza. Erik must have heard him approach, but he said nothing for several moments. "It was almost as if I killed myself," he whispered. Whether he meant anyone to hear him or not, Raoul wasn't sure. Raoul bent over the dead man and was about to rip the mask from his face, but Erik called to him in a sharp tone. "Leave it. Let the authorities unmask him." He couldn't explain why it was important. Raoul, too, had a strange feeling as they walked away from the corpse. Looking over his shoulder, he couldn't shake the odd sensation that they were walking away from the corpse of the Phantom.

"Meg?"

"She's all right. I think she was stunned in the fall." Erik looked sharply at Raoul, a hint of fear on his face. "A head wound is nothing to be treated lightly."

Raoul led him directly to the shop. The old man and his family gaped when they saw Erik's face, but he paid them no attention. The doctor had more presence of mind than to draw back in fear upon seeing Erik's disfigurement. His only concern was for the patient. When he saw the smile on her face, he assured everyone that the lady was fine, just a minor bump on the head. He then turned his attention to Raoul, who was deathly pale.

"You left me," Erik whispered near her face, a note of anger creeping into the hoarse sound. "You did a stupid thing!"

"I wanted to protect you from him." She defended herself weakly. "Once upon a time he had convinced me that he loved me. For the sake of that love, I thought he'd listen." She gnawed on her lower lip, fighting the urge to cry.

"When I arrived, he wasn't there. I waited and waited. Then he came out of the dark. The first thing I could see was the mask. I knew you were asleep in the dressing room, but it was as if he were you. It confused me for a moment and frightened me speechless. I realized he must be mad. He told me he was scarred, like you, as if that was what I wanted. Then he saw that I wouldn't go with him. He was nothing like the Giovanni I had known."

She lowered her eyes and looked away from Erik. "He told me things that I don't want to believe." She paused expecting Erik to dispel her worries. When he said nothing, she raised her eyes to his. He sustained her gaze, his eyes serious and steady. There was no denial or reassurance in those dark green orbs that watched her unblinkingly.

"We'll talk later," he said.

She felt cold inside. She had wanted him to reassure her, to embrace her and say it was all right. Instead, he held himself coldly aloof, by the door, waiting for the coach that one of the old man's sons had gone to hail.

Raoul offered to stay and deal with the authorities, but he was wounded. Erik insisted that Raoul and Meg be taken home immediately and said that he would remain if the officers insisted. That didn't prove necessary. The police were loath to impugn a French count's reputation. Besides, the lady explained that the dead man had kidnapped her and meant to do her and her husband harm. The final piece that convinced them that there was nothing amiss was that the dead man had a history of criminal activity. So the police officers were satisfied with the brief statements made at the crime location and said that they would be in touch if they needed more information.

The ride home was curiously quiet. Raoul assumed Erik was tired. Surely this day had exhausted him emotionally and physically. He himself was uninterested in conversation and only wished to collapse into bed. Meg consciously pushed her fears aside. She examined her husband. He had gone through hell, just like she had, these past months. If what Giovanni had said was true, it didn't matter. It couldn't change who the man by her side was. She had come to know him as Erik Fiortino, and she still loved him. Even if he had never regained his memory, she would have loved him.

Erik was exhausted. As he brought Meg to the bedroom, he caught a glimpse of a small figure down the hall. Having heard them arrive, Mario had wiped the sleep from his eyes, had dressed quickly, and was standing in the hallway, awaiting Erik's instructions.

Erik had no time to deal with the boy at the moment. He called down the hall, just loud enough for Mario to hear, "Go back to bed." The child drew back inside the room. Then Erik disappeared with Meg into the bedchamber.

He was upset with her for having been so foolish. She might have been harmed. Images of the brutalized women at Roderigo's flashed, unsolicited, across his mind's eye. Giovanni certainly would not have been gentle with Meg. He had hated them both too much. In the coach, on the way to Don Marcelo's, Erik repeatedly went over his encounters with Cimino until the pieces finally began to make sense. He had been played for a fool by his worst enemy! He didn't regret killing him, not really, but his death didn't erase the uneasiness that plagued Erik. The sight of Giovanni masquerading as the Phantom shocked Erik's sensibilities. Giovanni had been mad. And what of the Phantom? Had he, too, been mad?

Meg took the powders the doctor had given her for the headache and snuggled deeply under the covers. He couldn't be angry with her, not at this moment. He might have lost her! She asked him if he were coming to bed, but he declined. He had slept most of the day away, and there was something he needed to do.

He waited until she dropped off to sleep, and then he slipped down the hall to his children's room. Placing his hand on the doorknob, he paused. He didn't know where his mask was. He had taken it off during the fight. Even when the police officers arrived, he had not had it. They were shocked by his appearance, but he stared them down, daring them to say something.

Laurette had seen his face since the day she was born. He never wore it with the children. But it had been a long while since Laurette had seen him unmasked. Did she even remember him? Would he frighten her now if he stole in at night, and she woke to see his face? He was more confident that François wouldn't be afraid. He was old enough to remember Erik without the mask and to understand. Meg had explained to the boy Erik's lack of memory. He was sure his son would be delighted to find his father was back.

He thought Raoul might have picked the mask up. But everyone was asleep, and he couldn't go about the house searching for it at this late hour. He could wait until morning to find that mask or another one. Ambivalent, he stood by the nursery door. He so wanted to hold them both that he thought it would do irreparable damage to his heart if he waited any longer. The room would be dark. That would have to do. He quietly slipped inside, let his eyes adjust to the darkness, and made his way to his son's bed.

François lay twisted on his belly with one leg hanging over the edge of the bed. He had kicked the coverlet to the ground. Erik bent and spread it out over his son. He knelt closely to the boy's face and watched him breathe. He hesitated—he didn't want to wake him—before he raised his hand to stroke the loose dark curls that had fallen across his son's forehead. He'd be content with this for the time being. He loved his children almost painfully, but he had missed chunks of François's life. He hadn't been with Meg when she carried and gave birth to their first child. He had missed several of the early years of the boy's childhood. Yet when he looked at him, he felt that his tie to the boy could never be broken. François had his eyes, his brow, and the shape of his head. Meg had said that François had Erik's face. Erik preferred to consider the bits and pieces that he recognized in the boy's face rather than the face as a whole. For his own face, to him, was nothing but bits and pieces, good ones and bad ones, whereas François was beautiful. François had inherited more than his looks, too. He was undeniably the child of his heart, and he could no sooner deny him than deny himself.

He turned to the little girl. Laurette had stolen his heart and held it like a plaything in her pudgy little hands from the first breath she took. He couldn't look at her without wanting to hold her, without smiling with an emotion that was pure joy. Laurette had her mother's eyes, soft brown and filled with love. He had been there when she was born. He had seen her crawl and take her first steps. He had heard her first words. He carried her around whenever the nanny or Meg did not. And if she learned to walk late, it was entirely his fault! She was a piece of him.

He wasn't aware that his eyes had filled with tears until one fell onto Laurette's cheek and the child stirred. Quickly he whispered endearments to comfort her. He'd never forgive himself if he frightened her! But she wiggled under the tightly tucked blanket and hit him innocently with her outstretched fist on the mouth. "Laurette, mon ange, c'est moi, Papa," he crooned to her. When she heard him say that it was papa, she raised her arms to him, wanting to be picked up and held.

He pulled down the coverlet and lifted her into his arms, stood and walked around the room, talking to her in soft whispers. She leaned her face against his shoulder and within moments was asleep again. He could feel sleep sit on her like a cat, her body firm, solid, and heavy. She molded herself to him as if she were a part of him still.

"Papa, are you home now?" François had awoken as well. He must have watched Erik with his baby sister for some time, listening to the singsong rhythm of his father's voice.

"Yes, François, I'm home. I'm sorry that it took me so long to remember. I couldn't help it." He laid the little girl in her bed and made sure the barriers were securely in place to prevent her falling. François had gotten out of the bed and come to him. He grabbed Erik before he could turn around and hugged him tightly.

"I knew you'd remember if I played the song. I knew you'd come back. Maman said to be patient. She said you loved us, even though you couldn't remember us. Is that true?"

Erik thought back to the night Meg had brought him to see her children. "Yes, your mother is right. I always loved you even when I didn't know you were mine!"

A light filtered through the door. Madeleine had come to check on the children and had heard Erik's voice. "They need their sleep, Erik," she whispered.

He kissed his son once more and squeezed him tightly. "Tomorrow we start our lessons. I hope you've practiced?"

"Yes, Papa. Every day."

Madeleine closed the door after Erik left.

"Children are resilient, aren't they?" She accompanied him to his room, enjoying the intimacy she felt they both had achieved.

Erik didn't respond to this. He wasn't sure he agreed with her. "For some, it takes longer to recover." He bent, kissed her on the cheek, and said goodnight.

When Erik returned to the bedchamber, he found Meg awake, peering out from the covers, quietly waiting for him to speak.

"Meg, what Cimino said to you tonight about me ..."

Meg reached up and brushed his lips with her fingers to quiet him. "I don't need you to talk to me about it. I know the kind of man Giovanni had become. I can tell that what happened troubles you." She hadn't meant to ever mention the ugly things Giovanni had delighted in saying to her, but the words came spilling. "Before you speak, let me say something." Erik felt strangled by the need to tell her the truth, to lie to her, to beg her forgiveness, to vow he'd never again do anything to shame her, to stop her mouth with kisses, to run and hide forever somewhere where her eyes couldn't see him. But he held his tongue and waited, praying that she'd somehow know what to say to ease his guilt and make it possible for him to go on living with her. "I love you. You were a different man then. Now you've come home to me. You're my Erik."

"No, Meg. It's not that easy." He still felt a surge of anxiety and doubt rising to the surface even now, safe at home with his family. "I did things that I never would have done before." How could she still love him?

She swallowed her tears and groped for a clear, controlled voice. "Giovanni told me things about a night the two of you spent together at a certain place."

"He told you about the bordello."

"Yes."

"You must have been shocked."

"Yes, I think it was the violence more than anything."

She had trouble thinking of the right words to use. It did bother her to think of Erik with another woman. It nearly drove her mad with grief and jealousy to imagine him with Lucianna. But a visit to a bordello was not the same thing as his relationship with Lucianna over the past months. The night he spent with Giovanni at Roderigo's was just that—one night. It struck her as less significant than were the nights he had spent being a husband to Lucianna. And of course with Lucianna there might have been children, and it might have lasted his lifetime. But the sordid nature of the acts that Giovanni had described to her, she had to admit, shocked her sensibilities and threatened her belief that she understood Erik. She couldn't quite understand how to react to the debauchery Giovanni had described.

"I didn't ... I didn't do those things. I didn't hurt those women, but I didn't stop Giovanni from doing horrible things to them."

"But he said ..."

"He lied if he said that I did that. But ... I watched. And it should have sickened me." He couldn't go on. He couldn't let her know. She'd be disgusted with him, as disgusted as he felt with himself.

She was quiet. She must have already understood what he was about to say.

"I watched, Meg. I was excited, aroused. There was no difference among us. We were four bodies. It was as if whatever was done to one was done to all. I didn't stop him. I let him ... do ... things." He shuddered, overwhelmed by the risk he was taking in telling Meg about that night. "I felt vile." The worst was over. He waited for her revulsion. He could see her tremble. He wanted to touch her but didn't dare to reach out to her.

He wasn't aware that she had moved her hand until her fingers lightly touched the tips of his. He went to her, unable to hold himself back. She accepted him into her arms and held onto him tightly. She murmured into his ear, and he lay pressing his face deep into the crook of her neck, listening to the sounds she was making, sounds of love. She loved him. He knew it. He felt it deep inside—in a small, safe corner of his soul that nothing vile or ugly had ever been able to touch.

CHAPTER 10

❀

What Would You Do For Love?

When thou sigh'st, thou sigh'st not wind
But sigh'st my soul away;
When thou weep'st, unkindly kind,
My life's blood doth decay.
It cannot be
That thou lov'st me, as thou say'st,
If in thine my life thou waste
That art the best of me.

"Song," John Donne

Erik found Raoul at breakfast. The count's left arm was bandaged and supported by a sling. He used his left hand to hold the bread while he slathered its
warm surface with honey. Before him were the crumbs and residue of an
unusual breakfast for a Frenchman, thought Erik. It looked more like the heavy
repasts of the English—egg yoke oranged the porcelain, a meager crisp of sausage had escaped his hunger, seeds from the grilled tomato floated in a clear
liquid on the plate. Erik recognized the rumbling of his own stomach in
response to this evidence of plenty. He told the servant that he'd join Raoul in
breakfast.

"I awoke with an incredible appetite. Monsieur Costanzi sets a very generous table. If we stay much longer, I'll have to send to the tailor for new clothes
or at least have the seams of these let out." Raoul didn't refer to the fact that
Erik had found the mask and was now wearing it.

Erik smiled and poured himself a cup of tea with a heavy dollop of cream
and a generous swirl of honey.

Raoul nodded at the cup. "I see you never learned to drink your tea like a
man," he chided, holding up his own black cup, a crooked smile on his face.

"I cling to certain joys, I suppose," Erik replied almost in embarrassment. Raoul chuckled and nodded as he chewed a rather large bite of his honeyed bread.

"When I lived under the opera house, Madeleine brought me supplies, but they were monotonous and strange combinations of whatever was at hand." Erik stirred the milky tea, lost in the comfort of his newly remembered past. He smiled, one corner of his mouth higher than the other. "I had to sneak up to the dining hall in the dormitories to have anything as nice as hot tea or fresh milk. I used to sneak in after breakfast and before the staff came to clear up. I would go around the tables and drink and eat what was left."

Raoul put his bread down, his appetite dulled by what Erik had just described. He imagined Erik as a boy—for Madeleine had said he was perhaps about Mario's age when she helped him hide in the vaults—drinking the remains of other men's cups.

Erik saw his discomfort and hastened to assure him, "It wasn't as bad as you're imagining. The hall was clean, the food was healthy, and I didn't mind. I had had much worse in the cage." He wasn't sure just how much Raoul knew about his early childhood. Raoul asked no questions, and Erik was relieved he didn't have to explain. "Madeleine brought me what she could to make life comfortable. Her bundles were always exciting. I never knew what treasures she'd bring. She'd come only so far down the stairs." Erik didn't add that Madeleine was afraid to come any closer than the first underground level. "Then she'd leave the bundle on the stairs where I'd retrieve it. You have to remember that she was only a dancer in the company, had no money to speak of, and was quite young herself. One time she packed several tins of boot polish. At the time I had no shoes, much less boots. She must have packed it in the dark from the pantry and grabbed whatever she could. When she left fresh milk or bread, I ate that immediately, then the rest I would ration out to last as long as possible. I ate potatoes raw for a year or so until I finally set up the means to cook a meal. Between Madeleine and the dining hall, I managed quite well."

"No wonder you're a greedy bastard!"

Erik laughed out loud at Raoul's friendly insult. "Yes! Correct on both counts!" The servant set the breakfast tray before Erik who delved into the feast with unusual gusto.

"By the way, you and I deserve our hunger. Giovanni was a damn good fencer. Of course, all modesty aside, I'm the better swordsman. I would have been fine except …"

"Yes, modesty aside. Then what gave him the advantage last night?" Erik cast a meaningful look at the sling.

Raoul paused, seemed to think better of it, and proceeded, "To tell you the truth, it was unsettling to fight him in that disguise. It reminded me of our past encounters. I couldn't shake the sensation that I was fighting the wrong man. Then I was distracted by Meg."

Erik chewed his food thoroughly while he thought of Raoul's strange remarks. But he was more concerned about what had happened to Meg. "How did Meg get hurt? Did it have anything to do with the so-called distraction?"

"When I saw that she was in danger—at first she and Giovanni seemed to be talking and I hoped it would amount to nothing more—I rushed out of my hiding place to challenge him. Instead of facing me, honestly like a man, he grabbed Meg to use her as a shield. He actually drew his sword, ready to fight me, even with Meg trapped under his arm. Meg hampered his style, but then I was tremendously aware that I could skewer her if I made the wrong move. So I let my guard down, and he sliced me. At that moment, Meg bit him. He released her immediately, but he slapped her viciously across the mouth. She fell hard to the ground, and that's how she got the nasty bump she has."

"She was a stupid fool to meet him. You should have stopped her." The account of what had happened in the piazza brought Erik's anger back to the surface. He was annoyed with both of them. He stabbed his sausage with a bit more energy than was necessary.

"I did try, Erik," responded Raoul, seriously.

"I know." His anger lessened in intensity. "She can be … stubborn."

Raoul decided it was best to change the subject. "By the way, you displayed a rather remarkable control of the blade last night. Forgive me for saying so, but you never showed such skill when you and I fought. In point of fact, you weren't very good."

"Then why am I not dead, pray tell?"

"Touché. I suppose it was the element of sheer audacity that kept you alive. You were so damn erratic and, I confess, strong. Whenever you did connect well, the vibration was numbing."

"I imagine that I should thank you for the compliment. At least I think you meant it as a compliment, not an insult." Each man gave a slight bow of the head just over the breakfast plate. "I did fight well last night. Especially given the circumstances."

"At first you came on like you had in the past—all anger and madness. I actually debated leaving you. I thought for sure Giovanni would run you through eventually. Then when I came back, you were using a completely different style. Cold and calculating. I imagine it was difficult since the stakes were so high."

"It was easier once you got Meg away from us. As far as my skills, once we settled here, Marcelo arranged for a fencing master to teach me the fine points. Then Luci …" He felt lightheaded saying her name in such an off-handed way. "Lucianna encouraged me to continue. She hoped it would keep me occupied."

"It shows. Would you be up to doing a little fencing with me on occasion?"

"Yes, I'd like that very much. Perhaps I can give you a few pointers on your imbrocatta."

Raoul studied Erik. The mask hid what Erik wanted it to hide. Evidently he wanted to keep Raoul guessing as to whether or not he had spoken in jest, for his eyes were impassive.

"Well, I look forward to your kind lesson, Monsieur," Raoul replied with a touch of irony. Changing his tone, he ventured to ask, "You wear the mask now all the time?"

His formerly impassive eyes stared up at Raoul curiously. "No."

Raoul waited, expecting Erik to elaborate. But Erik sipped the last drops of his tea. Careful to assure the edges of the mask had not been dirtied, he wiped his mouth gingerly with a napkin. Finally Erik gratified Raoul's patience.

"I have normally worn it in your presence. I remove it in the privacy of my home, with Meg and the children. Mario is used to my face. The servants at the manor and in the apartments I shared with Lucianna became accustomed. It is worrisome for me to keep track of where and with whom I am at the moment, so it's more convenient here to keep the mask on."

"I rode back with you last night in the coach. You didn't wear it then. Indeed once you began to fight, you were without it."

"That was last night. And that was in the dark. But I do take your point. I hope to become comfortable some day without the mask. It's not for you that I wear it today."

After breakfast Erik strolled out to the garden to stretch his legs. Don Marcelo had sent instructions to Sig. Bianchi that Erik and Meg would not be coming today and to continue with rehearsals. The cast and orchestra could certainly work around the principals for one day. Erik felt completely restored and anxious to return to rehearsals. But, of course, Meg should certainly rest. There would be time enough tomorrow to work out the details.

He hoped that the headaches that had chronically plagued him would not be returning. The jumble of images that had flooded him had calmed significantly. He felt whole for the first time in months. There might still be lacunae in his past, but whenever he consciously tried to recall something about Meg or the children or even his life in the opera house, the pieces seemed to come into sharp focus. And although he knew that his time with Lucianna had not been a dream, its details were softer and less real to him than the history that he had just recovered.

Earlier that morning, it had amazed him to wake and find himself beside Meg. Everything about her hummed with life. A thousand vibrations rolled off her as he remembered details that he had not thought about for years. He recalled insignificant as well as significant moments with the same intensity and pleasure. Lying next to her, warmed by her, he had felt alive and joyful in spite of the bloodshed of the previous night, perhaps even because of it. He had not allowed the thought of Giovanni's death to mar his newly found peace. Reluctantly he had left Meg sleeping, driven by an eagerness to greet the day that he had not felt for some time.

As he stepped out onto the garden path, the realization struck him that the opera he was directing was his own. Such a remarkable gift he had been given: to work on the staging of his own creation and to cast his wife in the lead role. If only he could take the stage and play Don Juan. Erik hummed a few bars of Don Juan's first aria, a boastful song full of defiance. He stopped mid-note when he noticed that someone was sitting on a bench between two hedges. Erik glanced round and saw a pair of small dark shoes which he knew belonged to his young servant.

"Did you go back to bed like I told you to?" Erik startled the boy with his gruff voice and stern countenance. He immediately dropped both when he saw Mario's face. The boy's eyes were red, his nose inflamed. His bottom lip jutted out, and Erik could see that it quivered with each shuddered intake of air. He'd been crying. Quickly the child rubbed his shirt sleeve across his entire face expecting to wipe away the evidence of his recent distress.

"Maestro. Do you need me to do something for you?" He stood up alert and eager. He barely reached to Erik's waist. Seeing him next to his own children had convinced Erik that Mario was only a child. He had always known that, but children like Mario who lived in a certain class or fought for survival on the streets were not allowed a childhood. He knew what it was like from his own experience to have a child's mind, a child's needs and fears, and to be forced to live in an unforgiving world of men and women and demons. Victor and François were younger, but even at Mario's age, they would still be wrapped in the protective cocoon of childhood.

"No, Mario. There are plenty of servants here to do my bidding."

Instead of relief, Erik saw the return of despair on the boy's visage.

"Mario," Erik said sternly, "What is this? Why have you been crying?"

"Where will I go, Maestro?" The gates opened, and there was no amount of sleeve wiping that could stanch the flow of tears and mucus now.

"I wasn't aware you were thinking of leaving us."

"I don't want to."

"Then why are you talking about leaving?"

"There are so many servants around, and I've waited for you to send me on an errand, but you haven't sent me on any errands for days now. So I suppose you don't want me around anymore." The boy paused to blow his nose on the handkerchief Erik handed him before going on to say in a small, quiet voice, "I've gotten used to things. The street's not so bad, but I think I'll miss … things."

"Miss things? Like good food and a warm spot before the stove?" Erik asked softly.

"Those things, too." The child sniffled into Erik's handkerchief, wiping eyes and nose liberally, and wadded it into a tight ball to hand back to his master. Erik took the dirty cloth without hesitation and stuffed it into a pocket.

Mario looked up at him with such large, red eyes that Erik knew the boy meant something very different from the good food and warm spot by the stove. He pulled Mario to him and hugged him tightly. The child buried his face against Erik's waistband and grabbed his coat in two tight fists as if his very soul depended on his hanging on to his protector.

"Do you like it here?"

"Here at Sig. Costanzi's?"

"Well, yes. Here. I mean, Mario, with me and with my family whether we're in this mansion or in our apartment?"

He could feel the boy's head nodding fervently against his stomach.

"You could be a friend to my children? And you would obey Donna Meg as if she were …" He struggled to find the correct words. "As if she and I were the same?"

Mario stepped back and smiled up at Erik. "I'll be the best servant! Haven't I always been?"

"Yes, but now it will be a more difficult task. You'll take lessons with François and eventually with Laurette. You'll have to learn to talk and act differently. Like a gentleman."

"But that's not possible, Maestro. François and Laurette were born gentle."

"Mario, I'll tell you a secret. First answer this question. Am I a gentleman? Do people treat me as if I were a gentleman? Do I act like one?"

"Most of the time, you do, Maestro," he replied truthfully. For there were times that his maestro seemed not to care a wit for propriety. Yet he was an artist, so that seemed to explain it.

"Well, that's a fair answer. I wasn't born a gentleman. I'm a bastard and an orphan. Don Marcelo has taken me under his protection. If not for him, I wouldn't even have a name. Yet I am a gentleman—of sorts. Does that change your attitude toward me?" He eyed the boy suspiciously. Mario seemed a bit uncertain.

"No, Maestro. You've been very good to me. I think you're an excellent gentleman. But does Signora Costanzi know she's not married to a gentleman?" Mario whispered cautiously, should anyone hear them.

"Yes, she knows. I want you to stay with me, Mario. I want you to think of me not as your master ..." Again it was difficult to find the right language. He hadn't yet spoken to Meg about taking Mario in and treating him as one of the family. What if she were opposed to his idea? He couldn't abandon Mario, and he didn't want him to slip away among the servants. He was fond of him. He wanted to give him a childhood and a future. It suddenly was very important to Erik to give this boy what he himself had not had. "I want you to think of us ... of Signora Costanzi and myself ..."

"Mario, I think my husband wishes to adopt you." Meg stepped out from behind Erik and smiled at the child. "We'd be like a mother and a father to you. Would you accept that arrangement?" Meg took Erik's arm and squeezed it tightly. He began to say something, but she placed her fingers on his lips to quiet him. As if she could read his mind, she added, "I think it's a wonderful idea. François would so love a brother, especially an older brother, and Mario is very sweet with Laurette." She turned her attention back to Mario. "I know you're already fond of Erik. And he feels the same toward you. I can tell. Can you come to love the rest of us?"

Mario looked up at Meg with eyes of complete rapture. How could he not love her? And François? He'd teach François so many things. Of course, Meg might not approve of some of the skills he could teach François, but Mario was sure his master would understand their usefulness. And between him and

François, they'd take care of Laurette. She'd never have to lift a finger again with the two of them around. The only thing that made him hesitate was the thought of lessons. But if they allowed him to stay with Maestro, then he'd work very hard at them.

"Yes, Signora Costanzi, I think I should be very happy to have a family. I remember what it was like sometimes, when I dream."

Erik caressed the boy's head. Meg understood his silence. She, too, felt her throat tighten. "We'll have to talk about how you should address us. We'll set you up in the children's room and arrange for appropriate clothes later today. Now go on back in the house and get ready for the morning lesson."

Mario bowed from habit and ran back to the house in search of François.

"Are you sure?" Erik asked, staring seriously into Meg's eyes. This was too important for her to agree to without thinking it through. It was a lifetime commitment. And he didn't want her to agree to take in the boy just to please him.

"Yes, I'm sure. I want to fill the house with children. I want to have another child as soon as we can!"

A dark shadow fell upon Erik's face. He slipped his arm out from Meg's and walked over to the flowering bushes, agitated and somber.

"What is it?" Even with the mask, his face was terrible. She could see he was appalled. Why?

"I don't think we …" He stopped as if torn by some insoluble dilemma.

"That we …?" Meg was frightened by his unexpected change in mood. "You don't want me to bear anymore of your children? Are you aware what that would mean?"

Erik looked painfully at her. "Yes, I'm aware."

"You know that there is only one sure way to avoid getting me with child. You'd be able to live with me and never make love to me again?"

"No! No, Meg, I couldn't live with you and not touch you." As if he might prove it to her then and there, he grabbed her close, his hands firmly planted across her back and at the gentle slope of her spine. His face was pressed against her hair. His voice was strained and fearful. "I couldn't live without your touch, Meg. But women die in childbirth. I can't lose you!"

Meg was fully aware that bearing children was dangerous. She remembered how concerned he had been when she was carrying Laurette. But she had been fortunate. She was young and healthy; childbirth had been natural and uneventful for her. Perhaps it was Christine's recent troubles with Erica that made the dangers more substantial and real, even to Meg. Perhaps it was that the two of them had just found each other again. Then he had fought and killed a man. The threat of losing her had been quite real last night. She pulled away to look at him. There was so much pain and fear in his eyes that it nearly broke her heart. She didn't want to think how his concerns might also relate to his time with Lucianna. "I won't die. I'm healthy. My other pregnancies went very well." She tried to tease him. "You yourself have remarked many times on my hips and how suitable my body is for babies! I'm full of life and full of love."

How could he explain to her his sense of loss when he thought of the two babies buried next to Lucianna? They weren't his, but he had believed they were! He had accepted the same grief as Lucianna had experienced. And even the loss of the imagined child he thought she was carrying when she grew ill filled him with dread. He felt as if he had lost three children! And, as mad as it seemed even to him, he had not been able to separate Luci's death from the mistaken understanding that she was carrying his child. He hadn't told Meg the details of his marriage, his relationship to Luci. It was too complicated, even for him. It tortured him to wonder if she'd feel the same if he confessed that he had been overjoyed when Luci told him she was to have a child. What would she think if he told her that he had come to desire and even love Luci in those last months? He remembered how enthusiastic they both had been while preparing for the arrival of the child that never was. Could something like that happen to Meg?

He would have to tell her about Luci, about the child that wasn't, about those last days. He feared the telling would take as long as life itself. He was about to speak when a servant interrupted them. There was a solicitor begging to speak with Sig. Costanzi, Erik Costanzi.

Before Meg turned back toward the house, Erik pulled her into a warm, gentle kiss. As his lips released her, he whispered, "Forgive me."

When she smiled and turned again toward the door, he increased his pressure on her hand. He was in earnest. He wouldn't be satisfied by a smile. "Say it, Meg. Say you forgive me!"

"What? What am I to forgive?" she asked quietly, troubled by his urgency.

All the energy drained from his body, and he released her hand. He felt defeated. There was no way he could explain it to her. He didn't want to leave her in doubt. He'd have to find a way to live with it—everything he had done that he was ashamed of while he had been another man. He had been someone else—Erik Fiortino—and yet himself.

He wanted Meg. He wanted children—more children—with her. He couldn't abandon her bed, not even to save her life. The realization sent a cold blade through his stomach; he felt selfish and greedy. He clung to the hope that bearing him children didn't have to lead to death. "Meg, I fear for you. But whatever comes, comes. I love you. I'm not whole if I'm not with you. I couldn't live without ..." As he looked at her, the intimate nature of his thoughts made him shy and hesitant. "... your touch. I think I'd disappear completely without it."

For a moment, Meg desperately wanted to dismiss whoever had interrupted them and pull Erik behind the tall hedges and make love to him, under the sunshine, in the fresh air, on the closely cropped grass.

"Erik, don't worry. Nothing will happen to me." She promised him the impossible, but he decided to pretend that it was true.

The solicitor was waiting impatiently in the parlor. Raoul and Christine had joined him to keep him company until Erik came. The solicitor in a very matter-of-fact tone informed them that his business concerned only Sig. Erik Costanzi. Raoul and Christine rose to excuse themselves when Erik protested, "Anything you have to say can be said in the presence of the Count and Countess de Chagny. They're old friends. My wife, Signora Costanzi, will also remain." The solicitor acknowledged the brief introductions, and everyone took a seat.

The short, stocky man was all business. He placed several sheets of paper on the table in front of Erik and proceeded to explain that Signora Lucianna Maria Fiortino had signed over to Erik—before her death—certain properties that had been solely in her name, including the mansion by the sea on the island and the surrounding properties. Although his offices had been retained to handle the finances, he had come for Sig. Costanzi's instructions. He also informed him that Signora Fiortino had established an account at an associated bank in the name of Erik Fiortino with privileges allotted to both Henri Fournier and Erik Costanzi as joint owners in which the profits accrued from the opera, *The Stranger*, were deposited. As solicitor, he was fully aware that Erik Fiortino, Henri Fournier, and Erik Costanzi were indeed one and the same person. No fraud was intended in the use of these other identities, but he advised that the necessary papers be completed to simplify the ownership of the account. "Which of the three names would you prefer to use on the account?"

"Erik Costanzi."

"Very well. That concludes my business. The signed papers will be filed and available in our offices. Should you need anything further, here's my card. These bank drafts can be used at any time to withdraw funds or you may contact us whenever you wish and we will handle the transfer of funds to a local establishment."

Erik watched the solicitor leave. He was stunned as were the others in the room.

Finally the count shook his hand in congratulations. "Erik, everything you touch seems to turn to gold! You're a wealthy man in your own right now. A man of property." It was true. Although Don Marcelo had arranged that Erik inherit his estate—including the lion's share of the Teatro dell'Opera and a significant percentage of the Teatro Argentina—that lay far in the future. Erik hoped not to enjoy ownership of these properties for a long time.

But Erik was overwhelmed not so much by the economic windfall as by the fact that Lucianna had provided for his independence. And from the dates on the paperwork, it was apparent that she had done so well before she realized she was ill.

The final production of the season, *Don Juan Triumphant*, opened several days later. The critical reviews were cautiously favorable. However the opening night audience was evenly divided between those who thought the opera a work of genius and others who thought it the work of a madman. Everyone involved in the production was pleasantly surprised that the brouhaha surrounding the opera guaranteed that there was not an empty seat for any of the nightly performances. Don Marcelo was right. Financially there was no way for them to lose money on the venture. There was even talk of extending the run through another week, but Meg was showing signs of exhaustion, and Erik was anxious to move on to other things.

Erik decided that he and his family should spend some time on the island. There were matters to settle related to the running of the property, and the brief hiatus in the opera season was the only time that he could devote to such details. The thought of returning to the island was exciting. Yet he couldn't quite dispel a subtle anxiety that nagged at the back of his mind. Unfortunately, Marcelo would stay in Rome, and Madeleine had resolved, at the last moment, to remain as well. But Raoul and Christine agreed to accompany Erik, Meg, and the children.

If they were to spend time at Lucianna's island manor, it would be good to fill the rooms with life. Perhaps that would make the difference.

He knew it was a mistake to come back to Lucianna's manor the moment he stepped over the threshold. It had been his idea to bring them there. Several months had passed since he had watched over Lucianna's deathbed. He believed he had mourned her death sincerely and was even somewhat grateful to her for many things she had done for him. He had reckoned the debts he owed her time and time again, after his anger had cooled. He was alive. He had found his way back to Meg. He had his children. He had discovered new ground for his friendship with Raoul and Christine, and now he was rich on his own account, a man of property as Raoul would say, a successful composer, and the sincerity of his attachment to Don Marcelo was beyond dispute.

But when he walked into the house a shiver ran through him. He felt *her* fingers crawl up the back of his neck and around his throat. He choked momentarily, coughing to clear his lungs. The smell of smoke and burnt flesh came vividly twisting up inside his nostril's. No one else seemed at all affected by the mansion's ghost, so Erik brushed her fingers from his throat, greeted the staff, and introduced his family and guests.

Gretta had disappeared, as had Luigi and a handful of servants who had been with Lucianna since her marriage to Ponzio. They most likely feared prosecution as part of the fraud their mistress had committed. They had been loyal to Lucianna. If there was a crime, it lay at Lucianna's door, not her servants'. Now that Erik had his memory, Gretta and Luigi were of little consequence to him.

Raoul and Christine were placed in a beautiful and spacious bedroom overlooking the sea. When a dour replacement for Gretta, a Signorina Paglione, led Erik and Meg to the master bedroom, Erik felt his heart in his throat. Without so much as an explanation, he told the house mistress to close and lock that room. No one would be sleeping there. Instead he asked that their luggage be moved to another room at the end of the hall. It was smaller, but more private.

Meg had felt her husband stiffen immediately when they crossed the threshold of the main entrance to the mansion. But he seemed to have recovered once they greeted the staff. When Signorina Paglione showed them to the master bedroom, Meg wasn't surprised Erik balked. Casting an eye into the beautifully appointed room, she herself trembled slightly. This was the room where Lucianna and he had slept as husband and wife. It was also the room where Lucianna died. She pretended not to notice his nervousness.

He woke her in the middle of the night again. He was shuddering. A sound of distress, barely audible, occasionally escaped his lips. Meg nuzzled behind his back and placed her arm around him, hoping it would comfort him, help him make his way through the nightmare. His hand gripped hers and pressed it down hard against his body. Almost immediately his body jerked, and she felt the convulsions through her fingers and along her body pressed against his. Only when the last tremor subsided did his hold on her hand relax, and she slowly withdrew it. She listened as his breathing returned to normal, unaware that she was holding her own breath. She turned and rolled away from him. She knew he was not asleep. She waited for him to speak, but he lay still and quiet in the same position as before, his back to her. A quiet air of betrayal lay between them.

She must have dozed off, for she woke feeling him next to her. She recognized that he was observing her to know if she were awake. He wouldn't wake her if she were deep in sleep. She remained still and pretended. He knew she was pretending. She felt him turn back to his side of the bed. Eventually the weight shifted, and he rose. It was the twilight before dawn when it is both morning and night. She could see him, like a strange daguerreotype, go about his morning ritual. She almost spoke to him, but the crisp air around him was thick, and she couldn't come up with the words strong enough to pierce its armor.

He felt her hands on his body. He moaned as she stroked him. A strand of her hair fell across his parted lips, and he could taste sea salt. She whispered his name in his ear. Her voice was smoke and velvet, not the sharp sweet crystal of Meg's. He bolted awake, ran his hands down his body, finding no hands but his own. Meg lay on her side, her back cuddled up against him, asleep, safe. His eyes searched the darkness, like oil in the moonless night. It was warm, there was no fire, the curtains blew into the room. His eyes settled on a dark corner well away from the windows and from the bed. She was there! The darkness swirled, suggested a form, faded into undifferentiated darkness again. He held his breath to listen. He could hear Meg's soft breathing. It calmed him; his heartbeat slowed in the tranquility of knowing she was beside him. Then his ear twitched as he heard a hint of laughter—or was it crying? The only thing he knew for sure was that it was her!

The sound was coming from outside their room. He rose and threw on his breeches and shirt and went out into the hallway. There, too, it was dark, but he had often walked in the dark. His eyes were very sensitive to the light, and he almost thought he had the gift of seeing in the dark like other cave dwellers. He made his way easily down the passageway to the stairs. The laughter was coming from below. She was leading him somewhere. The air around him grew colder as he descended to the main hall. He shivered and fastened the buttons of his shirt. Where was she? A fluttering of air, a thickening and flow of shadow, drew him toward the back rooms. He found himself in the music room. The windows were closed and yet a soft wind blew past him, wrapping him in the fragrance of lilac and soap. His hair stood on end at the back of his neck. He waited and listened, barely breathing, his body taut like the strings of a violin. Then he heard her again. This time he could make out what she said.

"Play!"

"Luci?" he whispered tentatively, knowing that he must be insane but feeling her presence all around him. His eyes searched the darkness of the room. He could just make out the dark edges of tables and the cream brocade of the divan where one afternoon he had made love to her. Near the window, darker and denser than the enveloping night, stood the piano.

"Play!" The whisper—lingeringly sweet—came from the direction of the divan. *"Hush my babies!"* Luci wanted him to play, to play for her babies. He felt a tightening in his throat. They had, for a time, been his as well.

Erik fought the terror he felt rising from the pit of his stomach and did as she demanded. Very softly he began to play a lullaby. He would play them to sleep, Rafael and Sophia. Perhaps Luci, too, might rest.

Was it her fingers he felt on his cheek? He squeezed his eyes tightly shut. Such pain and loneliness. Her pain bent him toward the piano keys, pressed him in toward the music. Does anyone ever forget?

Under his breath, he pleaded, "Don't, Luci. Please, Luci. Don't do this."

"What would you do for love, Erik?" The words forced his eyes open wide, and his fingers froze on the piano keys. Were they not the words she had spoken on her death bed? What would she ask of him?

From the doorway, he heard Meg call out to him.

"Are you all right, Erik?" It was Meg, he was sure, but his heart pounded so fiercely in his chest he needed to be certain. He heard footsteps retreat and then moments later return and with them the light. Meg stepped into the room with the small lamp from the hallway that she had lit with her candle.

"Why didn't you answer me?" she scolded. "You had me frightened!"

Still he didn't answer. He was thinking of the fingers that had caressed him and the question the ghost had left. *"What would you do for love, Erik?"*

He remembered the reply. *"Anything."*

"Erik, you're frightening me. Let's go back to bed."

"She's here, Meg."

Meg hadn't expected him to say it out loud. She thought and prayed it was only her imagination under the persistent goad of jealousy. Hadn't Christine asked her if it was a good idea to go to the house where Erik and Lucianna had lived as husband and wife? She had dismissed Christine's concern. Now she regretted with her whole heart that they had decided to come. Meg insisted in a low urgent rush, "Erik, come back to bed. Let's go to our room! It's cold." She had just noticed how cold it was in the room in spite of the closed windows. Behind her in the hallway, it was distinctly warmer. She could see Erik's breath—small white clouds of vapor sprang, too quickly, from between his lips. She could see that he was shivering from the chill in the air. Why wouldn't he come?

She stepped forward intending to enter the room. But as she tried to raise her foot, to take the next step forward, her leg turned to stone. Even the air in front of her pushed her back! She retreated one step, and her body was once again her own. Terrified, she cried out, "Erik!"

He was listening to the babies. They cried softly. Luci was singing in that low, velvety voice of hers the lullaby he had just played. He was dimly aware that Meg was standing in the doorway, waiting for something. The crying began to fade. Meg's frightened call shocked him back to his senses, and he stared at her round, scared face floating eerily in the light of the lamp she held. He was freezing. It was the cold of death that touched him. *Why has she come back? What can she want from me?*

"Meg, she's here," he whispered. "She wants something. Rafael and Sophia are with her, but she wants …"

He was ranting like a madman! Meg's eyes had grown large and round in her fear.

Why does she linger in the doorway? Erik was tired. He felt no urge to rise from the piano. Why didn't Meg come to him? *Because she won't let her!*

Meg fought against the rising panic, the urge to run and leave Erik behind. The light fluttered as she held the lamp trembling in her hand. "I'm scared, Erik," she cried. "Come away from there," she pleaded. She barely recognized her own voice.

"She won't let me," he replied, expressionless.

He watched Meg recede, growing smaller and smaller until the distance between them stretched to miles. She wouldn't hear him from so far away, but he spoke anyway sensing that soon Lucianna wouldn't even allow him that. "She wants me, Meg. She won't let go. I promised her that I'd stay with her."

The room grew brighter, light from several lamps filling it with a warm, safe glow. Meg had brought the candles from the hall and the next room and lit each and every one of them. Erik blinked against the retreat of darkness. The air shifted and fell away from him, and he was surrounded by warmth. Meg felt the change, too, and emboldened by the brightness she stepped forward into the center of the room. Meeting no obstacles, she rushed to Erik's side.

"You heard her, didn't you, Meg?" Erik asked. "You know she's not left the house."

Meg urged Erik to follow her back to the bedroom. He saw the look of concern on his wife's face. It touched him that she was worried. She'd be sad if he left her. What was he thinking? He gathered her into his arms and squeezed her tightly to him. He would not go! The warmth from her body flooded over him, pushing back the chill that had settled deep into his bones.

He must keep his wits about him, or they'd lock him away in an asylum. He mumbled something about a dream and sleep walking.

Meg watched him undress again for bed. But instead of slipping in beside her under the covers, he sat in the chair near the window. She let the silence grow around them, waiting for him to speak. The candle still burned. He stared out into the night. Then he began to speak. He had to tell her. It hadn't been enough to say he had lived for nearly a year with another woman who forced upon him an identity that wasn't his own. It wasn't enough to say she had died. He had to tell Meg what it was like to wake with absolutely no idea of who he was, the slow filling of that void with false memories and lies, the construction of an identity. Could one live without memories? Without an identity? Without an identity, could one truly have a will, a soul?

Luci had wanted him to become the man in the portrait she had painted years ago. In the portrait, the mask was gone. In its stead was an unblemished face, the face he might have had. In another lifetime. That had been her first attempt. She had re-created him on canvas, as she wished him to be, or as she saw him, like a prince in a fairy tale. After the fire, she had meant to create him anew as she had done in the portrait. She filled her creation with the essence of all that was good. She granted him a charmed life. But there was always a worm lying in wait to corrupt her vision. She wanted to do with him what the paint had been able to do to his image in the portrait. But she could not paint away his true face. Even so she had made him feel differently toward it. His disfigurement was from an unfortunate accident. It was not who he was. Perhaps her creation would have been more fortunate if that had been the only sign of his creator's failure. Sadly she had given him the name of a monster. Like a drop of blood in a bowl of milk, Ponzio's story had spread through the fairy tale, and Erik was no longer the man in the portrait, the prince in the fairy tale.

Lucianna struggled to control her creation, but he escaped her hands. She forgot that he had a will of his own. She forgot that he constantly tried to make sense of all the pieces that made up his identity. How could those pieces fit together? How could he be whole? Luci's facile caricature of her beloved was twisted and out of control, at the mercy of unseen forces around it, and yet it sought to understand itself. When had he ceased to be an "it" and become a "he"? When he began to resent his creator, sensing her falseness, perceiving her failure to give him the paradise she had promised? And yet she was his creator! And he had loved her sometimes like a God, sometimes like a lover, sometimes like a mother. And then he saw Meg, and the world Luci had made for him was a prison. But that prison was inside him. He was what Lucianna had created, but not her ideal, not what she had sought to create. He was her flawed creation, her failure.

"I feel her hold on me still," he tried to explain to Meg who lay in the bed, listening.

She tried to imagine it through his eyes. She tried to imagine Lucianna, not as a demon, but as a woman who had intended to give Erik a perfect life.

"You don't owe her anything, Erik. She may have wanted to give you a better life, a happier past, but it was ultimately to serve her own purposes, not yours! She stole your soul, Erik, like a vampire!" Meg would *not* imagine her as a saving angel.

"She was wrong. But she wasn't evil, Meg." He averted his gaze and remained quiet for several moments. When he spoke again, it was a confession he wrenched from within. "I loved her. I hated her, too. But I can't hide from you that I needed her, I clung to her, and if she could have protected me from Ponzio and Giovanni and if she had kept me from you, I would have loved her still."

How could she respond to him? Why was he unable to tear himself from Lucianna's mad fantasy?

"Don't you see, Erik? You fought her. You weren't a lump of clay she could mold to her purposes. You lost the key to your memory, but it was always there, and you were always who you are. You found your music. You insisted on coming to Rome. You saw me at the theater, but you saw hundreds of other women far prettier than I and yet your soul recognized me. In spite of her lies, you found your own way back, back to me."

For the first time a glimmer of hope shone in Erik's eyes. He rose from the chair and came to bed. He wrapped her in his arms and held her.

"She had no right to force you to be hers. She lied, and she kept you from me and your children."

"Perhaps," he replied. Then he added, "But I can't hate her, Meg. Don't make me hate her."

Meg sighed. "No. I won't ask you to do that. She loved you. She did you and us a great wrong. Perhaps she didn't see how wrong it was. Maybe you're right to understand what she tried to do as a gift. But it was wrong of her to play with your life."

"You know that the saddest part of it all is that I think she loved the other Erik, not the one she tried to create. She did love me. She believed she was creating the man she loved, but it wasn't really me. When she rewrote my past, she lost me."

"But thank God, you're back."

Erik's fingers tightened convulsively on Meg's skin. A sharp stab of anxiety flashed through him "No, Meg. That's where you're wrong. I'm not the same. I can never be the same."

Meg whimpered in his arms, afraid to hear more.

"Erik died in the fire. I'm not him; I'm not Fiortino either. That's what's painful." He could not completely escape the story Lucianna had created for him. It had left its marks on his body and his soul. "I watched her die in that other room, the one Signorina Paglione led us to the first day. Luci thought she was carrying my child." His voice caught, but he swallowed several times, fighting the sorrow that welled up inside him. He didn't expect the feeling to be so raw. He had no right to ask Meg to console him as he cried for Lucianna. "The child was not a child. It was death, and I felt responsible for it. I lived with her as her husband. That will always be a part of who I am, Meg."

She brought her forehead close to his face and touched her brow to his. He could smell her sweet breath and feel its warmth flow over him. She gently caressed his chest with the palm of her hand. "I think I understand."

He hoped that she did. He whispered her name and kissed her. He prayed that Lucianna would allow him to sleep in peace for the few hours of night that remained to them.

Raoul bent the foil and tested its weight in his palm. He made small circles with his arm to limber the stiffness. The wound had healed well. The soreness was only a memory. "This is very, very nice!" He watched Erik put on the fencing mask. He had been strangely quiet since the other night. Actually since the day they arrived, Raoul had sensed Erik retreat.

Erik bent and stretched, his foil left on the sideboard next to the gloves. Christine had suggested that Raoul draw him out. Fencing practice seemed as good a way as any to loosen Erik up. Perhaps discharging some pent up energy would help ease him. However, if he didn't wish to talk, Raoul knew that there was nothing he could do to make Erik confide in him. He had never met any-one so able to hold his own counsel as Erik. The more upset he was, the less forthcoming he tended to be. Except when he became enraged. But Raoul cer-tainly didn't want to push him to that extreme. He had seen what Erik was like when he was irrational and angry and knew it was distasteful and dangerous to be within range of this barely tamed man under those circumstances. Yet that might be the only way to get at the heart of the matter.

"Your fencing instructor. Did he outfit the room?"

Erik looked around at the long rectangular room as if he had never seen it before. "Yes."

Well, that went well. Raoul answered Erik's silence with his own as he took up a position in the center of the long run of the room. He stood waiting for Erik to position himself opposite him. Once the two men had squared off, fac-ing one another, their foils raised several times in sign of readiness, Raoul became excited to see how much Erik had improved. "En garde."

It was like fighting a different man! Of course, Raoul reminded himself that they were simply practicing. There was no animus between them. No one's life was hanging in the balance. They intended no harm to each other. Fencing under these circumstances was completely different from using the blade in one's own defense or in the defense of a loved one. This was more an art or like a good game of chess where you test your mettle against a worthy opponent to learn perhaps more about yourself than about the other.

They were both working up a good sweat. Raoul stopped to catch his breath after a particularly long exchange where he managed to make the point with a punta riversa that met Erik's chest just below his collar bone. It was a good solid hit, and Erik conceded it in obvious displeasure.

"I see you still don't like losing," Raoul said.

Erik looked at him sharply, but then looked away before he spoke. His tone was chagrinned. "I lose so seldom that it's hard to become proficient at it."

Raoul could hear the grin under Erik's mask. It pleased him to know that he was still capable of sarcasm.

They continued for some time without speaking except to remark on a par-ticularly good move or to curse a misstep. After more than an hour, they stopped to figure out their score. They had become so immersed in the challenge that they had both lost count. They ran through the list of body parts that would have been cut and mangled, had they been in earnest, to find that they were separated by only two points with Raoul in the lead.

"I think my last point should count for more." In mock seriousness, Erik referred to a very nasty imbrocatta that would certainly have jeopardized any further progeny for the de Chagny family.

Raoul chuckled and told Erik he must not be greedy.

The atmosphere between the two men would never be more relaxed than now as they removed their protective masks and set the foils in their places in the cabinet along the wall. Even so, Raoul wondered how to broach the subject of Erik's troubled mind.

"Meg is concerned," Raoul said without preamble. Perhaps an appeal to Erik's desire to protect Meg from worry would draw him out. On the other hand, the count was convinced that direct questioning would likely place Erik on the defensive and guarantee his obdurate silence. "She says you sleep little, and when you do, you have nightmares."

"What other aspects of our private life does she share with you?" The camaraderie of the last hour disappeared. Raoul was quite aware of the anger behind the snide question. The implications were too obvious. Erik didn't want him meddling in what evidently was a very personal matter.

"Please accept my apologies," Raoul replied in earnest. If Erik preferred reserve, he'd get it. "It was not my intention to invade your privacy. I hoped that friendship might give me the right to be concerned for you."

Erik's face was always daunting. Raoul had become accustomed to his disfigurement over the past several months. The fact that Erik would remove his mask in his presence touched Raoul. He knew that it meant they had attained a level of friendship that was rare among men. But when anger sat on Erik's visage, it was a fierce thing to see. Raoul forced himself to keep his gaze fixed solidly on Erik's face in spite of the gruesome aspect the latter had assumed.

The tension in Erik's body slowly dissipated, and he took a towel from the sideboard and wiped the sweat from his face, neck, and hair. He cleared his throat, loudly and harshly, and Raoul could see the muscles in his jaw tense and relax several times. Erik turned so that his disfigurement was almost completely hidden from Raoul's view. "I'm sorry I was … so short with you."

Raoul bowed his head just slightly, enough to acknowledge acceptance of the apology.

"I know she's worried. I can't do anything about it, though," Erik continued. He sat down heavily on one of the chairs that lined the wall. They were in place for guests who might wish to watch an exhibition. Raoul joined him on another, turning it just so he could look at Erik without craning his neck. Evidently Erik had decided to talk. "You'll think I'm going mad, but I'm not. I've never been susceptible to ghosts or other superstitious tripe. For God's sake I lived for years off others' superstitions. I was as much at ease in the graveyard as in my own rooms under the opera house. The dead don't frighten me. At least not until now." He paused as if thinking of something. "Do you believe me?"

Raoul thought about what Erik said, and it did make sense to him. Erik had used superstition to protect himself, to keep the others from going too far down below the theater. He had made everyone, including Christine, think he was supernatural. He had been her father's spirit, the Phantom, the Opera Ghost. He had used magic and trickery, deceit and illusion, to reinforce their awe and fear.

"Yes, you've made a good point. I wouldn't believe you superstitious or gullible. But what is it that you think is happening?"

"I felt her the moment we entered the house." He edged closer to Raoul, his voice dropping to a low whisper as if he didn't want anyone else to hear him. Raoul felt gooseflesh rise along his arms. "I know what you think. Of course, I remembered her, and it seemed almost real to me. But it wasn't just memory. Later, in my dreams, she ... she was ... Oh God, I don't know if I can say it. If I tell you ..." Raoul waited, and Erik took several long and deep breaths before he continued. His voice was more controlled, less emotional. He would risk telling Raoul, whatever he might think of him. "She was demanding, unrelenting, and very powerful. I know no other way to say it: She took me—against my will. I would never have thought it possible. I struggled against her, even though I thought it wasn't real. I thought they were dreams. At first. I'm not sure anymore. I ... woke ... exhausted and ..." Again he paused overwhelmed by shame.

Raoul felt inadequate to help. He believed he understood what Erik was trying to describe. It was shocking that a dream could be so vivid, but Raoul had heard of cases, usually after many weeks or months of abstinence. But he was sure that was not the case with Erik and Meg. Why would Erik respond to an erotic dream so completely, so slavishly?

"Erik, I would think that you should ..." He had no right to refer to the private affairs of Erik and Meg's bedroom. It was risky for him to do so. "If you exert your energy as a husband with Meg ... I'm sorry I don't know a polite way to say this."

"You think I haven't made love to my wife? I have clung to her like a drowning man. I make love to her with a desperation that I know frightens her! I'm so exhausted when I fall asleep at last that I think I shall die when Lucianna appears in my dream. She's sucking the life out of me! She won't let me go!"

"We need to get you away from here." He placed his hand on Erik's shoulder and spoke with determination and urgency. He would take the decision out of Erik's hands.

Erik grabbed Raoul by the wrist before the count rose to leave. "But I can't leave them."

"Who?"

"Lucianna and the babies. They cry at night. She … asked me to play for them."

"Erik, there are no babies."

"She had two miscarriages. She gave them names. She buried them."

"They are in heaven then. They have no reason to haunt you. You weren't their father, and you didn't cause their deaths."

Erik seemed to absorb Raoul's argument.

"Erik, you have your own children to worry about. And a woman who loves you. Don't let guilt eat away at you like this." Raoul could see that Erik was wavering. He grabbed him solidly by the shoulders and spoke almost in anger. "You owe her nothing. Nothing! She nearly took your soul away!"

Mario broke into the room, yelling at the top of his lungs for Erik. He was dressed for riding, but his clothes were in disarray, and there was terror in his voice. "Maestro! Come quick! François is trying to ride Diavolo Rosso!"

Erik and Raoul bolted together and ran out to the stables. Erik had told the boys to stay away from the stallion. He was a fierce horse, nothing like the beautiful and gentle Charlemagne that Erik had taught François to ride. Even Erik had to fight to control Diavolo. The stable door had been flung open, and the stable boy was running up from the field where he had been exercising one of the mares. Erik looked about frantically for his son. Inside the dark stable Diavolo Rosso's stall was empty, the door swinging gently on its hinges. He heard something in the distance, ran around to the back side of the stable and could just make out the figure of his son, a small dark bundle on top of the demonic stallion, in the precise moment when the horse reared and jerked to the side throwing the rider dizzily into the air. Erik's heart stopped as the bundle fell heavily to the ground and did not move.

"No!" The sound was torn from his throat. He grabbed the mare the stable boy was leading and jumped to her back. He dug his heels into her flanks and forced her into a deadly gallop down the slope of the green field until he reached his child. He slid from her before she could come to a full stop and ran to François's still body. His arms and legs were strangely askew. His face was pushed into the grass, his mouth open, his eyes shut. His face was ghostly white. Erik screamed as he rocked back and forth on his heels, afraid to touch his son's bent body.

"No! Not my child! You can't! You can't!"

Behind him came the wagon. Raoul and several servants rushed forward as Erik ran his hand along the child's face, brushing the dirt from his cheek. He leaned in close and could just make out the sound of his breathing. Erik wouldn't let anyone else touch the boy. He carefully placed the child's arms along his sides and cautiously stretched his legs out straight. He lifted François gently and laid him in the wagon, surrounding his body with blankets so that he couldn't move. He got in beside him and held him in place as Raoul turned the wagon back toward the house.

Raoul had sent for the doctor the moment he saw the boy fall from the horse. By the time they reached the house and Erik carried the child inside, the women had come out into the hall and followed them into a nearby room. Erik released his son only after he had laid him on the sofa and Meg had knelt beside the unconscious boy. She broke into tears. She took François' hand and held it to her throat as she cried. Erik stood silently by, slowly backing away from the sofa, unable to drag his eyes away from his child. His child, not *Luci's*! *She* would not have him!

No one was watching when Erik left the room. Shortly afterwards, the doctor came. He told them to take the mother away so that he could more easily examine the boy's injuries. That was the moment they noticed Erik's absence.

you can't take him from me, he's my child, he doesn't belong to you, you have your children with you, let them go to their peace and leave us alone! if you want someone, then let it be me, let it be me you take with you, you always wanted me, you can't want him, not François, he's just a young boy, he won't love you, he'll cry for us, please, Lucianna, if you ever loved me, give him back and take me instead!

Erik had taken the mare. The stable boy saw the wild look on his face and thought for sure that the master's young son must have died. He went to the house, found Mario, and told him what he had seen. The master had led the mare out into the yard. Without a backward glance, he mounted her bareback and rode out in the direction of the cliffs. Mario asked to borrow one of the smaller horses. He told the boy to run back to the mansion and to tell the

Count de Chagny to come quick. Then Mario rode off in the direction Erik had taken.

Mario spied the mare pawing at the ground. She wasn't hobbled and for that reason might have drifted a fair piece away from where his master—he reminded himself that he was to call him Papa—had dismounted. He felt his chest tighten and heard himself sob painfully as he wondered where his newly found father had gone. He dismounted and quickly hobbled the small mount so she wouldn't wander. He might need to get back quickly. Then he went toward the edge of the cliff, dreading what he might find.

Down on the beach he saw him! He was taking off his clothes. His boots and stockings and coat had been discarded behind him, and he had been walking out toward the surf as he took off his remaining garments. He meant to plunge naked into the water. Mario was filled with dread. There was only one thought that rushed to his mind. He was going out into the water and had no intention of ever coming out again! Mario searched behind him to see if the count was on his way. Hopefully the stable boy had managed to get someone's attention. He called down to the beach below to Erik, but the wind carried his voice away. He was sure that it never reached Erik's ears. He saw him walk into the water and the water crash around him. The swells were high, and Erik was forced to swim in order to keep progressing out toward open sea. Mario was torn between waiting and rushing down to Erik. He thought of riding back to the house, but what good would it do? If someone wasn't on the way by now, it would all be for naught. He couldn't leave his father. He watched as Erik struggled against the waves, swimming farther and farther away from the beach, each stroke taking him closer to death. Mario thought his father would be safe as long as he kept his eyes trained on him, as if his gaze could buoy Erik safely over the water.

Erik would go to her. If he did, she would release François. He would beg her to take him instead. That's what she had always wanted. Since the first night she came upon him in the stable, she had wrapped her spell around him. She had led him to the fairy forest and in the moonlight she cast her net for him, but he had escaped. This time he would come to her willingly. Willingly, as long as she let François live. As long as his son could live. She had called to him before, and he had come. When she found him exiled from his land, estranged from the only woman who had truly loved him, she called him to her. And hadn't he come to her aid? Hadn't he protected her from Ponzio? Hadn't he risked his life to free her from her servitude to that monster? She had released him. She had let him return to Meg. They had parted friends. But she had lied. She still wanted him. She had forced him to live another's life, and yet he had held her hand and cried for her when she died. Wasn't that enough? Was anything ever enough for her?

Erik had ridden to the cliff's edge, left the horse to wander, had run down the path, almost falling several times, to the tide line. It would be here that he would find her waiting. He felt her fingers on François's neck. He searched the beach. There, sheltered by the rocks, they had made love. She had told him she was with child. Did she believe that he had planted death in her womb? Did she blame him for the growth that ate her life? Such pain and loneliness!

The salt breeze wiped his tears from his eyes before they could fall. Out there beyond the breakers she had floated carefree. She was waiting out in the water for François to die. She would wrap him in seaweed and hold him. François's eyes were Erik's eyes. She had been fooled, perhaps, by those eyes. She was still waiting, still waiting for him.

Quickly Erik stripped off his clothes. He kept his gaze riveted on the deep blue of the distant horizon. She would take him instead. If he went to her, she'd release the boy. She would open her arms to him, and François would slip away from her icy fingers.

"Oh, Meg, forgive me," he cried, unable to see any escape but this one. He walked out into the cold surf. He fought the push of the waves as they crashed against him, as if the ocean itself were rejecting him.

"*What would you do for love, Erik?*" He heard her voice like a high keening over the waves. As the sandy bottom disappeared under his feet, he swam out. He would have to swim so far that he wouldn't be able to make it back to shore. If he lost his courage, he wouldn't be able to make it back, and she would still have him. She must accept him. She would accept him. François would be free. Meg would be free. Laurette would be free. Mario would be free. No one would ever hear her crying in the middle of the night. The babies would sleep peacefully in their arms. She and he would sing lullabies to the babies. Meg would cry for him. But he must not think of Meg's grief. Wasn't she grieving now? Would she grieve any less if François died?

His arms and legs were numb from the cold. He continued to swim. Then he felt her soft hands on his body. He dived under the water to look for her. He could see her dark auburn hair floating up toward the surface. In her face her eyes—blue and green like the seawater—smiled at him. She was pleased he had come. She reached out to him, and he came to her. He felt her smooth his hair from his face. "*What would you do for love?*" Did he ask the question? "Please," he begged. Was she the one who answered, *"Anything, my love, anything"*? He was sinking into dark water, her hands were slipping away from him, her eyes were sad. It would be soon now. His lungs ached to breathe. Gently he felt her hands on him again. He closed his eyes and let her take him. She turned him. She pressed him up against the water's surface. The darkness receded. He opened his eyes and saw the light of the daytime sky above him. His lungs burned from lack of air. Were those her lips that brushed his mouth?

Someone grabbed his arm and pulled him roughly along the surface. He choked and sputtered. He struggled to get away. He struggled to sink down again into the water. The hands closed on him again, and then he felt a blow to his head, and he sank into oblivion.

Raoul had dashed into the water and swum out past the chopping waves to the last spot where he saw Erik go under. Several others had also jumped in and followed shortly behind. There was a boat down the beach, and he had sent two other men to get it. They'd set out as soon as they could so that Raoul and the others would not be forced to swim back the entire way. Knowing that, Raoul was unconcerned about swimming beyond his limit.

When he reached the spot he had last seen Erik, he searched the crystal clear waters of the bay for any sign of him. Finally he caught sight of something moving up toward the surface. Perhaps he was trying to swim up for air! He dived down and met Erik on the way up. But Erik did not appear to be swimming. Something had pushed him to the surface, had collided with him, sending him toward the light. Raoul grabbed Erik by the arm to drag him to the air. When Raoul started to haul him back toward the approaching boat, Erik twisted savagely in his grip and struggled to get away. He sank again below the waves. Having no other recourse, Raoul dived after Erik, latched onto his torso, and pulled him quickly to the surface. When they broke into the air, Raoul slammed his fist into Erik's face to subdue him. Better unconscious than fighting him and drowning the two of them! He positioned his hand under Erik's chin in an effort to keep the unconscious man's face above the water. Then he turned and began slowly to swim toward the shore.

The boat met them half-way to the beach. An hour later, the party brought Erik, still unconscious, into the house and up to his room.

they carry him in, wrapped in soggy blankets, water dripping like tears in their wake, Meg trembles, empty hands clenched tightly by her sides, she watches as they approach, her mouth fills with dust, scoured by salt and sand she watches, trembling, "he's alive," Raoul rushes to say, yet still she clenches her fists, nails cutting into the soft, unyielding flesh of her palm, he lives, she silently notes the broken words Raoul sprinkles before her like dates upon a desert, the sea, the briny depths, a struggle, Raoul looks at her, such kind eyes, seeking to ease her distress, a struggle? her heart shrinks, squeezing drops of blood, a shower of blood blinds her, she blinks away the crimson screen, the drops overflow and course down her hot cheeks, he lives? her fallen angel, how many times can he fall? how many times can he run from her? how many, many times will she soothe his brow? how many words shall it take? she brings her fists to her lips to keep from screaming, what more can she give him? her feet sink into sand as she follows them through the haunted passageways of Lucianna's grave, they carry him, wet and cold, his eyes—his beautiful eyes—are closed, they might always have been closed, picked and eaten by crabs and eels, sightless, another man's arms fold protectively round her, Raoul's voice, not his, not Erik's, whispers, woos her to his cause, "what would you do for love?" he says, as he seeks to reassure her, the drowning man had murmured those words, asked that question, made that plea, his eyes closed

what had she not done for love? a girl, practically a child, she had forged her fate to his, had descended to the damp bowels of a chimerical kingdom, surrounded by music, had stood before his terrible pain, the demon lover, the angel in hell, she had, with these same empty hands, wrenched him from his willful grave and forced him to live, she had given up the light to live in his shadow, to be his instrument, to lie in his passion, to rescue him from himself, who would have done what she has done? who would have had the courage to withstand that dreadful countenance? to love a man obsessed, enraged by fate, a man who cursed God and all humanity, a man who made love to death itself?

she could not bear the pain! she swallowed the bitter gall of her own despair, they carried him to their room, wrapped in soggy blankets, and it might have been her tears in which he had nearly drowned,

alive, alive, she lets the searing cry burst from her scalded throat, her body shakes with a rush of agony and fear, her fingers unfurl and reach out even as her heart swells with the knowledge of her own strength, he will not vanquish her! he cannot destroy her love for him, she is terrible in her beauty, her love grows, unbending, unbroken, monstrous, her hands touch his sodden skin, rip blankets from his body, clutch his bare arms, rough fingers punish him, rake across the plane of his chest, sweep the seaweed from his limbs, she claims him, "what would you do for love?"

What had she not done already? What would she not do for love?

"François?" he called out in the night.

"Ssshhh. He's all right, Erik." She comforted him. She sat grimly by the bed. François was resting on the small cot set up in the adjoining room. She listened for her son's cries as she watched over Erik's heavy sleep. "It's all right," she lied. Anger tugged at her still. Despair had finally gone. It had crawled away to some dark hole, disappointed by this reprieve.

Her lower lip trembled as she saw Erik slip again into sleep's warm embrace. She brushed the hair from his forehead, lingered on his brow, and, as so often before, reveled in his strange, sad beauty.

Erik tossed gently in his sleep, coming slowly to the surface from a pleasant dream. When he opened his eyes, he saw Meg brushing her hair at the vanity. He loved to watch her brush her hair. He wished he could do it for her. He lifted his head and fell back with a groan. His head throbbed and ached. Meg dropped the brush and came to his side.

"Don't think about it, Erik." She fixed the covers around him. "It's all right."

François! The memory came down on his heart like the blade of an axe. "Is he alive?" he asked. He vaguely remembered Meg's voice, her reassuring words in the stillness of the night.

"François is going to be all right. He's awake. He broke his leg, but it wasn't a bad break. He'll mend just fine. He wrenched his shoulder a bit and won't be able to play the piano until it's healed. He's very afraid that you might punish him. But I'm more concerned ..." She broke off with a sob. She pressed her fists against his shoulders, anger suddenly taking control of her, and demanded, "How could you? How could you mean to leave me?" She was so tired of worry. All night she'd watched over him, wondering what she would feel when he finally opened his eyes. She fell against his chest, sobbing in deep ragged gulps of pain.

Erik slowly brought his hands around her. The fingers of his one hand tangled in her freshly brushed hair while the other rubbed soothingly at her back. "Forgive me."

"No. I won't." She wrenched herself away from him, her tears forgotten, and stole away to the window. "I won't forgive you! You can't do something like that and then ask to be forgiven. It's too much!"

Erik fought the pain of the headache and sat up on the edge of the bed. He had almost drowned. Perhaps he had drowned! He was at least certain that he had been on the brink of death. "How did you know that I went down to the beach?"

"Mario followed you. He sent word to Raoul. Raoul brought you back."

Erik walked over to Meg. He could feel the waves of tension rising from her skin. He wanted badly to hold her, but he stood behind her, careful not to touch her yet.

She turned to face him. "He had to strike you! You didn't want to be saved!" Her body shook with emotion. Unwilling to wait any longer, Erik took her in his arms and held her tightly. She tried to get away, but her heart wasn't in it.

"I'm sorry. I was sure that François was ... I thought it was Lucianna."

Meg leaned against Erik's chest and listened.

"I thought she would take him from us. I thought she wanted our children since hers had died so young. I went to make a bargain with her."

A bargain with a demon! thought Meg. She pulled roughly away from him and crossed the room to stand by the bed. "What kind of bargain? No, don't tell me. I know what you offered! You offered yourself, didn't you?" She knew she sounded angry.

She stared up at him. He met her angry gaze. He needed her to understand. He had not run from her, never from her.

"She's been calling to me everyday since we've come here. I couldn't let anything happen to François, to you, to any of you. I thought that she'd only be satisfied if I came out to her. I thought she'd not rest until ..."

Meg turned her back to him. Erik stopped talking. He crossed the brief space between them, bent, and kissed the back of Meg's neck, brushing his lips softly against her skin. He buried his face in the long golden tresses and breathed her smell—cloves and vanilla and hyacinth and heather—long and deeply. His hands caressed her hips and glided along her waist to her breasts, to her throat, to the tender exposed hollow at its base. She was soft and light, nestled in his arms, her back wedged tightly against his torso. But he felt her hold back; she needed to know more. Would this ghost continue to haunt them?

"Do you think she'll feel cheated since Raoul saved you? Will she come back for you?" She tried to keep the fear and anger out of her voice. She didn't know if she believed there was a ghost or if she feared Erik's mind had invented her for some sad, tortured reason. Either way, she had to know what he thought, how he felt.

"No. We won't hear from Luci anymore. She's at peace now."

"How do you know?" She clamped her teeth to stop the hitch in her voice.

"I saw her in the water, Meg. She took me in her arms. I thought that I would end there." He was silent for a moment. He couldn't tell if it was Meg or he who trembled. But his voice was carefully hushed and steady as he tried to explain. "She kissed me. I closed my eyes and was ready to give in. But she didn't want me to die. She pushed me back toward the surface. She pushed me away."

"But you struggled against Raoul. Why?"

"I wasn't sure. I wasn't sure she had let me go or if she rejected me because she wanted my son. I didn't want to risk it. I thought she'd have no choice but to release him if I stayed with her. If I died for her." Meg had to believe him. If she didn't, then he thought he might go mad. "François is out of danger. She's let me go."

He turned Meg around in his arms and whispered into her mouth as he kissed her, "She's gone. She knows I love you. We're safe." Meg accepted his kisses. She let him carry her to the bed and lay her on the covers.

When Raoul suggested that Diavolo Rosso was a dangerous horse and should be put down, Erik scowled and replied, "Why kill the horse for the master's mistake?"

Raoul answered too quickly, "Does that mean we should put you down first?"

Erik arched an eyebrow. Raoul failed to swallow his laughter. Even François who still felt cautious around his father for having disobeyed him, smiled up at the tall figure whose hand gently squeezed his shoulder. Everyone knew that both Erik and Raoul had tacitly agreed to forget that the one who had made the mistake was not Erik but his son.

Christine led a bay out to the enclosure and walked her sharply around the circumference. Erik glanced at her fashionable riding dress. She would sit the bay on the imported English saddle as elegantly as she would sit in the parlor for tea. Raoul stood tapping his heels with the riding crop Erik knew was mostly for show. Erik looked down again at his son. The boy's leg was wrapped from mid thigh to ankle to impede movement. Erik's stern gaze starkly contrasted with his soft voice.

"Feed him so he comes to think of you when he's hungry," Erik coaxed François.

"Might the horse think François is his next meal?" Erik gave Raoul a sharp look. Raoul cleared his throat and smiled. "I was only joking, François. Train him to think of you with pleasure, to look forward to seeing you."

François nodded and stretched out his small hand below the velvet lips of the dark horse. He nearly dropped the small apple when the horse's lips tickled his palm. His father brushed his hand roughly over François's hair in approval.

"When can I ride him, Papa?"

"When the two of us say you can."

"But Maman won't let me."

"I wasn't referring to your mother. I was referring me and the horse. He has to agree." Erik thought for a moment, then added, "Of course, if Diavolo can't convince your mother to let you ride him, you and I might have to do so."

"But will he let me ride him? He barely puts up with you, Maman said."

Erik considered the boy for a moment.

"You must learn not to be afraid. Can you do that?" François studied the horse from the tip of his muzzle to the end of his tail. Erik could sense the boy's hesitation. He laid his hand on his son's shoulder and squeezed it lightly. "He's big and powerful. But he's just an animal. He's not a demon. He, too, must learn not to fear *you*."

"But why would he fear me?"

"Because, without you, he has nothing. If you don't feed him, he will starve. If you don't care for him, he will wither and die. You wouldn't want that to happen, would you?"

"No, Papa. I think he's beautiful. I wish he were mine."

"He can't be yours unless you belong to him, too. Touch him. Let him feel your hand, smell you. Let him know that you bring him comfort. Respect him, but don't fear him. Never fear him, because then he might think that he *is* a red devil, a diavolo rosso, and that he deserves the name."

"Good advice for anyone to follow." Meg strode forward into the enclosure. Erik's hand fell limp to his side as his eyes raked up and down the slim figure of his wife. Unlike Christine, Meg had not donned a gentlewoman's riding dress. She had no skirt, no short, tight jacket buttoned to the throat over a white blouse, her boots were not hidden under heavy skirts.

She stopped in the middle of the path, pleased by her husband's ravenous gaze. For a moment, she thought he might whicker like the stallion, for his animal pleasure was evident in every fiber of his body. She felt naughty standing with her feet slightly apart, aware of the lack of her skirt, the fact that the doe-skinned suede pants clung to her legs like a second skin, aware of the weight and warm caress of her loose hair, aware that the loose-fitting white blouse was buttoned low and did not disguise her feminine grace.

Erik was not the only one to admire Meg. Raoul's horse butted his head against his master's shoulder, tired of being ignored. Christine laughed to see her husband blush from the awkward moment. He turned and inspected the cinching on his mount. Christine had nothing to fear. No man in his right mind would step between Erik and Meg.

"I feel like a ride, don't you?" Meg's question might have been directed at any or all of them. But her eyes indicated that she was addressing only one—Erik.

Meg shut the door quietly behind her. The house was still, settled for the night. He stood waiting for her to come to him. His eyes were unwaveringly clear and calm. She could drown in those eyes. No, she had already drowned a thousand times in them. She went to him, stretched up to kiss his parted lips. Her hand disappeared in his hair at the nape of his neck. As he bent to kiss her, she felt the warm water rush over her yet again.

"Will we stay here or should we go back to Rome?" Meg asked.

Rehearsals for the first production of the season were still several weeks off, but Meg worried that Erik might still sense Lucianna hovering over them in dark corners or whispering along the sea breezes that fanned the curtains even now in their bedroom.

He smiled at her, knowing her fears were also his, but confident in his ability to protect her and himself from them. He would not lose her again. Whoever he was or might become, she loved him. They belonged to one another.

Slowly, he undressed her, touching her as he did so, kissing each exposed treasure as he found it. "It doesn't matter, Meg. Wherever we are, I love you. You're safe here." He drew her close. "And here." He brought her palm to his chest and laid it over his heart.

978-0-595-47236-9
0-595-47236-2

Printed in the United Kingdom
by Lightning Source UK Ltd.
130556UK00002B/288/A